In Sleep You Know

A Story of the Eleriannan

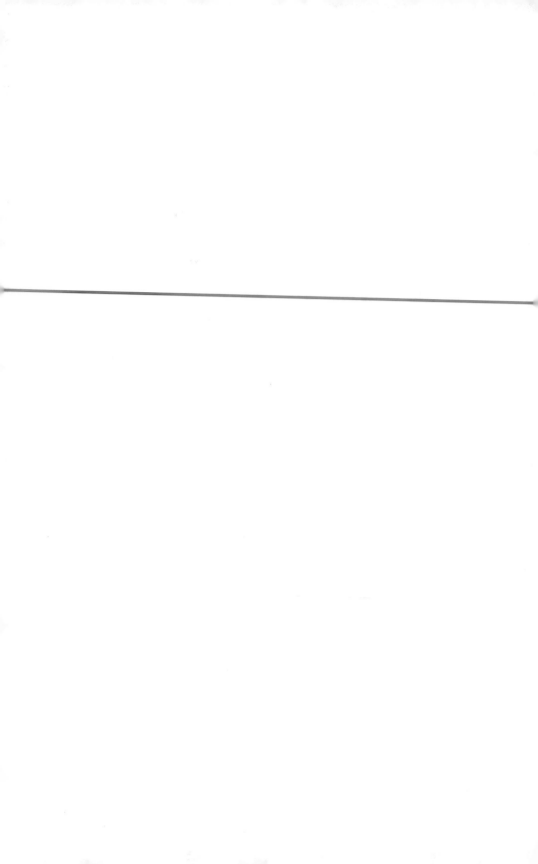

in sleep
you know

A Story of the Eleriannan

CHRISTIANE KNIGHT

In Sleep You Know
Published by:
Three Ravens Press
PO Box 502
White Marsh MD 21162
USA
Contact publisher for permission requests.

Front cover photo of man by Hamid Tajik from Pexels
Front cover photo of raven by kalpesh patel on Unsplash
Front cover photo of forest by Vlad Bagacian from Pexels

Front cover photo manipulation by Mohammed Hossain Polash
Cover design and interior book design & formatting
by Leesa Ellis ⟫⟶ *www.3fernsbookdesign.com*

ISBN: 978-1-7368503-1-2

Table of Contents

To Mom,
who believed in me
from the beginning.

To Christopher,
who was the first to read this.

SPOTIFY PLAYLIST

http://bit.ly/InSleepYouKnow

Music: Dead Can Dance
Mesmerism

Merrick took a deep breath before stalking boldly into the Halloween party. He had heard a lot about the people who lived in the big Victorian house on the outskirts of town; their parties carried the sort of legends that were fueled completely by rumor. No one he actually knew had been to one of them, but his friends all had stories, handed down until the teller couldn't positively identify the protagonist of the tale.

Well, he would be the first of his friends to make it in, and he intended to make it count. He'd managed to beg a ride to the edge of town and hiked his way to the place on dark back roads with barely enough room for two cars, much less a pedestrian. He figured that he had earned his chance to see what happened in the big house, by virtue of making it there without getting squashed by a SUV.

No one really seemed to notice that he didn't belong with anyone there. He had decided to wear an outfit that could go many places without too much comment: black BDUs tucked into freshly polished combat boots, topped off with an untucked white button-up shirt. A loosely tied black tie with skeletons dancing across it added an irreverent air that matched his spiky black hair perfectly. He looked every bit the musician that he aspired to be, without overstating it, as he'd carefully planned.

Merrick scanned around quickly to get his wits about him and headed for the likely place where the kitchen would be. He had brought two six-packs of the best beer he could afford, a rich porter from a local micro-brewery that he had discovered one night while in a bar in Fells Point. He had fallen in love with the taste and bought it whenever he could find it and afford it.

The way he saw it, he was crashing the party – the least he could do was to bring the beer he loved as a peace offering. Maybe the occupants of the house would notice his superior taste and tolerate him. Or maybe they would just kick him out and keep his beer. It was a difficult call at this point, really.

The people he'd seen so far were all rather... eccentric looking. They all seemed to be much more attractive than any one house full of people had a right to be, although none of them could be said to have a traditional beauty about them. From what Merrick had seen so far, they tended to be dramatic in dress, although that could have been attributed to the holiday, of course.

He found the kitchen and decided to take a beer for himself and anonymously stash the rest in the fridge. He should find someone to introduce himself to, he supposed, although he wasn't sure how he would answer the inevitable questions about why he was at the party in the first place. In fact, he wasn't really sure what had drawn him here. A sense of adventure, perhaps, mixed with an insatiable curiosity.

The refrigerator was full of strange food: odd fruit, weirdly lumpy packages with mysterious contents, and many dark bottles of liquid, corked and sealed with wax. There was a variety of beers on the top shelf, and he added the porters to that collection. Closing the door to the fridge, he was surprised by a small figure standing on the other side and took a step back with a gasp. The girl also shared his shock for a moment, before bursting into laughter.

"You look like you've seen a ghost! Never fear, stranger, I won't spirit you away...yet."

She opened her eyes wide and smiled innocently. Merrick gave in and started laughing, too. She looked at him carefully and said, "You're new here. Did you find us on your own?"

Merrick admitted, "I have been hearing the legends about the parties here for ages and decided that I would like to see them firsthand. I apologize if I overstepped my bounds, but I came a long way to be here tonight. I felt like I was drawn here." Why did he just say that? Damn, it was as if his tongue had a mind of its own!

"We like honest people here. We also have no call to argue with a call to join us; in fact, your tenacity honors us. And you brought beverages as well, yes?" Merrick nodded, mutely.

She smiled and said, "Good! You even follow the ancient formula of party crashing. Well, we didn't call it party crashing back then, but it will do for now."

She paused to give Merrick a glowing smile and winked at him. He was utterly enraptured at this point, he had never met a woman that had managed to captivate him so quickly. He could listen to her speak all night and never grow tired, he decided.

"You have to understand a few things before you enter the fray, as they say. Please let me be your guide, as you've made a favorable impression on me and I feel that I should get you through the evening unscathed. Do you agree?"

Merrick nodded, intrigued.

"Nay, nay, you must say aloud what you intend," she declared.

Merrick blinked at that, but complied, "I gladly accept you as guide."

She beamed at his wording and exclaimed, "Perfect! You did that quite well. Choose your words that carefully when dealing with us, and you will go far. Now, the next question: will you tell me your name? And be careful, here, when you are asked for it tonight from other than myself because names hold power. Never reveal all until you are sure, do you understand? I will give you mine first, as a token of good faith, but know this – there is a secret to the name that you carry; you should never give it away until you are sure. Give your common name, or a nickname, when you are asked, and then only if you wish. Names given are gifts."

She caught his gaze and held it, peering into his eyes until he thought he might have to either kiss her or run screaming. She broke the tension finally with a sweet smile, and said happily," I can see that this night will yield many surprises! I am Aisling, and I'm quite glad that I found you in our kitchen tonight."

Merrick felt, quite suddenly, as if he had been given a great honor. What was going on here, under the surface? He felt lost in the night's events, yet at the same time, this was exactly where he'd wanted to be. What could he do but go along with everything?

"Aisling. That's a lovely name. I'm Merrick, and I'm very pleased to meet you." He felt that to be an inadequate response, but Aisling beamed at his answer.

"Your name isn't very common, either. We are of a kind, then! This is pleasing." She practically bubbled over with excitement, then suddenly cocked her head to the side and looked a bit alarmed.

"Someone's coming, and you don't have all the information you need to make it through this evening safely. Come over here, quickly!" She grabbed his arm and pushed him onto a stool in the darkest corner of the kitchen, positioning herself between him and the wall.

"No matter what, keep your face hidden. Do you understand? If someone speaks to us, let me answer. Pretend to be engrossed in my presence, no matter what."

She slipped his arms around her and pressed herself against him. "Hide your face in my hair," she whispered, as the kitchen door opened behind her.

His head was spinning, dizzy from being so close to her so suddenly, her scent, her presence – and the suspense of the moment just added to the feeling until he could barely stand it. Her fingers were gently stroking the back of his neck, rather absently yet soothingly; he could feel her nervousness. Why was she so attuned? What were these people like, anyway?

There was some rustling and a low laugh from the figures who had entered. Merrick could only see the curve of Aisling's neck and her voluminous, curly hair, which under other circumstances would be more than enough. He realized that her hair was an unusual mix of deep, sparkling black and strands of delicate lavender. How did she manage that?

He must have made a sound, because Aisling tensed slightly, and one of the others in the room laughed again and said, "Oh, look. Aisling caught herself a plaything! Will you share, or are you greedy today, Aisling?"

Merrick winced at the condescending tone in the remarkably mellifluous voice. How could such a lovely voice become so bitter?

A second, more masculine voice chimed in. "I don't think I recognize it, Edana. Of course, I can barely see it. Him, Aisling? Did you find a boy? What a pleasant surprise!"

The other one sounded like he was teasing Aisling. He seemed rather more likeable. "We should leave her to her fun, Edana. I'm sure she will introduce us later, when they are... less involved." He laughed, lightly.

Merrick had the impression that he was trying to help Aisling, that there was some underlying tension that he was trying to defuse. Edana seemed to want to start trouble.

Aisling turned slightly, cradling his head and keeping him hidden in her hair, and replied in an even tone, "I am rather occupied, 'tis true. Edana, does the party grow dull enough to drive you to the kitchen for entertainment?"

Edana's answer dripped with ice, "Ah, those fools. They never tire of the same entertainments, you know. But rumor had it that some dark bird soared boldly through our threshold, and that waked my curiosity. Imagine when I find it roosting here in the shadows with you."

There was a rustling of fabric, and then a thin and cold hand had his chin, trying to wrench him from Aisling's protection. Merrick's heart jumped at the touch and started pounding. His impulse was to run away as fast as he could. Aisling laughed merrily and stepped away, though the look she shot to Merrick was full of warning.

"What you force, you do not command," she told Edana, a poisonous smile on her lips.

"Audentes fortuna juvat," Edana replied with a sneer, and Merrick's brain suddenly unlocked, and he knew what to say next. Bless those "useless" Latin classes!

"Lady," he addressed Edana, "as you advise, fortune might smile upon my boldness, and this crow does speak for himself, if you will."

She looked taken aback at his words but recovered with an ingratiating smile. "Ah, the dark bird has a tongue, and some wits, as well! What other surprises might this night hold, fledgling? And what say you to your presence here, uninvited and unknown?"

Merrick gave her his most engaging grin and answered, "Your gatherings are legendary, and I could not help but see one myself! I came through a small bit of adversity to get here, but I managed to bring a small peace offering of beverages. Aisling was kind enough to extend her welcome to me, and here I stand now, quite honored to be in your presence."

He had a sudden urge to bow, and did so, instinctively knowing that would impress.

Edana seemed rather taken aback, a look that seemed alien on lovely features that did not reveal her bitter personality. She took a moment to smooth the folds of her burgundy silken gown, and to toss back her shining black hair, before she turned to her tall, handsome companion and said, "What think you, Cullen? Shall we accept or exile this brazen one?"

Cullen laughed derisively at her and said, "It is not ours to decide, Edana, and you know it. He took matters into his own hands when he entered the door, and he made his amends with a gift and a well-spoken explanation. Aisling has befriended him, and there is naught for us to nay or yea at this juncture. Do not overreach."

He weathered Edana's evil glare with a guffaw and an eye roll as she pushed past him in a huff. "Do not think you have exempted yourself from my scrutiny, Raven," she threw to Merrick as a parting shot before huffing out the door.

A palpable chill seemed to lift, heightened by Cullen's imminent collapsing with laughter, which he managed to stave off by falling into Aisling. The shocked look that had not left her face the entire time Merrick had engaged the enemy, so to speak, finally faded into relief.

"That was an experience I most certainly do not want to repeat again!" she gasped. She reached for Merrick's hand, and held it tightly. "You handled yourself much more eloquently than I would ever have hoped. You are amazing!" Merrick's heart leaped in his chest at her declaration. When had he ever been smitten so quickly?

She gave him a smile as sweet as honey before turning back to Cullen gratefully. "And you! I appreciate you intervening; I know that is against your normal stance."

Cullen said, with a rueful look, "I have of late grown tired of those games, and I would distance myself from such as she if I could." He turned to Merrick and gave him a slight bow. "Well played, Sir. I am Cullen, pleased to be of service. Well met, and though you are welcome in our poison court, tread carefully."

Merrick considered his words and nodded slowly. "I appreciate your advice and assistance. I'm Merrick. I have to say I never dreamed that my little adventure of the evening would go this route, but I'm pleased to meet you on the journey."

Cullen threw back his blonde head and laughed at that. "Ah, Aisling, you found a keeper! Lucky girl. And you just found him today?"

She laughed, "Here in the kitchen! He brought us beer. GOOD beer."

"Marks for him, then." Cullen straightened himself out, adjusting the cuffs on his white ruffled shirt.

Merrick realized at that moment that Cullen was dressed as quite the dandy, with a red velvet frock coat to go with the ruffled shirt, and neat black pants tucked into pointed boots. His blonde hair was even pulled back into a tidy ponytail with a black ribbon. It made Merrick feel severely underdressed for the party. Even Aisling was wearing a silky black dress that looked made from some historic pattern, all ancient lines and flattering fit.

"Aisling, love, you should take him out to the party now. I think you've established for him from what cloth we're cut, if you gather my meaning," Cullen said, giving Merrick a measuring look. "If he can keep on his toes with Edana, he'll handle the others admirably."

Aisling replied, "This is probably true, but I'd like to have a few more minutes with him first before entering that mess, if Merrick is amiable, of course."

She looked to Merrick, who smiled and replied, "Of course."

"See you out there, then," Cullen gestured widely at the rest of the house and slipped back into the party.

Aisling looked down at the floor and muttered, "Well, I certainly screwed that up. My apologies, although you took all in stride. Forgive me?"

She looked up into his eyes beseechingly and laid her hands gently on his arms. She looked terribly fragile and sad, and the only answer he could see was to kiss her. Her eyelids fluttered shut as she rose up a bit on her toes to meet him. Their lips met, and his world seemed to shrink to tunnel vision for a moment; a heady feeling, like being drunk, or on a vertigo-inducing carnival ride, took over him.

He was practically reeling when she finally broke away and slid her arms around him in a gentle embrace. "I think that's more than enough for now, don't you? We cannot have you intoxicated so soon in the evening."

Merrick gasped in a breath, trying to catch his balance. "What... what just happened? That was... amazing. Wow."

Aisling gave him a mysterious little grin. "I have my secrets, to be revealed in time. I have to admit, that was an unexpected sweetness." She reached up and touched his face briefly, and said, "Now I need to impart to you this bit of importance – what you experienced with Edana, that is the rule rather than the exception. There are a few of us here who are of good heart, but some are ruled by the bitter hand of ennui and impatience. They like to play games. Words matter here, as I'm sure you've noticed, so mark what you say.

"Promise nothing that you cannot deliver and give as little as you can. Weigh everything you utter as carefully as you can, so that you say exactly what you mean. Shades of meaning can get you into much trouble with some of us. Trust your instincts; you seem to possess good sense about how to act around us. We are as quick to bless as to curse, so if you impress, you will do well. I will try to give you signs of who to trust, and who to mistrust, but stand by your instincts. And remember – I am there with you."

She stopped and gave him a look of amusement. "Is this the sort of adventure you were expecting?"

"Um... not quite. But I must admit, I don't think I could have dreamed up this scenario, so I'm rather pleased. Especially as I've managed to find you by coming here." He smiled, suddenly shy, and squeezed her hand lightly.

She laughed delightedly and said, "Then let us go conquer the party, m'dear!"

Music: Severed Heads

Heart of the Party

Merrick had been to a lot of parties in his twenty-seven years. He had seen debauchery, and decadence. He had been to gutterpunk gatherings that were as prim as church meetings, and soirees that his ridiculously rich and stuffy relatives had thrown that were practically orgies.

But this party seemed to have all of those wrapped up into one large package, and yet it felt like no other event he'd ever attended. The first thing he noticed was that everyone there was either incredibly gorgeous or utterly odd-looking. No one in the building could be described as "plain" by any means.

Cullen was in their direct path, sprawled in an overstuffed velvet armchair and surrounded by several small green-haired figures. He saluted broadly to Merrick and Aisling, and his tiny companions turned to see who Cullen had gestured towards.

Merrick was taken aback to see that they looked to be young girls, but they were dressed very provocatively, with filmy green gowns and black corsets, and elaborately done makeup and hair.

One of them spoke to Cullen, in a crystalline voice that resonated with adult tones, "Oh, who is this new blood that the waif has found? He looks... fragile." She eyed him lewdly, and the other two tiny women cackled and made suggestive faces at him.

Cullen sighed patiently and said, "Ladies, you see quite well that he has chosen his companion for the evening. Leave be, and perhaps you will have a chance at sweeter meat this eve."

The one who had spoken to Merrick turned on Cullen in an instant, and gave him a hungry, devilish grin. "Perhaps one who has resisted our charms? Perhaps the most handsome prince at the soiree?"

She licked her lips, and Merrick shivered. He was sure that Cullen could handle himself with those weird, rapacious females, but there was something in the undercurrent of that exchange that left him feeling that Cullen had tossed them a larger morsel than perhaps he'd intended. The look of careful calculation on Aisling's face reinforced his impression.

She inclined her head, very slightly, to the women flanking Cullen, and said in an even tone, "Ladies. Cullen."

The tiniest of the three stared up at Aisling with distaste and said, "Scion of Oneiros, none asked you here."

Aisling shrugged and replied, "Cullen would have otherwise, I say. But no mind; we need to mingle about and acquaint our Blackbird here with the Folk."

She turned to leave, and the smallest one reached out and grasped Merrick's wrist with sharp claws and hissed, "Not yet, I think. Let me look at this one."

She yanked on Merrick's arm and pulled him to his knees, a feat surprising given her small stature. He held back complaints, deciding that keeping his tongue quiet was probably the best policy at this strange juncture. The creepy little gamine stretched herself out, rather like a snake, until her face was so close to his that he felt ill. She smelled of licorice and something bitter and herbal, and he realized that her face, that had appeared so young at a distance, was covered in a maze of minute cracks. She looked as if she had been constructed by mosaic in fine detail. Her eyes were a shade of green that made him think of scum-covered ponds. Being this close to her felt toxic.

"Ah, I'll look into your soul then, boy, make no mistake...," she whispered, her voice colored with easy malice. He wanted to run away, screaming, but could not pull himself away from her. He could hear Aisling's sharp intake of breath behind him, but he couldn't even look her way. He was sucked into the pit of those green eyes.

He was in a dark room. He could barely see through the gloom, a dark cot and a thick oak door with a latch handle. He heard scratching at the other side of the door, and his heart started pounding rapidly. SHE was there, trying to get in, trying to peer into his secret places. The scrabbling intensified, and he could hear her cooing encouragement to him to open the door to her.

"I hear you in there, little raven. Open the door and let me in, let me see what you hide within... LET ME IN!" She started shrieking and pounding on the door.

He fled to the cot and cowered on it for a moment, found a small leather journal under the covers, cradled it in his arms. This was what she wanted, he knew, his secret dreams, his deepest thoughts. He took the book and placed it behind him, between his back and the wall, and spread himself out against the wall as if to cling to it. She would not get his soul without a fight.

"Ahhhh! The little wretch!" she screamed, and took a step back quickly from Merrick, still on his knees on the floor. The other little witchy ones gathered around their compatriot and clung to her, cooing reassuringly. She shook them off and pointed at Aisling. "What have you brought into this house?" she demanded.

Aisling flung back, "I brought nothing. He arrived of his own volition, and he is his own man, as you can plainly see. Give him your name; he earned it."

The small woman hissed and said, "You will pay dearly for your insolence, Aisling."

"Not to you, I won't. Give him what he earned, what you strove to take from him. You know the game."

She screwed her mouth up as if she'd bitten into something distasteful. "I am Morgance. They," and she gestured over to her companions, "are Ula and Morgandy. Proper address to us is 'The Ladies' or 'The Sisters'. We show little mercy, be warned. We will not forget this."

Merrick cocked an eyebrow at this. "You engaged with me, not the other way around. I wanted no part of that. I just wished to meet the people in this house."

Morgance sneered at him, "Well, and so you have! Did you think you had found some common garden party? You will find yourself severely mistaken and outclassed 'ere this night is ended, Blackbird. Don't expect us to abide by your rules, or you will not emerge unscathed. Not that I see that as an option for you, anyway. Too innocent. Aisling, take him from us. And Cullen, you have some reckoning with us."

Cullen laughed merrily, "You did not travel the road proffered to you, and now it is closed. As for me, I think I shall follow in the service of our young protagonist for a bit. This may prove to be more than mere distraction."

With that, he extricated himself from the grasp of The Ladies, and flung his arms around Aisling and Merrick's shoulders in a rather drunken way. "Off we go, into the depths now!" He dragged off the protesting duo, and muttered to Merrick, "Well done, lad, but now you've done it. They forget nothing. I was rather taken aback to watch Morgance go after you like so; rather unusual that. You burn like a candle in the darkest night to us, you see. Have you followed what has gone by so far this eve?"

Merrick snorted, "I have no clue what goes on here. I feel like I've fallen headfirst into a fantastic movie or strange faery tale. I keep thinking, 'There must be a reasonable explanation for all of this. Perhaps I'm on drugs.' I know that's not it though – is it? I'd love to understand…"

Aisling shook her head and warned, "Knowing doesn't always explain things, and sometimes one can know too much. I feel terrible that you've experienced this much already. Some things were meant to stay a mystery, Merrick."

Cullen offered, "Perhaps, but I think this one was meant to come here tonight. And what a night for it! You choose dangerously, friend, coming to a place like this on Samhain. You had no idea, did you?"

Merrick shook his head violently. "Not a clue that you would all be so mysterious and freaky, no. Did she do what I think she did? I didn't imagine that, did I?"

Aisling replied plainly, "I wish that you had. But we will talk more on this, as this is neither the time nor place. Ah! Here is someone you should meet!"

She deftly guided them over to a rather tall and regal woman, her dark skin offset marvelously by her blazing red hair. She wore a rich purple and black gown that would not have seemed out of place in a ballet – the skirt seemed to be made up of hundreds of layers of tulle that hung in artful tatters from an embroidered silken bodice, and her shoulders were bare under the tendrils of hair that hung down to her waist. She had tiny silver bells tied to braids throughout the red strands, and they tinkled softly as she moved gracefully to meet them.

"Aisling, you've brought a guest? Yes, I know, you found him in the kitchen. His bold tale has reached my ear already." The lady smiled encouragingly at Merrick. "I am Fallon, and I am glad to make your acquaintance. This is my house, and though it seems strange, there are some great and lovely folk to be found here. You have already attached to some of the best, I can see."

Aisling looked downwards with an embarrassed smile, and Cullen gave Fallon a little bow with a pleased grin. Merrick instinctively felt that he could trust Fallon. She seemed to radiate purity and light.

"I'm Merrick, and I apologize for coming to your party uninvited. Something just told me that tonight was the night to be here. If I overstepped my bounds, I'm very sorry, but otherwise I would never have met you, and Aisling, and Cullen, and for that I'm very glad."

Fallon laughed with delight and took his hands in hers. "You are officially welcome in House Mirabilis."

She raised her voice just loud enough to cut through the party chatter, catching the attention of all in attendance. "You may come to this house whenever you wish, Merrick. I'll tolerate no mischief done to you, and in return I ask only that you keep the things you see here sub rosa. Do you understand what I am asking?"

She looked at him and nodded. "Of course you do, you are a bright and quick-witted raven. Aisling, will you agree to stand by him and guide him through our ways?"

Aisling's eyes opened wide, as though she had not suspected what Fallon would ask, although Merrick couldn't see why. It wasn't as if Aisling had seemed inclined to abandon him so far, for which he was infinitely grateful.

"I agree, Fallon, of course," she answered, and she seemed to be blushing slightly, which just confused Merrick. What was going on?

"Perhaps someday I'll actually be able to understand everything that is happening in one of these conversations," he lamented, and Fallon laughed.

"Perhaps someday you will. Do not be too hasty to unveil all of our mystery, Merrick. You will find skeletons with the flowers, I warn you. Although perhaps that would be welcome to you, little raven?"

"Do I resemble a raven that much? I tried to make my hair more artistic than rumpled, but I suppose the trip here mussed it a bit..." He broke off his musings when the small crowd assembled started to titter.

A somewhat wild looking man, who looked rather out of place with the rest of the group, laughed and quipped, "Better a raven than a jackdaw! You cannot see the blackbird? What a shame. You will find out much about yourself here, I suspect." He grimaced and said, "Ah, pardon my rudeness. I have no pert excuse, unlike some here. I am Sheridan. If you like the outdoors better than this sort of revel, we might be grand friends."

Merrick smiled and said, "I don't know that much, a few trees and flowers, but I'm always interested to learn more. And I'm Merrick."

Sheridan laughed loud and declared, "I like this one! He doesn't know what he's in for, but I like 'im! D'you drink beer? Because if so, you've got my attention!"

Merrick's affirmative answer gained him a place at a large, dark wooden table that looked like it had been hewn directly from a huge tree trunk in one great piece. Animal faces and fantastical creatures were carved into the top's edge and down the legs of the table with amazing skill and detail. The giant, red velvet upholstered chair they'd placed him in matched the table.

He had a very large tankard of beer placed in front of him, and it seemed that everyone else at the table had a drink as well. Sheridan's mug was even larger than Merrick's. Aisling had a delicate goblet with a golden liquid in it; he looked at her questioningly and she offered it to him to taste. It smelled sweet and melted on the tongue with a faint honeyed aftertaste.

"Mead. We trade with another house like ours, Gentry House. They make the best honey wine around," Aisling explained. "You have the beer that Sheridan makes. Try to drink it slowly, although he will want you to quaff it. Trust me on this one," she advised with a wink, as Sheridan hollered, "She's telling you to take it easy, isn't she? Gah, women. Drink! You must tell me what you think of our beer, Merrick!"

General laughter ensued, and Merrick took an enquiring sip. The brew was thick and tasted of oats and hops and honey, and he noticed that though it was cool in his throat, it had not been chilled. It was utterly delicious. He closed his eyes and sighed appreciatively, and Sheridan howled in triumph.

"Ah, we have confirmed his good taste! That settles it; he's a keeper." He pounded his fists on the table with each exhortation. The rest of the group, including Merrick, laughed, and began to drink in earnest.

Aisling brought platters of food and set them about the table. There were rich roasts cut in finger-sized bits, and chunks of creamy cheese to match. Dusky, tiny plums crowded around sugar-dusted cakes and cinnamon cookies, and green apple slices circled the outside of that plate. There was a smoked trout and wheaten crackers to serve the bits upon, and mushrooms that had been anointed with herbed oils. Merrick looked at the bounty and was amazed. These people really could throw a fabulous party.

Aisling would lean over from time to time and whisper into his ear information about people or background on stories being told. He drank, and laughed at the stories, although he did not contribute his own tales. He wasn't quite comfortable yet, although the beer was certainly helping. At one point, a very rosy cheeked Aisling started feeding him morsels of food, which he would take with kisses to her fingertips. She had slid into the chair with him, and they were very closely entwined. At first, he didn't notice, as drunk as he was, but slowly he realized that she was softly pressed against him. A warmth – that was not one bit alcohol related – crept through him, and he smiled blissfully and sank back into the chair.

Sheridan caught his expression and started laughing. "You look like a cat that discovered a dish of cream!"

Merrick just shot him a grin back, and Aisling stuck her tongue out at him. Bliss, Merrick thought to himself. This was pure heaven.

Someone changed the music playing, switching from the deep vocals and guitar of *Fields of the Nephilim* to something melodically different – archaic, yet modern, with a lovely female vocal set to it. Merrick cocked his head, listening intently to the song, and asked, "Who is this? Her voice is amazing."

Aisling said, "A little-known group from New York, known as Mors Syphilitica. I have heard that the vocalist was classically trained. They are quite appealing to us – magical, distantly beautiful, a little cruel."

He answered her, "I don't think you're cruel."

She put a finger over his lips. "Say no more of that, Merrick. I can be as unkind as any here, and more hurtful than some. You've known me but a night, and though your heart is good, you don't know the whole of how it is with us. You can decide what you think of me later, and I will think you a smart man."

Merrick didn't know how to answer that. She took away his need to answer with a kiss, deliciously lingering.

She pulled away and put her lips to his ear, tantalizingly close, and whispered, "Mark everything that happens now, and don't be too afraid. I will be right here. I'm sorry that I couldn't give you more warning."

He pulled his head away from her, his eyes full of shock and questions, and Fallon was suddenly there, a hand on his chin. She forced his gaze to hers and said, in a resonant tone, "Merrick, down."

He felt extreme lassitude take over his body; he could not move. "Aisling, Cullen, take him hence," Fallon commanded, and he found himself drifting along with his companions, to a green brocaded fainting couch which was in the center of a round room with a vaulted ceiling.

In the back of his mind, somewhere amidst the fog they'd induced in his brain, he remembered the Victorian style tower on the left side of the house. He guessed that's where they were now. The walls were hung with tapestries that were crumbling with age. They all seemed to depict naked creatures dancing in the woods, rather like a series by Bosch put to fabric. Candles burned in tall wrought iron holders randomly placed along the walls, and there was a seven-pointed star painted in silver at the apex of the ceiling. The couch was positioned directly under it.

"Who will stand with this one?" Fallon demanded of the room, which had filled with the revelers.

Aisling moved next to him, protectively. "I will!" she declared, laying a hand on the back of the couch.

Cullen flanked him on the other side and said, "I will."

Merrick saw Fallon's eyebrow raise just a bit at that. "No more so uninvolved, Cullen?"

He had the grace to look a touch embarrassed. "I see something in this one, Fallon. I am willing to cast my lot with him."

She nodded, and then grew genuinely surprised to see Sheridan behind Cullen.

He said, simply, "I like the boy."

Fallon shrugged, and said, "That seals the bargain from our end, but we may not commence until we hear from Merrick. What say you, little raven? You get this offer but once, and then no more. If you decline to join our dance, we will vanish in the morning, and you will remember this night as if it were a fever dream. If you take our hand – which I must impress upon you, we rarely extend – you will as surely belong to us as we will to you, for at least a seven-year bond. We may teach you much in that time, but you will be bound to us, as well. Do you understand?"

Merrick felt the torpor lift enough to gain some mobility, and he said, "I hear what you are saying, but what do you mean? Who are you, and why would you want me to join you? I can't just agree to join a group of unknowns – will you please explain?"

Fallon closed her eyes for just a moment and inclined her head. "Let us that stand here be revealed. Aisling, show him who we are."

Aisling took a small, lacquered box from her waistband, and opened it to reveal a sweet-smelling ointment. "I must apply this; will you allow that?" she asked him. Merrick nodded, confused. What on earth was going on?

"Close your eyes," she requested, and lightly rubbed the balm across his eyelids. He felt her apply it to his lips and forehead, then to the palms of his hands. She reached inside his shirt and dabbed some gently on his chest, and murmured, "There. It is done. Open your eyes, Merrick!"

Music: Peter Murphy
All Night Long

He saw Aisling first; he knew she'd planned it that way. Out of all of those in the room, she looked the most normal, for what that was worth. Her features were wilder and more fey, she had more curve to her – a softer, pale voluptuousness that made her even more inviting looking – but overall, she looked as he had seen her all night.

She smiled at him and said, "I am myself. I think you saw me from the first with your heart, and so no glamour was ever evident. But what of the rest? What do you think?"

He looked past her to Cullen, who also looked much the same, except with much pointier ears and eyes that reminded Merrick of a fox. His canines were very pointy when he smiled, and he looked every bit the rascal.

Fallon, on the other hand, was dramatically different in appearance. She was older, but no less regal. She seemed to have gained a majesty that was only accented by the extreme slant of her eyes and fullness of her features. She brought to mind at first glance a woodcut he'd seen long ago, an image of the Lady of the Moon, only painted in golden and reddish tones. Her ears were pointed and curled up at the tips, and she seemed to have tiny horns that rose from her eyebrows and arched back into her hair. They looked like they belonged on her, somehow.

When she smiled at him, it was if the whole room lit up. She radiated power and benevolence to him, and deep in his heart he was glad she was in charge of these strange creatures.

He turned then to Sheridan and found him to be much wilder looking than he'd expected. He was ragged and wild-haired – even more so than he'd appeared before – and most notably, every inch that Merrick could see of him was covered with thin and spidery blue swirled tattoos. He had rings that went down the outside edges of both his ears, and he wore brown leather bracers on his forearms that had rings along the edges of those, as well. Merrick could well imagine him living at the base of a tree somewhere in a great forest.

Sheridan grinned widely and handed him a small circlet made of branches and ivy, about the size of a bracelet. "Put this on, friend. Oak and ivy will do you well." Merrick slid it on his left arm, to the approving nod of his friend, and he gasped as it melted from the air and burned into his skin. It left behind a gorgeous tattoo, completely lifelike, of the leaves and branches entwined around his wrist. Merrick studied it incredulously.

Fallon urged him then, "We await your decision, Merrick. Can you stay with us for the appointed time and be one with us?"

He looked around the room, at all the different folk there: a small pixy-like boy with feathers for hair. The green-and-black harpies that were The Ladies. A group of tall tree-people, who bent and swayed with grace. A round, spiky woman that was surely related to a hedgehog, he would wager. Their magic and their exotic looks were overwhelming, enticing – how could he say no?

"I will join, Lady. How could I walk away from all of you?"

Fallon nodded, as if she had expected him to acquiesce. "Cullen. Bring the vial."

Aisling told him, "Lie back, love. You'll want to be comfortable for this, trust me."

He gave her a funny look but did as he was told. At this juncture, and as muddled as he felt, it seemed prudent to follow her directions – especially as he'd more or less put himself into their hands.

Cullen had returned with a gleaming decanter that was finely made of hand-blown scarlet glass. It glittered in his elegant hands, and he seemed to treat it reverently. He took the small glass that served as a lid from the top and filled it with a sparkling, clear liquid, then handed it to Merrick carefully.

"Drink it quickly, like a shot of fine liquor. It will burn going down, and act quickly," Cullen advised.

Merrick took a deep breath and said, "Cheers," then downed the glass in one fell swoop.

Fire blossomed inside, and the world spun around him. He felt the glass taken from his hand, and someone's cool hands – Aisling's? – on his brow for a moment.

From very far away, through a burst of starlight and fog, he heard

Fallon's crystalline voice say, "It is done. Merrick, you are ours for one cycle, and we are yours. *Ad vivum!*"

There was a cheer, and he realized that they were all crowded above him, in a circle. Each one dropped something on him – a flower, a berry, a glass bead, a tiny key. He lost track. He noted in a tiny corner of his mind that Edana dropped a thorn, and gave him a maliciously, pointy-toothed smile. She looked as if she wanted to devour him.

After leaving their offerings, the folk filed out, leaving Fallon for last. She kneeled next to Merrick on the couch, and gently mopped his brow before speaking. "You are a brave little blackbird and your courage does you credit. Do not fear what happens now – we have given you gifts that will evidence themselves 'ere long, and I think they will make your heart glad that you chose this path." She laid a rainbow-sheened black feather upon Merrick's chest, and told him, "When you are ready, you will fly." She kissed him on the forehead and then left, with only a lingering scent of amber to note her passing.

Merrick suddenly felt very ill and convulsed violently. He knew he would have to retch, and tried desperately to get to the door, get outside, not soil this place... but Sheridan was there, holding him down, while Aisling provided a container for his sickness. After a bit, it passed, and Cullen brought in a goblet of water and gave him sips until he felt settled.

All during this, the walls moved around them, and the ceiling breathed. He could see shadows moving in the corners of his vision, but when he whipped his head around to catch them skulking, there was nothing to be seen. He sighed with frustration and confusion. What had they done to him?

Hours or days passed; he knew not which. Sheridan left, and returned with the remains of a fresh rabbit, and blood on his hands. He held it out to Merrick in offering, and Merrick grimaced and cowered in fear. The wild man laughed and left, but not before smearing a touch of the blood on the soles of Merrick's bare feet. Where had his boots gone?

He slept, and woke in a fevered dream state, and strangeness raged around him. Once he awoke to find the room filled with small blue birds; at his shout, they took to flight excitedly and started crashing about the chamber. One landed at the foot of his bed and morphed into the small boy that had been at his initiation. "Fortune favors the brave, blackbird," he whispered, then took off, half-winged. Merrick cried out and fell into blackness.

Falling into a deep pit, a consuming darkness that he thought perhaps he might never escape from... but then Aisling was there, and she had him in her grasp, pulling him towards sunlight. He opened his eyes and found that the room was bathed in daylight, the heavy curtains thrown back to allow the light in, blinding in its brilliance.

Aisling was asleep on the floor next to the small lounge, her thin hand stretched up from where she was to grasp his wrist. She looked exhausted, and he carefully disengaged her from his arm before trying to rise. He felt as if he'd been on that couch for days, and his equilibrium seemed to agree, as he could only achieve a stumbling, awkward angle once he made it up from his bed. He smelled awful, too. What a party!

He wondered what it was that they'd given him to drink. He was ravenous, but he was so dizzy that he doubted that anything he ate would stay down anyway. He shook his head to clear away the cobwebs, only to start another bout of vertigo – and rising up out of that miasma of brain-swirl, he realized something very odd. The walls of the room, which he would have sworn to be white when he first saw them, were covered with an odd pattern... no, not a pattern. Words. HIS words.

Somewhere along the time he could not recall, he had covered the walls – as high as he could reach – with writing. He stared incredulously at his handiwork, wondering how he could have done so much in a night... or two?

"Aisling, wake up. I need to know how long I have been here."

She groaned softly from her place on the floor, and said, "Merrick, what's wrong?"

He knelt down next to her and asked, "What happened here? I can't remember anything! How long has it been?"

Aisling muttered, "I am so not ready to deal with this." She gave him a hopeful look and asked, "I don't suppose we can have some breakfast first, could we? No, no hope of that I see. Ugh." She buried her face in her hands for a moment, then popped back up wearing a serious look. "Okay. Sit down, then, this might be a little weird."

She took a deep breath, and said, "We have always been here, but what we are is up for debate. People – your people – have given us many different names to bear. We were considered gods by much of the ancient world, the Romans and Hellenes and Celts. Then we became Faerie, Fae, Pixie... we slowly sank in stature in your minds, and by the time of the Industrial Revolution, many of our kind were gone, died off from being unable to adapt. The ones who remained learned that there were things we could still do here, ways to belong. There are pockets of us left, spread over the world, hidden in your midst and living along with you. Our presence brings creativity, beauty, artistry – but we need you, as well. Without your thoughts, your energy, your ability, we cannot live. It is a symbiotic relationship of the highest degree, but the rub is that you do not need us in the way that we need you.

"Without you, we will wither and die away. Without us, you will continue on. We merely spur your people to greater heights. We give you dreams and visions, inspire you to ideas and expressions you might not have found unaided. I will not lie to you – we need you. We can give you much, but we take, as well. What you give to us is valuable to us without measure. Do you understand?"

Merrick shook his head, slowly. "This is more than a little weird, Aisling, this is really fucking weird. So, say I just accept what you're saying: that you're some race of people who look like us, talk like us, and live off of our energy like succubi or something. And in return I'll get really fucking creative. Right?"

She mutely gestured at the walls. He exhaled hard, frustrated.

"What the fuck. You gave me DRUGS. I took them. Of course I did something crazy like cover the walls with my scribbling. I don't even remember what happened. And you still haven't told me how long I've been here! Aisling, I like you. I'm not angry, even – just very, very confused. I want to understand what's going on. I can't imagine a reason why you'd make up a story like that, but I can't say that anything that's happened in my life would support what you're saying, either."

She laughed at that, and in a cynical tone retorted, "You've never seen a black hole. Do they exist? What about mitochondria? Bristlecone pines, even. Have you seen one? They don't live as long as one of our kind can, if we wish. People talk about them, sometimes, but how many people do you know who have actually seen one? Trust me, they exist, and so do my people. You can see us easily, whereas most people cannot see our true shapes – we have given you this gift. We gave you the greatest gift we can give one of your kind. We gave you some of our essence, which opens your mind to the beauty around you, and will help you express it. We need you, but we won't leave you empty-handed, this I promise. Look at what you wrote! Look at what just a few days here gave you!"

He wandered to the wall, angry and just a little scared. He wanted to believe her, he really did, but her assertions scared him no end. What if this was all true? What would this do to his world? He felt like he was ready to step out into the abyss, and he was terrified.

He traced some of the words he had written on the walls. "Deep pool eyes, into your depths, I can see all around me but I do not understand. Will you make a path for me, blaze it with your clarity? Can you save me from myself?" He sang the words softly, remembering that he had created the song there on the spot. He had written it for Aisling, and she had cried as he sang it. "I have to go. This is too much at once."

Aisling looked alarmed. "You have to understand – you will come back. You pledged yourself to us. You'll be drawn until you have no rest, no peace. And what's more – neither will I. I stood for you, and I am bound to be by your side, do you understand? As you decline, so shall I. We will be miserable."

She turned suddenly at the hand on her shoulder, to find Cullen standing there. "He's a raven through and through, Aisling. He'll have to figure it out on his own. Don't despair." Cullen inclined his head to Merrick and said, "So she has given you the tale, and you choose to disbelieve?" Merrick looked trapped, and Cullen laughed dismissively.

"I will explain something to you, and just this once. I am not known for choosing sides. I am not usually the one to look to when you have a battle to fight. I see something in you, something rich and strange and desperately needed by us. I see that you need us as well, that you are searching for something that you have not been able to find. Here we are, and you run from it like we showed you your deepest fears.

"You may run, Merrick, but you cannot stay away from your dreams forever and be a whole man. I stood for you and continue to do so, but you must figure out what it is that you really want. I would hate to think that I finally took action on something, only to be proven wrong – I choose to put my faith in the belief that you will come to your senses. If you knew me, you would know this is quite the remarkable feat for me." Cullen stepped back, an unreadable expression on his face, and crossed his arms, waiting.

Merrick felt trapped, confused, and guilty. Why did they want him? How could they believe something so strongly of him, something that he couldn't see himself? He had to get away from this place, take some time to think. "Aisling, I... I need time. I need to get my head on straight. I'll call, come by, I don't know. I'm scared."

With that, he grabbed his jacket and ran out the door. Aisling looked at Cullen with the saddest expression on her face. "He might not return. He doesn't even understand what that will mean for him."

Cullen shook his head, sadly. "He will have to learn the difficult way, then. It isn't like you won't be seeing him, Aisling! Don't act like I didn't know what it meant when Fallon asked you to guide him. You'll be in his dreams; you can help to explain some of this. We may abide, Aisling, but we must have him back eventually, for the good of all. He will see this eventually; even a raven can only be so stubborn."

Music: Mira

Tick Tock

Merrick fled home in a panic. What had he done? Had he just tossed the perfect opportunity out the window? What if he could never go back?

He leaned his head against the cold pane of the bus window and let his thoughts turn over and over until he wanted to vomit. He hated being this unsure of anything, and he felt as if he might have walked away from the sort of opportunity that he had only ever been able to dream of before this. At the same time, the sheer strangeness of the folk that resided in that house, and the events that had happened there... well, it terrified him, to be honest.

Even Aisling, who had been nothing but wonderful to him, had such an aura of the supernatural about her that it confused him. The rational part of his mind knew that he was trying to assimilate foreign concepts. His grip on reality had been seriously compromised with the revelation of the strange people in that household.

The bus finally made it through its winding route to his neighborhood, which was a green and garden-filled oasis in the upper part of the city, well known as a home to artists, musicians and other artsy folk. Many of the rowhomes had large picture windows, which were decorated with wacky treatments that changed often. Merrick's next-door neighbor had a mannequin that he would dress in vintage fashions that echoed the seasons, complete with a vignette around it to reflect the theme. Right now, she sported a Puritan frock, and a giant turkey lurked behind her. Notably, the turkey sported rather psychedelic plumage, rather than the regular coloring. "Go figure," Merrick thought with a laugh.

Merrick's apartment was on the first floor, a decently spacious studio affair with vaulted ceilings and windows that ran the height of the walls.

He came in and opened the shutters, allowing light to pour into the space and set the dust motes to dazzling him. The floors were hardwood, covered here and there by some ancient Persian throw rugs, so he always took his boots off as soon as he could, to keep from scuffing the floor.

He decided that a shower would soothe him into a better frame of mind and stripped off all his clothing into a wilted little puddle. He looked down and started in surprise when he saw the tattoo fresh on his arm. He had forgotten it entirely. He brought his wrist up to inspect it closely, marveling at the intricate details in the oak and ivy leaves. He also found a small bag hanging around his neck; this he took off and determined that he would investigate later, after the reviving shower.

He let the water pour over his head for a long time, until he felt that he couldn't stay wet any longer. He shook his head at the amount of woody debris and leaves that washed out of his hair and off him in general. It looked as if he'd been rolling around in the woods for days.

He slid into dark blue flannel PJ pants and a black tee and decided that he needed tea in his garden. The garden was accessible from French doors that opened out from his main room, and it was a small but lovely courtyard-type space. There was a small fountain in the north corner, abutted against the house. Birds often frequented it, splashing about whether people were in the garden or not. There was a creeping rose arbor, with a few remaining roses clinging to the canes even at this late date in the year. The small maple was already devoid of leaves, reaching branches like fingers towards the sky. The rest of the garden was mostly herbs, left over from a previous occupant, and they often would emit delightful green smells when stirred by the wind.

Merrick had a small café table and chairs in the back of the space, where he would drink coffee or tea and escape from the inner city for a while. He made some chamomile tea in a colorfully swirled ceramic mug and plopped down in the chair that faced towards the fountain with a big sigh. Sipping the tea slowly, he realized that he was exhausted, and he still didn't know what day it was.

He figured that he'd already lost his job. He knew that he had lost at least a day, and he had been scheduled to work on Monday at the little convenience store down on Read Street. He wasn't too alarmed, as his bills were paid for the month, and he really wanted to get something better anyway... but it would have been nice to get the reference. Ah well, at least his adventure took care of one detail in an interesting way.

Merrick never even noticed when he slipped into sleep.

In Dreamtime

The forest was very dark, although Merrick couldn't tell if it was nighttime or overcast. No, there was the moon, desperately trying to shine through the branches that overlapped overhead and towered menacingly above him. He could hear water trickling from somewhere ahead of him, and he decided to make his way to the source, for lack of a better plan.

He kept tripping over roots and branches, and at one point a small animal ran across his feet, scurrying into the darkness and scaring the living daylights out of him. He needed a clue, a sign of what he was supposed to do! He saw two glowing eyes on the path ahead of him, down low. A cat, or a raccoon? It seemed to wink at him, and for Merrick that was enough of a sign. He followed it as it picked a path through the brush. They came to a clearing, and he finally saw the small guide before it ran off – a fox. Recognition dawned on him for just a moment... for one split second, everything made sense to him.

He fell down in the long grass, on his back to gaze into the stars above, laughing in happiness. He had the answers, he could choose whatever he wanted! He felt a soft touch on his forehead, hands on either side, and he found that he was looking up at Aisling, his head in her lap. She was smiling at him, but tears were running down her cheeks. He tried to tell her not to cry, but he seemed unable to talk, so he reached up and wiped away her tears.

He awoke to find raindrops coming down in quick bursts from the now overcast sky. He rose from the chair absently – and rather stiffly – and tried to figure out what his dream was about, exactly.

He wandered inside and splashed water on his face, trying to shake the fog from his brain. The phone rang, startling Merrick and making him jump. He picked it up and warily said, "Uh... hello?"

"Merrick! Where have you been all week? I've been worried sick! You got fired, you know. You stood me up for our coffee date. You just disappeared!"

Merrick sighed the sigh of the long suffering. It was his best friend, Lucee. She was very supportive, incredibly fun and cute, and unfortunately could come off as rather invasive and needy. This indelicate combination of traits left her on an eternal search for people to date, and when she was in a bad spell, Merrick would bear the brunt of social interaction. He loved her to death, but she could rub him the wrong way sometimes. Now he was torn, because what was he going to tell her?

"Hi, Lucee. I'm sorry that I missed our coffee meet. I suck, I know. I went to a party and ended up being very – well, out of it. Someone spiked my drink." That was true, in a way. "It was a crazy party," he added, weakly. "Hello?" She didn't respond. Merrick whirled around suddenly, at the sound of knocking on his door. He flung it open, and yelled, "Lucee! Why didn't you tell me you were on your cell phone and on your way here? I'm not in the mood for visitors!"

She barged past him, with a bag in her hand and a bottle of wine. "Shut up, you know you want to tell me everything, and I've got dinner, too. You look like you haven't eaten in a week." She pulled a variety of take-out boxes from the paper bag and made an offering gesture. "Lo Mein, Hunan Shrimp, egg rolls, some dumplings. Take your pick of whatever. I got all your favorites."

Merrick scowled, although secretly he was touched that she'd gone to the effort for him. "What if I hadn't been here? You would have bought all this food for nothing," he scolded, while he retrieved chopsticks from a drawer.

She shrugged and grinned at him. "I would have a lot of leftovers, then. And I called first, didn't I? Besides, you're just trying to distract me from your prime story. Where were you? Enquiring minds want to know!"

Merrick sighed, knowing that he was going to have to tell her something, if just to satisfy her curiosity. "You know the infamous party place, that big house out in the county with the super artsy people that we've all wanted to crash? I did." He waited for her response and was rewarded with a squeal of delight.

"Do tell! You went all by yourself? I didn't think you had it in you, Merrick! What was it like?"

Merrick considered this. "It was... a party. There were some nice people, and some rude and snotty ones. There was some magnificent food – the house is beautiful, too. I met a girl."

He looked up at Lucee and winced. "Shut up. Yes, she's lovely and witty. I don't know if I'll see her again. Something happened. Drugs. Some sort of hallucinogen. I don't remember a lot of the time I was there, it was bad, it made me sick. The girl tried to help me through it. That's really all I can say. I left this morning, came home. I'm here now, and I still don't remember most of it. Happy?"

She glowered at his tale, not impressed by the thought that someone had slipped him drugs, or that he couldn't account for most of the time he'd been away. "A week, Merrick! Did you have fun, at least? You sound pretty wiped out – was it bad? You're not giving me nearly enough information to make me feel better about all this!"

She swept her hair, tiny acid green and black braids that exploded from her head and hung to her chin, back out of the way. She only did that when she was extremely excited or agitated.

Lucee curled herself up in a ball in her chair, hugging herself tightly. He wished she wouldn't make herself look so vulnerable at a time like this. He remembered his promise not to tell about the people in the house; it burned in his brain as if it had been branded there.

"Lucee... it was really crazy. I seriously can't recall a lot of what happened. There were a few people that lived there that were really nice to me and helped me through everything, and I might go back again, I don't know. I'm still trying to sort everything out. I honestly didn't even realize a week had gone by, if you can believe that. Could explain why I'm so out of it!"

He suddenly felt like crying, so he grabbed the bottle of wine and took a swig to hide the emotion. If he started that, he might not finish for a while, and he hadn't felt like this since he was twelve and endured beatings from bullies every day at school. Lucee caught the expression on his face and wisely let the moment pass.

She looked up a few minutes later and said, "I got us a gig, you know. But you have to be able to show up, Merrick. You can't go gallivanting off to another adventure until the show!" She grinned at his astonished expression.

He stammered, "But we haven't practiced in ages! And... where did you get us a gig? That's fucking awesome!"

Lucee crowed with excitement, "Club Marcada! I know, I know – it is a hole in the wall. But they heard a practice tape and liked it, and they're desperate for people to take the stage on weekdays. I told them that The Drawback hadn't played a show before, and they didn't seem to care. Now we just need to tell Sousa, and we're good to go!"

Merrick gave her an exasperated look. "You haven't asked Souz yet? And when is the show, by the by? I might have a better time of keeping the calendar open if I knew!"

She rolled her eyes at him. "No, I just found out, dorko. The show would be this Thursday, we would go on at eleven pee-em sharp. Probably not much pay, but free drinks and food. We have to flyer, they'll put an ad in the papers. We're the real deal, Merrick!"

She squealed with joy and grabbed him for a hug. He automatically put his arms around her and hugged back, but she could sense his stiffness. "What's wrong, sweetie? You're still acting really funny. And you have a weird look to you, too. Are you still feeling off?"

Merrick nodded, answering, "I can't get back here, if you know what I mean. I feel really disassociated still. Like if I closed my eyes for too long, all of this would just melt away and turn into something else, something much stranger and foreign. Does that make sense?" He thought to himself, of course it didn't. She wasn't there this week; she has no idea.

Lucee looked at him, sadly. "I wish I knew what to do. I brought all my healing goodies – dinner, wine, good news – that's all I've got, Merrick. Should I just let you sleep it off?"

Merrick nodded slowly. "I think maybe a long sleep might help. Maybe I'll get my head together through the night, and wake up back to normal, eh?"

Lucee wasn't convinced, but she smiled and gave him a hug before she left. "I'll call Sousa and tell him what's up – band practice tomorrow, at eight! Bye!"

She shut the door softly behind her, and Merrick cleaned up the apartment in a daze. He felt like he'd been wrapped in cotton from head to toe – he wanted to feel and think, but he just was completely numb. Nothing would be better than going to sleep, he decided. He pulled his futon out from the wall, made a nest with blankets and pillows, and put on a CD from Sopor Aeturnus before he turned down the lights and climbed into the covers. He was asleep before he was in the bed for more than a minute.

In Dreamtime

Everything was dark, and he seemed to be hiding in a corner of a room; the walls were rough and damp. He heard whispers, male and female voices, in a language he didn't know, and then in Latin.

"*Finis coronat opus,*" the male voice whispered.

"*Omnia mutantur, nos et mutantur in ilis. Nom sum qualis eram,*" the female voice replied.

A soft touch on the arm startled him, but he made no sound as he whirled to find Aisling there beside him, finger to her lips. She pulled him through a hole in the wall that had not been there a second before, and into a small but lovely chamber. There was a burgundy velvet covered bed, and the walls were draped with tapestries that made the room feel sumptuous but cozy. There was a small table of dark wood with a fat candle burning on it. Merrick thought the place felt familiar.

Aisling said, "This is where we have met in your dreams before, when you were at the house with us. I tried to tell you many things there, but you were still confused. Do you remember?"

Merrick considered this. What did he remember of that time?

"Do you remember Sheridan? Cullen? Fallon?" she asked.

"Of course I remember them. Sheridan gave me beer. Cullen was there with that vile woman, Edana – right? I think we are friends now. Oh. Fallon... I remember...."

The room faded, and he was back in the room where he had stood before them all. "I... wrote things. I never really took the time to read any of them." He walked over to one of the walls, started reading aloud. "Like attracts like, this we know to be true. What brought me to you? Trust her, she means you no harm. Where shall I rest when my day is done? Her name means / a dream / she brings dreams / she came from dreams." Merrick looked up at Aisling. "You?" She nodded.

"I can bring you inspiration. I am a servant of sleep, a muse for the creative, a nocturnal helper. Although truth be told, I can come to you at any time. I was born from the Dreamworld, and there I am most at home. But I have something important to tell you, Merrick."

She pushed some strands of hair from her face, stood there looking at him earnestly. "You have to come back to us. We are like a drug in the system for you, as you are for us. The longer you stay away, the worse it will become, until neither of us will be very happy. Have you ever suffered withdrawal? You will not enjoy this at all, I promise you. I fear to see you come to this. You are afraid of us, and you need not be. We want you to be with us, we wish you no harm. Will you come back, Merrick?"

She looked so sad and dismayed, he wanted to go to her right then – but no. He had to think, he had to wait... he broke into a run, away from her....

Merrick awoke in a pool of sweat. What the hell? When did his dreams become this clear, this... weird? He usually had dreams about things that would never happen, or random, everyday things. Nothing like this, where people he had just met showed up and told him what was best for him or told him secrets about themselves that he could never in a million years make up on his own. He had no frame of reference for this.

He looked at the clock by his bed; only two-thirty in the morning. Damn! He tried to get back to sleep, but his mind kept mulling over the week he'd lost, trying to reconstruct what he was missing, and trying to figure out what the dream meant in relation to this. What had he written on the walls? Why would Aisling insist that they were like a drug? He thought further into things – wait, she'd claimed to be from the land of dreams. Obviously, he couldn't take all of this dream too seriously. There was a nagging feeling at the back of his mind that insisted that he should, though.

Enough of this, he decided. It was time for a stronger weapon. He rose up and shuffled over to the bathroom, took two valerian capsules from the medicine cabinet. He would go back to sleep, try to dream normal, healthy, non-confusing dreams. This seemed the most sensible solution for him at this point in the night, and he was ready to pass out and forget everything for a while. He sank into his bed with a sigh and pulled the covers up until he was almost under them. All he wanted was sleep, now.

In Dreamtime

He sat up in bed, cursing. "Why can't I just sleep! I just want to rest for a while, dammit..." He was startled by soft laughter, and he realized that Aisling was there with him.

"You have your wish, although I cannot guarantee that this will be a restful sleep. I'll try not to be too disturbing, though." She smiled at him, lovely and composed, perched on the end of his bed like she belonged there.

"Aisling. What are you doing here?" Merrick was utterly confused at this point.

"I'm here, but not where you think I am, Merrick. I'm in your dream, but not at your house. I don't know where you live. I've been looking for you, searching... Cullen says that you'll come back when you're ready, but I'm unsure of that, myself. I suspect that you have a hard head and will hold off as long as you can." She looked sad at that, infinitely worried for him.

"Merrick, you are vital to our survival. I hate putting such a burden on you so quickly – but there is so much to give in return! I haven't even begun to show you the magic of the Dreamworld, places you would have a difficult time getting to on your own, startling beauty and soul-shaking oddness that will give your music such inspiration to draw from! We gave you gifts, too, and you have not yet even begun to touch on what those have to offer you. Will you at least consider us without running away from me?"

Merrick frowned and replied, "Even if I wanted to run, I don't think I could right now. I took valerian; I'm stuck asleep until it wears off. That stuff always puts me out for ages." He snorted and added, "I can't believe I'm taking this seriously. Oh, I talk to people in dreams who I just met, and they give me advice and magical gifts – no one will believe me when I claim that."

Aisling chuckled and slid closer, gesturing around her as she did, "And you can control – to some degree – what happens here, too. We don't have to be in your bedroom if we wish; we can go anywhere you can imagine, or someplace that I have been that you don't even know yet. You can do whatever you can conceive of, once you learn to control yourself here, especially if I am with you. Most people would call this lucid dreaming. This is where I'm from, so this is second nature to me."

Merrick said, "You've said this before, and I remember that I wrote it on the wall – that you came from dreams. What do you mean? You can't literally mean you were born here..."

She put a finger to her lips, then answered, "If you remember to ask me in waking hours, I promise to answer to the best of my ability. Remember this, Merrick: those you encounter might lead you astray, or trick you with a quick hand, but they cannot lie in the Dreamtime. They can refuse to answer you, but we speak with our hearts here."

Merrick raised an eyebrow at this, and asked her, "Then I want to know: why are you chasing me around? What do I have that is so important to you and your people that you will go out of your way to haunt my dreams to get me back?"

Aisling closed her eyes for a moment, then opened them and looked directly at him while answering, "I've told you we need you, and I am not exaggerating. Our house is dying, the people around me cannot sustain without a vital, creative source to inspire. Like air and water to you, we need mortals – your kind – to give us belief and lend us imagination, or we fade away. The fading is slow and desperate, and we fear it with all of our being. They have grown bitter and jaded in their desperation, and only a few of us hold onto our cheerful dispositions as we search for one who might join us and benefit from a mutual partnership, if you will."

Merrick closed his eyes and sighed, confused and disturbed. Aisling said softly, "Can I help?" and slipped her arms around him, a comforting and gentle embrace that he resisted at first, but finally relaxed into with another sigh.

He thought to himself for a moment, this is a dream. She is a dream. I am free, in this moment.

He leaned back just enough to move her hair from his face, and kissed her gently, slowly, a kiss that grew in passion until they were crushing themselves together, clinging to each other as for dear life. Merrick's hands were entangled in Aisling's hair, and when he slid from kissing her mouth down to the curve of her pale neck, she tilted her head back in a way that made him mad with desire for her.

"Merrick," she murmured, her voice soft with ardor, "If we continue this, you will have put yourself in a situation where you will have to come to House Mirabilis. Do you understand? The further we go, the more you become entrenched in our pull, until you will burn with the need to be with us."

Merrick groaned, "Nothing is easy with you people, I swear!"

She sighed, "I do not like this either, Merrick. You should sleep some uninterrupted sleep, anyway. Here." She gently pushed him back so that he was lying in the bed, and she slid under the blanket with him. "Curl up with me, go to sleep. You'll awake in the Waking World, and you will feel more rested."

Merrick decided that holding her until he fell asleep wasn't so bad of a deal, and when she slipped between his arms and nestled her head against his chest, he was so content that he barely remembered falling asleep, there in his dreams...

Music: Bauhaus

Mask

H e awoke to the sun shining through the front windows onto his face, in what seemed a concentrated effort to wake him up. "Aisling?" he muttered, confused. She was not there, of course, she had never been there last night. She didn't even know where he lived! He sighed, both slightly disappointed and disturbed by his nocturnal activities. He was having a very hard time believing that he wasn't going insane or being fooled in some way. Obviously, this wasn't normal, and he'd never had a lucid dream like that before.

He dragged himself from bed and took a shower that lasted much longer than normal. He stood under the warm spray of water for forty-five minutes, just letting the water relax him. When he finally emerged, he was a bit pruney and not any closer to feeling better about any of the recent events.

He looked at the clock – eleven thirty, not too early to call Lucee and get some coffee, he decided. He threw on a black tee with the logo for the Deathrock band The Brickbats on it, some black jeans, and his tall Gripfast boots. It took a while to lace those up, so he called Lucee and put her on speakerphone while he laced.

"Lucee! Wake up! Coffee!" he yelled when she picked up.

She laughed and said, "Merrick, I was waiting for that call! Are we going to the Frisky?"

Merrick rolled his eyes privately, but replied in an upbeat voice, "Uh, where else, smarty pants? I mean, no one makes chocolate croissants like those freaks. And besides, I'm too cheap to spend my money at the corporate chain. Are you dressed?"

She was, and they decided to meet in fifteen minutes. Merrick looked in the mirror, stuck his tongue out at his reflection, brushed his teeth, and considered his hair before just dampening his hands and mussing it artfully. Good enough for government work, he decided. His hair obliged by sticking out at all sorts of crazy angles, as if he'd spent hours styling it, and he grinned at the look.

"Oh, you'd never look like that if I was going out to a club, stupid hair!" He laughed and grabbed his leather jacket before ducking out.

The Frisky Bean was the coolest coffee bar in town, hands down. They were open twenty-four hours a day, to start. They hired the freaks of town, so you could always find a great mix of Goths, Hippies, Rockers, Artists and Punks working behind the counter. They sometimes had live music at night, and always had good music on the sound system. There were giant, overstuffed velour couches in purple and red scattered around the back, and many tables in the front. They even had shelves with tons of classic paperback novels, poetry books, a dictionary and thesaurus, and board games. All the wood was dark and old and welcoming, and the place was perfect for spending long hours in, relaxing or working on a novel or paper.

Merrick and his friends had been coming to The Frisky for ages; it was especially popular to visit after a long night of clubbing or after a gig. Merrick had always wanted to work there, but they were never hiring when he needed a job, so he had decided that the fates wanted him to keep the place untainted from job associations.

For once, the place was rather deserted, which suited Merrick just fine. He found his favorite corner, where a red couch and purple overstuffed chair met and made their own little world and claimed it with his jacket before going to the steel counter to place his order. A large latte with a quad shot of espresso and a croissant later, he wandered back to his selected spot and found Lucee there, just taking off her jacket.

"Ah, you beat me to it. I was gonna treat," she said.

Merrick grinned and said, "You treated last night. I got this."

She shook her head vigorously. "Na, na. You're jobless, remember? I have a swank job – shut up, it's more than you have – and I can take care o' meself, bucko."

She bounced off, in time to the lilt of the ska of The Specials over the speakers, and came back with a giant mug of coffee, black, and an oatmeal cookie that was almost as big as her head. "I'll be eating this for the rest of the week," she quipped as she plopped down in the corner of the couch.

Merrick had claimed the chair as his own and had put his booted feet up on the coffee table in the meantime.

"So," she asked around a bit of cookie, "How are you feeling today? Anything new to report?"

He frowned, "Ever have lucid dreams before, Lucee? I seem to be having a very active dream life these days."

She raised an eyebrow and replied, "No, but I'm envious. Can you control the dreams?"

He shook his head, "Not really, although I'm talking and conversing while I know I'm asleep, which is weird enough, and the same person keeps showing up in these dreams, telling me that I could do more in the dreams if I tried. She even told me that they were lucid dreams and that I'd keep having them."

Lucee smiled and asked, "The girl you met this week, yes? You got a funny look on your face when you mentioned her. Any reason why it's her, I wonder?"

Merrick weighed his words carefully. He'd promised not to tell of the people at House Mirabilis, but this was his best friend, and he needed to test his sanity somehow, right? Aisling, he thought, I hope you don't get mad. God knows what you could do to me if you were angry.

He took a deep breath and said, "She claims to be a... well, a muse of sorts. One who works through dreams. And I guess at this point I'm inclined to believe her, because she's been showing up in my dreams since then, conversing with me just as you and I are right now."

Lucee sat there for a moment, looking at him. Merrick looked away, a bit sheepishly. He had stuck his foot in his mouth this time, oh yes. Lucee finally said, "Maybe she is, then."

Merrick shot her an incredulous look, and she retorted, "Well, we don't know jack about the world really, do we? I'm sure there are all sorts of things out there that exist that we don't know about; dismissing them as unreal just because I haven't experienced them would be rather egotistical of me. Then again, it could be the after-effects of the drugs you were slipped, but I have my doubts. More than likely it is just the power of suggestion, but again, I don't get that feeling."

She stopped suddenly, staring at his arm in shock. "Hey! When did you get that tattoo?" She grabbed his arm, looked at it closely. "That's really fucking cool looking! The detail is much too good for most of the local artists – where did you get it done? And when did you find time?" She gave him the first skeptical look of the day he'd had from her. "Did you just run off somewhere else for the week? Have you been making all this up to fuck with me? I bought you dinner!"

Merrick cracked up at that.

"Would you believe me if I told you that they put it there? The people at the party? I have no reason to make this crap up, you know. I wish I had been off having fun somewhere else, where I might have had a chance to hold onto the memories from the weekend!"

She gave in, "Yes, yes, you're right. I'm just as confused as you are, and I know there's tons you haven't told me yet, too. These people, man. They seem really strange. I can't figure out what they're all about. Tattoos? Really good tattoos, and people who show up in your dreams and give you directions on how to control 'em... who slip you drugs and keep you around for a week, incommunicado. What else aren't you telling me, Merrick? Next, you'll say that they've initiated you into some sort of strange cult, and that you've fallen in love with this girl."

There was an awkward silence, which Lucee ended with an expletive. "Merrick! FUCKING HELL!" The few people in the coffee shop all turned around and looked at them, and she waved a hand, dismissively. "Sorry, sorry."

She turned back to Merrick then, red in the face. "What the fuck? Look, you're my best friend. I'm fucking worried about you! Did you promise them that you wouldn't tell anyone anything? Gah!" She turned away, genuinely angry.

Merrick said softly, "I'm scared too, Lucee. But at the same time... I'm really intrigued. There's so much I want to tell you, and I promised – not a normal promise either, I swore that I wouldn't tell. I can tell you that weird in my head stuff happened before I swore not to talk about things. We're talking mental battles in my head stuff, Lucee. And yes, that was before drugs or whatever it was. I was off balance from the moment I walked in, because the people there are unlike any other. They're... otherworldly. Some are beautiful, others are just odd and they're all obviously different from you and I."

He paused, looked at Lucee very seriously. "Aisling – that's the girl – tried to help me from the very beginning. She warned me of the weirdness and tried to help me through. She's really great, Lucee."

He decided to tell her as much as he could and gave her a version that included the incidents with Edana and Morgance but left out the parts about his "initiation." She listened with a peculiar look on her face, as though she couldn't decide whether to believe him or slap him, insulted.

"So, you're saying that this Morgance went into your mind to attack you? And this was before you were given the drugs? Are you sure?"

He sighed, "I hadn't had a thing to eat or drink at that point; I'd barely arrived. And even when I had the strange confrontation with Edana, I had the feeling from those people – the ones who were unpleasant – that they held danger for me. I was not just feeling threatened by Morgance. I felt as though I was battling for my soul with her, that if I'd lost, I would have been in a world of trouble. Even Aisling didn't seem able to help me then. Cullen tried to lead her away from me, but she wouldn't be swayed – she wanted something from me, I have no idea what. And they kept addressing me as 'Raven' or 'Blackbird' as if this was a proper name for me."

Lucee said, "Well, considering the source, it probably was! Good grief. I think I'm having a harder time dealing with this than you are. And this Ashleen –"

Merrick interrupted with, "Ash-lin. Softer vowels."

Lucee rolled her eyes and retorted, "Aisling, whatever. Merrick – do you trust her? It sounds as if you do, and you just met her! What if they had just planned an elaborate ruse to make fun of the invader?"

She stopped and sat back, laughed softly at herself. "Listen to me. I'm berating you as if you weren't twenty-seven years old and perfectly capable of making these decisions on your own. All I'm saying is that events of the past week may have impaired your judgement. I'm just trying to cover all the bases here, so you don't fly off and get involved in something without seeing all the angles. Fair?"

Merrick inclined his head slightly and said, "I know. I don't resent your outlook; in fact, I appreciate it. I think I need to separate myself from them for a few more days, try to keep some distance while I gain perspective. Lucee, I think I need to stay awake during that, so she won't show up in my dreams. I think if I keep seeing her in my head, I'll get more confused."

She snorted at the thought. "Well, that should lead to a few interesting days, at least. Do you have what you need? You're going to need more than coffee, that's for sure."

Since practice was at eight, they had time to get what he'd need to stay awake. They refilled their coffee for the road, and as Merrick left, he told the barista, "I suspect you'll be seeing a lot of me for the next few days!"

She laughed and replied, "Bring it on!"

The first stop was the convenience store on Calvert Street, where they bought over-the-counter speed and tons of high-caffeine soda. They walked over to his apartment and dropped everything off. Lucee went to her place and retrieved her guitar, and they managed to kill several hours in Pepe's Music, looking at instruments they couldn't afford and getting Lucee's guitar a tune up, before heading over to Sousa's for band practice.

Joseph Sousa, or Souz to his friends, was an outright enigma – even to the people who were closest to him. He was independently wealthy, yet he dressed like a gutterpunk, albeit cleaner than one. He owned a large building on Park Street, a strange brick monstrosity that was slowly wearing down around the edges. It had turrets and huge dark wood staircases that curved around the inside. The place was huge, and always dark inside.

The part he lived in was broken into rooms rather badly, but Souz just used each section to store different things. One room was full of scooters and scooter parts, reflecting his love for rebuilding Vespas. Another big space was the band's place, which had an outside entrance and a balcony. They all had keys and were welcome to come at any time to practice or just hang out, as long as they stayed out of the rest of the building. They even had a complete kitchen, with a fridge filled with beer and soda and snacks. There were couches and chairs, a table, and a cheap big television and stereo. It was an unusual combination of swank and run down.

Souz was running through drum rolls when they got there, so they went ahead and got set up to play, not that it took much. They usually left most things out and ready for jamming. Merrick warmed up his voice a bit with some vocal yelping, punctuating Souz's cymbal crashes until they all started laughing.

Lucee said, "I think we need to run through 'A Million Years' desperately." She hit the opening chords, and Souz and Merrick came in, right on time. Souz let out a pleased howl, and Merrick jumped into the lyrics.

"I saw you on the street today,
wearing your same clothes
Everyone was staring, taking pictures.
All those people all around and no one seemed to know
That you'd been here yesterday, working the same tricks again...
You've been around
for a million years
you've done the dance and the drugs and the scene
nothing has changed
for a mil-ee-on years
you're no idol you're just the local drama queen!"

Lucee burst into a crazy guitar solo, very psychobilly, and they finished rocking out the song while jumping around like crazy all over the flat. Before they could break, Lucee started the next song, and before they knew it, they'd gone through their whole set with nary a break. Merrick hadn't realized he could hold his energy that high for so long.

After they stopped laughing hysterically, Lucee went to the fridge and got Sousa a beer, and said with a wink, "Now we'll be sure to kick all the asses at the show on Thursday."

Sousa gave her a wary look and asked, "Uh, Lucee – what show is this?"

She responded by singing, "We laid to rest, on Merrick's lap is slee-eeep-ing!" At Sousa's look of annoyance, she sobered up and said, "The one I got us at Club Marcada. At eleven, with pay. I just found out, or I would have told you sooner."

Sousa retorted, "Didn't you think to check with me on the date or anything?"

Lucee laughed, "It isn't like you'll have to work. You never go out and do anything except with us. And this is our chance to play the club we love!"

Sousa started laughing then. "I can't keep that up anymore. Of course I'm excited! Hot damn, did you get us free drinks, too?"

Even Merrick had to laugh at his straight to the point question. Leave it to Souz to worry first about the thing he loved – alcohol.

Lucee said, "We're getting paid, they'll give us cheap drinks, and we even get top billing, being as we're the only band. No matter what, we're going to rock it out then live it up!"

Merrick hung out with them for a while, and Sousa made some hand-bills with his computer so that they could give them out around town. Merrick said, "I want to go to Club Marcada tonight. A friend of mine is DJing there, and I can dance. What do you say, guys?"

Lucee of course was up for it, and Sousa decided that since they would be playing a gig there in a few days, making appearances would only be to their benefit.

They trooped out and made the short walk up Charles Street to the club. Being a Monday night, they knew it would be a mellow crowd, so they were looking forward to sitting at the bar or a little table and drinking some beers while they talked up their show to whoever would listen.

The Club Marcada was a well-loved hole in the wall sort of establishment that had gained considerable crowds once The Night Church, the big and flashy members-only nightclub around the corner, had gone out of business. The hip art folk crowd didn't transfer, but all the black clad underground types walked themselves right over to Marcada and never left. The club had a narrow entrance, and a bar that ran along the left, with almost no maneuvering room between the bar stools and the wall. Merrick had often wondered how they'd ever passed fire codes with an entrance like that. Once past the bar, there was a small DJ booth, then the dance floor and stage.

Merrick bought a rum and coke at the bar, then wandered over to the

DJ booth to say hello to his friend who was spinning, Dominion. As one might expect from a lady with such an unusual name, Dominion North was quite a character. A big girl, she made it her mission to become larger than life and did so with a variety of brightly colored hair extensions and wild club clothes, and of course giant platform boots. She was loud and brash and fun, and she had a heart of gold. She liked having a good time and liked it even more when she made the party happen around her. When she saw Merrick standing at the door to the DJ booth, she whooped with glee and threw him a kiss over the barrier.

"Merrick! You came out, after all!"

"Well, you're my pal and besides, we're playing a show here on Thursday, so we'd better show our faces around, eh?"

Dominion gave him a knowing nod. "Drink that fast, then get your ass on the dance floor. These jerks won't dance to anything, so I need you and Lucee to show 'em how it is done. Rock and roll!" She turned to get a request from someone else, shooing him towards the dance floor.

Dominion didn't go too far out to find her tracks to spin, mostly dipping into the club classics like VNV Nation or Covenant, but she would throw enough old school style Goth and Industrial into her sets to make you feel at home, rather than annoyed. So, the night was spent pleasantly enough, dancing and yelling and drinking until Merrick could feel the floor shifting under his feet when the bass would hit. They had managed to get most of the patrons of the club onto the floor at some point, and now that it was almost two in the morning, they were the only ones left.

Dominion put on "Temple of Love" by The Sisters of Mercy, and jumped out of the DJ booth so that she could dance around, too. Merrick really enjoyed this song, so he was very into dancing to it. Just as the song kicked into its big musical breakdown, something weird happened to Merrick. It felt like the world suddenly tilted, and for a second he felt like he had to curl up in a ball on the middle of the floor and writhe. Just as soon, it was over, but the next wave of strangeness came with a crunching pain in the midsection that made him bolt for the bathroom, where he vomited up all the drinks he'd had.

He emerged from the bathroom, pale and shaking, and Dominion took one look at him and ran to the bar for some water. "Merrick, I know you didn't drink enough for this to happen. Are you sick, do you think? Did you catch a bug?"

He muttered, noncommittally, "Could be. I should go home. I feel like ass!" Lucee volunteered to walk him home, and Sousa made sure that they could get that far by themselves before parting ways.

Dominion shook her head as she waved goodbye, then they were walking the blocks to his apartment. Luckily it wasn't more than seven blocks or so away, although Merrick felt like they'd walked forever. He had to keep stopping because he was shaking so much.

Lucee got him in the door and out of his jacket, and said, "You should go wash up, but leave the door unlocked in case you pass out in there or something. Merrick, I want to stay here tonight and make sure you're okay, if that's alright with you. I'm worried!"

He waved his hand weakly at her. "I'll be okay. I think."

In the bathroom, while he was splashing water on his face, the realization dawned on him what might be happening, as frightening as it was. He emerged from the bathroom and said, "Lucee, I have a theory, and it isn't one you're going to like."

"Oh no. If this has to do with what I think you're going to say it does…"

"Aisling told me that I would start to feel it if I didn't return, like withdrawal. Like I'm a common junkie. And this isn't a normal thing that's happening to me now, you see – it just came upon me, and I can't stop shaking. I feel itchy all over, like I'm missing something vital. I can barely touch myself, I'm so sensitive. I don't know what the hell it is, but I'm betting this is what Aisling was talking about. And I can't go back yet. I have to do the show!" Merrick started weeping, to his own disgust. What the hell was going on, that he couldn't control himself?

Lucee said, "No, no, don't cry about this, it'll be okay," and she went and gently led him to his bed and made him get under the covers.

"Here, try to go to sleep, because then you'll feel better, I think. I'll stay here on the floor and make sure you don't choke on your own vomit or something, okay?"

He tried to laugh at that but could only muster a weak sound. He laid down and closed his eyes, listened to the comforting noises of Lucee getting ready to go to sleep. He could see that she'd turned out the lights by the increased darkness behind his eyelids. Then he heard her breathing change as she drifted off. He wondered briefly if Aisling would get confused and visit her in her dreams.

Then it dawned on him.

He'd taken all those uppers. There was no way he was going to sleep any time soon.

Music: The Cure

If Only Tonight We Could Sleep

The next few days passed in a blur for Merrick. Lucee couldn't stay with him the whole time, as she had to work during the days. She tried to get Sousa to go over and check in on Merrick but getting Sousa to do anything responsible was a faint hope at best.

Merrick knew that he was going to have to give in and go to House Mirabilis sooner or later, because this could not keep on this way. He couldn't sleep, he gave up trying after a while. He decided the best he could do was try to hold it together until their show, then find a way to go back to House Mirabilis and see what could be done.

Lucee had other plans. She decided on Tuesday night that Merrick wasn't going to get better any time soon. She needed to take things into her own hands and find Aisling on her own. She knew as well as any about where the house was supposed to be, the only thing that was stopping her was transportation.

That was it! She knew what to do. She went to Sousa and demanded a scooter from him. He looked at her and said, "You know how to drive it? And you do know that it will be much colder when you're moving, right?" She just looked at him until he capitulated and gave her one of the bikes. She decided that back roads were the way to go, and that she should wait until Wednesday morning to go, since it would be warmer as the sun rose higher. Also, she would have a better chance of spying the house as she drove by.

She set off the next morning, wearing two pairs of long johns and some holey jeans, and a sweatshirt under her leather jacket. Never too many layers, she figured. After a shaky start, she got underway.

The back roads took forever, but the scenery was lovely once she got to Roland Park. The houses became bigger and more pastoral, and the air felt cleaner. Finally, she got out of town and on the road that she had been told to look for, and she started looking around for the house. That had to be it, on the left, almost hidden from the road.

It was a Queen Anne style monstrosity, which Lucee immediately loved. She decided to pull into the driveway, and after parking the scooter, cautiously walked up to the front door. "Ah, fuck it," she said quietly, and knocked boldly.

There was a rustling behind the closed door, and then it opened just a bit, wide enough for a grandly handsome man to stick his head through and ask in a voice that was rich despite the annoyance coloring it, "And who do we have here? Too large to be a mouse, too bold anyway. You have a familiarity about you. Have we met?"

Lucee was taken aback. Merrick hadn't prepared her for just how oddly these people talked! "I'm a friend of... your blackbird. He doesn't know I'm here, but he is having a bit of a bad time right now, so I decided to see if I could do anything."

The handsome man's amused visage changed to one of alarm, and he quickly stepped through the door and closed it behind them. "Not the place to speak of this, please come with me," he said tersely, and led her around the house and to a gazebo in the back, filled with overstuffed cushions. "We'll have a modicum of privacy here," he assured her in his mellifluous voice. "Is he very badly off, then? The sickness upon him?"

She nodded. "I don't know how this happened, how it works, but it needs to stop. He looks like he'll die!"

The man looked pained. "How much did Merrick tell you?" he asked, cautiously.

Lucee grimaced and replied, "He was afraid to tell me too much, because he didn't want to break his word. He gave me the barest details, just enough to know that something very odd and possibly disastrous happened to him here. And he told me that he made friends, though he gave me little in the way of detail. I'm his best friend. I have to help him. He trusted me more than you people might like, but we're like brother and sister. He has no one else to turn to."

The man turned away for a moment, considering. Lucee noticed that the weak November sun glistened in his hair like gold; he was indeed very handsome. She then became annoyed with herself for becoming distracted by something as trivial as a good-looking man and looked away.

He turned to her then, and said, "Twice in a week I'm at a loss and leaving myself vulnerable. What will the world come to?" He shook his head in self-disgust, and said, "I am going to do something that I do very rarely, my lady. I am going to help you. I do believe I have become soft in my old age."

She tilted her head, considering what he'd said. Well, wasn't that why she'd come?

She mentally rolled her eyes, but stuck out her hand gamely and offered, "My name's Lucee. And you are...?"

He looked scandalized. "Ah, Merrick didn't tell you quite enough about us, I see. Be careful who you offer your name up so casually to, m'dear. Names hold power. We often give nicknames for that very reason." He looked mollified at her candor, though, and said with a smile, "You gave so generously that I must certainly do the same. I am Cullen, and I helped Merrick muchly while he was here. He also left an excellent impression with me, although I wish he had not run off the way he did. Do you know the stories of those who partake of the hospitality of Faerie, and wither and die when they have it no more?"

Lucee nodded, gravely. She didn't like the sound of this.

He continued, "That is what Merrick suffers now, and we suffer with him. We made a bond with him, and he has stretched it tight in his flight from us. We can be rather terrifying, I admit, but now that he has joined us, we would not harm him. Even the worst of us would do ill to break that bond."

Lucee said, "The worst? There are some of you who do harm?"

Cullen snorted, bemused. "We are no different than you in this. We have those of us who do good works, and those who would disrupt and harm, often out of boredom. We are not saints. We may hurt or heal at whim."

She looked at him seriously and asked, "What are you, then? Merrick didn't tell me. In fact, he did a very good job of leaving you shrouded in mystery!"

Cullen actually looked pleased at that, and replied, "Well, that's a bit of a tale, but for now I can say that we answer quite well to The Gentry, or as we call ourselves, Eleriannan. If you are familiar with the old Celtic myths, we correspond nicely with their concept of the Fair Folk or Good Neighbors enough to tell you that they refer to us explicitly. And now I've told you more about my people than I've revealed to any one person in a very long time. I might ask for some stories about you in return, when we have less of a task ahead of us, but for now we must tend to our Raven."

Lucee had to shake off the fascination that she'd fallen under, listening to Cullen talk. Oh, this guy was dangerous, she thought wildly. She was much too attracted to him. Best to keep moving, stick to the job at hand. She could have sworn that Cullen wore a slightly self-satisfied smirk, as if he knew exactly what was going on inside her. Ugh! Smarmy boy.

Cullen said, "Now how will we attack this problem? The logistics of getting to Aisling and managing to travel to where Merrick is... hmmm. Your vehicle is too small for all of us. No matter, if you can show me where he is, we can come to him. After that, we can plot a way back to this house."

She said, "We have enough time to take you all the way there and back, before helping him? That seems hopeful at best."

Cullen smiled and answered, "No, which is why you need to show me where he is. Much different than taking me there, I assure you."

She looked confused, and he said, "You'll see in just a moment. Will you give me your hands?" She obliged, grudgingly, and he took them so that hers sat in his cool ones, resting gently. "Relax, and don't be afraid," he murmured, and the world suddenly shifted.

There was a sudden feeling of vertigo, then she closed her eyes and things straightened out a bit. She heard laughter, but it wasn't her voice, and it was inside her head. What the hell?

Cullen's voice, in her ear – no, in her head too! – said, reassuringly, "I am here. If you show me where he lives – how you see it, in your heart – I can find my way. Think of Merrick, his home, how you feel when you are there."

She felt light, lulled by his voice in her head, and she started thinking of Merrick, having dinner with him, in his comfortable and surprisingly spacious apartment... the garden out back, where they would sit and have tea, and the sun shining off dust motes in the big front windows. She thought of them curled up on his couch, discussing the destiny of the band and their lives once they would become rock stars.

She became aware of Cullen's amusement at this recollection, and that shook her reconstruction so that instead of Merrick, it was Cullen there. He gave her a wicked little grin and said, "Aisling will be glad to know that you could be so close to Merrick and still stay friends. Not all of us are so well-behaved!"

She gave him a shocked look. "He's my best friend!"

Cullen leaned very close, and suggestively said, "Well, I'm not."

Lucee almost gave in and kissed him, but at the last second, she jumped up and said, "We have to rescue Merrick. Enough of this."

She refused to show Cullen any remorse at not surrendering to his kiss, although she certainly felt it inside. Guys as good looking as him usually didn't pay attention to girls like herself.

He had the grace to look nonplussed before she made herself pull her hands away from him. "Well," he muttered, "That was unusual."

For a moment she truly regretted her choice, but then she made herself shake it off, dedicating herself to helping her friend, and worrying about flirting with hot guys later.

"Did you get enough to work from?" She asked him, forcing her voice to be cheery, as if the past events hadn't completely freaked her out.

He replied, "I believe so. Aisling will be able to use it more than I, so between us, we will find him. You should go to him now, but wait you here a moment, and I will give you something to take to him that will help."

As much as she didn't want to be left alone in the garden, she had come here to bring back help, so she nodded and put on a determined face while Cullen went back to the house.

She sat there, nervously, and tried to lose herself in her thoughts until she was distracted by a snuffling noise nearby. She whirled around to see what was nearby and found herself being inspected closely by two very lovely women. One, the taller and darker of the pair, wore a disdainful look that even her fine clothing – red gown and black cloak – couldn't distract from. The other was smaller, dressed all in green velvet, with a sunny look about her, and a pleasant smile on her face.

The lady with the shining black hair tossed it back before pronouncing to the smaller one, "It seems that all sorts of refuse gets blown into our property these days! What have we here?" She made a distasteful sniff, and said, "I feel Cullen's involvement in this. What say you, Tully?"

She looked at the other woman with an air that proclaimed that she didn't really care what Tully thought, but it was better than speaking directly to Lucee.

The smaller woman looked directly at Lucee and gave her a warm smile before asking, "Are you here with Cullen, stranger?" Lucee wasn't sure what to say, so she decided that just nodding was the best option.

Tully turned to the other woman and said, "See, Edana, a guest of Cullen's. Best to be kind to her, even if that seems difficult to you."

Tully seemed inordinately pleased with her statement, as if she'd made a joke. Lucee knew that something was going on under the surface and wondered just what she was missing. She made a mental note to ask Cullen why it was that those two were so free with their names, when he'd cautioned her about giving away hers. It made no sense.

Edana did not seem a bit placated by this. "Look, you," she snapped at Lucee, "You just sit there not saying a word, in our garden, in front of your betters as if you had a right to be here. Speak now, tell me who you are and why you are here!"

Tully looked alarmed and shot Lucee a look of warning. By this point, Lucee was angry – how dare this woman walk up to her and start insulting her without grounds? Especially as she knew that Lucee was there to see Cullen!

She said, in an even of a tone as she could muster, "I am here to see Cullen. My business is with him; I mean you no disrespect, but he asked me to wait here, so here I am. Waiting. Anything else you need to know, Cullen will have to tell you, I am not at liberty to say more." Lucee was impressed that she'd managed to stay so calm and even-tempered while speaking. It had taken all she had not to let her voice shake with the anger she was feeling.

Edana, on the other hand, seemed even more livid. "How dare you tell me that I must wait for Cullen? Insolent whelp!"

A masculine voice cut in, surprising them all, "Indeed, she was correct, Edana. She is here on private business, and it is between her and me. You are being nosy and out of line, and your temper tantrum is wasted on me."

Cullen stood there, arms crossed, and gave Edana a disapproving glare. She sneered at him, "When did you care about such proprieties as this? Ever since that blackbird crossed our threshold, you have changed, and not for the better I wager!" She tossed her head angrily and said, "To the depths with all of you, then!" She stalked off, leaving Tully and Cullen looking as if they were choking back giggles, and Lucee ready to spit nails, she was so angry.

"Cullen, may I kick her ass in the future? I think she needs it," she said, to a chorus of Cullen and Tully's no longer suppressed giggles.

Tully gasped, "She is so very full of herself! She needs taking down a rung or twelve, I think."

Cullen replied, "If I thought you could beat her, I would allow it in a second. She makes our lives here rather difficult sometimes, as you might imagine." Lucee just made a menacing face and shook her fist at the retreating Edana. Cullen and Tully burst into laughter again.

Tully got herself together, finally, and said, "I like you! I am Tully, at your service. I can't say I can easily go against the likes of Edana, but I respect those who do."

Lucee gave her a grin and said, "I'm Lucee. I'd stay and talk longer, but I have an urgent need to get back to the city – Cullen, did you bring me what you went to retrieve?"

Cullen nodded and said, "This will help, for now. Aisling and I will be there as soon as we can." He handed her a small package, very light and compact. She put it in her jacket's inner pocket, where it would be safe. "Don't be tempted to try any, understand?" Cullen asked her, concerned. She nodded, and he smiled brilliantly. "You are a brave one, Lucee. You are a good friend to our Raven."

Realization slowly dawned on Tully's face as she figured out why Lucee was there, and she nodded approvingly. "If only we all had friends like you, Lucee," she said, pleased. "You should go before anyone else comes along. When you come back with the Blackbird, you will be quite welcome!"

Lucee considered that. Coming back? She wasn't sure, but she gave a smile of thanks anyway. Cullen walked her to her scooter, and said, "We will follow, I promise. I look forward to seeing you again," and gave her a kiss on the cheek quickly before hurrying off.

She kicked the scooter off, grinning like a fool. Damn him for being so attractive, she thought yet again. I'll have to guard myself carefully around that one.

Merrick was a walking zombie. He spent hours pacing around his apartment, trying to find anything to soothe his nerves and get him to settle down, to no avail. He tried to take a shower, but the water felt like it was burning him, even when he ran only the cold tap. Attempts at eating went disastrously, as anything he tried to ingest came right back up. He could keep tea down, but that was all that he could stomach.

He tried cleaning up his place, which succeeded for a short while, until he realized that instead of dusting, he was slowly shredding the rag into little bits while standing in the middle of the room. He even attempted to use the feelings he was going through to write, but all his phrases came out disjointed, painful. Finally, he collapsed in the center of his garden and rocked back and forth while he watched the ants scurry amongst the tile stones.

Lucee found him like this, in the darkness of the evening, with no shoes or coat on even though it was in the forties outside. "Merrick! You're crazy!" She exclaimed and dragged him inside. "I brought something very important for you, something that will make you feel better," she told him, as she propped him up at the table.

"Don't believe you," he muttered, pathetically.

"Well, you don't have to, but I'm telling the truth anyway. I went to that place –"

"House Mirabilis? By yourself?" He shot up suddenly, afraid for her.

"Yes, yes, by myself. I met Cullen; he was very nice." She could feel herself starting to blush, so she blurted the rest out quickly. "He gave me something to help you. He gave me his name, too, as you were telling me that they do. He was worried about you!"

She pulled the package that Cullen had given her out of her pocket and gave it to Merrick. He took it with trepidation and opened it slowly.

It was a piece of bread.

Lucee gave Merrick a look of "I have no idea" and shrugged helplessly. "That's what he gave to me. He said it would help you until they got here."

Merrick yelled, "What!" He jumped up from the table, knocking over his chair in the process, then crumpled to the floor as the room spun around him.

"Hello, dorkface, you can't keep fighting this off," Lucee scolded him. "Cullen told me why you're freaking out, and boy did you put your foot in the shit this time. You're going to have to go back, Merrick. You're not going to be able to deal otherwise." She added, sarcastically, "Good for you that you manage to crash a Faerie party and get yourself stuck with them!" She shook her head, baffled by her friend's adventures.

Merrick righted the chair and sank onto it like he was sinking into the depths. "So, I eat this and everything's better?" He asked skeptically.

She confirmed, "Cullen said that it would hold you until he and Aisling could show up."

Merrick couldn't help but feel his heart leap a bit at the mention of her name. He decided that it was just a piece of bread, and if it helped him feel better, well, more power to him. He lifted it to his mouth and took a cautious bite.

Lighter than air, sweeter than honey, creamier than any loaf had a right to be – the bite of bread melted across his tongue like a kiss or a wish, and he felt a sense of well-being creep along every limb until he was positive that he was glowing. The look on Lucee's face didn't contradict it, either – she looked shocked and amazed.

"It must be better than sex, with the look you're wearing," she breathed.

He looked at her, eyes aglow, and offered her a bite. Her mouth watered to taste it and she almost took it before remembering what Cullen had warned. "Na, na, Merrick. It's for you, you eat it. I was told that you needed all of it," she told him, and the moment passed. She breathed a sigh of relief. That was uncanny!

He tried so hard to eat it slowly, but by the end of it, he was shoving it in his mouth, desperately. Lucee watched him and was glad that she hadn't tried the morsel. Bit by bit the color returned to his cheeks, and he regained the glow of health, until finally he sat across the table from her, restored to his normal self.

"That was... really fucking weird," he breathed.

She nodded, in agreement one hundred percent. Trying to get over that awkward moment, she grinned at him and said, "So does this mean we're good for the show tomorrow?"

He looked at her, considering. "I... I think so, actually. If I can stay feeling like this until the troops arrive, I assume. Lucee, how did I manage to get myself into this one?"

She shook her head, saying, "Only you, Merrick. This stuff never happens to me – or anyone else I've ever known, either. So, you fell into a faerie tale; does this mean you get special powers?"

Merrick considered this before answering. "I can see what they really look like." She asked, "You mean they look different to you than to, say, me? Not as pretty or majestic, maybe?" Lucee didn't like the sound of this.

Merrick smiled and answered, "Different, in some cases markedly different. Aisling is more ethereal, for example."

Lucee cocked an eyebrow and said, "And what of Edana, or Cullen?"

Merrick looked surprised. "You met Edana? Oh, no!" Lucee grinned, "And a right bitch she was, too. Cullen had to put her in her place."

He frowned and said, "Cullen seems to be doing that a lot lately. And to answer your question, Edana looks much more bitter and sullen to me, rather as if she were made of branches and thorns and other sharp things, and Cullen... well, Cullen reminds me of a fox, honestly. Crafty, sly, and he's got pointy ears too."

He watched Lucee's reaction to that and laughed. "Hey, you should see your face! The others are even more wild looking, honestly. You'll be amazed." He hugged her, happily. "I didn't thank you yet for helping me. You really went above and beyond the call of friendship. And now I can talk to you a bit more about this, since you've been there and met some of them."

Lucee shrugged and said, "That's what you do for friends, Merrick, and you're my best friend. Besides, I love you! I couldn't have just sat there and watched you suffer while I did nothing. And now I do understand a bit more what you were telling me – Merrick, those people are so amazingly weird, even your tale couldn't do them justice. If I hadn't had your story to go by, I would have been utterly confused."

He nodded, slowly. "The only thing that got me through was to stay on my toes and keep completely polite and civil at all times. They respond very well to courtesy, which makes sense in retrospect. Good thing we've both read a lot of Mythology and Celtic tales, eh? And they seem to like to speak in Latin sometimes, too."

"They are very old, aren't they? I'd be really interested in hearing their history."

"From what they told me, they are incredibly old, and dependent on us – humans – to keep going. They need our energy to remain, and in return they give gifts."

"And you don't know what other gifts they've given you yet, do you, Merrick?"

He shook his head, curious himself at what would manifest in the future.

Music: Mors Syphilitica
A Lullaby of Sorts

They decided that Lucee should stay over, just in case things got weird again. Merrick tried to give her the futon, but she wouldn't agree to it, insisting that he hadn't slept in so long that he required it. He finally got her to concede to share it, and they each claimed a different end of the bed for their heads, as Lucee insisted that if she wasn't spooning, she hit people a lot in her sleep. Merrick found this hilarious and claimed that they were both going to be miserable from their smelly boot feet. Of course, their feet weren't smelly, but that didn't stop them from trying to attack each other with toes until Lucee fell off one end of the bed.

She noticed when Merrick slipped into dreams, because he started to mumble, then thrash about violently in the bed until she decided that she'd better wake him. "Merrick! You're having a nightmare, wake up!" She shook him until his eyes finally opened and he groaned.

"Ughhhhh. Get all the mud off of you before you hug me, okay?"

Lucee said, "Huh?" and Merrick sat up suddenly.

"Shit!" He exclaimed. "I thought you were Aisling, pulling me out of the stream!"

Lucee said, "I'll say it again: huh? You were dreaming, dude. You started freaking out, and I woke you up before you hurt yourself or more particularly, me."

He groaned again, and said, "Sorry, Lucee. I'm really freaked out now. I was with them – House Mirabilis – and we were riding horses across a field, to visit some other great house. Why we were on horses, I don't know. I ride for crap, and I hate horses. Anyway, we got near a creek, where trees lined the water in places and it was very shady, and my horse really wanted to drink. Aisling saw me headed that way, and called for me to come back, but I couldn't control the damn horse. And right as we got to the stream, these horribly scary things jumped out of me, tall men made of sticks and branches and brambles, and they tried to pull me off the horse. The next thing I knew, the folk were rallying around me, and they were fighting the stickmen with swords and magic – I swear to the sun, I saw blasts of energy flying from them. They fought the stickmen, and Aisling tried to get to me, and I fell off the fucking horse and into the water. Then you woke me up, and that was that."

He shook his head, as if to clear the images from his mind. "What's worse is that I have no idea if that really happened or if it was merely a dream. Ever since Aisling has come into my life, I dream things that are as real as can be. What if they're all hurt? What if they lost me, and now they can't find me?"

Lucee looked at Merrick in shock. "Do you think that could happen? No, no, Cullen has good directions on how to find you – he got them directly from me. I'm betting that he could even find me now if he couldn't find you."

Merrick asked, "How do you figure that?" She stammered, unsure of how he would react to this admission, "Well... he... went into my head and got directions, so to speak."

Merrick looked confused, so she rattled on. "He asked me first! He said I had to show him where you were, and that was the only way. He saw where you live, through my eyes and thoughts."

Merrick raised an eyebrow at that and said, "Be careful, Lucee. Remember what I told you – he's a sly one. I like him, and it might be that I owe him my life. But if he hurts you in any way, I'll be very angry. I don't want to feel that way about him, and I don't want you to get hurt, either." He sighed and flopped back on his pillow.

"So, did I wake you up, or were you just lying there, staring at the dusty ceilings?" He asked her, then yawned hugely.

She shrugged, "I was awake. I have a lot on my mind, and this is pretty crazy stuff to deal with, you know. And we have a show in less than twenty-four hours, and that's freaking me out a bit, too. Will everything work out okay? Will you hold up and not turn into a quivering faerie-addicted blob before we get off the stage? Are they going to take you away so that I never see you again? Because that, I couldn't stand."

She looked terribly sad, and Merrick gave her a hug, murmuring, "Everything will work out. I know it will. As scared as I am, I know that we'll make it through, and no one's going to separate us, either. If I have to kick asses to assure that, I will." The hug muffled Lucee's laugh at that pronouncement.

They finally got back to sleep, Lucee passing out first this time. She remembered hearing Merrick humming, and then nothing else until the sun shining in her eyes woke her in the morning. She heard noises in the kitchen area and turned to see Merrick making eggs and bacon. She could smell coffee. "Am I in heaven? Because it definitely smells like it," she exclaimed.

He laughed and pointed to the table. "Sit down, shut up, stuff your face." She obliged, eating until she thought she would explode.

They both expressed some worry that Cullen and Aisling had not shown up yet, but Merrick seemed to be hanging in there, so they decided that everything would be okay if they just went about the regular duties of the day. Regular duties included figuring out their clothing for the show, then going to restring their guitars and run through a quick practice if they had time.

Merrick decided that he was going to wear his outfit all day, so he went ahead and picked out his favorite clothes. If he wanted to get through this day, it would be as himself, one hundred percent.

He picked out his black leather jeans and a Joy Division tee shirt. Over the tee, he loosely buttoned a soft black shirt and rolled the sleeves up, and he felt ready to go. He realized that rolling up the sleeves of his shirt revealed his new tattoo, and he liked the effect. He spiked his hair, brushed his teeth, and then went into the other room and pulled on his "fancy boots" as he called them – they were taller than his combat boots, and they buckled up with five shiny buckles in the front. He felt every bit the dandy, and pretty much ready to handle anything.

Lucee nodded approval, and said, "You're gonna knock 'em dead in that, Merrick. Damn." He grinned and bowed to her, and said, "Now it's your turn, lady. Let's go."

They went to her small apartment, which was a double flat shared by several people. She had the upstairs room on the end of the row of rooms, a long and narrow chamber. She loved it and had even strung tiny Christmas lights around the perimeter of the sleeping room, and there were photos of close friends taped to the walls.

The room was a pleasant cream color, but the walls were so covered with posters and show flyers, one could barely see them anyway. There was a small desk, and a bookshelf with a tiny stereo, and the rest of the room was rather bare of furniture. There just wasn't room for it.

Lucee pulled a surprising item from her closet, a punky ballgown of ripped black satin and tulle. It was the ballet kind, that had a satin bodice and a full skirt, one that she'd obviously tattered to her own liking. She flounced off to the bathroom with it and emerged wearing it with red fishnets and combat boots. She'd even put on dark eyeliner, which she only did these days for very special occasions.

He whistled appreciatively. She twirled around and said, "Just a little something I've been saving for a special occasion."

He said, "Well, with the way we look, it can't help but be special. Now let's get moving, the day's getting short and we have lots left to do!"

The rest of the day was spent in a flurry of activity. They restrung their instruments, and tuned them, and practiced a little bit. They took their equipment to Club Marcada and set up on the makeshift stage the club provided and did a quick sound check. Souz declared that they sounded as good as they were going to get, and that they should get dinner.

They went to a ratty diner that they often frequented, right around the corner from the club. Merrick, who felt that he couldn't eat much, settled on fries and bad diner coffee. Lucee settled on the same, except she covered her fries in ketchup until they looked as though they'd been in a horrible accident. "That's gross, man," Souz commented, as he wolfed down a ridiculously rare hamburger, leaving a greasy mess on his plate in the process.

Lucee stuck her tongue out at him, and said, "Couldn't you have dressed up even a little, Souz? I mean, you don't have to look as dapper as our man Merrick, here, but jeez. You could at least have put a clean shirt on!"

He shrugged and replied, "I'm not keeping it on when we're playing, anyway. Too hot. Besides, I'll be behind my kit, no one'll see me. No big deal."

He went back to his greasy food, and Merrick shrugged and said, "He's got a point. We'll just have to be the fashion plates of this band, Lucee."

Finally, it was time to head back and do the show, and so they trooped over to the club. As soon as they walked in the door, Merrick could feel something different in the air, something expectant and energetic. Lucee gave him a look that told him that she felt it, too.

"Wow," she breathed, "Something is going to happen tonight. I don't know what, but I hope it's good and it has to do with us, Merrick."

He grinned and got them all a beer, "for relaxing purposes," he asserted. They drank them nervously, looking around at the crowd.

"Lots of people here tonight, you'd think we were popular or something," Sousa muttered. The others nodded in agreement, amazed.

Merrick spied a face in the crowd that made him look twice. "Lucee, do you see that guy?" He grabbed Lucee and gestured as subtly as he could.

"Huh? What, the guy with the mohawk? His name's Jerry," she answered.

"No, no, the tall and thin one? Looks like he could bend over like a reed? Lucee, he's one of them. He's weird as hell looking, like he's made of sticks! You can't see that?"

He couldn't stop staring. He knew that he'd never seen the strange looking man before. Merrick felt with all certainty that this strange apparition was not a member of House Mirabilis. Something felt... off, strange.

The man turned, looking for all the world as if he was sniffing in the crowd. Suddenly their eyes met, and the stickman smiled, a wide, disturbing grin meant only for Merrick. He felt like his heart was going to stop. He remembered his dream suddenly, the stickmen and House Mirabilis fighting for him, while he fell from the horse. Was it now his turn to fall for real?

Lucee turned to him and said, "Merrick, what? You're gripping my arm like a vise! What's going on?"

He whispered, barely audible over the din around them, "Lucee, there were a bunch like them in my dream, the one I had last night, the bad one. There's at least one here now; what does this mean?"

Lucee looked worried, searching the crowd for what Merrick saw. Sousa looked over and said, "What are you guys looking for? What's going on?"

Merrick said, "Souz, I'm afraid that things might get a little weird tonight. Whatever happens... uh... we just keep rocking. Okay?"

Sousa snorted and answered, "Of course, that's what I do. Besides, we know enough people here that no matter what, we've got friends around us. Nothing's gonna faze me tonight, Merrick. Don't you worry."

Dominion came running up to them, and yelled, "It's time, guys! Get up there! You've got until the end of the song."

They all visibly blanched a bit, but Merrick said in a voice full of bravado, "Let's rock!"

They made their way up to the stage, but right before Merrick could get to it, a hand grabbed him. He whirled and found Cullen standing there, with a half-smile on his face. "We found you, at last. Be warned, things are not safe here – but do your utmost on stage, and we will be here guarding. If you do well tonight, you will do well by us also."

Merrick said, "What do you mean, not safe? Do you mean the stickmen that I saw? And where's Aisling?"

Cullen frowned and said, "You've seen them, then. Aisling is bringing more of our kind, those who wish you well. The better you play, the more the stickmen will want you, but the more we will be able to defend you.

Aisling will be here soon, you shall see. Now go, make your music!"

He gave Merrick a push towards the stage, and Lucee gestured wildly for him to follow. She caught sight of Cullen, and Merrick saw her blush a little. "Oh no," he thought. "Another one smitten by the Fae. Look at my example of where that gets you."

As he jumped up on the stage, he realized that a good number of people were already lined up, waiting to hear them. The front row teemed with the stickmen, interspersed with people that Merrick knew. He grimaced internally but put on his rock face for the crowd. The song that was playing on the PA ended, and the lights came up on the stage. Merrick turned to Lucee and Sousa and said, "Let's kick some ass for rock and roll, eh?" They grinned back, and Souz started the drum beat for the first song, as Merrick stepped up to the mic and said, "We are The Drawback. Here we go!"

They kicked in the guitars right then, a sonic assault with rhythm. He and Lucee bounced around up front for a moment, then he stepped to the mic again and started singing the lyrics, shooting them out to the audience like arrows in a war. It was a good song to start the set with; people were starting to dance, bounce around. Not a bad start, he thought, then lost himself in the song.

"We got a fight on our hands
It was something we didn't plan for
You want to run away and hide
That's something that I've already tried
You want it
We got it
You called it down
You take them out!"

He realized that the stickmen were nodding along, smiling malevolently, and Cullen was towards the center of the room, gathering beautifully odd-looking people together, pointing in different directions.

For a second he thought he'd spied Aisling, and his heart jumped happily. Lost in the crowd again, he turned his concentration back to the song, which had a difficult bass riff he needed to do soon.

He pulled it off and threw his head back, lost in the music, while Lucee crowed in joy. Souz just grinned and kept the percussion coming. They ended with a flourish, and the crowd went wild. Merrick yelled into the mic, "Thank you!" and they pounded right into the next song, a cover of Joy Division's "Heart and Soul" with nary a break. Merrick pounded the bass, then started in with the lyrics, keeping his eyes lowered this time, brooding and intense. He tried to invoke the feeling of Ian Curtis, the vocalist for Joy Division, in his performance.

He could see people dancing, singing along with them as he performed. He felt transformed, transported to a magical place where all his rock and roll dreams were reality, and all the people in the audience had been kind enough to come along with him.

He finally looked out, and then he saw the nature of the battle this evening. The stickmen had mostly scattered from the front row and were circulating in the crowd. Where they went, people tripped, or spilled things, or tried to start fights. They were sowing little seeds of discontent amongst the listeners!

As they did their work, the House Mirabilis folk went along and tried to cause good things to happen. He spied Cullen, dancing with a girl Merrick knew to be rather plain but incredibly nice, and the look on her face was one of amazement and sheer pleasure. Another pretty woman with lovely blonde hair was wandering around, smiling and talking to people, and as she passed through Merrick could see the happiness spread through the crowd. Lucee spied her and cried, "That's Tully!"

Even Edana was there – of course, with the pretentious Uber-Goth crowd, he noted – but she seemed to be flirting and bringing smiles to peoples' faces, to his surprise. When they ended the song, she even clapped her hands and made approving gestures to those around her.

The band started a slower song, a love song. Merrick had to sing his heart out on this one, a song he'd written ages ago about a woman in a dream. As he sang the lyrics, he found Aisling in the crowd, as she had suddenly become visible by standing in the very center of the room, staring up at him with a look of complete adoration. She was positively glowing, and he could feel himself reacting to that and becoming even more intense. It was if the energy in the room was swelling and growing as he sang, now directing his words only to her.

She practically lit up the room, in his eyes, and evidently something rather similar was happening to him, because Lucee shot him a rather surprised look. "What the hell?" she mouthed at him, and he smiled beatifically at her. Everyone at this point was entranced by the song, not that Merrick would have noticed, he was lost in a private world with Aisling.

People were swaying back and forth, caught in the magic of the moment, some even dancing with each other. At the end, the crowd just stood there for a moment, awed, before breaking into tremendous applause.

Merrick's heart leapt in joy as he saw the stickmen scowl and start to walk away, in disgust.

One of them pointed up at Merrick and hissed, "Next time will not be so painless for you. Watch yourself, mortal – we have marked you now, and we do not give up easily." It turned and stalked out, causing a recoil of small accidents and confusion as it went.

Aisling came running over, but Merrick shook his head and said, "Last song, and thank you all for coming out and supporting us! We are The Drawback, and we are nothing without our friends!"

They kicked into a hard, upbeat number about sacrificing all for friendship. It was the sort of song that got people singing along with the chorus immediately, and soon enough the entire bar was involved, swinging drinks in time, dancing around, and yelling at the top of their lungs. The band finished the song by all screaming, "Good Night!" and were answered with a chorus of screams of approval.

They jumped off the stage, and were immediately surrounded by the crowd, who all seemed to need to touch them. Sousa looked both overwhelmed and rather pleased, especially given the attention he was receiving from the ladies who had gathered around. Lucee smiled and nodded and was hugged by many. Merrick was grabbed at and pawed, but he was making a beeline for the only person in the crowd he was interested in finding at that point. He heard his name and turned, looking anxiously to see if it was Aisling, and then suddenly she was throwing her arms around his neck.

He closed his eyes happily for a moment, and breathed, "You found me," then she was kissing him, and they were the only two people in the world.

MUSIC: TONES ON TAIL
Real Life

They were finally interrupted by Cullen, pulling on Merrick's shoulder. He laughed when he saw their faces, and said, "Far be it from my intentions to mar your happy reuniting, but shouldn't we adjourn to someplace more private? You two are lighting up the room in a most obvious fashion."

Lucee was standing next to him, and she nodded in accord. "Seriously. Like you have a spotlight on you or something."

Cullen glanced at her, obviously not realizing she was there until she spoke. He smiled, a little grin of expectancy, and said, "Ah, Lucee, wonderful show. You have quite the glow up there, yourself. I was entranced."

She blushed a bit, but shot back with bravado, "I rock. That's what I do. Buy me a beer on our way to wherever? I suggest the table over there in the corner." She waved at Merrick and Aisling to follow, and left Cullen in her wake.

Aisling practically broke down in giggles at this exchange, and commented to Cullen, "Ah, you've met your match there, Cullen! Get the lady a beer, she won this round fair and square." They followed Lucee over to the table, leaving Cullen standing in the middle of the room, flabbergasted. He sighed and walked over to the bar, bought the darkest beers they had – one for each of them – and walked over to the table.

Lucee smiled and moved over to give him some room next to her as she grabbed her beer, and said, "So what the hell just happened? There was a lot of stuff that I just didn't catch."

Merrick said, "The stickmen – what were they? Why were they here?"

Aisling answered, "There is a lot going on here, more than we bargained for when we brought you in, certainly. It was never my intention to put you in danger, Merrick."

She leaned her head against him for a moment, reassuring him. He kissed her on the head, soothingly, and said, "I didn't think that. But what's going on with them? First in my dreams, then here. And they threatened me when they withdrew, saying they would be back."

Cullen shook his head, frustrated. "Once they have the scent of something of power, their desire for it is not easily assuaged. They are but the outlying minions of a greater evil, too. We have quite the battle on our hands looming."

Aisling interjected, "Merrick, we are all in the same situation, all of our people. We all search for the bright lights of the world to keep us sustained, but although we are all of the same kind, we are not all family. House Mirabilis is an outpost, a fortress in the dark wilderness of negativity and hopelessness. There are more of us, such as Gentry House that I mentioned before, and Tiennan House, and many more... but we are opposed by those of us who have lost the light and succumbed to iniquity. They are called the Gwyliannan. They are not satisfied with their own fall; nay, they want to perpetuate it by dragging all of us there, mortal and my kind alike.

"The stickmen, as you call them – we call them ArDonnath, which means 'of the mud' – they were here tonight to test your strength, and cause mischief. They are the scouts of the Gwyliannan. But it is inevitable, now; they have seen your power, and they want you for their own. We cannot let this happen. Not only do we not wish to lose you, as you are now one of us... but we cannot afford to let you fall into their hands and tip the power structure that far to their side. More than the fate of the Eleriannan rests on this, as if they gain power, this whole land will change, and not for the better. Despair will take hold, beauty will cease, and all will suffer."

Merrick looked shocked. "This is much bigger than I ever dreamed, Aisling. I found it weird enough that you would want me for the basic value of a writer and musician, that I could help you at all there. But this – this is beyond any imagining I could have. I feel like I'm in a fantasy novel, a paperback story. And somehow I've become the most important pawn on the board in this struggle... unbelievable."

Lucee nodded, amazed. "I've always felt that you were special. I mean, you are my best friend, that says something." She winked at Merrick, who rolled his eyes. She continued, "I have to admit, Merrick, any doubt I had at the beginning of this has just disappeared after this evening's events. What a crazy fucking night."

Aisling smiled at her, and said, "I never properly introduced myself, although I am sure you know who I am, after this week's events. I am Aisling," and she extended a hand, smiling warmly.

Lucee smiled back and answered, "Lucee, and I'm glad to see that this week's madness was worth it!"

She took Aisling's hand as if to shake it, but Aisling put her other hand over Lucee's and said, "There is something I need to give you, because without it, you are severely handicapped in your dealings with us. And seeing that you are a true sister to Merrick, I feel you will be with us as much as he is." She left a small pot, like a tin of balm, in Lucee's hands. "Put a tiny bit on your eyelids sometime tonight. You will see the difference. And keep the unguent with you, for reapplication if needed. You shouldn't need it often, but there may come a time when you'll need it. I made it for you."

She smiled at Sousa and said, "And I know you do not need it, or I would offer. Well met, cousin."

He smiled at her, sheepishly, and Lucee whipped her head around and stared at him, sputtering, "You're one of them? And you didn't tell us?"

He laughed at that and said, "And what would I have said, silly? You wouldn't have believed me, and there was no reason to reveal myself. Merrick, you knew, did you not?"

Merrick shook his head, slowly. "I should have. I can see it now. But familiarity blinded me, I think. A good lesson to learn." He laughed, then, and chortled, "It explains a fuck of a lot about you, though!"

There was a muffled snort, then Lucee burst into giggles. She tried to repress them several times, then finally gave up and collapsed into a little pile on Cullen's shoulder, laughing. Cullen, looking nonplussed, patted her helplessly. That made everyone else at the table burst into laughter.

They all fell silent for a moment, then, and sipped on their beer, each lost in their own world of thought. Sousa looked rather satisfied with himself. Cullen was restless; Merrick caught him stealing glances at Lucee from time to time. He was amused with that, the strutting peacock made nervous by the exuberant waif. Lucee was studying her beer intently, tapping the glass to force more bubbles to rise to the surface. She seemed oblivious to Cullen, although Merrick knew this to be a ruse.

Aisling was also twitching in her seat, but she seemed more moved by the music the DJ was spinning than by boiling emotions. She finally bubbled over and jumped up, helplessly drawn to the dance floor by the Early Music/dance hybrid sounds of a Helium Vola track. She spun around and swirled about on the floor, looking so blissful that Merrick had to join her out there.

They danced near each other, not touching; but they were intimately aware of one another, trading joyful looks from time to time. Despite the full dance floor, they seemed alone out there, as if the whole place was theirs. The magic they were generating seemed to slowly infect everyone in the club, and soon enough more and more people were drifting onto the dance floor.

Cullen looked at Lucee meaningfully, then rose and offered her his hand. She took it after a second's hesitation, and he pulled her up and onto the dance floor in one graceful move.

Not so far away from them, Edana swirled and swayed with a tall Goth boy who couldn't have been much more than twenty years old. The look on his face was almost obscenely passionate; when Merrick spied him, the fleeting thought passed through his mind that the young man might possibly never have a moment like this again. It was the sort of feeling that one could spend the rest of his or her life trying to recapture. In fact, many of the people around him – often partnered with one of the Eleriannan – had that sort of look about them. This was going to be a night that would live on in legend for quite some time, he decided.

The music changed to a slower tune, "Passion of Lovers" by Bauhaus, and Merrick instinctively knew that it was the last song of the evening. Aisling twirled elegantly towards him and reached him just in time for the faster part of the song. They were suddenly dancing together, Aisling caught gently in his arms, one of her hands resting on his shoulder, and the other fluttering about gracefully. He never danced like this, ever! He usually hated dancing with other people, as it was awkward at best for him, and never as pleasant as it seemed it would be. This was different. This was magical.

The song wound to its end, and everyone there spontaneously broke into applause and cheering. Merrick found himself kissing Aisling, quick and sweet, with a promise of more to come. She poked him gently and indicated with her head where Cullen and Lucee were in a similar passionate embrace.

Aisling looked at Merrick with wide eyes and said quietly, "That's something I'd not expected. She should know that he's a handsome cad, good in heart, though not one to pine over."

Merrick nodded, thoughtful. "I'll talk to her, I suppose. She doesn't fall too easily usually, but this isn't a usual situation." He kissed her once again, a quick one, then said a bit louder for the benefit of those in their party, "What now, people?"

Cullen and Lucee looked up, both with the same guilty look on their faces, and Merrick had to choke back a laugh. Edana – who looked almost soft and gentle after the events of the evening – said, "I am not quite ready to end this revelry. What say you, shall we take some of this to our abode?"

Cullen's eyebrow shot up at that, but he replied in an even tone, "Choose those most deserving, I say." He murmured to Lucee in an aside, "It isn't as if they'll remember much in the morn, anyway." She looked puzzled but resolved to ask later. She hoped this wouldn't apply to her.

Edana took her bewitched Goth boy and his two bedazzled Gothling friends, two girls dressed in typical velvet club gowns. They clung together as if they were terrified the evening would leave them behind and lost.

Sousa had not only managed to put all the equipment into his van while they had been dancing, but he'd taken it all back to his place and dropped it off. "I have room for many in the van, if you're not too fastidious," he declared.

Lucee laughed and said, "I didn't think you knew words that big!"

Souz stuck his tongue out at her and said, "Well, obviously you haven't been paying attention, or you would have realized there's a lot about me you don't know."

She made a funny face at him and said, "Okay, I concede, at least this time. Suppose I'll be riding in the van, yes?"

Cullen nodded and said, "If we may ride together, that would be pleasing to me." He still looked nervous, like he was on very unfamiliar ground.

Aisling said, "The others have their own ways to get to the House, let us go with Souz in the van, shall we?" She slipped her small hand in Merrick's, nested comfortably, and he knew he was smiling like an idiot because of it.

They tumbled into Sousa's van, and found various places to curl up for the ride. Tully was in the front seat next to Souz, chattering merrily about life in the city versus living at House Mirabilis. She seemed set on trying to convince Souz to move to the House, which he was vehemently against.

Cullen rolled his eyes at their conversation, and said, "She should get a commission for each one of our kind that she convinces to live at House Mirabilis. Never mind that many of us are loners, oh no."

Lucee, who was curled up near – but not quite next – to Cullen, asked, "Are there many of your kind who live separate from the houses, then?"

Cullen nodded and said, "We don't all get along, even if we're on the same side. Some of us are social creatures, and others not so much."

Sousa chimed in, "And some of us prefer to live amongst the mortal folk, you know. Much more fun, unpredictable."

Lucee nodded, then remembered what she'd wanted to ask. "Cullen, you said the Gothlings probably wouldn't remember much from their visit. Why is that? Will I remember?"

Aisling answered her question, smiling, "You will remember because we want you to, and because I have opened your eyes. Speaking of, if you have not used the balm, you should now."

Lucee obediently fished the tin from her pocket and applied a tiny bit to her eyes, while Aisling resumed talking. "They will have a beautiful, amazing evening, and after they leave and go home, all they will remember from tonight is the marvelous, magical party. Anything odd they've seen will be chalked up to drink or drugs or a faulty memory... and then they will write stories, or poems, or perhaps create some other art that was inspired by the events of tonight. And in that way, we have fulfilled our function, inspiring creation and imagination. From their imaginations, we will continue on."

Lucee said, "I see, I think. Amazing. Merrick explained it to me a little bit, but now I really get it."

Aisling replied, "Good. And do you see me differently yet, or Cullen? Look closely, I know it is rather dark in here."

Lucee peered at Aisling and said, "You are even more beautiful, damn. Merrick, you lucky dog!" They all laughed at that, but Lucee's laughter broke off as she turned her attention to Cullen. "Your... your ears are pointy. I'm hoping you're aware of this," she said, mustering all the bravado she owned.

He grinned at her and said, "I have been aware of them all my life."

She replied, "You remind me of a fox, Cullen. Very cute."

Up shot one of his eyebrows – noticeably pointier now that she could see how he really looked – and said, "I've been compared to Reynard before, 'tis true. And some say I share his appetites. Others appreciate my craftiness. I suppose it is all how you look at things. Glad to know you find me... cute." He seemed torn between disgust at being called cute, and jubilance at not being spurned.

Aisling giggled and said, "At least she seems to have taken your appearance in stride, buffoon! Remember the maid in Killarney who let out that unholy shriek when she saw your true skin for the first time, then tried to slay you with a cord of wood? That was too rich for words!" They both collapsed in laughter at that, leaving Merrick and Lucee looking at each other in puzzlement.

"When was this?" Merrick asked, knowing full well that the answer was going to freak him out.

"Oh, that was not so long ago, before we came here. Two hundred years, Cullen? It wasn't long before we came here on that cursed ship. Do you know, even ones such as we can have seasickness? It was terrible, terrible, I say. Cullen was rather brave, even climbing to the crow's roost from time to time. I hung over the rails all the live long day."

Cullen guffawed at that. "She was a miserable sight. Aye, but you were so young then, Aisling. Things have changed much since then."

She smiled, and Merrick detected a tinge of sadness in her voice as she said, "Omnia mutantur, nos et mutantur in ilis, yes?"

Merrick suddenly had an overwhelming sense of deja vu, and said, "Wait. What does that mean? I heard that in a dream, while I was running away. I remember it clearly. Something about change, that much I get."

Cullen said, "It means 'all things are changing, and we are changing with them' – it is something we say often, because the mortal world shapes us as much as we shape the dreams of the mortal world."

Aisling added, "We have been here for a very long time. Many of us resist change, sometimes with some very undesirable results. Witness the Gwylianan as testimony to this. Part of their horde is formed from those of us who could not adapt properly to the changes that time wrought on the world. They would rather throw their lot with those who have no desire to support the world around them, than work with what we are given now. They cannot tear their gaze from the past. The Eleriannan recognize that we change, no matter if we will to do so, or no. We hold no illusions when it comes to this."

Lucee said softly, "How long have you been alive? You sound ageless, from the way you talk."

Cullen smiled and said, "Truly, we do not figure time in the way that you do. I am considerably older than Aisling, but younger than Edana or Tully. I can tell you that I remember a time when we spoke Latin as a matter of course; I remember Rome quite well. That was a time of splendid changes, I must say."

Lucee blinked and said, "You remember the Roman Empire? You've gotta be kidding me."

Cullen chuckled, "Well, mostly the ending of the Empire, truth be told. I can tell you this: people were much cleaner before what you call the Middle Ages. Suddenly there was this dearth of bathed peoples and dealing with your kind became much less pleasant! It wasn't until the Industrial Age that the smell began to disperse. Of course, the trade-off was the beautiful land... mortals became clean, and instead polluted the world."

Lucee just sat there, her mouth slightly agape. Merrick looked at her and started to laugh, although he was mindful that the idea that his new friends were so ancient was a bit disturbing to himself, too.

Aisling poked him and said, "I'm a little younger, at least. I wasn't created until after the great plagues. I escaped from the Dreamlands around then, at least." She seemed to have a hard time remembering, and Merrick looked at her, questioningly.

"You were created? That's really strange to think, Aisling. Is this a normal thing for your kind?"

She shook her head and answered, "No, I'm an odd one, even for our people. I'm the rare and unusual offspring of Eleriannan and Mortal flesh, conceived in dreams. I was begot in the Dreamtime, which is why I can move back and forth through it so easily, but my respective parents were of the Waking World, and I reside here now."

She looked slightly embarrassed by this, and Merrick gently asked, "Why do you look like that? Is there something shameful in being the mix of those two things?"

She nodded, absently, and Cullen added, "To our people, being a changeling or Eleriannan/Mortal mix is difficult enough. But Aisling comes from such unusual circumstances, many of our folk do not know how to fit her into their world view. She is no different from me in my eyes, although she has different skills and gifts than I. She is truly special, even if some of our people can't comprehend this."

Merrick said, "Is that why some of the people at the party were so rude to you?"

She made a small, derisive snort, and said, "Well, that's in their nature, to be rude to those that they feel are beneath them. But yes, they are often particularly rude to me because of my lineage. It will be interesting to see how their attitudes change now that you are with us. They are going to be surprised by you, I suspect."

He said, defensively, "Well, if I'm as important to your people as you say, I'll do my best to put an end to this. I won't have them talking badly about you if I can help it. If it wasn't for you, things wouldn't have gone the way they did that night!"

A look of pure adoration blossomed on her face at his declaration, and she slid her arms around him in a gentle hug.

Cullen looked at Lucee and said, quietly, "I must admit, I am glad that he came into our lives. He has already wrought positive change in our people, and now we are doing something we have not done in many years – we are inviting unknown Mortals into our House, we are starting the great exchange of dream and energy and creativity again. This was the way for us, and then we slipped away from our ways – and the world – bit by bit."

Lucee said, "It sounds rather like the salons of the late Eighteen and early Nineteen hundreds, where artists and writers would come together to inspire each other."

He smiled and nodded, "Exactly! Except for us, we are rejuvenated in life, not spirit alone. The Mortals who spend time with us walk away with amazing creations that can enrich others in the world."

Sousa interrupted them by announcing that they had arrived, and Aisling said, her eyes sparkling with excitement, "This is what we live for! Now you will see how it is supposed to be."

Music: L'âme Immortelle

Close Your Eyes

Somehow, someone must have told the inhabitants of House Mirabilis that guests were arriving, because it was obvious that pains had been taken to make the place even more beautiful since Merrick's last visit. The door was decorated with a great swag of evergreens, holly and ivy that hung to the ground, and candles were scattered around the path and entryway in glittering glass holders. Cullen opened the door for their party with a grand flourish, and Aisling led them all inside, pulling Merrick by the hands.

Cullen grabbed Lucee as she walked through the door and swung her over to his side. "Will you stay near me for a bit? I would like to give you a proper introduction to the members of this household... and I would like to be close to you, truth be told." He gave her an engaging look, and she was helpless to say no, even if she had been inclined to deny him.

She said, carefully, "You are a dangerous man. I don't let dangerous men near me, usually. Just so you know."

He nodded, and said, "I deserve that, I suppose. I will be honest and say this: I promise nothing. My nature will allow no less. We are not faithful creatures by disposition, in most forms of Mortal reckoning. We love freely and rather wildly, and we do not often stay to one partner. I am worse than most of the Eleriannan in this, you must know." He laughed in a self-depre-cating manner. "I am a philanderer by any standard, I suspect."

Lucee made a face and said, "Well, there's something to be said for honesty, I guess. So, you're the king in the den of Free Love?"

He sighed and said, "If you like. But you must understand this: just because we do not adhere to the Mortal standards of relationships, this does not mean that we do not love deeply and fully. Fidelity is in the heart, not the bodies as far as we see it, and love is not an exclusive emotion or act, either."

Lucee nodded at that after a moment, and said, "I think I see. I might take some time to truly comprehend it though, Cullen. This isn't anything I was expecting to ever deal with, you know."

He smiled and said, "Well, it isn't as if I am going anywhere, Lucee. I am here, and here I remain. But the party – that is another matter! Shall we?"

He gestured towards the rest of the house, then offered her his arm, which she took with a grin. Inside, her head was swarming with thought – what had she gotten herself into? This was why she never dated! But on the outside, she presented a festive air, and they strode boldly into the large room where Merrick and the others were.

Lucee was overwhelmed by the casual opulence of the house. The room, which Cullen told her was their main gathering court, was divided into sitting space with overstuffed velvet chairs and couches, and a huge hewn wood table that was laden with food on platters. There were plenty of odd-looking folk in the room, all of whom seemed to be staring at her and Cullen. He puffed up a bit and said, "Lady, let me introduce you to House Mirabilis. Folk, she is a sworn friend of Merrick's, and thus a friend to us. She put much work into bringing him to us. Will you give us your name, m'lady?" He looked at her, expectantly.

She looked to Merrick, and he nodded subtly, so she smiled and said, "I am Lucee Fearney, and I am pleased to meet you all." She felt infinitely stupid introducing herself this way, but the crowd reacted with smiles and nodding heads. Cullen put a comforting hand on the small of her back for a moment, but stepped aside when a stunning, commanding woman stepped up to them.

She was a comforting vision of reds and golds, with deeply slanted eyes and delicate golden horns. She looked like a goddess and carried herself like a queen. Lucee's instincts told her she should bow her head, so she did.

The woman spoke to her in warm tones, "You may raise your head, Lucee Fearney." Lucee did, and met the woman's golden eyes, which seemed to glow with warmth. The woman took Lucee's hands in her own, and held them while saying, "Lucee, I am Fallon; this is my House, the House Mirabilis. You are certainly welcome here, both as a friend of Merrick, and as a friend of the Eleriannan. You have proven yourself to us, so let no other here doubt you. We hold you in great esteem."

She let go of Lucee's hands gently and signaled a small boy that seemed to have hair made of feathers. He came up, rather shyly, and gestured for Lucee to bend down. Lucee did, and the boy put a necklace around her neck, then backed off. Lucee noticed in that moment that his feathery hair was colored in shades of blue.

She stood up and took the necklace in her hands, inspecting it closely. There was a long chain, hanging down to her chest, and made of fine yet substantial links of silver. The pendant was a small silver locket, shaped like a book, and engraved all over with intricate Celtic knotwork. She opened it, curiously, and saw that it actually had tiny pages inside. The first one had the word "hello" written on it. She smiled and said, "Hello, I'm Lucee, your new wearer." She looked up and said to Fallon, "It is beautiful!"

Fallon smiled secretively and said, "I hope it will be of great use to you. It is but a small token of our appreciation. But now, you must join the festivities!" She turned and clapped her hands, and the group broke into smaller groups of revelers, each who moved off to different parts of the house with much commotion.

Merrick came over to Lucee and Cullen and said, "Lucee, come sit at the table with us! That way people can come over and meet you if they like, but it will be less intimidating for you. You'll have the table to grip if you get nervous." He gave her a wink after that statement, and she punched him, lightly, which made him laugh out loud.

"C'mon, c'mon. You have to try the beer here, anyway. And you have to meet the man who makes it!"

He led her to a seat to the right of the one Aisling was in, and he plopped down with Aisling. The chairs were certainly big enough for two, and solid enough for twelve. Lucee wonderingly traced a finger along the carvings in the tabletop and edge, and said, "This is gorgeous!"

A loud laugh drew her attention to the doorway, where the doors swung open to reveal a rough-looking creature – an untamed mane of hair, flashing eyes, and the swirl of blue tattoos were the first things that caught her eye. He was a muscular man, and different from all the others gathered there, in that he was unkempt and savage-looking, as if he'd been living in the forest his whole life. He stopped when he spied her at the table and shouted, "What is this? A lovely lady at my table, to try my beer, I wager!"

She looked startled and Merrick, laughing, said, "May I introduce my dearest friend Lucee?"

The man set the pitchers he had carried into the room on the table with a bang and crouched before her, grinning from ear to ear. "So, did he tell you anything about me, lass? I would be Sheridan, although if he gave you the tale already, you would know that. Pleased t'meet you."

Lucee raised an eyebrow and said, "You make the excellent beer, yes? And you stood by Merrick when he was here last. Your reputation precedes you!"

Sheridan looked at her for a second, then burst into laughter. "This one can hold her own. Give her a mug, yes, yes!" He pulled a chair over to their group and then poured beer for all of them.

There was a commotion across the room, then they saw Sousa break through the crowd and stomp over to the table, visibly frustrated. "I need to hang out with people who talk sense," he grumbled and guzzled the beer in his hand.

Merrick and Aisling exchanged confused glances and Merrick asked, "What's going on, man?"

Sousa exhaled loudly. "Tully told me that you got yourself sworn to these folks for seven years. And I called you a dumbass, because that really was a dumbass move and you're lucky it turned out as well as it did. And not only did she laugh that off, she tried to press me – AGAIN – into moving out here, abandoning The Maithe and the city, because to these...," he broke off here and paused a second to get himself under control, "To these folks, the city is a wasteland of negativity and should just be abandoned to the Gwyliannan. Which is ridiculous. There's so much good in the city. The fight is there, the real reason we should be gathering together, but they left me alone and I can't do much on my own!"

Merrick sat there, with his mouth open a little, shocked. "Wait a sec. What are you saying here, Souz?" Sousa pulled out a chair and sat down heavily, then slumped a little and turned to Merrick to explain.

"I'm going to tell you a tale, Merrick. You might know a little about this, I don't know how much they have told you, but this is how I saw it happen, so I'm sure they haven't told you that part of the story.

"When the Eleriannan established themselves in this area, we were at first a small group, as these lands weren't that populated by us yet. I'm sure you know that we have traveled here from across the sea with your people, although there were some of our own kind here, unbeknownst to us, who have always lived here and were connected to the indigenous peoples of this land, but that's a story for another time.

"We at first banded together, and I knew Fallon and Sheridan and some others well; we all worked together to inspire the mortals around us, to bring beauty and creativity into the world through their hands thanks to their proximity to us and the inspiration we provided. As time went on, we started to see the Gwyliannan's marks on the city and other cities in this country that was so new to us, and we were saddened and frustrated. We didn't agree on how to handle it, either. Some of us wanted to fight. Some wanted to withdraw and let the mortals figure it out on their own. And some... well, some became bitter and jaded for a variety of reasons, and actually defected, they went over to join the Gwyliannan!"

Sousa stopped for a moment, both to let that sink in and to finish off his beer.

Sheridan leaned over and handed Sousa another one, and commented, "We lost powerful friends in those days. So much was lost."

Sousa shook his head. "It was foolish on their part. Or perhaps not. I don't know anymore. We made so many mistakes."

He sighed and went on, "This ended up breaking up the band, so to speak. We broke off into the great Houses, each with their own philosophy and ways of staying connected with the mortals we need so much. House Mirabilis became a haven for the more unique of our people, the ones who might need more glamour in order to fit in with the mortal world. Gentry House was where the highborn went to live, and they have the closest connection to what we call the Misty Lands, or what you might call Tír na nÓg, which is where our people came from. Tiennan House was a bit of a mix between the other two – but it fell to the Gwyliannan and now they own it and the lands around it. And Maithe House is the only one that remained in the City, the beacon of light for a long time, fighting off the darkness that wants to eat up the city so badly."

Merrick asked, astounded, "Wait, you mean The Maithe was once a house like this? And more people than you lived there?"

Sousa nodded. "Once every room was filled and the building was majestic. There was – well, there still is – a ballroom there, and people would come to dance and perform, human and Eleriannan alike. And our people and those who were in our circle would come and stay at the House, like an inn of sorts. But all that slowly stopped as our people started to die off or disappear. Eventually, the other Houses cut off communicating with me and The Maithe, though I have kept the House ready for the day when they would need me again. They've forgotten what's there. They've forgotten what we had, what made life good. And I guess if you look at me, you can see that the mortal world has had its way with me a bit as well."

Sheridan shook his head, sadly. "I never agreed with that, even though I am not one for an urban landscape. But then, I know what you keep safe behind those mighty walls, brother."

Lucee interjected, "Dust? A room filled with scooters? Souz, what else are you hiding in there?"

Sousa smiled slyly. "Wouldn't you like to know?"

Lucee was shocked. "Actually, yes! I thought we were friends. And here you are keepin' all these secrets including being some sort of magical being...."

She trailed off, making a face that conveyed perfectly that she knew the words coming out her mouth were unbelievable at best. Sousa, as one of these eccentric, beautiful creatures, was just too hard to swallow!

Sousa responded, frustrated, "We are friends. But how much deeply personal shit do I know about you? And when everything came down with Merrick, who knew about it? Not me. You guys didn't even let me in, I had to start piecing together what had happened while we were playing a damn gig! So, forgive me if I didn't tell you a bunch of things about myself that you wouldn't have believed, anyway." He sat back, arms crossed, looking about as mad as Lucee had ever seen him look.

She immediately was chastened, because she loved her friend and had always felt a little special that he wanted her, of all people, in his circle. She knew she was a good guitar player and that was some of why he was her friend, but he had always been good to her.

"I'm sorry, Souz," she said, genuinely contrite. It's just a lot to take in. To know that you had this connection all this time."

He snorted. "Barely. Remember, I was persona non grata! But keep this in mind – I gave you and Merrick keys to The Maithe. That meant something. Until you two, I hadn't allowed anyone into the building in years. Putting the band together and becoming friends with you and Merrick gave me the most hope I'd had in ages."

He paused and took a long swig of the beer in front of him. "Ah, Sheridan, your brewing skills do nothing but improve!" Sheridan raised a mug in thanks, a big grin on his face.

Sousa continued on, "I don't want to give the City over to the Gwyliannan. There's so much good there! The arts and music scenes are really beginning to take off again, despite losing some of the venues. People are trying to get re-inspired; they're trying to fight back against injustice and the decay that's been allowed to spread. I see hope.

"I don't want to turn my back on that; honestly, I can't. I am part and parcel of that city now. I saw our band as a way to help spread that energy, to assist the music scene to get re-invested in local music and keep the magic growing. Every action has a ripple effect, you saw that played out at our show with the battle between us and the ArDonnath."

Merrick asked, "Is it always that literal? Or do you actually fight with weapons, too? Because in my dreams, there were weapons."

Sousa blinked, surprised. "You saw us with weapons? Tell me about this dream, would you?" He raised his voice and called out, "Hey Fallon, you might want to hear this."

She drifted over to the table and sat down, a questioning look on her face. Cullen followed, curious about what was being discussed.

Merrick continued, "It was at the edge of a field bordered by a stream, I am guessing behind the house somewhere? And there were horses, we were mounted, which I was mad about, because I don't like horses. I was riding next to Aisling, but many in the court were there, including Cullen and Edana, and Fallon, you were leading."

She nodded, and Merrick went on, "There was an attack by stickmen, and you fought with magic and swords. And the horse threw me in the river, and Aisling tried to get me out. Then I awoke, but it was so real..." he trailed off, remembering.

Fallon's face grew solemn, hearing his tale, and she spoke quietly. "This is disturbing. Merrick, this is one of the gifts you received when Aisling stood with you at your initiation, but I never dreamed it would bring an ill portent this soon. I fear that dark times are coming." She looked incredibly sad. "We have not prepared adequately for such a threat if things come to pass that I feel are awaiting us."

Sousa said, angrily, "That's because you retreated away from everything, stuck your heads in the sand, like the Gwyliannan would be satisfied with the City and never advance their conquests farther out! Mirabilis and Gentry Houses were complicit in this situation by their lack of action, Fallon!"

Fallon closed her eyes, then slowly opened them, nodding. "Alas, Sousa, I fear that you are correct. I know you take no comfort in my admission, but now I – we – are faced with decisions that will shape the future of the Eleriannan in this part of the world. How do we defend ourselves? We have the house. We have the Blackbird. I do not know what they bring to this battle."

Sheridan spoke up, "I can make weapons for those of us who recoil from iron still. I can also create traps around our lands, make it less hospitable for those who wish to harm us." Fallon nodded, pleased with his offer.

Sousa said, "I know it's not what you want to hear but facing off in the City would stave off attacks on these lands for a while. They won't want to cede what they have already won, and they will fight to expand those claims in a way that makes the plots they rule more defensible. They won't want to fight on multiple fronts, they will pool their attacks in the area that means the most to them."

Fallon wrinkled her nose and said, "I care about this house and the people in it more than I do a bunch of urbanites."

Merrick's mouth fell open at that, and Sousa bolted up from the table so fast and angrily that his chair fell over with a loud clatter. The room fell to a dead quiet and everyone turned to look at what was happening over at the big table, looks of shock and surprise on most of the faces there.

Merrick stood up said quietly, but with steel in his voice, "I live in the city. It's my home, and I love it. It has helped to shape me into the person I am. A lot of people bag on Baltimore, and it definitely has problems. But you all tell me that the problems it has are being exploited by creatures that use that negativity for their own benefit, just like you would use my creative energies to your own. How can you dismiss a place, a whole city of people, who are being used by beings as powerful as you are, who are encouraged by them to be their worst in order to power these beings? It defies explanation.

"You should WANT to stop this. And not just because it threatens your idyllic lifestyle, but because it is WRONG." He paused, and cast his gaze around the room, meeting the eyes of as many as he could before he continued. "I cannot stand by and let this Gwyliannan corrupt and take over my city. And it is sick and sad that any of you would allow this."

He turned to Fallon and said, "I don't know what this will do to me, if I choose to leave here without all of you, to go fight. But it's not right. If I have to suffer until I die, at least I'll die knowing that I fought against the darkness as long as I could. I've never been someone to take a stand, but this seems like the moment and the cause."

The first voice to speak up after Merrick surprised them all.

Cullen let out a long, exasperated sigh, and said, "Again, why is it that I am the one to speak up first? You have heard the Blackbird speak more eloquently than any Raven should, and he has shamed us all. He calls for us to unite and fight for the Light – is that not what we were born to do? We have grown all too accustomed to sitting by while the world changes around us, refusing to be a part of that change because we were comfortable, and scared! Shame on us, I say. I, for one, will follow where the Blackbird leads." He walked over and stood next to Merrick, his hands clenched in fists at his side. Merrick nodded approvingly at Cullen.

Aisling said nothing, she just stood up at Merrick's other side, and looked at the rest of the room defiantly.

Lucee came around the table to stand next to Cullen. "I'm just a mortal who doesn't know much about your world yet, but this is a no-brainer," she declared. "You always fight for goodness. You always fight with your friends at your side."

Fallon assessed them, then addressed the room, "Is this what we want, then? I am your leader, and I know you would go where I say, but this is a decision I care not to make for you all."

Sheridan spoke up, "We do not all have to go fight in the City. Some of us will need to stay here and protect the House, and some are not suited for a fight, but might lend a hand in other ways. We all have our strengths and skills. But I feel that this is a matter that we must take a stand on, else we find all we love destroyed."

There were nods and sounds of agreement around the room, and Fallon said, "It is decided, then. Merrick, you have spoken well, and Cullen, you as well. Sousa, your words are true and we will strive our best to heal the rifts we have caused, whether through choice or inaction." She bowed to Sousa, and the whole room reacted with small gasps and whispers.

Merrick pulled on Cullen's sleeve and Cullen murmured, "She just acknowledged him as a superior in front of all. Unprecedented." Merrick's eyebrow shot up in surprise.

He said, to no one in particular, "Okay, so now what?"

Merrick's question was answered by Sousa. "Now, we finish partying. Tomorrow, we plan. How does that sound?" A feeling of relief that was tangible washed over the crowd, and there was a cheer. Sousa threw back the rest of his beer and yelled, "I need like 10 more of these!"

MUSIC: FAITH AND THE MUSE
In Dreams Of Mine

The night wound on, but Merrick could feel himself wearing out around 4am. Aisling looked at him during one of Sheridan's rambling tales, and murmured in his ear, "You are practically asleep. We should get to bed, I think."

He groaned and stretched languidly, and agreed, "I am wiped out. All this trying to stay awake really starts to cramp one's style, you know?" That made both Aisling and Lucee laugh.

Merrick turned to Lucee and said, "Are you staying? Is that... is that an appropriate question to ask? I know you're an adult, I just want to make sure you're okay and if not, that you get home safely."

She shrugged and answered, "Unclear as to what's going on. I'll be fine, though, don't you worry about me, Merrick. I can sleep anywhere. And I'm not leaving, I need to be at this planning session. I am part of this now, you dope." She punched Merrick lightly, and he winced and pretended like it hurt. "Don't you humor me, you butt!" she exclaimed, and pretend punched him again, much to Aisling's amusement.

"Alright, you two. If you don't behave, I'll give you both something to complain about! That's weird dreams, in case you didn't guess." She winked and pulled Merrick up. "Come with me, my Blackbird. Let me show you where to roost."

He waved, helplessly, as he was pulled from the room, while his friends at the table tittered. Sousa went back to a deep discussion about beer with Sheridan, and Cullen turned to Lucee and quietly said, "You are more than welcome to sleep with me."

Lucee made a face. "That's absolutely not the way to ask me that, you know. Ugh."

Cullen looked aghast. "I meant in my bed! Not... well, I would love it to be more than sleeping, I think that's obvious. But I am not that sort of cad, and it pains me to think you see me as such." Lucee snorted. Cullen's eyes widened as he continued to protest, "I'm more suave than that, lady! I believe that I am insulted."

Lucee rolled her eyes. "I have a hard time buying that you can't hear how that statement sounded, Cullen. Anyway, I'm fine sleeping in a chair or the floor, whatever. It's not my first house party rodeo, whatever that is."

He actually did look insulted at that. "Not on my life. What sort of host would I be otherwise? You will sleep in my bed, and I will sleep on the floor. Does that suit?"

She sighed deeply, tired of having to navigate their exchanges, and said, simply, "That's fine."

Cullen stood and extended a hand to her and helped her up. "Follow me, then."

Cullen's room was upstairs, in the back of the house. It wasn't large by any means, just a room with a bed, a chair, a few shelves, a steamer trunk, and a full-length mirror next to the closet. Lucee almost made a snarky comment about that when she saw it but decided that she was just over sparring with him for the evening. It had become too much to deal with until she had some sleep.

She sat in the chair and took off her boots, trying to keep her expression as blank as possible. At this point, she just wanted to get some rest, and then she would have a better handle on everything.

Cullen sat on the bed and watched her for a moment, considering, and said, "I'm sorry. I don't mean to make things difficult. It's in my nature to be like this, but that doesn't make it right, or something you deserve. And I could say that I warned you – and I did – but that also is less than fair to you."

She had stopped, in the middle of pulling off a boot, and was watching him with a blank look. He paused, biting his lip, then continued.

"I like you, Lucee. There's something about you that strikes me in the same way that Merrick does, in that it spurs me to act against that nature of mine and take risks that I never have before. I do not understand it, and to be honest, I do not like it, because it makes me feel vulnerable in a way that I don't understand or know how to manage. You are special and I think you should not waste your time on the likes of me – but I also must admit that saying that, that thinking about you choosing someone else, causes an ache inside me the likes I have never felt. It is utterly foreign and completely terrifying.

"So there. You have as much candor from me as anyone has seen in many an age, perhaps ever." He stopped and sat there looking at the floor.

Lucee wondered if he was embarrassed. She couldn't have imagined a speech like that ever coming from him until she heard it herself.

She took a deep breath, and told him, "I appreciate you sharing all of that with me, but I'm not sure what you want me to do with the info, what you want from me. I am the kind of girl who gets guys that try to play me all the time, so I stopped dating so much. I just grew tired of all the games and bullshit, you know? So, I'm going to tell you this and let you decide how you want to play it: this sort of speech is nothing new to me. 'Oh, you're so special Lucee,' like that's enough to get me to drop my pants." She laughed, not a mean laugh but more one of self-deprecation. "Truth? It worked well enough when I was young, and who doesn't want to be special? But it's funny how I'm never special enough to be exclusive to, to commit to. That's not the kind of 'special' that Lucee Fearney is, oh no."

Cullen muttered, almost to himself, "I am an ass."

Lucee shrugged. "Oh, but that's how you are made, right? No way to change that if it's baked in." She got up and climbed past him, into the bed. "It's fine. It's exactly what I expected, anyway. I am a sidekick and I'm lucky to even be invited along to these fantastical adventures, so I'll be grateful that the handsome rogue even gave me the time of day and live off of that. So, if you'll excuse me, I should get some sleep. No need to sleep on the floor, there's plenty of room here."

She turned away from him, and laid her head down, trying her best to not let him see the tears in her eyes. "It's always this way," she thought. "I got cocky and thought it could be better, but I was fooled by faerie glamour."

Cullen sat on the edge of the bed for a moment after she laid down. Lucee wondered what he was thinking. She heard him get up, walk over to turn out the light, then come back. He laid down next to her as if he was trying to make the least amount of fuss possible, then she heard his voice, almost a whisper.

"I'd really like it if you'd let me hold you. I understand if you say no."

Lucee considered this for a moment, then reached her arm back, found his hand, and pulled his arm over her so that they were spooned up, her hand over his, pressing it into her waist gently. He moved a little closer, but kept the distance between them respectable, and she heard a little sigh of contentment." I have no idea what to do with this," she thought, before falling into an exhausted sleep.

Elsewhere in the house, the party had wound down for the most part, with both Sousa and Sheridan passed out, heads down on the table. On a big brocade sofa across the room, the Gothlings were all asleep, curled up like a bunch of kittens with Edana in the middle, surrounded by them. She looked ecstatic. There were some other people, mortal and Eleriannan, crashed out in chairs or on big pillows on the floor. And upstairs, Aisling and Merrick were finally able to sleep together, in a bed – and in person, not in dreams.

Aisling's room was next to the tower room. Merrick had really wanted to ask to see it again, but the night was so late and he was utterly wiped out – between the party, the show, and all the lack of good sleep, he was running on fumes at best.

He was delighted by her little room, though, when they entered it. It was painted all in a dusky sort of mauve, with deeper mauve, purple, and mossy green accents in her curtains and bedclothes and rug. On the wall behind the bed, there was a random pattern of iridescent copper dots that meandered up the wall and onto the ceiling over the bed. She had an overstuffed velvet chair in that same mossy green in one corner, and what looked like an ancient armoire. And at the end of the room was a bay window with a bench seat, framed with tattered, lacy curtains. It looked exactly how Merrick expected, and Aisling looked perfectly at home in it.

"This is beautiful!" he told her, and she beamed.

"There's a really nice little balcony porch on this floor, too, I'll have to show you tomorrow. I sit there sometimes and watch the birds," she told him. "But now, we should sleep! You look half transparent!"

He smiled, "I feel half transparent. And I don't have anything to sleep in or change into – ugh. I'm sorry."

Aisling laughed at that. "Let's sleep first, it doesn't matter about what we're wearing, this is not the time to be fastidious. Tomorrow, we'll sort out clothing. We have a plan for that." She winked at him. "Let's get you into bed now."

After he'd pulled off his boots and climbed into the cloud of bedsheets and blankets, he turned to her, apologetic.

"I feel bad that we're finally in a bed together and all I can manage is to sleep! I mean... I guess I'm assuming a lot. But –"

She cut him off, "Merrick, you silly raven. I want you to sleep now, and we can revisit this once we are rested." She kissed him gently, and said, "There. Go to sleep." And she slid into his arms and wrapped hers around him, her head on his chest. He sighed happily and felt consciousness slip away.

In Dreamtime

He stood up abruptly, disoriented. It was dark, and it took his eyes a few moments to adjust and for him to realize that the faint light he could see was coming from the street, and that he was in an alley. A moment after that, he recognized that the alley was behind The Maithe, Sousa's place, and that he was not alone.

A flash of bluish light revealed a woman with purple hair, surrounded by four stickmen and a man who could have only been Fae, he was so handsome and striking looking. He was tall and thin, almost angular, and his face had the sort of pointed features that made Merrick think of one of Brian Froud's elves. His hair was silvery-white and reminded Merrick of starlight. The woman was standing with her back to the wall, her fists up. At her feet were cans of spray paint; the half-finished graffiti behind her looked like some sort of sigil to Merrick.

She looked familiar, for some reason, and Merrick knew he needed to step up and defend her. He yelled HEY and put his hands up like he was going to fight, and the alley exploded into neon rainbow colors, throwing all of them back. The last thing Merrick saw was Sousa running in, fists flying and what looked like lightning cracking around him, and he heard yelling –

He woke up, sitting up in the bed with his heart pounding. The sun was shining, and Aisling was squinting up at him from the pillow, confused.

"Merrick, are you well?" she asked, touching his arm gently.

He nodded, taking a moment to catch his breath before answering. "It was another dream. This time you weren't there, but Sousa was. And some stickmen –"

Aisling stopped him, "Wait, let's tell everyone together. Your dreams have been instructive to all of us, let's see what the others think of this one. But it is yet early – will you lie back down with me? We have had so little time together, without some emergency or another interrupting us."

That made Merrick smile. He snuggled back down into the bed next to her and reached out to move a strand of her hair away from her face. "I am lucky beyond belief," he said to her, softly.

She put her arms around his neck and said, "We always say, 'fortune favors the brave,' and you are very brave, my Blackbird."

She kissed him sweetly, and he couldn't help but pull her closer, their kiss growing in intensity. He pulled back for a moment, looking her in the eyes, and asked, "This is real, right? Just... all of what's happened, and now I'm here with you, and it all seems too perfect. I keep expecting to wake up naked and alone in an empty field."

Aisling giggled. "To be fair, that's the sort of thing we are known for. But this IS real, and I am not disappearing. Especially if you are naked." She winked at him, and he felt himself blush a little.

"Well, I guess even if that was how it ended, it would have been worth it." This time, he was the one to kiss her, and when she started to push his tee shirt up, her hands on his bare chest, he sat up and pulled it over his head. When he turned back to her, she gave him a flirty look and pulled her dress over her own head, then laughed as his eyes grew wide with delight. She pulled the covers over them both with a laugh, and they collapsed into a tangle of their naked bodies.

When Lucee woke, she was alone in the bed. She rolled over and the first thing she saw was a small bouquet of flowers on the pillow next to her. She wrinkled her nose, confused. Where in the world did Cullen find flowers like this in late Autumn? They were tied up neatly with a pale pink velvet ribbon, and they were the oddest choice she'd ever received – chamomile and what looked like... cherry blossoms?

There was no sign of Cullen anywhere, but at the end of the bed was a neatly folded pile of clothes with a note on top. She picked up the note to read it and shook her head in wonder. The paper was smooth and creamy, obviously very fine. Cullen's handwriting, written in a sepia ink that no doubt came from a fountain pen, was showy, full of flourishes.

It read:

Lucee,

Please pardon my absence. I am contemplating the error of my ways.

Tully found these clothes for you; I hope they suit. If you wish to bathe, you will find all that you need in the bathroom. When you are ready, you may join me on the balcony porch, if you like.

Yours,
Cullen

Well. That was a thing.

She took the note and tucked it into her boots, so he couldn't take it back while she was showering. Scooping up the pile of clothes, she found the bathroom, and was delighted to find a claw footed bathtub with a shower. Then as she turned to close the door, she spied a set of wooden shelves with baskets, and one of the baskets had her name on it! She noticed Cullen and Sousa both had baskets, along with other names she recognized. How nice!

She found in the basket everything she needed to clean up, all in neat packages or bottles. She grabbed a herbal smelling bar of soap, found a clean and fluffy towel, and went to town scrubbing up in the shower. It felt amazing.

The clothes were perfect. Tully had found her a long skirt made of fabric that was woven to show black from one direction, and a green that matched her hair perfectly when she turned the other way. It had big pockets like cargo pants as well, and she was thrilled. A black woolen tunic topped that, and Tully had made sure to include some black tights that were the softest thing she'd ever worn. After she'd gone back to the room and pulled on her boots, she took the note and wrapped her clothes from the night before around it, then she grabbed the tiny bouquet and went on a quest to find the balcony porch.

She found it on the other side of the stairway, through a small sitting alcove with more of the soft, overstuffed sofas that the occupants of the house seemed to favor. She opened the French doors and walked out, and found Cullen sitting at a café table, in a chair that looked much more comfortable than it should have.

Arrayed before him on the table was a tray filled with breads and muffins, and there was butter and jam for the bread. He had set out two plates and mugs made of beautiful hand thrown clay and glazed in blues, and there was a carafe of what she assumed was coffee, with cream and sugar cubes in a dish. Despite the sunny sky and the delicious looking food in front of him, Cullen had a hangdog look about him, and he stared into his coffee, only looking up when she sat down across from him. Then for a moment, a smile flashed across his face before it went back to that woebegone expression.

Lucee tilted her head, curious, and asked, "Did something happen? Are you okay?"

Cullen replied, once again studying his coffee, "Just spending some time in deep self-reflection. It has been brought to my attention of late that I am, well, deficient in some areas. And when I examine that, I do not like what I find."

She murmured, "Oh."

He shrugged a little, then took her cup and poured her some coffee. "Please do eat something. I brought this up here just for you. Well, and

Merrick and Aisling if they ever drag themselves away from bed."

He rolled his eyes, and Lucee snickered. She set her little bouquet on the table and reached for some bread, and Cullen said, "It makes me happy that you accepted the flowers."

She nodded while she added butter and jam, and looked up from her task to ask, "But where did you get them? It's the wrong time of year!"

Before Cullen could answer, Aisling and Merrick walked onto the porch, and Aisling said, "You're asking one of us where we found anything? That's funny." Cullen laughed at that and gestured at the pair to pull up chairs. She leaned over and inspected the flowers and her expression changed to a puzzled one. "What did you do, Cullen?"

He looked sheepish. "Of course. You know what the flowers mean." He stood up abruptly. "I'll go get you mugs, and more coffee."

Merrick raised his eyebrows, and Aisling made a face at him. She said to Lucee after he had left, "What do you know about the Language of Flowers? The nosegay he gave you means something, and he is embarrassed that I know it."

Lucee's hand flew up to cover her mouth. "What? Will you tell me what it means? I doubt he will."

Aisling smiled. "I guarantee that he expects me to tell you. Here is what I know: chamomile means 'patience in adversity' – which is why I asked what he did. The apple blossoms surprised me. They say, 'I prefer you above all others.' For Cullen, that is a quite bold statement. It is also a very odd combination of flowers; he would have never chosen these for aesthetics, which told me immediately that they were carrying a message."

Cullen, standing in the doorway, cleared his throat awkwardly. "I admit that I hoped the others would read my intention as well. No one here sees more in me than the scoundrel and ne'er-do-well. It becomes a self-sabotaging trap. I look at you, Lucee, and I want to be more than what everyone expects of me." He put the mugs and coffee down on the table and turned to go.

"Oh no you don't!" Lucee exclaimed. "You absolutely do not get to run away after a statement like that. Sit down with us while we eat. I'll think about what you said. And, um, flowered."

Merrick had to stifle a chuckle at that. He covered by reaching over for a muffin and stuffing it in his mouth.

MUSIC: THIS COLD NIGHT
Blackout Rift

After two pieces of buttered and jammed bread and a cinnamon muffin that she shared with Cullen, Lucee was utterly stuffed. The four of them had shifted the conversation to less embarrassing things, and Lucee and Cullen managed to laugh together as Aisling teased Merrick about his new rock star status in Baltimore. But there was a tension hovering over breakfast, and finally Merrick addressed it.

"I know we are gathering to talk about it later, but except Sousa not being here, I would consider you all my inner circle." Cullen elbowed Lucee, none too subtly, and she swatted at him and made a face.

Merrick continued, "Anyway, what should I expect? I am worried that having time to think over what Sousa and I said will give some of them time to change their minds. And I don't really know what our next steps are. To be fair, I don't even know much about our enemy, other than they look like they were built of sticks, and they seem to hate fun."

Aisling replied, "They don't all look like sticks. That's just their scouts, the ArDonnath. Many of them look like us."

Her voice grew soft. "Some of them are – well, were us. You truly can't judge us by our looks, just like with mortals. To be honest, I don't know what many of them look like these days, we have avoided confrontation with them for so long that it was a shock when they came at you as they did. I think when we brought you into our fold, your light shone even stronger than before, like we unveiled it in a way. And it drew them like a beacon, just as it did us."

She paused, sipped her coffee. "I wish I could tell you what their endgame is. All I know is that they have always been the harbingers of bad things, and they are diametrically opposed to our views on the world. We have been at odds forever, and where we sow joy, they sow sorrow."

Cullen nodded, and added, "As for the others, I also am unsure what their plan will be. As you can see, we have grown complacent. There was a time when we would ride out, engage with the world, fight to bring beauty into the world. Now, we need an interloper to sail through our door in order to kick us into action. You, and now Sousa as well, are the ones pushing us to be better. Left to our own devices, I believe we would have become insignificant and then just faded away."

Aisling gave Cullen a searching look. "You have been thinking deeply, my friend. I hope I am not too bold in saying that I like the changes come upon you of late." Cullen answered with a wry smile. Lucee shot a look at Merrick behind Cullen's back and made a face, which Merrick did his best to ignore.

Eventually, they made their way downstairs. Amazingly, the entire place was spotless again, though by the looks of things, neither Sousa nor Sheridan had moved much all night. They were somehow still drinking beer and were snacking from a plate of meats and cheeses set in the middle of the table while they yelled at each other.

"Tiny toadstools, you two, did you even sleep?" Cullen exclaimed.

Sousa laughed at that, and Sheridan bellowed back, "This table makes an excellent pillow!"

Aisling shook her head, and both Merrick and Lucee managed to stifle their laughter.

"Have we any thoughts on what our next steps are, guys?" Merrick asked, taking a seat next to Sousa. Sheridan offered him a tankard, but Merrick waved it off, and Sheridan shrugged and took a swig from it himself.

"The way I see it, we have one of two ways to handle this," Sousa said. "We can wait until they come to us, or we can go to them."

Aisling looked alarmed. "Go to them? That seems foolhardy at best. We know next to nothing about their strengths, their numbers."

Sousa took another swallow of beer and replied, "Not to fight them. To talk to them."

The whole table fell silent, and Merrick said, "Whoa. How is it that I didn't even see that option?"

Sousa raised his tankard and answered, "Power of beer, man. Power of beer."

Merrick snorted, then asked, "But what do we ask them? 'Are your intentions to fight us, or are you just mad we didn't invite you to the party?' I'm sure that will make us popular."

"Listen, you geniuses, you cannot just walk up to the Gwyliannan and ask them their plans!" Cullen snapped, incensed. "How do you think that will work out? They aren't going to invite you in for tea! What are you thinking?"

Merrick shrugged. "What if they do? What if they don't? Either way, we learn more than we know now. Would you really go to war without finding out why, or what they want?"

Cullen scowled and shot back, hotly, "What if they capture you? What if they kill you?"

Merrick took a moment to breathe deeply. "From what I understand, hospitality is a thing with you, correct? Does that go across the board?"

Cullen furrowed his brow and answered cautiously, "Yes, generally. Some of us on both sides are brutish, but to insult a guest or treat them poorly is looked upon with distaste." He looked then to Aisling. "Surely you aren't supporting this idea?"

Aisling made a pained face. "Do you really think that I love this plan? But Merrick is right. We have assumed many things, but that is all they are. If we come to parley, we will at least know more about their motives and goals. Perhaps we may both gain understanding of each other. Merrick has proven himself to have impeccable manners, let us use that to our advantage."

Cullen countered, "Fallon will hate it."

At this point Fallon walked into the room and said, "And what is it that I will hate?"

They pulled out a chair for her, and then they filled her in on their plan. Fallon's expressions went from confused, to worried, to resigned as they explained, and Cullen continued to push back against the plan.

"Hush now, let me think," she murmured, waving them back with one hand. They all sat quietly, with the tension so thick one could cut it with a knife.

Finally, Fallon spoke. "Merrick and Sousa are right. We have assumed much and we know little." She raised a finger to Cullen as he started to protest and continued. "Yes, the risks are great. But Merrick has the right of it; if he goes as an emissary from our court, they will have to receive him and listen to what he has to say. I hope they will decide to give as much as they get."

She looked at Sousa. "You will be going, as the representative of Maithe House, I assume?"

He nodded and said in a voice that was quiet, but with steel behind it,

"They caused strife among mortals who were under my invite. That needs to be addressed."

Fallon tilted her head in agreement. She turned to Cullen, then. "I know you do not agree with this. But I would ask you to stand again with our Raven and show the Gwyliannan that we give him our support."

Cullen scowled, but answered, "Fine. In for a penny and all of that. What else do I have to do, anyway?"

Merrick leaned over and put his hand on Cullen's shoulder. "I am glad you'll be there with me," he said, carefully avoiding any mention of gratitude or being indebted.

Aisling said, reassuringly, "You'll be with people who will have your back, Merrick."

Fallon shook her head, "Not you, though, Aisling. You know how poorly that would go."

Aisling looked crestfallen, and Merrick asked, "Why would that be?"

Aisling said, in a small voice, "She is afraid they will think me an abomination and take insult. Don't get angry, Merrick. She's right. I don't want her to be, but she is, as usual."

Fallon shrugged and said, "You don't become the leader without learning how to be right as much as possible. Leaders who make too many mistakes pay for those mistakes."

It wasn't much later that Merrick and Cullen found themselves in Sousa's van, driving South, headed to what had been Tiennan House. The neighborhoods in Baltimore changed quickly as they went – some blocks looked more prosperous, then the next block immediately over would look almost deserted, buildings falling down and boarded up.

Cullen whispered, "Surely no one lives here?"

Sousa replied, "Sadly, they do. The disparity in this city is heartbreaking, and it is almost impossible for those born into these areas to successfully escape, because of the social and economic factors that keep them trapped. You can see that things used to be different here, but it feels like it's getting worse every day. That's why I won't abandon The Maithe. I know we could help stop the spread of this damage."

Cullen looked away, chastened.

They made a turn from a run-down boulevard onto a small side street, and suddenly everything changed. The entire neighborhood was full of large houses that had once been magnificent, but now were showing the ravages of age, time, and a lack of maintenance. There were many trees – in fact, the entire neighborhood felt like it was slowly being claimed by the trees and shrubbery around it. As they came around a bend in the road, what could only be Tiennan House came into view.

It was atop a small hill, so the roof and second floor rose above the trees. Like the houses around it, the building was somewhat worse for the wear, but it was still imposing in size and faded grandeur. It was a Queen Anne style with a small tower on one side, and a big circular window on the second floor that was flanked by small balconies. A peaked roof hid a third balcony and a lot of gingerbread-style trim under its eaves. The house was painted various greys, but Merrick could almost see that there had once been other colors, as well. He turned to Cullen and they both shared a moment of exchanged nervous glances.

Sousa pulled up to the front, and they gathered next to the van. There was not a soul in sight; not only around the house, but they had also seen no one while driving through the neighborhood. Everything felt eerily deserted, which just added to Merrick's nervousness. He closed his eyes for a moment, balled his fists, and took a few deep breaths. You can do this, Merrick, he thought as he tried to breathe through the anxiety.

Finally, he felt calm enough to do what he came to do, or close enough, and he started up the front path to the door. It was painted that grey color, with the palest green trim, and there was a knocker in the middle of it that was a frog, sitting on a lily pad. When Merrick lifted the frog, it was obvious that you banged it against the lily pad, and it made a deep gonging noise. Merrick really wanted to look to Sousa or Cullen for reassurance, but he kept his focus forward, and that paid off – when the door opened, he was looking the house's occupant directly in the eyes.

Merrick tried not to show his surprise. The being facing him was tall, stocky, muscular, with dark skin and short hair that stood up in small spikes. His eyes were almond shaped, with an extreme tilt, and were a surreal golden color. And besides having ears that ended in points, he also had two graceful horns that started at his forehead and curved back to end in a small curl upwards.

He quickly schooled his face from surprise to a neutral expression, and said to Merrick in a deep, resonant voice, "What have we here? What brings you to boldly knock on this door?" He eyed Merrick up and down, sizing him up.

Merrick took a deep breath and said, with a small bow, "Greetings to you, lordly one. I am the Blackbird of House Mirabilis, and I have come on their behalf to ask for parley with this house." He bowed again, then moved back so Sousa could move forward.

Sousa added, "I am the leader of Maithe House, and I am also here to parley." He looked to Merrick like he was holding himself back.

Keep it together, Sousa, Merrick thought.

Cullen bowed with a flourish, like the dandy he was. "I am also from House Mirabilis, here to stand with the Blackbird and represent our house. We seek your audience to discuss urgent matters, if you will."

He was met with melodic laughter from the man on the other side of the threshold. "So formal, you all are! And I know that must be chafing to at least one of you!" He shot Sousa a knowing look, and Sousa frowned in return. "So brave of you to come right to our front door!"

He laughed again, then gestured to them to enter. "Come in, come in. You are bold enough to knock on the door, you are welcome here. Sit in here and I will gather the court."

He led them to a bare room – there was only a fireplace with a fire going, and a circle of many wooden chairs. They stood together next to one of the chairs, unsure of how to feel about how everything had gone so far.

After what seemed like an excruciating amount of time, they were joined by a small group of the Gwyliannan, who looked Merrick, Cullen, and Sousa up and down as they entered. In turn, Merrick knew he was probably gawking. They were uncanny looking, stranger than most of the Eleriannan that he'd encountered.

Leading the group was the one who had answered the door, looking no less impressive next to the others of the house. There were four others, each wild and beautiful in their own ways.

Merrick heard Cullen's startled reaction as one of them pulled back a hood to reveal a wide, yet somehow delicate feminine face, curtained by wild, shining black hair. She had a rosy golden complexion, which made her icy, almond shaped eyes really stand out. Her pointy ears poked through that cascade of hair in a way that looked quite natural on her. Each ear had many small silver rings around the edges. She was the tallest of the group, lithe as a dancer.

Cullen exclaimed, "Genaine! We thought you were gone forever!"

Merrick quickly pivoted to look at Cullen. "You know each other?"

The woman laughed, and to Merrick it was as pleasant as tinkling bells, though the words that followed were tainted with bitterness. "So, it is Cullen, who has always been good for a laugh or a tumble, but never when circumstances are dire. You might have known more of my fate if you'd bothered to come fight when we needed you. But do tell why you are here now, suddenly concerned with the power struggles of the city beyond your House."

Cullen bit his lip, looked away for a moment, then turned to face Genaine. "I was many foolish things before. And the chances are good that I am still foolish, but I endeavor to become a better man, if not a wiser one. I cry you mercy." He went to one knee, head bent.

Merrick covered his mouth with a hand in shock and surprise. How much had this weighted Cullen's decision to champion him, he wondered?

She laughed again and waved a hand in dismissal. "Cullen, what you did is unforgivable, but for the sake of your companions I will let this lie – for now. There will be a reckoning between you and I, believe you this."

Cullen rose, his head still bent, his face white. Merrick didn't like any of this.

She addressed Sousa next, "I know who you are. You are the keeper of Maithe House. You didn't come either, but I heard you were waylaid in transit. Is this true?"

Sousa nodded. "I fought ArDonnath near the Great Hill. They destroyed my transportation; they beat me senseless and left me to die. I returned, defeated and alone, to The Maithe. Until quite recently, I had seen or interacted with none of our kind. Then this one," he gestured at Merrick, "decided it would be a grand lark to invite himself to a party at House Mirabilis."

Genaine made a pained face, and addressed Merrick, "And you, mortal, you knew not what you were taking up with."

He nodded. "I'll be totally blunt. I was clueless. But I somehow managed to endear them to me, and now I am here as their representative, but at my own insistence."

That made the Gwyliannan murmur to each other, surprised. The one who had opened the door originally said, "I think we need to sit down and hear this tale. All of it. And we will repay you by sharing our own tale."

He paused, and added, "I am called Daro. I, for one, appreciate bluntness, not the hollow formalities in which your friend there is well versed. Let us sit at a table, share food and drink, and our stories. But I wish to hear yours first."

"I am Merrick, known as the Blackbird. I was told that giving names is a big deal with your – now my – people. But it seems right to tell you who I am, I don't know why. But I'll tell you the whole tale, and why we are here."

Daro smiled at that. "It is a big deal to steal a name or trick it away. But given as between equals, it is an honor, not to be abused." Merrick nodded, and Daro continued, "Come with us and we will come to some understandings."

They moved into a room that once was a grand dining area, but had obviously seen better days, like so much of the house. There was a long wooden table that dominated the room, surrounded by chairs that had once been upholstered in fine silk velvet, now threadbare, the green faded to a mossy brown. Everything looked like it had been there as long as the house had been around.

There was another fireplace, on one of the long walls, with a carved marble mantlepiece that had obviously been a point of pride long ago. There was still wallpaper on the walls, once elegant, now faded and covered with drawings and swirls from floor to ceiling. Merrick was reminded of how he had covered the tower room at House Mirabilis with his dream-addled writings.

They sat down, and one of the Gwyliannan – a small, dark haired guy with pitch black eyes and hands that were like a hunting bird's talons – brought them drink and food. Merrick noted that everyone had wine except Sousa; they'd somehow known to bring him beer. The food was a tray of fruits and cheeses, nothing as fancy as the spreads that always seemed to appear at House Mirabilis, but still quite nice.

Daro said, "Even though you came to parley with us, let us be the first to tell you who we are. Then you may tell us your story, Merrick."

Besides Daro and the willowy Genaine, there was Brenna, who had warm brown skin, large rounded eyes, and feathers where one might expect hair. They started as tiny ones at her forehead, and lengthened as they went down, giving them the appearance of a flowing mane. She reminded Merrick of an owl.

Dermot was the name of the one who had brought food and drink. He seemed shy. Karstyn was a bit of a surprise – muscularly buff, with a pale complexion that looked like they never went out during the day, and with a long mohawk that was made of tendrils that moved independently. Merrick couldn't be sure they were not actually snakes.

All of them seemed to favor piercings and tattoos and clothing that wouldn't look out of place in an apocalyptic movie-scape.

After Sousa introduced himself, Merrick told them a carefully edited story of how he came to be bonded with House Mirabilis, and Genaine leaned forward with interest when he explained how he and Aisling had connected. "She is the dream born one, yes?"

Merrick nodded, and explained, "She wanted to come along, but Fallon – the leader of House Mirabilis – was unsure if her presence would be welcome or offensive. Evidently she is objectionable to some."

Genaine's eyebrow shot up. "For something that she had no active part in? How very Highborn."

"I honestly don't know what that means. I am still learning."

She snorted. "There are a lot of important things you don't know about us yet, Blackbird." She pointed at Cullen. "You. You should be educating him, as you stood for him."

Cullen said, "You are correct. Things have progressed quite quickly as of late and much of his education has been slapdash, or entirely postponed, I fear."

She waved her hand in the air, dismissively. "Always excuses with you."

Cullen sighed, beaten.

As Merrick described the events that happened the night of the Drawback's gig, the Gwyliannan all looked shocked, then Dermot said, dismayed, "That was none of us! We have a few ArDonnath attached to our House, but not a one would have gone on their own to create such mischief, and we did not send them!"

Sousa and Cullen both looked taken aback. Sousa said, "I don't think I understand. There's another group of Gwyliannan here in Baltimore?"

The others all looked at each other, visibly upset. Brenna spoke, "We have suspected there to be another faction afoot as of late but had no proof. Until now."

Merrick's heart was pounding now. "This... this changes things considerably." He downed the wine in his glass in one gulp. His hosts all nodded, made noises of uneasy agreement. He said, after making sure he'd left not a drop behind, "Why don't you tell us your story now, and perhaps that will help us understand where we are now."

Genaine replied, "Fine. I'll start."

MUSIC: THIS MORTAL COIL
Acid, Bitter and Sad

Genaine sipped her wine, looked at each of the visitors in turn, and began to tell her tale. "As Cullen knows, I was not always Gwyliannan. In fact, despite the way that some of the Eleriannan frame things, we are both the same, with just different alignments and missions."

Cullen sputtered, incredulous, and Genaine's brow furrowed. "Will you let me tell this without your interjections? After all, there are more things in heaven and earth than are dreamt of in your philosophy; open your ears and you might learn more than you expect."

Merrick turned to Cullen and gestured to him to keep his lips zipped, and Cullen made a sour face and indicated that Genaine should continue.

"As I was saying: I was Eleriannan, and I lived here at Tiennan House with a cohort of others like me, like you. We believed that we were good, light in the world, put here to bring inspiration and beauty. We did much as you did at House Mirabilis, and once long ago at Maithe House – we found mortals, pulled back the glamour long enough to tease them with marvels and turn them back out to use that glimpse as fuel. Or we would choose one or two special mortals, those with a white-hot shining light, and we would take them as our own for a time. Like you, Blackbird. I am sure they sold you a bill of endless wonders and all the creative output that being in that house could offer, yes? And maybe they told you that we need you more than you need us. If they were feeling magnanimous, of course."

Merrick's face was unreadable as he slowly nodded.

She continued, "As I thought. That is how we have done for many an age. But what they don't tell you, Merrick, is that despite making it sound so charitable, so noble, the ones we touch are never able to return to the lives they led, and many of us believe that our case is quite oversold. The Gwyliannan are made up of many of us who saw what was really being offered and objected to it.

"The Gwyliannan walked away from the idea that we should imbue select mortals with the gifts that we offer, which all too often ended poorly for the mortal involved. We instead started working in the shadows – indeed, it is implied in our very name – to affect the world in ways that create broader change, starting with our neighborhood. We are regarded as protecting angels to those who live here, despite them never actually knowing exactly who their benefactors are.

"We keep the divisive elements out, encourage the denizens to grow gardens and have street parties and slowly work for positive change as a small community. They only know of us as the odd artists who live in the old house on the hill, and that suits us perfectly."

She stopped for a moment to take a long sip of her wine, and Sousa asked, "So you move among them, and they suspect nothing? How do you work to protect them?"

Daro spoke up, "We have driven off the gangs, quietly chasing them down in the night and putting fear into their hearts. The rep of this neighborhood is one of 'do not fuck with them or else' and that was what we intended." Sousa looked at him with respect.

Genaine went on, "As I said before, when the House was attacked, I lived here with other Eleriannan. Some fought alongside of me. Others fled, leaving us to fare as we might. A few were killed. I thought I was going to die. I fought with a Highborn who was leading them, one who goes by Camlin. He offered me the chance to join his side, and then left me to die when I refused.

"He was powerful, not like anything I had ever seen before. And here's the most interesting thing: the ones he leads are neither Eleriannan nor Gwyliannan. They are both, and yet neither. They call themselves Grimshaw, those of the dark woods, and they have a deep hatred for all of us.

"When they left, those who were injured and could not follow were left behind. Most had been Gwyliannan before he had swept them up and enthralled them, twisted them to his purposes. They were appalled to find their minds free, and their consciences burdened with what they had done.

"We healed each other. We tended each other's wounds, learned about each other, and grew close. And I learned in turn how they view the Eleriannan's place in the world, and I felt shame for that. We could have been doing so much more! Now, that is what Tiennan House is doing, even if it is on such a small scale. And the Grimshaw have never returned, nor had we seen sign of them in the City – not until now."

Genaine grew silent.

"No one ever came to check on this House," Merrick whispered, visibly upset. Cullen stared off to one side, his jaw clenched and his hands balled up in his lap.

Sousa sat there a moment in silence, then said, "I get all of this. I let The Maithe sit dark and dusty because I wanted no part anymore of why we had been. Merrick and I had been friends for a while before he stumbled into House Mirabilis, and he had no idea who or what I am. And if I had known what he was going to do that night, I would have found a way to keep him from doing it."

Merrick swiveled abruptly in his chair to face Sousa. "You would have stopped me?"

Sousa immediately replied, "In a heartbeat. Genaine is right. We have a way of destroying those who get too close to us. It's why I have never seemed like more to you than a dirty punk drummer dude who happens to be your friend, which is exactly how I wanted it to be. I would have been fine if we had just kept playing songs in our practice space forever, until you got tired of being in a garage band and found some girl to marry and have kids with and went off to live your normal, safe mortal life. That would have been great.

"Now, you are The Blackbird, pledged to others who I barely know – no offense, Cullen – and in the middle of something that could be fucking perilous as hell. And to be honest, I hate it. I wish you'd just stayed the singer for The Drawback, my friend who works at grocery stores and coffee shops and dates goth girls. Sorry, but I do."

Merrick was breathing heavy at this point, emotions running wild. He got up out of the chair and walked behind it, pacing wildly behind his friends. "I didn't know any of this. I had no way to know."

A soft, melodic voice broke in, "These things are all what have gone past us. We cannot change them, and we can only ever see the board and pieces that are revealed to us at the time we make those choices. To rage against that now is futile at best. Let us try to move forward with the knowledge we have gained and choose wisely from here." It was Karstyn, their sinuous hair moving gently as they spoke.

Merrick stared at them like he'd just noticed them, and murmured, "Fair enough."

He took a breath and said, "So is it fair to say that we are not enemies?

I feel that we have more in common than we do not, despite some of the issues presented here."

Genaine pressed her lips together, considering, before she answered, "We are not enemies. We have wildly convergent views on things, but we are not enemies."

The others nodded. Daro added, "I think with some deep self-reflection on the side of the Eleriannan, we could become allies. But they need to face their biases, and it will be up to you, Blackbird, to make that happen. Do you think it possible?"

Daro turned to Cullen. "What about you? You came here and have said little, which I find wise. Have your eyes been opened?"

"I... I have had my entire world upturned of late. This was the finishing blow. I am shamed, and that is no easy thing for me to confess, but I will do so to you, and to my people, who will understand even more than you, how rare and impactful this is."

He stopped and looked at each of them in turn, before speaking in the humblest of tones. "Before today, I would have said that Merrick coming into my world was the most important thing that had ever occurred in my long life. And truly, he has been the catalyst for all of this. But what you have told me today has opened my eyes to everything I have conveniently ignored, what I didn't wish to see or think upon. I will not forget that."

He pushed back some of his blond hair, which had started to escape its ponytail, out of his eyes. Merrick thought that maybe there were tears in his eyes also- it was hard to tell, but Cullen was definitely affected in a way that seemed foreign to him, and he was having a difficult time navigating his feelings.

Everyone seemed a bit emotional, actually. Merrick decided it was time to move things along a bit. "So, what are our next steps? Cullen and I will need to recount all of this back to House Mirabilis and try to navigate their response. What will you do?"

Brenna sat up a little, her eyes wider than ever, and said, "You have the harder path, I fear. We will inform the others in our house what has transpired and hold a council to decide what path we would like to take."

Daro added, "I think it wise if we reconvened in a week's time, both sides together, and share what else we might have learned, and what steps we will take. What say you?"

Merrick and Cullen looked at each other and said, "Yes" at the same time.

Sousa said, "It's not exactly neutral, but we can convene at The Maithe.

It has no ties to either group, not exactly, and there's plenty of space – even space for both groups to confer in private, away from each other."

Everyone liked that plan, and the Gwyliannan seemed excited to be able to see the inside of The Maithe. Karstyn said, in their soft voice that was at odds with their looks, "We will adjourn until the New Moon. Let us come to The Maithe when evening falls."

Merrick said, "I just want to address one thing before we leave." Genaine indicated that he should go ahead.

"You didn't have to sit down with us, or discuss any of this with us, but you did. You welcomed us into your House, and allowed us the time to explain ourselves, as well as to share your own story. I know better than to thank you for that opportunity. But I will tell you that it means so much to me, personally. I respect that now, and I will in the future."

Genaine nodded solemnly, and answered, "I think I can speak for all of us when I say that we respect you as well, Blackbird. And you, Sousa of House Maithe. You came to talk when you could have warred or withdrawn further." She shot a pointed look at Cullen, who set his jaw and looked to one side. "But Cullen, I will say this: you have taken ownership of your flaws. That is no small feat. Continue down that path and great things could happen."

He nodded tersely. "I'll take that under advisement," he replied, but there was neither heat nor sarcasm in it.

As the van drove away, Merrick turned to look back. For a moment, the house seemed to gleam in the last rays of the sunset, like it might have in its former days of glory.

They were silent as they drove to Merrick's so that he could check on his place and grab some clothes. As soon as Merrick had entered his building, Sousa turned to Cullen. "I always wondered why Mirabilis didn't join the fight. I thought you didn't know until it was too late."

Cullen sighed, "No, we are just so conflict adverse that we couldn't be bothered to stand for what was right. Getting them to see that our choice makes us the villains is going to be a tough sell. They – we – are so caught up in spinning the Gwyliannan as evil, the antithesis of what we are, that the revelation that everything we know is wrong is going to destroy everything. And I fear we deserve that."

"What of your part? How will you cope?" Sousa asked. "I'll be honest, I knew of you by reputation and wasn't impressed. I really hated that you were nosing around Lucee, who deserves the best and rarely gets it. But I can't shit on someone who sees that they've done wrong and not only admits it but takes steps to change."

Cullen snorted derisively. "I don't know if I can ever make up for what I've done, or not done. I have been the way I am for a long time. And I am not doing this to prove anything to Lucee, who deserves much better than myself. But I will confess that if she looked at it favorably, I would have the smallest balm for the way I'm feeling about myself."

Sousa raised an eyebrow. "Don't fucking hurt her. That's all I'm saying. Change for you, change because it's the right thing to do, change because you hurt other people and that's a way to make amends. Don't change because you think it'll make her favor you."

Cullen's voice was so quiet, Sousa had to strain to hear the answer. "I don't think I deserve her even if I become a better man. I need to do this because it is how I redress the balance. It is not about her, or even about me. It is about doing what's right. Finally."

They were interrupted by Merrick climbing back into the van, and Sousa drove off to House Mirabilis. Merrick said at some point along the way, "You know that Lucee is going to need to get more stuff and come back out. I mean, if she wants to." He trailed off, seeing the stricken look on Cullen's face.

Sousa, oblivious, said, "I'll drive her. Or she can borrow a scooter again. She did great the last time." Merrick, in one of the back seats, nodded, but no one saw him.

When they got back to the House, it was solidly dark out, Sousa was starving, Merrick was a nervous wreck as he anticipated the awful conversation that he was about to have with the Eleriannan, and Cullen was ready to go find a hole to hide in. They walked in and were greeted by Lucee, Tully, and Fallon, which was as odd a trio as any in that house.

Fallon looked anxious, Tully was as serene as ever, and Lucee was furious.

"WHY? Why did you go without ME.? I am supposed to be at your side, you dumbass!" She was seething with barely restrained anger, and Merrick threw his hands in the air.

"There was never any chance we were going to take you! It was too dangerous for a mortal, dumbass. Yes, I know, I'm a mortal too, but at least I've supposedly got some powers, and I have a little clout. Or notoriety. It was more than you had, and I wasn't about to endanger you."

She glared at him and growled, "Fine!" And then she turned away, her fists in little balls.

Merrick caught Sousa's sigh, and privately he echoed the sentiment. Hadn't they been through enough today already?

"Look," he said to the group, "We are tired and starving and stressed out. Can we eat and regroup a little before we address the house and talk about what's happening? I know everyone is anxious to know our news, but we are just exhausted."

Fallon said, "That is a good plan, and we will do this. I just need to know one thing: are we at war with the Gwyliannan?"

Sousa spoke up then and said, "No." Merrick bristled a little at that – it was so unlike Sousa to maneuver the conversation in that way – but he let it be, because obviously Sousa has his reasons for that blunt, terse answer that told Fallon nothing about what actually was happening. He was definitely going to have to grill Sousa about what he was up to before they talked to the House, though.

Fallon nodded once, a queenly acknowledgement, and said, "Go take care of yourselves. We will meet in the later evening and much will be discussed." She turned to Lucee. "I would very much like you to be here for that discussion. Your insight will be valuable."

For a moment, Lucee's face softened, and she said in a gentle voice, "I will be there." She shot a defiant look at Merrick and Sousa and stalked off toward the kitchen.

Sousa shrugged at Merrick and said, "I need a beer."

Merrick wandered off to find Aisling and to wash his face and get himself together. And Cullen dashed up the stairs and into his room, where he closed the door hard and stood there a moment with his back against the closed door, trying to get his feelings under control. After a moment, he went to his closet and dug through all of his garments, finally pulling out a pair of plain black jeans and a black linen button-down shirt. "I don't deserve anything nicer today," he said to himself, as he scooped it all up and fled to the shower.

After a long shower, just letting the water pour over him like it could absolve him of all the guilt he was feeling, he got dressed and went to the balcony porch to sit and think for a bit. He was hopeful that he would be alone, but after about five minutes of sitting on the edge of his favorite reclined chair, he heard a small noise, and turned to find Lucee standing in the doorway. "Of course," he thought.

She said, with the smallest smile, "And the hits keep coming, eh?"

He tilted his head and said, "I have no earthly idea what you mean."

She snorted. "Judging by how you looked when you all got back, something really shook you up. Not them, YOU. So... want to talk? Or should I go away?"

For a minute, she thought she saw his lower lip tremble. He turned to her and said, "I don't want you to go away. But you probably should. I am not fit to even be in the same room as you, to be quite honest."

She bit her lip, then said lightly, "Well, good thing we're outside then. Move over and tell me what's going on. Surely it's not as bad as you think."

He slid back so his back was against the chair, and she was sitting at the long part where their legs might have gone. He answered her, "Oh, it is worse than I ever suspected." He paused, then continued, "I am going to tell you things about what we discussed today that no one else but us has heard yet. I trust that you will keep them between us until tonight."

She responded by getting up for a moment and going to make sure the door to the balcony was closed, and the curtain pulled. "There. We are alone. I won't say anything, even if you tell me the worst thing in the world. I promise."

He told her everything, unvarnished and raw, including how being called out for his lack of action had affected him.

"I have always known that I have been lazy, unreliable, a cad. These are all pathetic enough, but I never thought I truly hurt anyone, just disappointed them. But now I see that I am a coward as well; I am a heel. And I have no one to blame but myself. I don't tell you all this in order for you to reassure me or to swear I'll redeem myself to impress you. I hope you believe me.

"I just... I want to say it to you as a way of holding myself accountable. You are braver and bolder than I will ever be, Lucee. I hope one day I'll be as good and as strong as you. Even if you disdain me for a thousand years – which I would understand! – I hope one day that, at least, I might be worthy of you. But at the end of the day, I need to be better for myself, first and foremost."

He stopped for a second, realized he was crying. Great, just great. Then he saw that Lucee was, too, and his heart sunk. Surely everything was ruined with his reveal of the terrible person he truly was.

She managed to surprise him when she turned around and slid up on the chair, then pulled him close to put her arms around him. "Awesome, now we're both crying," Lucee murmured into Cullen's hair, and she was rewarded with a half-hearted laugh from him.

"I beg your pardon, I don't cry. I weep, like a gentleman."

That started her giggling. Then they both were laughing, holding onto each other. Eventually they got it out of their system, and they found themselves leaned back in the chair, Lucee's head on Cullen's shoulder, while he wiped the tears from her face gently.

"Look, if we can't be lovers, can we at least be friends?" he asked bluntly. "I don't think I could bear to not have you in my life in some way, Lucee Fearney. I think that would be a punishment I might deserve but could not endure."

She moved a strand of hair out of his eyes and said, "You've been un-characteristically unkempt lately for a fashion plate like yourself."

He shrugged. "I haven't felt much like being a dandy."

She tilted her head upwards and kissed his cheek. "I'd like to be friends. I'd also like to be more than friends. But I don't have any intention of being some sort of conquest, or someone who you sometimes have sex with. I'm a one person at a time sort of girl, despite the efforts of some to get me to change my ways. I can barely handle one man, what makes you all think I'd want to try multiples?"

She snickered at that, but Cullen was very serious. "Silly girl, don't you know that you're the only one I can think about? I don't want anyone but you!"

Lucee's eyes grew wide. "Oh," she whispered. "Are... are you sure? Me? Truly?"

He cupped her face with one hand, gently. "Truly. As broken and flawed as I am, I still dare to dream that somehow you might want me someday, when I am more deserving."

She leaned over and kissed him, lightly but lingering. When she finally pulled back, she told him, "Don't be ridiculous. You are deserving. You made mistakes, you owned up to them, and you intend to atone for them. You move ahead with your head held high. And if any give you grief for that, I will school them."

She looked so fierce in her defense of him that he had to laugh, and then kiss her.

After a while of that, he said to her, "I think it would be wise to take my time and court you properly. You deserve nothing less, and it would give us time to learn how to understand each other. I don't want to mess this up, Lucee."

She nodded in agreement. "I am guessing you mean taking it slow, but does that mean I should find someplace else to sleep?" She looked disap-pointed. "I liked falling asleep with your arm around me, I have to admit."

He grinned and said, "We can share a bed. I will be a gentleman. And I would miss holding you, as well."

He pulled her back again, leaning back into the recline of the chair and nestling her against his chest. "We have a little time before we need to meet back with the others. Shall we just lie here for a bit, together?"

She sighed, "That sounds wonderful." And they were together, silent, just enjoying being with each other, and with no other cares in that moment.

Music: The Sundays
I Feel

As it grew closer to the late evening hours, the residents of the house seemed to naturally gravitate down to the main room downstairs. Someone had taken all the chairs in the room and placed them in a loose circle around the big room, with plenty of space in the middle. When Merrick saw this, he glanced at Aisling and said, "Is this something your people do often?"

She shook her head vigorously, "No. Not at all. We haven't had something this important to debate in a mortal lifetime, for certain."

She gestured at the table, with its usual array of finger foods and mead, ales, and other drinks set out. "Be sure not to drink aught but water or juice tonight, Merrick. Keep your head clear. I know you are going to have resistance to what you are going to say, and having your wits around you will be important."

Merrick sighed and agreed, "When isn't it, right? That's standard operating procedures nowdays. After all is said and done, I'm drinking all of Sheridan's stock."

She tittered at that, her hand over her mouth. "You won't move for a week after!"

Sousa, of course, was already there, drinking beer as usual – and surprisingly, deep in a conversation with The Ladies. Merrick shot a look at Aisling, who mouthed "I have no idea" at him. When Sousa saw them, he waved them over. "Merrick! I need you to discuss something with us!"

Merrick could feel his heart start pounding. Whatever could this be about?

He decided that impeccable manners, as always, were the best way to approach this. He bowed to Morgance and the other Ladies, saying,

"Greetings, fair ones." Then he went down to kneel on one knee before them, a way to both show respect and also that they were equals.

Morgandy and Ula made approving faces, and Morgance said, in her chiming, small voice, "Greetings, Blackbird. I see that you are as charming as ever."

He smiled to hide his tenseness. "I am sure to spend all my charm when you are involved, Ladies." Ula actually laughed a little at that.

Morgance held up a hand and addressed Merrick, "You are a talented Raven, but there is something you lack. We can help you with that. "

Merrick tried to school his face to hide his surprise but failed. "Help me? You? This is unexpected. In your opinion, Ladies, what is it that I lack?"

Morgandy spoke up, "You were given gifts, but no training."

Morgance continued, "We can assist with teaching you what each gift is capable of, and what you might do with each. Normally, we would expect you to learn on your own, with plenty of time to explore your gifts. But this is no normal time, and you may need the skills that these tokens may offer."

Sousa added, "The Ladies are most talented at this sort of work, as I think you know. They tell me that you are very strong willed and capable of the sort of magic they could help you learn. I suggest you cash in on their offer, dude."

Merrick had to stop himself from laughing at Sousa's "dude" tacked onto the end of what otherwise would be a rather unbelievable statement. "You know, every time I start to get the hang of the weirdness of all of this, something comes along to mess with my mind all over again, in some new and unexpected way."

Morgance waved a hand in dismissal at that. "You came to us, not the other way. It is your responsibility to adapt."

Merrick objected, "Oh, I don't mean to say that I wish you all would be... well, less weird. That would be ridiculous and probably terribly offensive." Morgandy and Ula nodded in unison at that.

Merrick continued, "I am just lamenting over something I probably shouldn't be, because if things suddenly became more normal, I would miss how they are now. You are correct, Morgance, it is up to me to become adaptable." She looked pleased at that.

"So, does this mean that you will accept training from us?" She asked.

"Will you promise to stay out of my head?" he shot back.

She grinned in a way that was extremely unnerving. "Of course not. In fact, I will promise that I quite likely will be going into your head more than you would enjoy. But that is part of what you will need training in,

Blackbird. You are our champion. I would not send you out onto a battle-field without all the weapons you require."

Merrick gulped. Weapons? Battlefield? He knew she was right to frame it that way, but he honestly hadn't thought about it like that before now. "Seriously, Merrick, you really are getting good at inserting yourself into the stupidest situations," he thought to himself. To Morgance he said, "I accept your kind offer. When do we start?"

They agreed that first this night's conversation with the entire house needed to happen, then they would begin training. When he went back to Aisling, who had stayed away because she knew Morgance disliked her, he told her everything – and to his surprise, she seemed pleased.

"They will prepare you well, Merrick. And since you have gone toe to toe with Morgance previously, you know how powerful she is. She will make sure you are well versed in using all your gifts." She added, "I must admit that seeing them with Sousa is jarring to my eyes."

Merrick stifled a laugh. "I'm learning to roll with these things."

The room was slowly starting to fill with people, and Merrick and Aisling grabbed seats in the front, because he knew he was going to have to stand up and talk quite a bit, so having a nearby chair when he was not speaking would be smart.

Aisling whispered in his ear then, "Here comes Cullen and Lucee. I wonder if he told her all that you told me?" Merrick wondered the same.

"She doesn't seem upset, but Cullen still has that fragile look about him. And... he's not dressed up? That seems unlike him, yes?"

Aisling agreed, "Very much unlike him, to the point that I am shocked he even owns clothes that plain. Others are noticing it, too." It was true, there were whispers as Lucee and Cullen made their way over to where Merrick and Aisling were sitting and took seats next to them.

Merrick leaned over and poked Lucee as a way of greeting, and asked Cullen, "Are you ready for this? I have been talking it all through with Aisling and neither of us know what to expect."

Lucee made a face, and Merrick couldn't tell if it was intended for him, or in reaction to what he'd said. Cullen replied, "I am in no way ready. However, I don't think I would be, no matter how much time I was given, so onward we go. Is Sousa about? Has he been drinking?"

Aisling laughed, "When is he not? Ah, there's Fallon, it must be time to begin."

Lucee squeezed Cullen's hand; his face was pale but he looked determined. Telling their tale, and the reality of who and what the Gwyliannan were went better than expected, all things considered. When Merrick explained that those who had attacked Tiennan House weren't actually representative of the Gwyliannan at all, but something other, the Grimshaw, Fallon interrupted to say, "That name is but a legend! None have ever seen or known one of the Grimshaw that I am aware. It is always rumors and dark tales."

Merrick said, "Lady, all I know is that their leader's name is Camlin, and he seems to have great powers of persuasion, because he had those fighting him under his control. And it wasn't all Gwyliannan, either. When those folks were able to break free, they stayed with the few left from Tiennan House and became the caretakers."

Cullen took over then, and his passion was evident. "We let those cousins down. We did not go to stand by their side, we did not even go after all was done to give aid to the wounded or secure the lands! We sat here in our fancy house, safely surrounded by wealthy mortals, and we danced and drank and stopped functioning at all in any way resembling how we love to paint ourselves." He cast his gaze around the room, looking at each of the folks sitting there. "We have called the Gwyliannan our enemy, when they were actually out there serving a purpose that we could only pretend to claim."

"And what purpose is that, Cullen?" Fallon asked, the expression on her face unfathomable.

He cried, "Making things BETTER! They protect the mortals around their House. They inspire, they assist, and they support the community surrounding them. Their house and the lands around it are quite visibly a bubble of prosperity in a section of town that is otherwise struggling. What benefit can we claim? Before Merrick waltzed into our House, we were moldering away, living to entertain ourselves alone!"

He took a deep breath. "I talked to these cousins of ours, these people we disdained and outright accused of nefarious deeds, and I felt the deepest shame. We should all bear this guilt. We turned our back on our purpose, our meaning, and our people. We have sat here long enough, derelict – if we want to claim that we are truly beneficent, we must change our ways. Starting now."

Sousa stood next. "When you stopped coming to the city, you allowed a void in power to happen. And that void has been filling itself steadily with negativity, gloom, malfeasance. I haven't given up The Maithe and just left for a number of reasons – one, I am not a fuckin' quitter. Another is that The Maithe is the fortress that holds the goodness of the City Center together. It's my job to protect that, and to keep fostering the good energies as much as one being possibly can on his own."

He cast an angry eye around the room. "No help from any of you. Just hiding here, fuckin' cowards."

Merrick looked around the room. The overall energy was one of shame and regret. Even Edana, usually so proud, looked crestfallen. Sheridan had somehow bent the metal armrest on his chair into a twisted mess. No one said anything.

He looked at Lucee, and she made a face at him that plainly said "DO SOMETHING" so he opened his mouth, entirely unsure as to what was going to come out.

"House Mirabilis." Heads turned their attention to him. "You have had a mirror held to you, and you dislike the reflection you see. But that is a reflection of what was and what is, but not of what will be. Do you understand? You can change who you are. Not regress, not become the vision you once had – no, you can become bigger and better versions of that best vision of yourselves.

"You cannot change if you don't know what needs to be changed. Now, you do. You have the opportunity to do better, to be better. You have the chance to make a difference and right the wrongs of the past – and to create the best possible future as we move ahead."

He took a second, put his hands on his chest. "When I first came to you, I was aimless, full of big dreams but without drive to get there or do anything better with myself. And you showed me marvels, you saw something bigger than who I was at that moment inside me. You saw possibility, and you invited me into a pact with you that would allow me to truly improve and expand on the raw talents I have.

"That is just the first step. When we entered into this partnership, I didn't think I had much to offer in return. But now? Now I do. I can offer you the chance to see things with fresh eyes, to look beyond the roles and definitions that you've been working with for so long, so that you can see the truths under those myths. You need only give me that chance."

There was a silence in the room as Merrick stood there, one hand outstretched, offering or begging, he really didn't care which they thought.

And of course, it was Aisling who broke that silence, standing up and saying loudly and clearly, "I do."

Then Cullen turned to him and said, "I do. Without hesitation."

Sheridan next, completing the triad who had stood by him at the beginning. "I do, lad!"

One by one, they began to stand and declare themselves. Merrick saw Cullen's face register surprise when The Ladies not only stood up, but came to stand next to him, surrounding him, as they spoke for him. Merrick raised both eyebrows and shot Cullen a half-smile.

Lucee came to stand next to Cullen, and he took her hand and smiled at her. Eventually, they were all standing; the only one left to speak was Fallon.

"When I invited you to join our ranks, never did I guess a day like this would come to pass, Blackbird," she said. "And now, I must exchange a pledge with you in return, it seems. How oddly fitting." She came to stand in front of him. "You are our champion, our hope. And now, it seems, our conscience as well."

He shook his head slowly. "No, that's Cullen. I think you'll see he's been remade, transformed."

She smiled, and observed, "Who could have predicted that?"

She reached out to take Merrick's hands. "Of course I stand with you, because you stand with us. But now what do we do, Raven?"

He made a small bow over their hands, turning it into a show of respect for her. He could hear from the crowd how well that was taken. "Now," he said as he stood back up, releasing her hands, "Now we meet with the Gwyliannan."

Murmurs circled around the room.

He continued, "We have arranged a time and place; The Maithe, at New Moon. It is neutral ground; Sousa says there is plenty of room and that it is an appropriate place for this sort of meeting."

Sousa spoke up, "Some of you remember the place, I'm sure. It's been a while, but it's still great." He got some titters around the room for that.

Sousa added, "The plan was to give us enough time to recover and recoup, to decide what you want from this meeting, and to think about possible next steps. Also, I gotta be honest, I need a couple of days where absolutely nothing dramatic is happening." Merrick choked back a laugh at that.

Fallon agreed, "I think this is a capital idea. Do any here have questions?" Silence around the room. "I know it may take some time to fully absorb all that we have discussed. Let us rejoin at Maithe House at the new moon. And of course, Merrick, Lucee, Sousa, you are all welcome to stay here as long as you like. That is an ongoing invitation."

Sousa grinned in response, and Lucee said, "That's so kind of you to make me feel welcome."

Fallon flashed a big smile at that response. "Well said, Lucee Fearney! You are like our Blackbird, constantly full of surprises. How refreshing."

Lucee looked confused. "If I might be bold – how am I surprising?"

Fallon laughed and explained, "We have found that most mortals are very bad at being a good guest. We care a great deal about politeness and hospitality, and despite the fact that mortals whisper in fear the things that have happened to other mortals when they flout our social rules, they continue to be so, so bad at them. So, when one who found herself amongst us unexpectedly can manage to navigate our rules so brilliantly, we take notice. Does that help?"

Lucee replied, "I – I guess so? I'm glad that I haven't managed to offend anyone yet."

That got laughs from around the room, and Lucee smiled with them, but Merrick could tell that she didn't really think it was all that funny. He leaned over to her and quietly said, "Let's talk later, okay?" She nodded, gratefully. Merrick was pretty sure she just needed to pour out everything that had been happening lately – so many changes, so fast, was a lot for anyone to handle.

The gathering finally started to disperse, and Merrick took advantage of that momentum and gathered up Sousa, Cullen, and Lucee and pulled them over to the big table, still piled with plenty of food and drink.

"I don't know about you all, but I am starving! All that talking and stress was enough to make me forget that I've eaten anything at all," Merrick said, and took one of the chairs at the end of the table by the back wall of the room and set up a small plate of food for himself. Aisling sat next to him on his right, somehow curled up in her chair in a way that would have been awkward if it was anyone else. Lucee and Cullen sat to his left, Sousa was next to Aisling but with his chair angled into the corner so that he could see the entire room.

Merrick asked Cullen, "Does this table ever not have food and drink on it? I don't think I've ever seen it not piled full."

Cullen looked amused. "You do know that there are a multitude of stories and ballads about this sort of thing, yes? An endless bounty is one of our trademarks!"

Merrick rolled his eyes at that. "Yes, but how? Are there members of your household who come and fill the table? Does it just appear?"

Cullen's amusement grew, but he answered straightforwardly. "Like Brownies? Well, yes and no. We each have our talents. And one of the talents we might have is to always have abundant food at a moment's notice. Domestic magic is considered humdrum by some of us, but it is quite useful, as you have seen, and no great House would want to be without those who can perform it. However, you'll rarely spy those who prefer the domestic arts – they tend to be quite shy and secretive."

Merrick said, "So... like a Brownie. I mean – I hope that isn't an insulting term! No offense meant!" He looked around, ruefully.

Cullen laughed outright, then. "Brownie is a mortal term. I suppose you could use Bwbach or Shellycoat. That's more acceptable." He leaned in and mock whispered to Merrick, "If you'd like to get on their good side, they love a good dark chocolate. Back in the day, the mortals used to leave cream, but once they discovered the deliciousness of chocolate, they really developed a taste for it. The darker and finer, the better. Don't give them aught besides food, though. You'll insult them."

Merrick thought about it a moment and replied, "I can't tell if you are teasing me or telling the truth. But either way, I am certainly enjoying their efforts!" He made a mental note: go get some fancy chocolate bars this week.

Aisling said, "So my question is: what will each of us do until our meeting with the Gwyliannan? Sousa, I know that at some point you will need to go home and prepare your house. But is that right away? And Lucee, what of you? Are you going to stay with us until the new moon?"

Sousa answered with what was basically a full-body shrug, which made her grin. "I was going to leave tonight, but between the length of our council and the idea of watching Merrick spar with Morgance this week, I just might have to stick around a bit longer."

Lucee and Cullen simultaneously said, "What?!" and Cullen added, "On whose advisement was that decision made? Or did you forget what grief she put you through last time?"

Merrick answered, "It was her idea, actually."

Sousa added, "It's pretty brilliant. She's not going to be soft on him, and she actually wants him to do well, so -"

Cullen broke in, "And why would she care if he does well?"

Sousa rolled his eyes and spoke to Cullen as if he was a small child. "Because how would it look for her reputation if he managed to best her, but went out and had his ass handed to him by someone else? It's an investment for her." He added, conspiratorially, "And I suspect she's grown to like our boy, but don't tell her I said that."

Cullen was flabbergasted. "Well, I certainly could never have predicted that."

Aisling nodded. "After seeing how she went at him in the beginning, not at all something I could have guessed."

Lucee questioned, "But is she to be trusted? If she went at Merrick before, I mean, what's not to say she wouldn't again?"

Cullen patted her hand. "No, I don't think that's anything to fear.

Basically, she'll get a chance to test him to her heart's content as his teacher, that is generally the sort of sport she loves. And he is now one of us, she's honor bound not to hurt him."

Lucee sighed in relief. "That makes me feel a little better, then."

Cullen asked Lucee, "What will you do? I know you probably want to go home for a while..." He trailed off but flashed her a brave smile. She leaned over and kissed his cheek, and Merrick swore he saw Cullen blush.

She replied, "I do need to get clothes and things. And talk to my boss at my job. I suspect I might have lost that, I got so carried away with all of this. Damn."

Cullen said, "Don't worry about that. We have ways to take care of things."

And Sousa added, "You can move into The Maithe if you want, you know. I have more room than you can imagine. And you'll be seeing that soon, so you have time to think about it."

Merrick thought to himself, "He doesn't want Lucee to move into this house. I wonder why." He made a note to ask Sousa about it later.

Sousa went on, "I can run you back home and out here again tomorrow, Lucee. If you want."

She smiled and told him, "That would be above and beyond, Souz." He responded by saluting her with his beer before he downed it.

They spent some more time eating, drinking, and then Merrick and Lucee found themselves sitting there listening to Sousa, Aisling, and Cullen trading stories of their adventures and misadventures from long ago.

Lucee leaned over and asked Merrick, in a low voice, "Is this what we should expect for the rest of our lives? History lessons from a first-person point of view that might have been heavily influenced by being under the influence?"

He chortled at that. "There definitely seems to be a theme of drinking extraordinary amounts of alcohol threading through these tales!"

He checked to make sure the trio weren't paying attention to them, and asked Lucee, "Are you okay staying here again? Is everything alright between you two?"

She made a face at him. "We have an understanding. We're taking things as slow as molasses, at his insistence, which I think is a first for him. I really need to get some one-on-one time with you soon though, Merrick! I miss talking all of this through with you. You're always my beacon of common sense."

He groaned, "Oh yesssss. Such common sense from me, the champion of a house of immortal supernatural beings who picked me because I crashed their party."

Lucee busted out laughing at that. "Well, you've always given good advice to me, anyway, even if you don't know how to follow it yourself!"

She yawned hugely, and Merrick interrupted the reminiscing of the others with a poke at Cullen. "Hey man, your girlfriend is falling asleep. I'm not saying that it's related to this line of conversation, but..." He trailed off and winked at Cullen.

"She's never going to actually be my girlfriend if I keep doing that, is she," Cullen said. "Lucee, do you need to get some rest? I'm ready if you are."

She nodded, then yawned again. "Let's go to sleep. We can reconvene in the morning. Maybe there will be waffles or something," she said, hopefully.

As they all started to troop upstairs, Cullen hung back and addressed the empty room. "Waffles would be so nice. I might need to go out to the grocery tomorrow and get some chocolate bars later, too." He made a quick bow, smiled, and turned to catch up to Lucee.

Music: Ships In The Night
Dark Places

There were waffles in the morning. Lucee couldn't figure out why Cullen was so pleased, but she was definitely thrilled. Not only were waffles her favorite – and these were huge, thick Belgian style waffles – but there were also all her favorite toppings. Bacon, and eggs, and a whole tray of muffins in various flavors completed the spread.

Cullen brought her a giant mug of coffee and said, "You should take one of those muffins with you when you run back home. That would make a grand snack."

She pulled on his sleeve and asked, "Wanna come back with us? As far as I know, we're just running there and back."

Cullen said, "I would love that! Do you think Sousa would let me stop at the upscale grocery on the way? I need to pick up something for the house."

Sousa did agree to stop, and Cullen bought all of the dark chocolate bars they had. Then they swung by Lucee's place, and Sousa waited in the van while Lucee dragged Cullen in by the hand to show him her room, and show him off a little to her roommates, who looked suitably awed by his good looks and demeanor.

When they got into her room and she closed the door, Cullen started to laugh. "Was that strictly necessary, or is it normal for the residents to show off their arm candy?"

Lucee shot him a sly smile. "Don't tell me you didn't love it, Foxy. Speaking of, is it wrong of me to take great delight in knowing what you really look like, and that they can't see things like the pointy ears?"

Cullen answered, "Wrong might not be the word I would use. Though it is tragic that they don't notice my magnificent ears." He winked at her, and she reached over and pinched one lightly.

Cullen busied himself by looking at all the posters, flyers, and photos she covered her walls with, as she dug through her clothes to find some suitable things. "Make sure you bring something rough and tumble, and something appropriate for a party," he said, then added, "I love this photo of you." It was a shot of her at a band practice; she was jumping in the air, playing her guitar, her green braids flying everywhere. There was a look of tremendous joy on her face.

She said, offhandedly, "Oh yeah, that's one of my favorites. You can have it if you want, though, I've got another copy of it." He smiled to himself as he carefully took it off the wall and tucked it into an inner pocket of his jacket.

They made one last stop, where Lucee learned that indeed, she had been fired from her job. She met this news with a shrug and a "See ya around, then!" Cullen just shook his head at that. "It was a pay-the-bills job, that's all," She said.

Last stop was The Maithe. Sousa pulled the van into the building's parking area, and said, "I'll be right back."

Cullen looked up at the huge building in awe. "I forgot how big Maithe House is," he muttered.

Lucee asked, "You've been here before?"

He explained, "Long ago, but I don't think I ever met Sousa face to face then. I was part of a group from House Mirabilis that would often come to events here. Sousa used to throw some amazing parties."

Lucee remarked, "I always thought that Sousa would be great at having parties and wondered why he didn't. So much makes sense now." Then Sousa jumped back into the driver's seat, threw a ratty looking duffel bag in the back, and they headed back to House Mirabilis.

When they arrived, Fallon met them and said, "If you go to the tower room, you will find Merrick and The Ladies starting his first lessons. Sousa, I know you wanted to observe, and I think it would be wise for all of you to be there. He will need you in the coming days." She turned to Lucee. "I think you might be surprised at the things you will see, so this is especially important for you. Be not afraid, Lucee. Our Blackbird is still your Merrick."

The tower room was still covered in all of the words that Merrick had written, the night he committed to the Eleriannan. The fainting couch he had lain upon in a haze that night was now in the corner, and instead there were four velvet chairs in a circle in the middle of the room. Merrick sat in one, and Ula and Morgandy flanked Morgance, who sat directly across from him. Aisling sat on a pillow on the floor next to the couch.

Morgance noticed the group standing in the doorway, and said, "Come in, or leave. If you come in, sit you down and do not move until we are finished, because this is potentially dangerous work."

Aisling waved them over, and said as they sat down, "You must stay quiet, do not distract him. I am glad you are here." She smiled at them brilliantly.

Morgance was speaking to Merrick. "The first thing you must learn is to protect yourself. I believe this will come easily to you, as you did admirably well against me previously, not even knowing what you faced."

Merrick nodded, not trusting himself to speak without showing nervousness in his voice. She cackled at his reaction and told him, "I can read you like a book, boy, you are fooling no one! But never fear, I would think you cocky if you were not nervous right now."

Merrick replied, "Well, that is definitely not reassuring at all." Aisling, out of eyesight of The Ladies, stifled a laugh.

Morgance pointed at Merrick's chest, where the small bag rested that held all of the gifts that they had given them, and said, "Show me what your bag holds."

Merrick took off the bag and set each item out on the floor in turn, after holding them in front of Morgance.

A small key.
A black feather.
A clear glass bead.
A small flower.
A berry.
A thorn.
An acorn.
A leaf.
A tiny, corked vial of what looked to be water.

Morgance nodded as she was shown each one. "That last one is from us. You will find it quite useful."

Merrick said, "What does it do?"

She laughed, tiny chiming bells. "It does nothing, boy. You are the magic. If you drink from it and imagine it bottomless, you will never thirst. If you put a drop down and envision a body of water, you can cast that illusion. It will not actually be a lake, but it will look and feel like one. You must believe in it with your whole heart, though, or the mirage will be broken."

Merrick looked suitably impressed. "So how do I learn that? Will you show me?"

Ula spoke then, "You must practice. Belief is something you must learn on your own. But what we will show you are all steps to help you find that skill."

Morgance pointed at the bead, which was about the size of the end of her small finger. "That is what we will start with. You should string that and wear it around your neck, long enough that you can see it. It is for focus, to keep a clear mind. You can call on it to envision a protective shield, as well."

She turned and pointed at Aisling. "You. Craft a string for this when we are finished here. Your connection will add power and an air of calmness."

Aisling nodded and asked, "Is there a preferred material?" Morgance waved a hand, dismissively.

"Now," she said, turning back to Merrick, "Take that bead, place it in your palm. Look at it, but let your mind feel loose, unfettered. Do not panic." She leaned forward and placed her small hand under his, cupping it. Everything suddenly shifted.

He could feel her presence in his mind, but not forcing or pressuring him, merely there. Her voice whispered in his mind, "see the form... feel the strength of the glass, how you can see through it but it is impenetrable. set your mind inside that bubble, know you are surrounded by calm that no one can touch... good, good."

He envisioned himself surrounded by the bubble of the glass, safe, untouchable. And when he felt Ula strike at him with her mind, he saw her attack roll off that bubble, ineffective and unconcerning to Merrick.

He hadn't noticed Morgance moving out of connection with his mind, but when she suddenly attacked him, he did not falter. He breathed slow, long breaths, and stayed centered in his bubble. He could feel her scrabbling, looking for any weakness she could exploit, then slammed into the glass wall several times, full force. The wall held, and so did his composure, somehow.

"GOOD!" he heard Morgance say, and he came back from inside his head. He exhaled deeply, and realized he was exhausted.

Morgandy said, "This work will take much out of you until you master it, mortal. What comes naturally to us is much harder on you."

Morgance advised, "You should rest, eat. We will come back to this tomorrow. Between now and then, you should practice this with the Dreamling. She has the skills to properly challenge you."

The Ladies stood as one and swept out, leaving Merrick sitting there a bit dazed by all that had happened.

Lucee piped up, "So... what just happened? It was hard to tell from here, and I can't even decide if the – The Ladies – were pleased, angry, hungry..." She trailed off as Cullen guffawed at that.

"Though it is always fair to assume they are angry, I believe they were quite pleased with Merrick's efforts today," he said, adding to Lucee, "I know they seem small and young, but they are ancient and very powerful. But I am sure Merrick explained how they introduced themselves to him."

She nodded and said, "They seemed terrifying in his story, less so in person. But I know enough to know that appearances mean nothing with you lot." She poked him and made a face.

Cullen winked at her. "Yes, it's true that I have to hide how handsome I am to the mortal world, for your own safety and sanity."

Lucee rolled her eyes at him and Aisling made retching noises. Sousa, unexpectedly, hooted with laughter. "Now THERE is the Cullen that I know!" Cullen responded with an exaggerated bow to Sousa.

Merrick grumped, "Just a reminder that I'm starving."

They ended up in the big room downstairs, flopped on some of the velvet chairs and couches, with small tables to hold their food and drink. Merrick had eaten a plate and a half of meats, cheeses, fruit, and bread, much to his friends' amazement. "I am ravenous!" he exclaimed, as he started on the second plateful.

Cullen managed to slip into the kitchen and place one of the chocolate bars on the counter, saying, "I brought you a treat. Breakfast was wonderful, Lucee loved the waffles."

When he joined Lucee on one of the couches, she asked, "Where did you go?" and he answered, "Just needed to take care of something, what did I miss?"

Lucee snorted and said, "Only Merrick inhaling food like it was air. That's it."

Merrick added, with a mouth full of food, "Is so good!"

Aisling said, "This sort of work burns up a lot of energy. You'll want to get a good deep sleep soon, too. But The Ladies were right, we should practice on this skill before you fall asleep. We don't have to work with the bead, we can just work on your visualization skills. No attacks." She smiled sweetly at Merrick.

He sighed with relief. "I'm glad for that. It wasn't that what I did today was hard, or at least it didn't feel difficult. I'm just so wasted now. You'd think I ran a marathon or something."

Someone laid in a fire in the fireplace, and the lights were down low. A few more of the residents of the house had drifted in; Lucee grabbed

Cullen's hand in alarm when she spied a being that looked like it was made of twigs and branches, swaying across the room in graceful half-circles. She whispered, "What iiiisss that?"

Cullen replied, softly, so only she could hear, "That is one of our own, what we call a Ffyn. Basically, 'sticks.' They are quite nice, good dancers – as you might guess from their movements – and mind talkers. They do not have speech in the way that you or I do. They are relatives of the ArDonnath, the mud and stick looking beings that were at your concert."

Lucee reminded him, "Ah, but I never got to see the stickmen, remember? I did not get the sight salve until after they left. Surely they aren't as pretty as the – Ffyn – is?"

She stumbled on the name, and he nodded at her, encouragingly. "No, the ArDonnath look sinister, where you can see that the Ffyn are lovely."

He paused, and added, "The Ffyn gave Merrick a rowan berry as a gift. Some of us can't even touch those. It was a potent present to give him."

Merrick perked up at that. "What does it do, Cullen?" he asked.

Cullen said, "It's protection from magic being used on you. It doesn't differentiate, so you have to be judicious about when to use it."

He paused for a moment, then continued, "You might find that instincts are your best guides with many of these gifts you carry. The Ladies will train you well, but they can only take you so far. Trust your feelings, and they will tell you what tool to use at the proper time."

Aisling laughed, "You know they would have your hide if they heard you, for presuming to school their student!"

Cullen shrugged. "Ah well, they have pronounced me vexing before, and I am sure they will again."

Lucee joked, "You are consistent, at least."

Merrick asked Cullen, "Do you remember who gave me each gift? I was definitely pretty out of it by that point. I remember that Edana gave me a thorn."

Lucee made a surprised noise, but Cullen defended it. "A thorn from the Hawthorn is a potent gift! It is strong protection and a weapon as well. She can be very annoying, but that was a solid prize to award you, Merrick."

He thought for a moment. "I think I cannot reliably say who gave each item. But it truly does not matter. The gifts are from us, that is the important part. Also, as Aisling said, The Ladies will eat me if I keep telling you everything." He winked at Aisling, who laughed.

She looked at Merrick and said, "I think my Raven is ready for his roost. What say you?"

He just nodded sleepily and gave a general wave at everyone.

"Goodnight, good day, whatever it is," he mumbled as Aisling guided him to the staircase.

She grinned at him. "I don't think I've ever seen you this tired, even when you ran away and weren't getting sleep at all!" They stumbled into Aisling's room, and he fell heavily on her bed.

"I really hope you're not going to say that we should practice more now, because I will probably just curl up and die."

Aisling snorted at that and answered back, "Right now? Not on your life. But I'll know when you're rested, and if you are amiable, I would like to work a bit on visualizing then. It will be easy, not draining like working with The Ladies, because you and I already have this connection. If you don't object to me coming into your mind like that, of course."

He frowned and asked, "But isn't that what you've done already, with the dream visits? Or is it different?"

Aisling snuggled into the bed next to him and explained, "It is not the same, though it might feel like it. The Dreamtime is... well, it is a thing apart. It is made up of bits of this world, and parts of the worlds we build in our minds and sometimes share. I can meet you in that mutual space, and when you wake up, I can remain or leave at will, because the greater space is communal. But in your mind, there might be the elements I saw in your connection to the Dreamtime, or nothing at all similar.

"It can vary wildly depending on the person, and how their mental mindscape is constructed. Some folks are completely non-visual in their mindscapes, and that makes navigating them difficult for creatures like me, or the other Eleriannan. There's nothing for us to connect with."

Merrick sighed, and said, "I wonder what my mindscape is like? Comparatively, I mean. To me, it is home and what I'm used to, so I really have no idea what it looks like. If that makes sense. I know when I think about things, I see them... is that what you mean by a visual mindscape?"

She said, excitedly, "Yes! That's also going to be helpful for you to understand in this work. Honestly, I knew you were visual – a non-visual thinker can do magic and glamour, but it is infinitely more difficult. They need to develop other ways to connect with their desired manifestations." She sighed then and leaned over to kiss him. "You need to sleep. We can continue this later, okay?"

Merrick nodded, and drifted off.

In Merrick's Dream

They were in a forest. No, a Forest – something that felt old, primordial… sentient. It was watching them, judging them. They – himself, Lucee, Cullen, Sousa, and someone he did not know – were standing in a clearing under the great trees. There was a rough path leading away from them, made of mossy stones that sunk into the ground in a way that said to him that they had been there forever.

Aisling appeared suddenly, from behind one of the enormous tree trunks. She looked surprised to see the woman they did not know, standing now next to Sousa, who had a look of great joy on his face.

He turned to Merrick and said, "This is my great secret, and I couldn't even get here to show it to you. Not until now!" He spun around like a small child, his face upturned to the sky.

Merrick realized that although he could see just fine, it was actually dark above them, with a sky full of stars – he could actually see the Milky Way!

He said to Sousa, "Where are we? How did we get here?"

Sousa said, "This is my home! You know where you are, Merrick. You just don't recognize it."

The woman beside Sousa turned to him and said, "Mine." The word reverberated throughout the Forest.

Lucee gasped and said, "I know who you are!"

Cullen stepped back, shocked – no, awed – and went to one knee. Aisling took a deep breath and grabbed Merrick's arm, and as he turned, he saw the woman glow with power, an aura of green and a purple so deep that it was almost invisible.

She pointed at Merrick and said, "You will be the bridge" and Merrick woke up with a gasp.

Aisling startled awake a moment after, and said, "What in tiny toadstools was that, Merrick? It all felt so familiar."

He shook his head, his eyes wide. "I have never had a dream like that."

He took a deep breath, and added, "My dreams got a serious upgrade when I started dating you, but this felt different. Or maybe not. It felt like the dreams I had about stickmen, in that it felt like a prophecy. But this? Was so much more intense. I don't know. And I have no clue who the woman was that was with Sousa. Totally random."

He looked around the room and realized that it was early morning already. "I must have been sleeping hard. I actually feel pretty refreshed, despite that weird-ass dream."

Aisling said, "Did you want to sleep more, or would you like to work with me a little bit? This early morning hour is a really great time to do these sorts of exercises, as there's so little distraction."

He made a snuffling sound and burrowed down into the covers a little more. "If I don't have to get up or open my eyes, I'm in."

She snickered and cuddled in with him. "Here we go," she murmured, and then Merrick sensed the softest touch across his consciousness, like a feather dragged across his mind.

"I am here," her voice said, softly, in his head. "Can you try to hold my image in your mind, how you see me? Don't expect it to be a mirror image, just let impressions of me run through your thoughts."

He thought of her, his Aisling, the scent of her, her soft cloud of hair, her small features and big eyes, the swirl of the skirts she was perpetually wearing, always velvets or silky material... and she seemed to form before his mind's eye, an even truer version than who laid in his arms.

"There I am." And his vision of her moved, speaking with the voice in his head.

He was amazed. "Did I do that, or did you?"

Aisling's double smiled. "You gave me a vehicle to carry my voice... It is easier for you at first to have that visual to work from."

She said, "Now, take us to the club where your band played... take us to that night."

As he remembered Club Marcada, it rose up around them – the dark room with the flashes of dancefloor lights, shadows of others dancing around them, the feel of the bass from the sound system pounding in his chest, even the smell of the fog machine. Aisling took his hand and spun around him, pulling him into dancing with her. They were once again moving across the floor to "Passion of Lovers" by Bauhaus, getting lost in each other as they traveled around the room.

And then suddenly, there were stickmen surrounding them, out of nowhere! Merrick gathered Aisling against him in a protective stance, and instinctively put out a hand and pushed with it. Stickmen flew back in every direction, and he heard Aisling say, "Ouch!"

He opened his eyes, lying there in the bed, and breathed, "Damn! That was intense!"

Aisling made a pained sound, and he realized she had a hand to her forehead.

"What happened?" Merrick asked, and she grimaced.

"You hit me hard! Which is great, but I did not expect that at all." She sat up, still holding her head a little, and touched Merrick's arm. "You are a natural, Merrick. You should be able to do that face to face too, as strong as that strike was."

He frowned. "In person... like not in my head?"

Aisling nodded, carefully, so that she didn't hurt her head more. "Not in your head. This is such a good sign! You didn't even think, you just let your instincts guide you. You are such a natural."

He looked skeptical but said, "If you say so. Hey, but I'm not tired like I was yesterday! I wonder why that is?"

Aisling answered, "It might be that I didn't actually attack you. I just threatened with the image of the ArDonnath. So, you lashed out but you didn't actually have to guard yourself against harm. Does that make sense?"

He snorted, amused. "As much as anything in this crazy house, Aisling. I'm learning to accept whatever and just roll on, you know?"

MUSIC: COCTEAU TWINS
But I'm Not

Aisling wanted to show Merrick the grounds around the House, before he had to meet The Ladies for what he was now privately calling "Magical Bootcamp."

He asked her why, and she told him, "It's actually a long tradition with those we bring into the House. We create a connection between you and the land, and our family, as you pace out the borders in your steps. I'd like Lucee to come as well, since she is certainly connected to the house, too, at this point."

In the end, the group consisted of Merrick and Aisling at the front, with Lucee and Cullen. Sheridan joined because he had, as he put it, "an interest in fulfilling his commitment to th'boy."

He was trading a flask back and forth with Sousa, who said he was along to see what would happen. And for some reason, Tully had also joined them, looking like a sunflower left in a late Autumn field with her blonde hair and a deep yellow dress that glowed against the dead grasses and trees.

It was one of those November days where you know snow is just around the corner; the chill in the air made Merrick glad that he'd grabbed his leather biker jacket. Aisling was actually wearing a cloak, which on her, looked exactly right. Merrick realized that they all looked a bit more festive than you might expect for a chilly stroll around the property.

Lucee was jumping up and down as they walked, bouncing in front of Cullen and making him laugh. "You are going to fall, and then who will be the one carrying you back?"

She joked, "Probably Sousa! Hey Souz, remember the time that slam dancing guy knocked me down at the Damned show and you had to carry me out to the van?"

Sousa hooted, remembering. "You were SO mad! You wanted to fight him but you sprained your ankle so bad you couldn't even stand up. Hoo boy, that was hilarious!"

Cullen was aghast. "A man knocked you down and didn't even help you? I am glad Sousa was there!"

Lucee bounced up to him and kissed him on the nose. "Such a gentleman, foxy fox. I was fine! Just mad – usually we help each other up if we get knocked down in the pit."

Cullen gave her a quizzical look. "The pit? You dance in a hole? Or do you mean like the orchestral pit?"

Sousa started laughing even harder, and Lucee said, "Actually, you could technically say it was happening in the orchestra section, funny enough. But it comes from the concept of a 'mosh' pit. Sometimes you feel like you're in a hole, especially if you get caught in the center. It's fun! Aggressive, but fun."

Cullen's eyes were wide at this point. "Does this happen at your shows? I do not think I would enjoy that."

Lucee started to answer, but she was cut off by the loud sounds of horses galloping up to them. "Oh!" she exclaimed. "They are beautiful!"

It was Fallon, with Edana, the feather-haired boy, and some other Eleriannan folks that Merrick didn't know. The horses were huge, and to Merrick's untrained eyes, they looked spirited to the point of being barely tame. The horses shone like silk in the late November sun, and their long manes and tails floated in the air like they had a life of their own.

Fallon called out, "Merrick! Aisling! Surely you would much rather ride out with us, on horse-back? You can see much better from here!"

Merrick suddenly had a sinking feeling in his guts. "Aisling," he said in a low voice, "remember the dream I told you about?"

She turned to him, "Were we not already on horses in that dream?"

He nodded, slowly. "Is there water nearby?"

She exhaled sharply, and answered, "Right before us. We are almost there."

Before he could call a warning to Fallon, the ArDonnath appeared out of nowhere. Fallon yelled out in alarm, and the feather-haired boy shrieked in fear. Merrick didn't stop to think, he just started running toward them, as fast as he could.

Somehow, he was there in an instant, and a tall ArDonnath was swinging a huge wooden club at him. He crossed his arms in front of his face, as much as to protect him as to ward off the blow, and as the club came down, there was a bright flash and both Merrick and the stickman were blown back off their feet.

He heard yelling from behind him, and he knew that Sousa and

Sheridan had caught up and were also fighting. There were flashes of light exploding all around him, and some of those bolts were coming from him! He looked away for a moment to try and find Aisling and Lucee and make sure they were safe, and spied them standing back-to-back with Cullen, trying to fight back two stickmen who were attacking.

Merrick yelled, "Over here you bastards!" and, amazingly, shot a fiery beam at one, who burst into flames and ran off screaming. The other charged Merrick, and he decided that he should get it, and the others, away from his friends as much as he could.

He started running away from the melee, shouting curses at the ArDonnath as he ran. He was so fast! The stickmen were also fast, and they were starting to gain on him, he couldn't run any faster – and then his foot hit a rock embedded in the ground, and he flew up and tumbled forward, rolled uncontrollably, and flew over the riverbank and into the water.

He could hear Aisling screaming his name, as if from a great distance, as he was pulled along by the current, bashing into submerged rocks and logs as he went. He heard a loud boom from behind him, and for a moment he was really afraid of what was happening to his friends, and then he was too busy just trying not to drown.

The water was running fast and was so cold! He went under for a moment, then popped back up, sputtering, trying in desperation to get a purchase on anything he was being swept past.

Finally, he got a purchase on something – no, it had him. He didn't know anymore. All he knew was that he was moving toward the shore, pulled by his jacket collar so that his head was above water. When they got close to the riverbank, Merrick used his hands to protect himself from the branches at the water's edge and found himself deposited on a small strip of muddy earth, his back propped against the rise of the riverbank. He started coughing, and in between the spasms, he realized he had been pulled out by a very red, very wet fox.

Another coughing fit took him over and doubled him up, and when his eyes reopened, it was no longer a fox sitting there, but a naked and wet Cullen.

"Holy shit!" Merrick exclaimed, and drew back in surprise. Then he started to laugh, because really? This was both no surprise and at the same time almost too much to deal with.

Cullen crouched in front of him, at first concerned – then he started shaking his head. "This is the thanks I get for saving your life, you laughing at me. And me, naked and freezing, too!"

Merrick tried to get himself together, but at that, he burst into another round of laughter, punctuated with big gulps for air. Cullen's worried look returned. "Do I need to slap you to bring you back to earth, my friend? You would think those big rocks in the river had done enough to you."

Merrick finally gathered himself somewhat and sputtered out, "You have to be naked to change shapes? I just didn't expect that. At all."

Cullen sighed. "Neither did Lucee, let me tell you."

That set Merrick off again, and Cullen rolled his eyes. "Yes, yes, vulpine man who saved your hide is hilariously nude. And you sit here, soaking and probably ready to catch your death of cold, having forgotten about your friends and the battle behind us."

That silenced Merrick immediately. "Oh no. Are they safe? I must be delirious, to not even have thought about their welfare!"

Cullen shook his head. "You had your sense knocked right out of you. You were magnificent until that fall, Merrick! You drew them off and Fallon was able to cast an orb of protection, while Sousa and Sheridan fought the ones that had not chased you. And I chased them, and saw you fall. I have never flung my clothes off so fast in my life. I thought I would lose you."

Merrick exhaled deeply. "I am lucky that you went after me."

Cullen inclined his head, humbly. "You are under our protection. More importantly, you are my friend. At least, I think we are becoming friends."

Merrick smiled, then said, "Well, my friend, we need to get back to our other friends. How far away do you think we are?"

Cullen decided that the best course of action was for him to change back to his fox form and walk with Merrick that way. "I'll be able to sniff anything dangerous before we see it, as well," he explained. "I hope that it is not too uncomfortable for you to be accompanied by me in this guise."

Merrick assured him, "No way! Anyway, if I'm ever going to learn that trick, maybe watching you will help?"

Cullen tilted his head and answered, "I'm honestly not sure if Fallon meant you would actually learn a Raven shape or fly in some other way. But as much as I hate changing guises in front of others, if it will help you -" and he stepped back and began his metamorphosis.

Merrick watched, frowning slightly, because it was just so... odd. It wasn't like a special effect change, which Merrick had sort of expected, like a werewolf. Nor was it instantaneous. It was more like there was a blurring where Cullen stood, as though Merrick's eyes themselves had become unable to focus.

He blinked, and for a weird moment he could see both Cullen and fox, and then another blink and the fox remained. "Damn," Merrick breathed. "That was uncanny."

Fox Cullen sat down and looked up at him, and Merrick said, "Oh, you can't talk. Of course. Duh, right?"

The fox that was Cullen tilted his head and made a small whuffing noise.

"Yes, I know. I'm brilliant. Shall we go? I'm sure you're just waiting on me."

It took Merrick a couple of tries to get up the bank of the river. As the sun sank low, he was really starting to get cold, and he could feel every bruise and scrape. His boots were squelching with every step as he limped through the underbrush and then into a field. They started trudging back, Cullen loping out in front then ranging back to Merrick to encourage him, then bolting ahead again.

At one point Merrick said, "I'm sorry I can't move as fast as I did earlier, this must be maddening for you." Cullen made a little yip and brushed past Merrick's leg as he circled him, and Merrick knew Cullen was trying to reassure him.

There was a fence to climb – thankfully, wooden and not wire or worse, electrified – and then some woods. Merrick was stumbling by this point, and Cullen nosed him toward a pile of stones under the trees.

"If I sit, I might not get back up, Cullen," Merrick objected, but sat anyway, on the ground with his back against the smooth stone surfaces. "I'm just so tired, I'm sorry. Maybe I should rest for a minute? Would that be okay?"

He felt his eyes closing, and no matter what he tried, he couldn't keep them open. Cullen sat there for a moment, swiveling his ears around and sniffing, trying to sense any potential dangers. He wasn't sure what to do – if he left Merrick, that would leave his friend vulnerable. But he knew the House must be worried beyond belief at this point, too.

The potential to choose disappeared when he heard the slightest crunch of leaves, and he went into a protective panic. He positioned himself between Merrick's sleeping body and the woods in front of the stones and felt the fur on his neck and back rise as he prepared to defend his friend.

He was growling, a quietly deep, visceral sound – and then he heard something familiar – a tinkle of bells, then the sudden scent of a horse and people. The horse came into view and carefully riding it were Edana and the boy with the feather hair.

Cullen felt relief wash through him as the boy jumped from the horse's back and ran to them. "Is he hurt?" he asked in his soft voice. Cullen shook his head, and the boy tried to gently wake up Merrick.

Edana called out, "Cullen? Are you hale?"

Cullen let out a small bark, then shook his head, frustrated. He took a moment and moved back into his regular form. "I am unhurt, though cold in this guise. How did you find us?"

Edana laughed and said, "And well you should be cold, in that state! The boy sensed you; he has been casting about for the Blackbird for hours. Quillan feels quite a connection to our Raven."

They worked together to help Merrick get up on the horse, Quillan insisting that Merrick use his hands to step up, Edana and Cullen on either side so that he wouldn't just fall back off.

Edana said, "It is just my luck that I get to ride behind a cold, wet mortal."

Cullen didn't hear the spiteful edge that he usually associated with her voice, and thought to himself, "Even she can't resist our Raven's charms for long. There's something endearing about him."

He said aloud, "Will you be able to handle him and the horse as well? He's a bit of a sack of potatoes right now." Merrick made a sound like he wanted to object, but it was half-hearted at best.

Edana waved dismissively. "This is hardly the most challenging task I've faced. However, I'll be slow going, so let me send you ahead to alert the House of our imminent arrival?"

Cullen did not like that idea much, and after much insistence on his part, they decided to send Quillan ahead. "He will be much quicker than I, anyway," Cullen said. "Our pace will be more suited to my level of exhaustion."

Quillan took off, a flock of small birds that could barely be seen against the darkness. Cullen reverted to fox form and they began to pick their way through the trees and back to House Mirabilis.

When they arrived, Quillan was waiting with Fallon, Aisling, and Sheridan. Aisling was holding Cullen's clothes, which she brought around to the other side of the horse and left for Cullen to change into in private.

"Finally," he said as he changed, "Someone who respects my personal space!" He expected some sort of relieved laughter, and got silence so deafening that he stepped around to where his friends were, even though he only had his pants on at that point, and said, "What's happened?"

Then, as a sense of dread started to rise, "Wait. Where's Lucee?"

Aisling said, quietly, "Cullen... don't panic..." and Cullen didn't even wait to hear the rest, he took off as fast as he could run, no matter that he was shirtless with no shoes.

He burst in the back door, through the kitchen, and found everyone in the main room in a loose circle around Sousa and Lucee. Souz looked like he was going to cry. He was hovering over Lucee, who was unconscious, carefully laid out on one of the velvety couches.

As Cullen burst in, the whole room turned to look at him, and his heart sank to his knees. He stopped and blurted out, "Tell me."

Sousa looked up, and gestured to Cullen to come close, and said in little, broken sentences, "One of the ones who had been chasing Merrick. It turned back. It charged at me and Sheridan. Our backs were turned, fighting others. She came at it, yelling. Screaming, like that would stop it."

Cullen gasped, a sharp intake of breath. "Oak and Ash! My brave, foolhardy girl."

Sousa nodded sadly. "She leapt on it, like a madwoman. Beat it in the head. It finally threw her off, and she struck the ground hard. We think she hit her head. She's been out since. I carried her back myself."

Cullen sank to the floor next to the couch and took her hand in his. He turned to ask Sousa a question, but was interrupted by Sheridan, Edana, and Aisling helping Merrick in.

Sousa said, "Oh man. Is he okay? Hell, are YOU?"

Cullen nodded, distracted. "He's beat up but he'll be fine. I'm fine. How long has she been like this?"

Sousa answered, "A couple of hours. I wanted to take her to the Hospital but I was vetoed."

Merrick limped up, propped up between Sheridan and Aisling, and murmured, "Oh no." He turned to Fallon and said, "Can't you do something to heal her? Isn't that something you all do? Or can I, somehow? Surely I have some way to help her."

Fallon put her hand on his shoulder and said, "None here are healers, but having her in our midst will help. And Cullen being close to her will help more." She turned Merrick to face her. "You need to rest, too. Take a shower, then come lie on the other couch and we will stay close. All will be well, Blackbird."

Aisling took Merrick off to get him into the shower, and he was grateful for her help, because at this point, he was so stiff and sore that he could barely move on his own. He stood in the shower for a very long time, while Aisling waited for him patiently. She had offered to help, but he insisted that he just needed a few minutes where he could collect his thoughts on his own. When finished, he put on an incredibly soft pair of black pants and a black tee that she had laid out for him, and she shadowed him as he slowly went down the stairs.

There was no change in Lucee, but Cullen had managed to pull one of the chairs and an ottoman up so that it was parallel to the couch she was on, and he stretched out on that, a hand on her arm. He was staring into space, a forlorn expression on his face.

Merrick sank down on the other couch and said, "No change?"

Cullen shook his head, ever so slightly, and sighed. "Maybe she'll feel better with you here, too."

Aisling said, softly, "You know there is a thing you can do, Cullen. You know how to reach her."

Cullen's jaw set, and his forehead wrinkled in frustration. "I don't want to do that unless it is absolutely necessary, Aisling. You know why."

Merrick snapped, "Well I don't! What could you do that you are not, and why?"

Cullen turned his gaze to meet Merrick's, and said in a cold, flat tone, "I will forgive you that, because I know you are grief stricken and afraid. But do not speak to me again as if I would not do anything possible to help Lucee. Because I would. This is just... delicate."

He closed his eyes, took a deep breath, and spoke in a more pleasant tone, "I can touch her mind, go in and sense if she is able to find consciousness, or if there is more injury there. I cannot heal any injuries, I do not have that skill. However, there is an ethical issue to just going into her head like that. She can't give me permission, and she probably cannot push me out either. That breaks our moral code."

Aisling said in low, reassuring tones, "She gave you permission previously. I do not believe she would be angry if you did this now."

He replied, "You could do it. Easier than I, at that."

She shook her head. "You know quite well that I do not have the leeway that you do."

Merrick broke in, "Really? You are arguing ethics while our friend lies here unconscious? Cullen, she would want you to do this. Or if it makes you feel better, let it be on my head. I will take the blame. Just bring her back!"

Cullen looked down at Lucee, then at Aisling, who nodded and said, "I'll be here if something goes wrong. I can find you. Go on."

Merrick said, "Wait, something could go wrong?" He realized that Cullen had already closed his eyes and slipped away, and Aisling was zoned out, he assumed following Cullen's progress. Merrick felt like he was going to throw up. "What did I do?" he thought. "Did I push them to do the wrong thing?"

Music: Kristen Hersh
w. Michael Stipe
Your Ghost

Cullen found himself in a dark place, and for a moment, he was very afraid. "Where is she?" he thought. He felt the light tug that was the thread of connection Aisling was keeping on him, and he was grateful for that. It was easy to get lost in the thoughts of another when they were not in their usual state of mind. He thought he could hear something, like music coming from down a long hallway, and he pushed toward that – he could see light coming from around what looked to be a doorway, and he pushed through and found himself at the threshold of a small bedroom.

He looked around and noted the holiday lights along the ceiling, the band posters, the black curtains and bedding, and black clothes all over the floor, and decided that this surely had been Lucee's bedroom as a teenager. Where was she, though? He decided to sit on the bed, and he began talking to her, wherever she was.

"Lucee? Where are you? I know it feels safe here, but we need you to come back to us. Please?" He heard his voice crack a little. "We need you."

A small pause. "I need you."

He heard a soft noise, and then realized it was crying. He stood up and tried to pinpoint where it was coming from, and finally opened the closet door, and found Lucee curled on the floor, weeping. He sank to the floor and whispered, "I found you. I found you, and I'm not letting you go." He reached over and managed to scoop her into his arms, where she cried into his shoulder for a while, as he stroked her hair.

She finally snuffled a bit and said in a teary voice, "I am afraid to go back, Cullen. I hurt so much, and it was so scary. I act brave but inside, I'm just a terrified little girl. And when Merrick went down and you went after, I was so angry, but it wasn't enough! I couldn't take down the stickman that went after Sousa and Sheridan. It won. And here I am now."

He shushed her, gently.

"You know we're all scared when those things happen, right? You weren't the only one. I went after Merrick but I was frightened, I was just more driven to try and rescue him than I was afraid. I acted, I didn't think. You are braver than you know. And if you'll follow me out of here, I promise to show you every day how amazing you are. But you need to come with me, come back to us. Will you do that?"

She sat there a moment, her head still buried in his shoulder, then she nodded quickly, like she needed to do so before she changed her mind. He helped her up and said, "Hold my hand, and we'll figure out how to get back out of here. Aisling will help, too. She's keeping track of me."

They left the room and trudged through the darkness. Lucee held his hand tightly, and whispered, "Is it supposed to be this dark?"

Cullen said, hesitantly, "This is odd. But I've never gone into the head of someone who was knocked unconscious, so maybe it isn't odd at all. Look over there – is there a light?"

There was a tiny spark of a sparkle, and they headed that way – and were gratified to see it grow in size as they neared it. Lucee said, suddenly, "You should go ahead, let me wake up without you in my head. I don't know why, I just feel it very strongly."

Cullen asked, "Are you sure? Do we know if it's the right place? I feel nothing, honestly. I can stay here –"

She cut him off. "No, go ahead. I will be there in a moment, I swear."

Cullen opened his eyes, and the first thing he saw was Aisling's concerned face above his. "I tried to follow but you just seemed to vanish! Did you find Lucee?"

He said, "She's not waking yet?"

He ran through what had happened, and Aisling said, "That seems weird. But inside the head can be a pretty weird place. Hey – I think she's stirring now!"

Lucee moved steadily towards the twinkling light before her, until she stood before it and saw that it wasn't exactly a light at all, but a glittering portal. On the other side, it was light and she could see misty shapes that looked like familiar things.

She started to step through, and a voice – low pitched, soft, and full of concern – said to her, "You know if you go through that, you'll be changed.

Nothing is ever going to be the same. You will not be the same. Is that what you truly want?"

She hissed in frustration. "Voice, you are about a month too late for that nonsense, you know? Everything changed when Merrick went to that party, and anyway, nothing ever stays the same! I'm awfully tired of my head trying to keep me safe by locking me away."

The voice countered, "You were not changed until today. If you go back, you will find yourself a new, unknown version of Lucee Fearney. If you don't believe me, ask your book. It knows what happened. But of course, you can't do that until you are awake. What a conundrum."

At this point, Lucee was fiercely angry. "You know what? I know who you are. That's my Da's voice in my ear, and you know what else? He never gave me a reasonable piece of advice in my life. Thanks for the warning and now I'm getting back to my regularly scheduled life." And with that, she dove through the portal.

Lucee gasped and sat up abruptly, then said, "Owwwwww," and put her head in her hands. "I feel like I tried to fight a tractor and not only did it win, it backed over me and fought me again."

Cullen covered his mouth with a hand and made a muffled noise that could have been a laugh or a sob, it was hard to tell. Aisling sunk to the ground in relief. Merrick grumbled, "Oh DAMMIT, Lucee,"and nearly fell out of his chair trying to get over to her to gather her up carefully in a hug.

Lucee said to him, "No squishing please! Jeez, you'd think I was at the brink of death or something."

Sousa fussed, "You've been out for hours, you dingdong. We were worried sick! I can't believe you attacked like that; you saved my hide. Don't ever do that again, do you hear me?" Sousa's voice cracked at the end, and Lucee looked at him, stunned. Sousa, upset over her? She didn't know how to process that.

"I love you guys," she said quietly. Cullen kissed her hand, gently, and Merrick patted her shoulder and gave her a crooked grin.

Cullen didn't want to leave Lucee's side, but she insisted that he get a shower and some fresh clothes.

"You need a moment to get back to yourself," Aisling agreed with Lucee, "And we will all be here to keep her company until you return."

When he hit the shower, he realized how wise her words were; everything hit him at once, and he ended up sitting on the tub floor while the water beat down on him for quite some time. Getting out and into fresh clothes, he felt every sore spot on his body, and his stomach was rumbling, too. "I am a real mess," he thought, disgustedly.

Coming back to the great room, he found the lights lowered, with a fire roaring in the fireplace, and some small tables loaded up with food and drink. Merrick and Aisling had curled up together on one couch, Sousa was in the chair that Cullen had been in earlier. And Lucee was on the couch, waiting for his return.

She moved so that he could sit at one end, and he slid in so that his back was against the arm, with his legs stretched out. Lucee smiled and cuddled against him.

"It's a grand thing that these couches are so generously made," Cullen joked, and reached over to grab something to eat from the table. It was all his favorite things – he knew who was probably to thank for that. "This is delicious," he sighed happily.

They spent some time just relaxing, catching each other up on the things that had happened to each other on that day while they were separated, and eventually everyone began to nod off.

That is, except Lucee, who had something very important she needed to do, and had waited for this moment to be able to try.

She made sure Cullen was dozing – he was adorable with his mussy post shower hair, she decided, but of course, when wasn't he? Once she was sure everyone was out, she took out her book necklace and held it for a moment, contemplating what she was about to do. When the voice in her head told her to ask the book, surely this is what it meant? This was the only book she had.

She opened it and self-consciously addressed it. "I don't know if I'm doing this right, but here goes. What changed in me tonight? My Da's stupid voice in my head told me to ask you. I hope that's okay."

She shook her head, feeling incredibly stupid, but to her surprise, words began to appear on the page.

You are more like them now than like you were. As the Blackbird, but not.

"Wow," she breathed, "it did work." But she didn't understand any more than she did before. "Please, Book, I don't know what you mean. What happened? I am not as clever as some of these folks, please keep that in mind."

You might ask The Lady. It was she that worked a change upon you.

And it was Cullen who responded with, "What?!" Lucee turned and saw that he had been awake and had read the responses from her book and was none too pleased. "Lucee, what is this all about? What does it mean – a change?" He looked at her, tilting his head, assessing. "Something is different about you. I don't know why I didn't notice it before, but I knew something was off when I went into your mind. What is going on?"

She sighed and explained to him about the voice in her head and what it had said to her. "And it was my Da's voice, Cullen; trying to advise me, but that man has never done anything but belittle me and try to make me be things I am not. So, it told me to ask the book, and I wanted to do that on my own, and not worry anyone else until I knew what was going on. But now I'm more confused than ever. The Lady? What does that mean?"

Cullen looked angry. "That is Fallon. Your book is never going to use direct names, it is one of our objects. And now it seems that she has given you other gifts, ones that were unknown to you. And I am guessing, to anyone else but herself."

He took a second, collecting himself, before he went on. "This voice said you were changed."

She said, "It said if I went back to consciousness through that portal, I would be a new and unknown Lucee Fearney, which is weirdly specific. Well, let me clarify – it never actually said 'don't go back through that portal' specifically, but this whole conversation didn't start until I was ready to pass through it. And it sure never offered an alternative way to wake up – I mean, was I supposed to just stay unconscious forever? It was all suspect and odd."

Cullen took the hand that wasn't holding her book and squeezed it gently. "Look, whatever it is – it is done. And you don't seem like a new and unknown Lucee to me. I think at this point I might notice if you were wildly different, right?" He winked at her and was gratified to see a small smile in return. "So now we wait until Fallon is awake, and we ask her what she did, and what moldy moondream told her that it would be okay for her to do it."

Lucee said, "You're trying to make me laugh."

Cullen nodded solemnly. "Always. It is one of my most potent tools."

She did snort then, amused, and said, "So... we wait? The Book told me to ask her, so I guess that's the right move. Ugh. I hate waiting."

And at that, it was Cullen's turn to snort. "I am fairly sure that every single being that knows you is aware of that, m'lady."

She laughed, but then her face grew serious, and she closed her book and put her other hand on his. She said, "Look me in the eyes and tell me that you are okay, would you? I mean – you are okay? You would tell me if you weren't?"

He pressed his lips together and looked away for a second, then met her gaze. "I have been better. I have not been this beaten up in a very long time. I was afraid for my friend's fate at the hands of the ArDonnath, and then I was afraid we would both drown. I spend a remarkable amount of time either in my fox guise or naked and freezing – " Lucee tittered at that, then slapped a hand over her mouth. He continued, "The last bit, walking next to Edana's horse, was excruciating. And then I thought I lost my love."

Lucee sat there for a moment, a nervous look on her face. "Um… I don't know how to respond to that."

Cullen nodded, a gesture that seemed more for himself than for her. "I also find myself at a loss for words. I just know this: somehow it seems that I am falling in love, which is a thing the old me would have regarded as ridiculous. And confessing it to someone, even more so. But here I am, doing both."

He paused for a moment and looked away, and when he looked back, she thought that he might not have looked that vulnerable before in his life. He said, so softly that she had to strain to hear him, "You need not feel the same, or feel an obligation to say those words. I am telling you this because it is true, and I need to say it, not because I need to hear it in return. It will not change how I feel. And I am sorry if I have made you uncomfortable."

He breathed out, a sound of relief. It occurred to Lucee that telling her this must have been releasing such a weight from him. She still had not said a word – her head was spinning with emotion and she didn't trust herself to say anything at all.

Cullen smiled at her, a soft, caring smile. He said, "We should try and get a little more sleep. We have some things to get to the bottom of tomorrow." He leaned forward and kissed her gently, then reclined back and encouraged her to snuggle back in with him. She did, lying her head against his chest, and putting her arm around his torso with a deep sigh.

Lucee heard his breathing slow, and before she, too, fell asleep, she whispered, "I think I love you too."

She couldn't see that Cullen was smiling.

When Merrick woke, the early morning light was coloring the room with warm tones, and he could hear soft voices in the other part of the room, where the big table was. He laid there on the couch for a while, enjoying the feel relaxing, snuggled into blankets. Aisling was somewhere else, he suspected either in the kitchen or one of the voices at the table – so he stretched out fully, wincing as he found all the sore places from yesterday's adventure.

He turned on his side and looked around to see who else was asleep. Sousa was starfished in the overstuffed chair and on the ottoman, lightly snoring, which made Merrick snicker to himself. He was surprised to see Sheridan sprawled, face down on a blanket on the floor in front of the fireplace. He looked like he was recovering from some all-night rager, which also made Merrick laugh.

Across from Merrick on the other couch, Lucee was on her side facing the room, with Cullen spooned up around her. He had to admit, they were adorable. He wondered how they were both feeling, and if they felt as rough as he was.

Just then, Lucee opened her eyes, saw Merrick, and grinned and winked at him. She tried to slide away from Cullen carefully, so she wouldn't wake him when she sat up, but she stopped with a wince. "Ow!" she whispered to Merrick. "That is NOT how I wanted to wake up!"

Cullen made some grumbling sounds and said, "Wind and water! Whose idea was it to rise now, with the sun barely in the sky? Ughhhhh."

He groaned as he tried to pull the blanket over his head. "Everything hurts. This is not what I was told to expect from immortality."

Merrick commiserated, "I am not really enjoying the after-effects of yesterday, either. You can go back to sleep! I just smelled food and I seem to be starving."

Lucee added, "I smell waffles. I'm gonna get fat if I keep eating here. Gloriously, wonderfully fat."

She stiffened up, then, because she saw Fallon walking towards them, holding a big tray of breakfast foods. Cullen felt it and turned to her, putting a hand gently on her arm. "Steady, love," he said quietly. "Keep a cool head."

Merrick didn't see her reaction, and greeted Fallon warmly. "Greetings, good morning! I don't suppose there's coffee on that tray?" He gave her an earnest, begging look.

Fallon laughed and set down the tray on the small table, and said, "What sort of host would I be if I did not offer coffee?" She turned to Lucee and Cullen and said, "And I heard that Lucee likes waffles, so I made sure to bring some with all the good things to put on them. Lucee, I hope you are feeling better this morning?"

Lucee took a deep breath, and before Cullen could stop her, she blurted out, "What did you do to change me?"

Fallon stood there a moment, blinking. Her face was perfectly blank.

"Where is that question coming from?" she asked, stiffly.

Lucee said, "From me. I asked the Book what happened and it said I needed to ask you. That you changed me, that I am not now as I was. And you know…" She stopped for a moment, gathered herself. "I understand that things happened fast, and I am sure whatever you did, it was out of concern for me. But you didn't tell me after the fact. Or anyone else, I am guessing?"

Fallon looked away, then looked back. "I am the leader here. I made a decision without asking the leave of any, and I take responsibility for that on my own. But I could not have you die under my care, and you earned that accord at any rate for your valor on the battlefield."

Lucee felt Cullen's quick intake of breath. "You gave her the gift."

"What does that mean? Would it kill y'all to just speak plainly for once?" Lucee snapped.

Cullen turned to her and explained, "It is like what we did for Merrick, though yours would have been given in the heat of the moment, and without the ritual that we gave Merrick, so the effects are more sedate, and will take much more time to develop. But it means that she thought you might die, she wouldn't have done that otherwise."

Lucee looked at Fallon with her mouth agape. Fallon nodded solemnly. "I should have told you. You are correct. But in the madness of everything happening yesterday, I just – well, I wanted to wait, break it in gently. But your subconscious must have had other ideas. Tell me what happened?" She pulled up another ottoman and sat with them.

Lucee explained the whole sequence, and Fallon nodded. "You have a part of you, deep inside, that is resisting. It has chosen a voice that has made you feel small before, to bully you into keeping yourself small. But Lucee, you are as bright and compelling as Merrick! You deserve as much attention from us as he, you are brave and loyal and strong. I wish I could have had the leisure to ask you properly to accept these gifts."

Lucee asked, cautiously, "So I am bound to you? For seven years? More?"

Fallon smiled gently and answered, "No. There was no ceremony, no oath. I gave this to you freely, without bond. You will have life as long as you desire it, or unless you are caught in a mishap. You have strength from me, as that is what I imparted with the potion. And you will develop your own strengths. If you left us now, these gifts would not fade. So, you are both like and unlike Merrick."

Merrick's eyes were wide, and so were Cullen's. Sousa, who had quietly woken up and started listening at some point, said, "Whoa."

Lucee blinked a couple of times, trying to take it all in. "So... when Merrick leaves, this all wears off? But if I decided to bail now and never see you again, I would be fine?"

Fallon replied, "That is what he agreed to."

Lucee's face turned stony; she was not pleased at all. "Fix it." She pointed to Merrick and said, "He's supposed to be the special one, not me. Either take it away from me or bring him up to speed. I'm just the frickin' sidekick, this is all wrong!"

Merrick looked aghast, and Cullen's hand was over his mouth in shock. Sousa, on the other hand, cheered, "Hell YES, Lucee. You go, you badass!"

Fallon leveled her head to give Sousa a disapproving look, and then said to Lucee, "Do you reject my gift, then?"

Merrick held his breath. He knew she needed to reply carefully – she didn't want to insult Fallon, that was a one-way ticket to ruin – but she was so mad! Lucee looked like she was considering what to say next, and Merrick was sitting on the edge of his seat, anxious, as she paused and mulled over her answer.

"Fallon, I have no desire to reject such a kind, generous gift. I just feel that the balance of things has been shifted with your largesse. Merrick pledged himself! He should be the one receiving such gifts before me. And –" Her voice broke here a little. "And I honestly can't imagine eternity stretching out before me without him being there, too. He's more than just my friend. He's my family, the one person who has always been there for me. You talk about my loyalty, but having a friend like him makes it easy to be loyal, you know? I would be betraying him to not speak up at this moment."

She took a moment to breathe, then continued softly, "I'm sorry, I never wanted to disparage your kindness to me. But I can't get something better than Merrick got. If it wasn't for him, I wouldn't even be here now."

Fallon took a deep breath, then exhaled audibly. She looked around the room at each of Lucee's friends, seeing how much each of them loved her in their own ways. Then she spoke, her rich voice carrying throughout the room. "Lucee, even if I wanted to take it back, I could not. I gifted you from my own essence, something I have never done before. In a way, that makes me like a mother to you; and like a daughter, I find you endearing and vexing in turn. I could not bear to see you die on my watch, so I made the decisions that a ruler makes, the ones of life, and death, and transference of power. Do you understand? I know that Cullen does, I can see it in his face."

Lucee turned to look at Cullen, who was quite pale, then turned back to Fallon. "You... gave me some of your life? And... some power?"

Fallon inclined her head. "Yes, that is a very simple explanation. The deeper one is that you and I are now connected. When I finally pass on, to the Misty Realms or into oblivion, you will inherit my power. As things change, we change with them. So, it is now."

She turned to Merrick then. "Lucee spoke from her heart, and you had nothing to do with this request." It was a statement, not a question, and he nodded agreement. "She is the best companion you could ask for, Blackbird. And I believe she is correct: we must balance the scales. You two? You are our hope for survival. I have, as they say these days, gone all in on you."

Music: David Sylvian
Orpheus

Lucee said, confused, "But... I'm mortal. Not – I'm not Eleriannan, not Fae in the slightest. How do I do what you do?" Fallon laughed, delighted. "You make good decisions. That's really all I do. You lead. And here's something you seem to have missed – you are, for all intents and purposes, now Eleriannan as well. You belong to us, and we to you. Just as we swore with Merrick. But now we must correct the imbalance you so perceptively caught."

Cullen raised a hand and said, "Obviously, I am still and will be at his side, and will give whatever is needed."

Lucee whirled around to look at Cullen, who smiled sheepishly at her. She mouthed "you rock" at him, and his smile spread across his face.

Sheridan, still on the floor with his blanket over his head, yelled, "Of course I will, now will y'let me sleep?"

Fallon pressed her lips together, suppressing a laugh. "We need two others to lend themselves to this task, and then we may proceed. What say you, Aisling?" She turned, facing Aisling, who had been quietly standing behind her for some time. "Heard you all of this?" Fallon asked her, and Aisling nodded slowly.

"Heard enough to agree and wonder what took us so long, honestly. Lucee, you see clearer than any of us do."

Lucee made a face. "I just have an overbearing sense of fairness," she demurred. "But who is the last person you need?"

Fallon laughed and said, "Why, Merrick must agree, of course! He has been uncommonly quiet through all of this – dear Raven, are you willing?"

Merrick cleared his throat a little, suddenly nervous. Why did this feel more momentous than his original pledge? He said, in a soft voice, "To be honest, I have never thought about a day that I wouldn't be with all of you, once I got over my fear of the pledge I made.

"I know we agreed on seven years, but I've built so much with you – love, friendship, community. A feeling of family – even if I don't understand all of you yet, I am connected to you all and would defend each of you with my life if need be. I guess I showed that yesterday. I didn't even think about it, I just acted, because that's what you do to protect those who mean the most to you."

He paused, twisted his hands together, looked off into the distance for a second. "I won't lie: I take this decision seriously. It's no small thing. But I couldn't walk away now. You, all of you... you hold everything precious to me. I could never go back to who I was, and I don't want to either.

"So yes. I agree."

He looked to Sousa, the only one there who he expected might object. Souz shrugged and said, "You'd better not break up the band, man. I will be mightily pissed if that happens." He pointed at Lucee and added, "You either, Fearney."

She rolled her eyes at him and popped back, "Sure, because you'll never find another guitarist who can roll with your goofy ass."

Merrick fell back against the back of the couch laughing, and Sousa snorted. Sheridan, still on the floor but now sitting up, grumbled, "I guess I'm awake, then."

Fallon declared that the ceremony would be that evening, and that Merrick and Lucee should take it easy during the day, because they would need their strength for that night. And then she said to Sousa, "You know you must leave, yes? Just for tonight?"

Sousa agreed, "Of course. I need to take some time to spiff up The Maithe anyway."

Lucee said, "Wait, what? You won't be here?"

Souz said, "You'll be fine, girlie. I can't stay, I'm not part of this House. Each house has their own mysteries, and they don't share. It's fine, I'll see you soon." He gave her a hug and clouted Merrick on the arm, then headed back to the city.

Lucee tried to lift the strange mood that lingered by joking. "Guess I'd better eat some of these cold-ass waffles, then... HEY!" She had taken a plate and found them to still be as hot as freshly-made, and it shocked her. "How on earth are these still perfect?" She took a bite and mumbled through it, "And they're delicious, too!"

Cullen looked at her, with her mouth full of waffle, and busted out laughing. "You have already forgotten that we're magical beings, I see! I'm actually surprised you didn't notice before, with a table always piled with food and drink that is always the perfect temperature."

Lucee shook her head, as she continued to shovel bites of the waffle in her mouth. "Nope! But I like this kind of enchantment, yummmm." Merrick and Aisling both cracked up as well, and they dove into the food like they'd all just realized how hungry they were.

After breakfast, Merrick stepped outside to get some fresh air, and Aisling followed, and sat on the steps from the back porch, looking out at the sky. "I do think we might get snow today," she said, sniffing the air.

A sharp, crackling voice behind them said, "Unseasonably early snow, at that. But when did the Dreamling become a weathervane?"

Aisling didn't even turn her head as she answered, she was too busy staring out at the sky. "Well met this morning, Ladies. It is rare to see you out here in the daytime, what brings you?"

The Ladies said, in unison, "The Blackbird does."

Aisling tore her gaze away from the sky for that, turning to look at Merrick, who looked less surprised than she would have thought. "Greetings, Morgance, Morgandy, Ula. I was expecting to see you. Have you heard of tonight's plans already?"

Morgance waved a hand, dismissively. "Merely a formality. You have been ours since the moment you stepped foot in this House. No, we are here to finish your training. We believe you will need those last skills sooner than we expected."

Merrick's face reflected some confusion. "Do you think that's something I should do before tonight's ceremony? And after yesterday's challenges?"

All three of the diminutive ladies threw their heads back and laughed at that. Morgance answered, "Indeed, that is the best time for us to pursue your training! Do you think your challenges will only come when you are well rested and ready?"

Merrick said, "Fair enough. What do you have for me today?"

Ula turned toward the open door and whistled, a sweet yet piercing sound. Out came Quillan, looking down at the ground humbly. Morgandy said, with a challenging look in her eye, "Do you think you can do better than this boy at flying, Raven?"

Merrick addressed Quillan, softly, "You helped me when I was hurt. I remember your kindness."

Quillan raised his head and met Merrick's gaze. He said, in a quiet but clear voice, "It is my honor to help you, Blackbird. I would show you how to take to the skies, if you will allow me."

The Ladies directed Merrick and Quillan to the yard, and they stood a bit away from Aisling's perch on the stairs. Morgance commanded, "Boy, show the Blackbird how you change. And you, Raven, you watch the process and tell us what you feel as you see it happen. Use your heart, not your eyes, do you understand?"

Merrick nodded, thinking about it. "I believe so."

Quillan said, so quietly that Aisling could hardly hear his voice, "Watch my eyes, not my wings. That will give you the clues." And then he just melted into a small, blue bird form right before Merrick. He hovered there for a moment, as if he was showing Merrick the entirety of his avian form, then he expanded back into a human shape again.

Merrick exhaled loudly, and said, "Well, that's a thing, isn't it."

Quillan smiled shyly and said, "Did you see the way? Shall I do it again?"

Morgance said, "Let him try his hand first. Merrick, if you feel uncomfortable, just imagine yourself at the moment you feel most at ease with your human self. That is your doorway back to your own body."

Quillan whispered, "Think of lightness, of moving through the sky."

Merrick bobbed his head, acknowledging the tip. He closed his eyes, imagining what birds felt as they flew, their light-boned bodies, the sound of their wings – all the things he saw in Quillan as he changed. He let his mind wander to how it would feel for him to grow wings, spread them wide, open his beak and caw..."

His concentration was shattered by the loudest CAW he'd ever heard, and he fell to the ground on his rear so hard that he went "OOF!" and Aisling gasped. "What – what just happened?" Merrick stuttered, feeling completely confused.

Quillan was clapping his hands and jumping up and down, and even The Ladies had something like a smile on their faces. Aisling exclaimed, "Merrick, you were truly a raven for a moment! How did it feel?"

He looked from side to side, brought his hands up to look at them for a moment, then said with a shaky voice, "I want to do it again."

They were out there for long enough that Cullen and Lucee came to find them, only to see a large black bird and a small blue one soaring back and forth across the yard, swooping over the heads of Aisling and The Ladies. Lucee, awed, said, "Wow! Wait – is that Merrick?"

Cullen whooped loudly and yelled, "The Blackbird flies!"

Lucee clapped her hands, excitedly. "I couldn't even have dreamed up something this amazing," she said to Cullen. "My friend flies in the sky as a bird, who gets to say things like that? My boyfriend turns into a fox! What even is this life?" She laughed, throwing her head back, reveling in the moment.

Aisling saw the couple and waved them over, pointing up at Merrick and Quillan as they swooped and performed aerial acrobatics. "Look at those two fools! They are having a blast. They've been at this for a while now."

Morgance turned to them and said, "He is a natural, I must admit. We have had to do little to assist him. He is quick and clever, as a Raven should be."

She paused and then addressed Lucee. "We know what Fallon did. We would have questioned her choice if given the option, but we must concede that none of this House could take her place successfully, and you have a certain... charm about you."

Lucee said, uncertainly, "I am not sure how to take that."

Ula spoke up and said, "We will be at your side tonight for the ceremony. That is unheard of and will be remarked on."

Morgandy added, "We expect it will lend legitimacy to your status, which you well may need when the rest of the House finds out Fallon's intentions. They will not speak against you if we are by your side."

Lucee was taken aback, and unsure how to answer. Cullen, sensing this, spoke up. "Ladies, your wisdom is remarkable. Lucee, they are working to ensure that no one objects to Fallon's choice as you for her heir. This is a high honor, as The Ladies are not known to take sides, especially not where mortals are involved. Though we know, you are not truly a mortal anymore. The rest of the House will find themselves having to agree to this path."

Lucee said, "I don't know what to say. I... I appreciate and welcome your offer, Ladies." She felt like she needed to add something, so she dropped a curtsey awkwardly. The Ladies seemed pleased with that, and Cullen took her hand and squeezed it lightly.

She smiled at everyone self-consciously, realizing suddenly that she really had gotten in over her head and that she had no idea what she was doing. She was grateful that Cullen was with her to help her through, and she squeezed his hand back, as a flush of affection for him washed over her. "How do I even rate all this?" she wondered.

She decided the best way to break her awkwardness was to divert attention back to Merrick, so she yelled up at him, "Get down here, birdbrain! Aren't you finished showing off by now?"

Aisling broke up at that. "You two are so funny together," she said, giggling.

Lucee grinned and replied, "Years of refining our comedy act. We bring out the goofy in each other."

Merrick-the-Raven swooped down to land in front of them, and morphed into his usual shape, something that fascinated Lucee to watch. "That is so weird!" she exclaimed. "I don't know how to process that. Like – I saw it happen in front of my eyes, but if you asked me to describe it, I don't think I could." She turned to Cullen. "Like when you become a fox, though your process is different. Which is also weird. Why are they not the same? Is it because you are different animals?"

Cullen shook his head, laughing at her childlike interest. "We are actually not animals at all, exactly. We are ourselves, in different form. We still think the same." He tilted his head and asked her, "Did you notice a key difference?"

She thought for a second and said, "He kept his clothes!" Then, to herself, "Thank goodness. I don't think I'm ready for naked Merrick." That set Aisling off again. Lucee was confused by this revelation. "I don't get it. How come you have to be naked? I mean... I don't mind you being naked, but it must be super annoying..." She trailed off as both Merrick and Aisling started laughing, Cullen looked immensely pleased with himself, and even Quillan was trying to hide a smirk.

The only ones not laughing were The Ladies, of course. Morgance said in a matter-of-fact voice, "One is shapeshifting into another inherent part of a being. The other is shapeshifting through cunning and skill. Cullen cannot change his clothes because he IS the fox. Merrick is the Raven's shape only in those moments that he takes it on, despite our title for him."

Lucee considered that. "Of course, I know nothing, so forgive me if I'm talking ridiculous things... but it seems so arbitrary."

Morgance sniffed, "If there is one thing you will learn about us, it is that capriciousness and inconsistency are the rule, rather than the exception. Magic and glamour are very fluid and there is no one way to get to any goal. You'll see."

Cullen added, "I do wish I could shape like Merrick does. But my shape came built in, you might say. I can change with no thought or preparation. Merrick, on the other hand? He is not necessarily limited to the Raven's guise. In time, he might master many guises, even those of other mortals." To his surprise, both Merrick and Lucee stared at him, mouths agape.

"What, you never considered that?" he asked.

Merrick stumbled over his words as he blurted out, "Wh-why would I? I was surprised to learn that I could take a bird's shape, and now you suggest that's just the beginning? I am definitely blown away by that idea!" Lucee just nodded emphatically.

Cullen said, "You would need a talisman that represents that form, at least at first. Like your Raven feather. It is something to explore in the future, my friend. You have quite the ease in shapeshifting."

The Ladies agreed with nods and an affirmative from Morgandy, "You slipped into the Raven's guise with hardly an effort."

And Ula added, "As of now, you have excelled as a student."

Morgance sighed, "Do not let it go to your head, however. These powers will need to be practiced and expanded every chance you have. Even natural abilities' needs must be honed, Blackbird."

Merrick agreed, "I hear that and agree with you. I will honor your efforts to teach me."

The Ladies looked pleased at that. "We will take your leave until the ceremony tonight. Remember, Lucee – we will stand with you." They swept off, impressive despite their small size.

Lucee shook her head, unbelieving. "They are something else. It's hard to believe that Morgance attacked you so when you first met, Merrick."

He snorted and said, "It's a thing I won't soon forget!" He turned to small Quillan, who had patiently been standing there the whole time. "I owe you much for all your help. And I know, I'm not supposed to be talking about obligations. But you... I won't forget."

Quillan looked at the ground, but he had a pleased smile on his face. Merrick continued, "I have to ask, though, and obviously don't answer if you don't wish to – but in the tower, when I went through the ceremony... well, there were many blue birds. Yet only one turned into you. Are there more here like you, or was I just out of my mind?"

Quillan dragged a toe across the ground, nervous or embarrassed, it was hard to tell. "Only one is the real me. The others are a sort of protection glamour, a projection from me. If I am prey, it is much more difficult to capture the correct small bird that way. If I am scared or excited, it may happen without my control. Only in my bird form, though. I might be able to teach you; I am unsure but would gladly try."

Merrick smiled and thumped his shoulder lightly. "That would be a treat to attempt with you."

Quillan looked up and Merrick and smiled the brilliant smile of one who was praised by his hero. He turned to Lucee then, and she was a little surprised to see that he was pretty big on her, too. "I did not give you my name," he said, shyly. "I am Quillan. I serve Fallon and would be pleased to do the same for you and the Blackbird."

Lucee covered her mouth with her hand, trying to conceal how touched she was. "I am Lucee Fearney," she said solemnly, "and I would be honored to have you by my side whenever you choose." Quillan looked up at her with pure adoration in his eyes, and Cullen and Merrick exchanged a look and a smirk.

Quillan excused himself to go take care of the horses, explaining that it was his favorite chore. As soon as he left, Cullen teased Merrick and Lucee, "Look, you have your first groupie. Or lackey, I suppose. Henchman?"

Lucee shoved him gently and said, "More than you've got, Foxy. Or are you jealous?"

Aisling bit her lip and made a face, and Merrick snorted. "We are a regular bunch of goofballs, we are."

As they headed back in, he asked Cullen, "Hey, here's a question. So Quillan's bird guise is like your foxy one? But he kept his clothes! How does that work?"

Cullen shrugged and said, "Mysteries upon mysteries, Merrick. My guess is that it is shapeshifting like what you are learning, but he inherited the connection to the bird guise. Our magic is, as Lucee pointed out, quite arbitrary in its rules. Or better yet, we might say that there are no rules, only suggestions and practices for best usage. Much of what we do is based on the power of our minds and the strength of our suggestions."

Lucee piped up, "If you believe it, you can be it?"

Aisling answered, "Ye-e-ssss. Somewhat. Belief and the ability to tap into the energies around us that most mortals ignore or deny. Some are born with the ability, but all can learn it – however, most don't. A flexible mind is the key, and a certain innocence helps greatly as well."

Lucee chortled and said, "Well, that explains Merrick, then."

Merrick made a shocked face, but Aisling said, "Absolutely. It's a really pure sort of quality that the two of you share. He also has a natural talent for it; I am not sure about you yet, but I have my suspicions."

"Really?" Cullen and Lucee said at the same time.

Aisling tittered, "That is adorable. Cullen, you haven't thought she might have a talent for it? Or is it that you are too close, too dazzled by her brilliance?" She winked at Cullen, but he didn't respond how she expected. He looked thoughtful.

"I think you might be right." He sat at the big table and poured himself a glass of water from a pitcher into a crystal goblet. "Both that Lucee may well have a talent and that I was – am – dazzled. And as that is a state which I am quite unused to being in, it would affect my judgement accordingly." He took the glass, raised it in a toast to Lucee, and drank from it. She tilted her head and smiled at him, but she seemed puzzled by his reaction.

He finished the glass and said, "I'll be back shortly," and kissed her on the forehead as he left and headed upstairs. She looked at Aisling and Merrick, confused, and said, "I guess I shouldn't follow then? Also – what was that?"

Aisling shrugged and said, "I speculate that Cullen is perhaps feeling out of sorts. You have caused a number or remarkable changes in him, all for the better. But he isn't used to the person he is becoming and might not be sure where he belongs in the scheme of things as that person. It might be a topic to explore when things are less frantic."

Lucee laughed, a little bitterly. "Is that ever the case here?"

A bit later, Merrick went up to get "spiffed up," as he called it, and Lucee said, "I guess I had better pull out the nice clothes Cullen told me to bring. It's a good thing he did. I hope he's done with needing alone time."

Aisling said, "Actually, I have something for you, if you like it. Tully and I put it together. Want to see?"

Lucee was pulled into Tully's room, which was on the first floor, and seemed to be made entirely of closets and flowers, from what Lucee could tell. Tully squealed with excitement and said, "I can't wait to see how this looks on you!"

She produced a dress that, on the surface, reminded Lucee a lot of her deconstructed prom gown that she'd worn to Club Marcada. But this was all cotton and tulle mixed together in a riot of layers, with tiny sequins and small gold bells dotting it throughout the broad sweep of the skirt. It was a mossy green, mixed with a silvery grey and touches of deep brown, and it looked like they had pulled it from the forest floor. Tully shoved Lucee behind a dressing screen and demanded she try it on, so Lucee slipped out of her current clothes and threw the dress over her head.

"Does it suit?" Aisling asked, so Lucee came around to the other side, a little unsure, because she never wore colors like this.

"Lucee, look in the mirror," Tully urged, so Lucee obliged, and gasped with delight at the image of herself there. The dress seemed to have a life of its own, with layers floating up around her here and there. It went beautifully with her green braids and her warm brown skin and made her feel like she had never been more attractive in her life.

"Ohhhhh. Oh my," she whispered.

Aisling nodded appreciatively, and Tully said, "That is exactly the reaction everyone will have. Aisling, I do believe we outdid ourselves!"

Lucee twirled around and then, spontaneously gave each of them a hug. Aisling felt as light as a bird, but Tully was solid and earthy, and squealed with delight at getting a hug. "Now go and show off!" she urged Lucee.

Music: Second Still

I t was time to gather in the tower chamber. Lucee and Merrick were both nervous; Merrick, because he had ideas about what to expect, while Lucee's nerves were all about not knowing at all what was to come. They found themselves standing in the middle of the room holding sweaty hands, and Merrick said quietly to Lucee, "This should be interesting. But I'm right here. I promise." She gave him a sick sort of smile and squeezed his hand.

There was a soft sound of music, then the Eleriannan started to file into the room. At the head of the line was Fallon, resplendent in a red-orange and brown gown trimmed with gold that shimmered as she glided across the floor. She had painted her dark skin with swirls and symbols that neither Merrick nor Lucee recognized. Quillan trailed behind, playing a primitive looking flute.

Fallon stopped before them, facing the pair, as the rest of the Eleriannan took their places.

The last ones to enter were those who were standing with Merrick and Lucee for the ceremony. Aisling, wearing a dress that looked like a stormy cloud – which utterly suited her – came to stand at Merrick's right. Merrick dropped Lucee's hand and moved aside so that Cullen could come stand between him and her.

Lucee felt a flutter in her chest when she looked at Cullen, who had totally outdone himself in his garb for the evening. He was in a suit of all black – the pants were woollen and the jacket had to be silk velvet, she was sure. His shirt was some silky material she didn't recognize, and it shifted from a deep red to brown and back again as he moved. His hair, loosely pulled back into a ponytail, seemed even more golden than usual. He turned to look at her and gave her a courtly sort of nod, though she could see a smile playing at the edges of his mouth.

Behind them stood Sheridan, looking wilder than ever. On his head was a circlet crown of oak leaves and acorns, and he had some sort of animal skin thrown around his shoulders, over a tunic that would have looked at home at a medieval re-enactment.

Lastly, The Ladies came to stand at Lucee's left, and they looked much as usual, though their green and black dresses were velvets instead of a lesser material, and they each wore black veils over their faces. Fallon, seeing them stand by Lucee, raised an eyebrow and murmured, "Unexpected."

The door to the chamber shut, and the lighting in the room changed, became darker and more expectant, like house lights in a theatre before they went dark and the play began. Fallon began to address the room.

"Brothers, Sisters, Others: Eleriannan. I stand before you today with two you know, mortals who have become our own. Merrick Moore, our Raven, has come to have his bond deepened with us, from one cycle to a bond that will never be broken. He has done well by us, and we by him, and we claim him as ours.

Lucee Fearney, his faithful friend and friend of the Eleriannan as well, has recently joined our number. It was I who gave her the essence needed, as she was sorely hurt and I feared she would not survive. More importantly, I see a more noble and celebrated path for her future; she is to be my chosen."

There were whispers of shock, excitement, interest among the Eleriannan. Obviously not many had known Fallon's plan, and they were taken by surprise. Fallon raised her arms and a hush fell over the people.

"*Absit invidia*. This is not up for debate; truly, it is done in all but name. She received the essence I would have saved to give my successor hence she is now the one to succeed me. And she is a good choice, this will keep our ranks balanced and unbiased, and more in touch with the mortal world that we have a need to properly rejoin, so that we once again may be *amicus humani generis*. Lucee and Merrick will be the ones to guide us into a way to survive and thrive again. Understand?"

She cast her gaze around the room, and there were no objections. Lucee realized that her heart was pounding. She had been sure someone would have complained. Next to her, Merrick let a breath out with an audible sound.

Fallon stepped to Merrick first. She spoke clearly, in a tone that rang out in the room, "You have done well, our Blackbird! Let us bring you forevermore into our circle now; I expect that these before me are to stand for you once again? Though truly, you have proven yourself to need none to vouch for you."

Merrick felt prouder of that statement than just about anything he'd ever accomplished, and he was admittedly bemused by this. The one great success in his life was something he hadn't planned on and couldn't tell anyone about. Ironic.

Fallon addressed his friends flanking him. "Aisling. Cullen. Sheridan. You continue to stand with Merrick." It was more a statement than question, but they each nodded.

Aisling added, "There is no place else I would rather be."

Fallon smiled at that. "You are well matched," she said. "Now, Dreamling, our vial. This time we will seal the deal properly, for all time." She took the decanter from Aisling, and said to Merrick, "No fear, this will not be like the first time you tasted this. The greater work had already happened."

She poured the liquid into the glass that served as a lid for the vessel and handed it to Merrick. Despite remembering what happened the last time, he held it up in a toast to the room, then downed it in one gulp, as before.

This time the effects were much less startling – he felt a warmth creep through him, and he felt elated. Honestly, it felt like taking a shot of extremely high proof alcohol, though it didn't have that taste. He felt his face flush, and for a moment his head spun – but then everything settled and just left the sort of "overly bright world" feeling that he associated with the hallucinogens he'd tried once or twice. He caught Lucee intently watching his reaction, and he shot her a brilliant smile and gave her a thumbs-up. She gave him a nervous grin in return, then schooled her face, because it was her turn.

"Lucee Fearney. You have already received elixir from me that brings you into our circle, but only as connected through me. I wish for you to connect with all of our House, as Merrick has, so it is important for you to drink from this vial as well."

She addressed The Ladies then, "I did not expect your involvement here, Sisters. I do not believe you have ever stepped up in this capacity – what moves you now?"

Morgance tilted her chin upwards, haughtily, and answered, "We have never known a candidate we found acceptable until now. Also, as you have said, Lucee is our future, and we cannot allow just any of us to stand for her. She will need extra guidance."

Fallon agreed, "You speak truth, of course. Your stance pleases me." She started to speak to Lucee, but Cullen spoke up first.

"I would also stand with Lucee. If she, and you, will permit it."

Fallon's face only changed subtly, but Lucee saw Cullen's crestfallen expression in reaction and her heart sank for him. "Cullen, we remarked in surprise when you volunteered for this responsibility with our Raven. But I fear you outpace your current ability and resources, my friend. I do not recommend this."

Cullen replied, chastened, "I will be at her side anyway. Officially or no."

Fallon nodded once, acknowledging Cullen's stubbornness as well as his devotion, and said, "Duly noted."

She turned to Lucee and said, "I laid this obligation at your feet, unasked for and without bargain. In return, you called for a balancing of the scales by admitting The Blackbird fully and forever to our ranks, which we have fulfilled. Do you agree that we have upheld our end?"

Lucee nodded and answered, "I do." Fallon continued, "And do you accept the mantle of inheritance?"

Again, Lucee answered, "I do." She then added, "I am accepting with full respect of what you are offering, and with awe at the prospect and honor." Fallon looked quite pleased with that response, and from the sounds she heard from the others in the room, they did as well.

Fallon offered her the drink from the decanter, as she had to Merrick. Following his lead, she toasted the room, and slammed it down in one draught.

Unlike Merrick, she felt downright odd from the drink. Everything narrowed to tunnel vision for a moment, and she staggered a bit, lost her balance, and Cullen reached over to steady her.

"Oh, this is weeeeiiiird," she intoned.

Fallon laughed lightly, saying, "It will settle momentarily. You missed the jarring effects of the first dose, being unconscious when it was administered. You can ask Merrick how that went for him – I believe you have got the best of it."

Merrick nodded solemnly. "That was the most intense time I ever had. Worth it, but wow." That made the whole room break out in titters and giggles. He smiled and said, "Oh yes, laugh at it now – I definitely do!"

Lucee looked at Merrick and Cullen, trying to focus on them and get her bearings, but they seemed to keep morphing back and forth in her vision – from themselves to their animal guises and back again, never fully, just enough to make her question what she was seeing.

Cullen said, "Focus on what you know. Look at your hands, see if that helps you."

She looked down, spreading her hands out in front of her, and she concentrated on her long fingers and smooth, oval nails that she always kept super short, thanks to her guitar playing. He was right, it did help.

Morgance said to her, so quietly that only those standing by her could hear, "None of us have changed. Only you have. So, if you see your hands as normal, know that when you look up, your mind has nothing to rebel against that it has not already seen. That is the key."

Lucee's gaze shot up, and she met Morgance's green eyes. "That is brilliant advice. Nothing here has changed but me."

She turned to Cullen, and his features clicked into focus for her. If she tried, the fox guise seemed overlayed on his regular handsome features, but now she knew the trick to make her mind obey. "Yours was, too. I am glad you are all by my side." He gave her such a brilliant smile back that she felt a flush of emotion rush over her.

She turned to Fallon and said, "What else must I do?"

She threw her head back and laughed, "Is this not enough? You are one with us, Lucee Fearney! Well met!"

The Eleriannan cheered, and Quillan started playing his flute again, and suddenly there were creatures of all types dancing around in the chamber. She was grabbed and spun around with one of the twig people – a Ffyn – and a sense of being so welcomed, so wanted washed over her that she could have cried.

Something deep inside told her "This is the Ffyn telling you this" and she blurted out, "I am so happy to be here!" and the feeling around her deepened until she laughed and cried at the same time, she was so overwhelmed.

She was rescued by Tully, who hugged her tight, and a man who looked like he was covered in bark and moss bowed to her, and then so many more that she thought she couldn't take much more... and then there was Sheridan, who gave her a huge grin and said, "Aye, I think it's time we got you out of here and down to more comfortable surrounds, right away!"

He grabbed her hand and practically pulled her out of the chamber, down the hall, and to the stairs.

"Y'looked like you were gettin' overwhelmed, so thought it might be kind to rescue you," he explained, releasing her hand then patting her shoulder. "Yer foxy boy is most likely waitin' for you down the stairs. I'll be down soon," he added and headed back to the chamber. She could hear Merrick's voice echoing down the hall, then he and Aisling were there with her.

"Let's get away or they'll pull you two right back in," Aisling said, and Merrick and Lucee were happy to heed that warning.

Downstairs, Merrick turned to Lucee and asked, "Are you okay? I know how overwhelming all of that felt to me, and it's not my first time at that rodeo."

Lucee snorted at that. "So many jokes I could make there. So, so many jokes."

He rolled his eyes and said, "So you're fine. Okay then."

She laughed and said, "It takes more than that to phase m-"

She was stopped dead as she turned the corner and caught sight of the main room. Someone, somehow, had transformed it while they were upstairs in the chamber room. The chairs and sofas were pushed back to the edges of the room in small clusters, and there were little tables here and there with the chairs, most of which had candles on them. The entire ceiling was sprinkled with twinkling white lights that were so small that they reminded Lucee of stars strewn across the sky.

There was a fire going in the fireplace, and the room smelled of oakmoss and woodsy resins. Music was playing, and it was obvious that the room was set up like a small club so that people could dance or chat in small groups. It was perfect and lovely, and Lucee and Merrick both looked pleased about the transformation.

Standing next to the fireplace, roughing up the logs with a poker, was Cullen. He turned and saw the trio standing at the edge of the room and smiled, his face turning from brooding to brilliant in that instant.

Merrick heard Lucee make a small sound, and said to her, "You really like him, don't you."

She turned to him, grinned, and said, "Next I'll tell you that they've initiated me into some sort of strange cult, and that I've fallen in love with this guy."

Merrick's eyes grew wide, then he busted out laughing. "I don't think you can call yourself my sidekick anymore, you know," he gasped, while Aisling looked at them both like they were crazy, and Cullen, still on the other side of the room, held up his hands like he was asking, "What?"

Lucee shot back at Merrick, "I'll always be your sidekick, duh," then ran off to throw her arms around Cullen, who looked delighted and picked her up and swung her around.

"Our future leader is looking quite fetching this evening," he declared, giving her a kiss.

"Does this make you my shapeshifting consort?" she asked, giggling.

Aisling nudged Merrick and said quietly enough for him to hear, "It eventually just might, actually. I guarantee he never expected such an elevation of status."

Merrick confided, "I'm having trouble dealing with all of this. We're just these two goofballs with a totally unknown garage band, you know?"

Aisling slipped her hand around his arm and moved close to him. "You have upgraded, love. You are now two quite important goofballs who rub elbows with the Fair Folk, quite a change."

Music started playing over the invisible sound system, the keyboard opening of "A Day" by Clan of Xymox, which made Lucee comment, "The Eleriannan have wonderfully unexpected taste in music."

Cullen replied, "We enjoy many different styles, but most of House Mirabilis is quite fond of things with a more melancholy, darker edge to it. You will find that each House tends to favor certain styles and eras. I am not sure why that is, it just is."

"I wonder what music Tiennan House enjoys now," Aisling mulled.

Merrick noted Cullen's expression change in reaction to what Aisling had said, and he said, "Perhaps I will ask them when we next meet. But for now, let's enjoy the tunes we have tonight!" He swept Aisling into the middle of the open floor and started dancing.

Lucee laughed, and said to Cullen, "No matter what club we're in, Merrick's always one of the first on the floor, dancing. He loves it! Our friend Dominion calls him 'the DJs best friend.' She gets excited whenever he comes out to her gigs, because if he dances, other people always follow."

Cullen asked, "Should we stick with tradition and do as our Blackbird, then?" and he offered her his hand with a flourish, which she took with a grin as he led her out.

Merrick heard laughing as the rest of the Eleriannan came down, then found their esteemed mortal friends happily dancing in the middle of the room. The volume of the music ticked up considerably, the open floor filled with dancers, and the party was underway.

He looked over later and saw Lucee swaying about to some Cocteau Twins song with a group of the twig people, a look of delight on her face. Cullen was in a plush chair, surrounded by The Ladies, deep in an animated discussion about something or another. At the table, Sheridan and Fallon sat with a variety of Fair Folk surrounding them, all drinking and eating.

Edana was by the fire, with the woman Merrick privately referred to as Hedgehog Lady – he really needed to learn her name – and a few other Eleriannan that he didn't know. They were laughing, and Edana was making some gestures as she talked that made Merrick wonder if she was talking about his attempts to fly.

She glanced over at him and caught him watching, and visibly colored – but he laughed and shouted across the room to her, "I bet I looked ridiculous!"

She looked relieved and laughed along with him, and a wave of affection for her washed over him – even as annoying as she could be. He walked up to her and said, "In a way, you're the reason I am here today." He bowed to her, smiling.

"Ah, a throwback to the first night we met! You are correct, Blackbird, our interaction was just the beginning. Has your time with us brought you what you expected?"

Merrick answered, amused, "I could never have dreamed all of the wonders the Eleriannan have shown me! My only expectation is to never know what will be next."

Edana looked pleased with his answer. "I believe I am getting soft, but you are growing on me, Merrick."

He looked at her and cocked his head. "Did you actually just use my name? You really must be getting fonder of me!"

She made a face, and said, "Do not read too much into that, your crowing does you ill." But Merrick saw her heart wasn't really in it, and he threw her a wink. "Gah, you are learning all of Cullen's bad habits!" she said, throwing up her hands.

The party went on until the late hours, until the room only had a few small groups of people left. Merrick had walked to the kitchen to get some water and happened to look out the back door's window. He called to Aisling, and she came over with Cullen and Lucee.

Merrick pointed out the window and observed, "Look at the snow coming down! I haven't seen it snow like this in ages, much less this early in the season. I am glad we are in here. Though I hope it clears up before we need to go back to the city. Sousa is a good driver but I don't know if even he could get the van back here in this mess."

Cullen sniffed and said, "You vastly underestimate his skill, let me tell you. He is unlike many of us in this house, in that he not only is not repelled by iron, he can manage modern machinery well. We can be near iron and even touch and handle it, but some of us still dislike it, and few of us enjoy or know how to operate things like cars. Though we do love our stereo system, I much admit."

Merrick looked surprised, and Lucee asked, "So some of you do drive, though? And do you think in Sousa's case it is because he decided to stay in the city and near cars, and modern buildings, and things like that?"

Cullen nodded. "I remember the first time I stepped on a locomotive. I thought I was going to die during the entire trip. But when I came back the same way, it was less distressing. Repeated exposure does help. And a willing disposition, I believe. Some of us are certainly more adaptable than others."

Lucee looked at the three of them, and said, "This is all very interesting, but THERE IS SNOW!" And she pushed past a laughing Merrick to open the door and run across the porch and down the stairs, so that she could fling herself into a snowdrift. "AH THAT IS COLD!" she yelped, then cracked up laughing.

Cullen stepped out onto the porch and said, "Clever girl, I would never have guessed!" He was silenced by the snowball Lucee pelted him with.

This started a four-person snowball war in the yard, until Merrick looked at Lucee and said, "Your lips are blue! Cullen, we need to get her inside, she's going to get frostbite!" He turned to Aisling and said, "Surely you are cold, too?"

"I am having too much fun to be cold!" She kissed him, and he could see snowflakes in her hair and melting on her nose in the eerie light that snowy nights always seemed to have, despite there being no moon's reflection thanks to cloud cover. She swept some snow from his hair and said, "I think you might be a bit blue, as well. Let us all go warm up!"

They came in to find hot chocolate waiting for them on the counter, and Lucee couldn't contain her delight. "This is perfect!" she cheered. "I don't know how they always know just the right thing, but they do."

Merrick said, "They? What did you call them, Cullen, the Shellycoats? Tell me they do it without coercion?"

Cullen sighed and smiled sadly. "I promise we force none to perform any tasks. Though at one time, that would not have been a promise I could have kept. Long ago, it was common to keep beings like them in thrall, doing all we did not wish to waste our time with. When we came to this land, those old bonds were broken, but they found it difficult to assimilate into homes here.

"Many came to the Great Houses, looking for shelter in exchange for what they have always done. We ask nothing of them, in fact we seldom communicate at all, which is how they like it for the most part. In return, they use their talents to help this House run better. A symbiosis, you might say. Coming to these lands was a huge challenge to many of our kind, though some adapted more easily than others."

Lucee said, "It must have been very strange, coming here from Europe. Though not all of you are from there, are you? You don't all look the same. Or is that very different than it is with humans?"

Aisling answered her question by pointing at herself and saying, "Well, I am an oddity, but I am not even from this realm or Cullen's. So, you truly cannot tell by looking at us. But no, our kind exists all over this planet, and each area has its own names, practices, and types that are found more often than in other places. We have often adopted the names we are called and some of the culture from the lands we have spent the most time in. It is our own way of belonging, of assimilating."

Lucee looked at Aisling with a sad look. "You really don't have a home, do you. You are truly unique among everyone here."

Aisling smiled brightly, but it was obviously a strained smile. "I have tried my best to make my home here, at House Mirabilis. But yes, I am a woman without a land or people. I am, as far as I know, one of a kind."

Merrick said, taking her hand, "I will be your home."

Cullen added, his voice shaking a little with emotion, "And I will be your people."

Lucee agreed, "Me too. I would be honored."

Aisling sniffed, a tear rolling down her cheek as she said, "I am so glad you came to us, Merrick. You changed everything for me."

MUSIC: GANG OF FOUR

What We All Want

The Frisky Bean was deserted. Then again, it was 3am, and Sousa had seen exactly zero people on the way over to the quirky coffee shop. The Frisky, as the regulars affectionately called it, was tucked away on a tiny back street in the City. It was in the Arts district but not frequented by the students from the Art College down the way. Sousa liked the place because the folks who frequented the coffee shop were the salt of the Earth – the weirdos and the misfits, the people who were everyday odd and not "trying to make a point" odd.

The people who worked there were the sort who had trouble getting jobs anywhere else, whether because of their looks and style or because of the hours they liked to keep. They were artists, writers, musicians – Goths, Hippies, Punks and Rockers. Several former baristas had gone on to gain publicity for their various projects. Working or frequenting there seemed to have the cachet of rubbing shoulders with celebrity.

Sousa hadn't been to the shop this late at night in a while, so he wasn't on a first-name basis with the woman who was currently behind the counter. There was something familiar about her, though – she had this attitude that caught his attention, even if he didn't exactly recognize her. Plus, she had some stand-out hair – short, crazily tousled, and very purple – it matched her attitude, which seemed very self-assured.

She was bouncing around behind the espresso machine in time to The Damned song that was playing on the sound system, cleaning the brass while she sang along under her breath. Sousa chuckled at her quietly, and said, "Hey, can a guy get coffee in this place?"

To her credit, she didn't miss a beat. "And what kind of coffee does a drummer drink?" She tossed the rag into the service sink with a flourish and spun back around to face him, a crooked smile on her face. Sousa got the impression that she was amused, but it was hard to be sure. "Well? It's late, I'm guessing you run on full octane. Am I right?"

"Um, you're gonna laugh."

She grinned at that. "I do not judge, I am here to make the coffee. Besides, I doubt there's anything you can throw at me that I haven't heard before. Even from a burly drummer dude like you."

He schooled his face to a very serious stare. "I would like a very large, very hazelnut breve latte with an extra shot of espresso. And whipped cream." And he raised an eyebrow, keeping the rest of his face in Very Serious Mode.

She mirrored the look back at him, saluted, and said, "Aye aye!"

They couldn't really chat over the sound of the espresso machine, and she seemed to concentrate fully on what she was doing, so Sousa turned toward the large window in the front. When he'd walked down, the night had been clear, but now huge snowflakes were falling from the sky and starting to stick to the sidewalk out front.

Once the espresso machine stopped, he said, "Hey, look at that snow coming down! I didn't know they were calling for snow tonight, did you?"

A flash of concern showed on her face, but she made a dismissive noise. "It'll never accumulate enough to be an issue. Never does here, right?"

She handed him his drink with a smile. "I'm Vali, by the way. You met me at that show that you did a couple of weeks ago. I suspect that with all the people that were there, you probably don't remember, but you bought me a beer, and I don't forget stuff like that." She grinned and added, "It was a GOOD beer, too."

"Oh! That's where I know you from! I knew that I'd seen you around, but not from here, and it was really bothering me. I'm Sousa – I live down the street from here, so I come in here a lot." He looked around at the empty coffee shop. "Can you sit down and hang out for a bit, or do you have stuff to do? I never get to talk with pretty women in coffee shops in the middle of the night, and I really don't want to walk home in this snow shit yet."

"If it was snowing shit, walking home would definitely be unappealing."

Sousa laughed at that. She grinned and walked around from behind the counter. "No one will want to be out in this. It's a Thursday morning, well after last call – I'll probably be farting around until I clock out. So, you should entertain me by telling me all about you."

She grabbed a bottle of water from the counter and gestured to a very purple, overstuffed couch that faced the window. Sousa claimed one corner and she plopped down into the other, turning sideways to face him at the other end.

"So, why are you awake at 3-something in the morning?" she asked.

"Nothing better to do? I'm a night owl, I guess. Plus, I can never sleep after band practices, so I tend to work on stuff or get into trouble around town. I'm evidently also driven by a strong urge to drink overly sweet and fatty coffee drinks in the middle of the night."

"Where do you guys practice, anyway? This isn't the neighborhood that I'd think would be welcoming to rock bands."

Sousa shrugged. "Can't say much as long as we don't break noise ordinances, and I have the space soundproofed pretty well. We're down the way at The Maithe. I have a big space there for us to make noise – you should come by one night and check it out. We're pretty silly, and we love having guests."

She tilted her head, curious. "Don't you live in that place, too? Is the practice space your apartment?"

"No, I have my own living space there. I... um... I have a lot of space there."

She gave him a questioning look. "It always looks so dark in there. Does anyone else even live there?"

"...no?"

"And how did you manage to get a place there? Isn't it weird to be the only one?"

"I – well, I own the building."

She sat there for a moment, a stunned look on her face. "How? Should I even ask?"

Sousa sighed and answered, "I know, I look like a dirty punk. Hell, I AM a dirty punk. I'm a dirty punk with an inheritance and a huge building in the middle of the city. Welcome to my weird-ass world, Vali. That's why I'm awake in the middle of the night – because I can afford to be without having to be at a job. Though if I had to work, I'd definitely want something like this. I'm all about the late-night vibe. And maybe I'd still be able to sit on the couch and talk to people sometimes."

"I'm so sorry. I didn't mean to sound like I was judging! I guess I have more preconceived notions than I thought I did." She looked thoroughly embarrassed. "I feel like a total jerk now."

"You're not a jerk! Honestly, I have to confess this. I almost never tell anyone about my situation because when I do, most people don't believe me. At least you didn't accuse me of lying, you just didn't expect someone like me to have circumstances like this."

He took a huge gulp of his drink, using the moment to try to decide what to say next. Vali sat there, biting her lip. He sneaked a look at her from over the lip of his huge cup. She was so pretty! He hated seeing her so uncomfortable, especially when it was at least partially his fault. He decided to turn the conversation her way.

"Now you know a bit about me: I'm a drummer in a two-bit rock band, I live down the street, and I own a freakishly big house. So, what about you? Are you secretly a zookeeper, do you jump out of airplanes, are you a speaker of five obscure languages? 'Fess up!"

She laughed and replied, "The only languages I speak are fluent American English and poor Pig Latin! Sometimes I feel like I'm a zookeeper when I work here and it's busy, and I'm scared of heights. Whoopsie! Three strikes!" She poked him in the arm, leaning across the cushion between them to do so, and laughed again when he pretended to flinch.

"Oh look, I flirt like a third grader. There's something to know about me." And then she blushed, and quickly added, "I'm an artist. I do murals. On walls. Usually illegally. Because that's how I roll. With spray paint, that is. Holy crap, look at that snow come down. Can you even see the street?"

Sousa blinked at the switch of topic and turned to look as he was directed. "Daaaamn. No, I definitely cannot see the street. Or the curbs, or the sidewalks, or the freakin' SKY. I can't remember the last time that I saw it snow that heavy here. Can you?"

She shook her head emphatically. "No, me either. Crap. It's so pretty, and so inconvenient." She sighed, "I need to call my coworker and make sure that he's going to make it in soon, and I need to straighten up real fast so that I can get out of here when he does. You going to be here for a while?" She looked as though she thought that she already knew the answer, so when Sousa responded with a yes, she broke into a big grin and bounced off to make her call.

Sousa alternated between chatting more with her about various funny things, and watching the snow come down at dizzying speeds. When Vali's coworker finally showed up, shaking off snow all over the clean floor and looking terribly annoyed to have had to go out in the mess, Vali looked a bit disappointed. Sousa realized that she was having as much fun as he was, and he felt disappointed, too. He had this feeling inside that once the night was over and they parted ways, he might not see her for a while, and he did not like that thought at all.

She went to the back of the shop to count out her register and gather up her things to leave, and the guy who was taking over leaned over the counter to talk to Sousa. "I'm glad she has somewhere to go tonight. It's way too cold to sleep out there."

Sousa blinked, taking a second to decide that he'd heard what he thought he had, and said, "Outside? She sleeps outside?"

"You didn't know? She's a gutterpunk, dude, don't you guys all know where each other squats? All I know is that she has a sweet deal here, since we have a shower and all that, which means that we don't have to smell gutterpunk either. Though I have to admit, she's never smelled, you know? She'd be cute if she wasn't a punk, I guess."

Sousa had a sudden urge to punch the guy, but reined it in. "Good thing that I happen to like gutterpunks. You know, being a punk and all that."

"Yeah, dude, she's like perfect for you," the clueless guy answered, cluelessly. Sousa decided that being smart was definitely not a prerequisite for this job. Luckily, Vali reappeared before her coworker said something else that was rage-inducing, and Sousa turned to her with relief.

"Oh yay, I get to talk to my own kind again," he joked, and rolled his eyes. She tilted her head to indicate Clueless Guy, and Sousa made a face, to which she laughed.

"Yes, let us now go and converse in our own secret punky language," she joked, and pulled him away from the counter and toward the door. "He's such a dumbass. Sorry you had to talk to him."

"Well, he did tell me one important thing that YOU didn't tell me." Sousa frowned at her. She looked confused, then got a very angry look on her face.

"He didn't."

"He did. And I'm glad that he did."

"That ASS!" She balled up both of her fists and screwed up her face angrily, then breathed out in one long breath, relaxing a little. "So now you know something about my situation that I almost never tell anyone. We're even. I think you have the better end of the deal, though."

"Look, this is going to sound bad, but at this point, fuck it." He took a breath. "You should come home with me."

"Um... I like you. But dude -"

"I have a huge house. A huge, warm house. There's so much room that you could stay there and never see me at all if you wanted."

"I -"

"Vali, it's cold. Really cold, and I don't think it's going to stop snowing for a while. Please? Won't you please let me feel better, if you won't do it for yourself? Because I will feel like total shit if I let you go sleep wherever it is that you sleep in this weather. Seriously."

She looked like she was going to cry. "Fuck. I hate this. I hate feeling this way, I hate being embarrassed, I hate that my pride wants to say no. But I... shit. Okay. Okay, fine."

Sousa sighed with relief. "I have food. And beer. And drums. It's like the trifecta of awesome. And I won't have to worry." She looked uncomfortable. "Let's just go, okay? Before I kill my coworker and have to pull another shift. No one else will come in to cover it if I murder him."

She zipped up her jacket and grabbed a decent sized Army-style backpack. Sousa looked at it, then her. "I know what your answer is gonna be, I think, but I also would be an ass not to offer to carry that."

Vali rolled her eyes and said, "It's my life, I'm used to carrying it."

Sousa shrugged and said, "Like I said. But the offer's there, anyway. Sometimes it's okay to let other people help you out, just saying." He grinned and added, "Besides, having freedom to move means you won't get hit with as many snowballs!"

She had to laugh at that and ducked as he threw one her way. "If that one's any indication, I am totally safe!" she shot back.

They slogged through the snow to The Maithe, which was just far enough to impress on them that this snow was serious business. Vali looked over at Sousa at one point and said, "Seriously, you didn't even zip your leather up? Are you a glutton for punishment or just inhumanly impervious to the cold?"

"The latter, of course. Although possibly the former as well. I run really hot, though. My bandmates laugh at me all the time because I don't have sleeves on anything, and during practices I usually don't bother with a shirt. So, it's a practical as well as a stylistic choice."

Vali tried hard not to laugh at that and said, "I'll be honest, I haven't been this amused in ages. You are a funny guy, Sousa."

Souz grinned and said, "There's something about you that definitely brings it out in me. That and you didn't hold it against me that I own a giant building in the middle of the city." Vali started to answer, but tripped over something buried in the snow, and Sousa was just able to keep her from face-planting. "See," he teased her, "If you'd let me carry your backpack, you would be more agile..."

She groaned and fussed at him, "If you shoveled the sidewalk as we went, I'd be less likely to trip!"

He chuckled and retorted, "Next time I'll make sure to bring my shovel to the coffee shop!"

He led her around to the alley that ran along the side of The Maithe, and started unlocking a big, reinforced steel door. She asked, "You don't use the front entrance? That explains why this place always looks deserted."

"I don't use most of the building much these days," he answered, as he opened the door and fumbled around for the light.

The light clicked on and flooded the room, revealing a practice space filled with guitars, drums, and other gear. The room was huge, and there was also a full kitchen, a big table and a bunch of chairs, and a couple of couches.

"Nice space!" Vali said.

Sousa gave her a thumbs up and said, "There's plenty of food and beer in the fridge and cabinets – nothing fancy, but a good mix of decent stuff and junk for any palate." He waved her over to where he was. "And come back here and you'll find a full bathroom, and a couple of bedrooms. Pick whichever you like, you'll know which one I'm using because it'll be a mess."

She looked into each room – he was right, his room was obvious, because there was a pile of bedclothes on the unmade bed, and the chair in the corner was covered with discarded tees and pants. The other two were about the same, but clean. Vali chose the one next to Sousa's and hoped he wasn't a snorer. She realized something about the rooms – the windows were high up, and not big. They must face the alley, she thought. Nothing to see, and safer that way.

Sousa stuck his head into the room and said, "Cool, this one's yours then! I've got laundry down the hall, if you wanna throw your stuff in there please do. If you need quiet, there's a door between the bedrooms and the practice space, feel free to close it. Or tell me to get lost if you get tired of my face."

She made a raspberry noise at him. "I think I will wash all this stuff. It all smells like coffee shop."

"Hey, wait a sec, I probably have some stuff that you can borrow so you can put everything in a load, if you want," Souz offered.

He ducked back out and came back with some black sweatpants and a Cramps tee shirt that, predictably, had the sleeves cut off. "My standard at-home uniform," he said, with a grin. "I'll let you do your thing, if you need me, I'll be chilling out on the couch for a while."

She traded out what she was wearing for the things he'd given her and was gratified to find a tank top in that pile as well. "Half my torso could fall out of these armholes," she said to herself, with a chuckle. She dumped out everything from her backpack on the bed, scooped up the clothes, and managed to find the laundry.

Once she had that going, she wandered back to the practice room, and found Sousa sitting at the end of one of the couches, his back against the armrest. He was playing a guitar, just noodling on it from what she could hear.

She cleared her throat a little as she came into the room, so that she wouldn't startle him. That was a trick she'd learned from her time living on the street – when to make noise, and when to be absolutely quiet. He stopped playing long enough to wave her in, and then went back to playing while she sat at the other end of the couch, more or less mirroring his position. They spent another hour or so talking about the music they liked, the local bands they'd seen, other people they might both know, and the merits of different types of coffee.

She managed to get her clothes in the dryer and came back in to hear him playing a song she didn't recognize at first. After a while something connected in her brain and she realized she had heard it before at a Ren Fair ages ago. He was singing along softly – lyrics about a man who was sent over the seas to deliver a message for the king, knowing that the journey would likely be one that sent him to his death. "Lovely," she thought, and then she slipped off to sleep, unaware that it was happening.

When she woke up again, she realized she had no idea at all what time it was. She sat up, squinted while looking around the room until she found the clock on the back of the stove, which said 10:08.

"So, is that morning or night, stove? And are you even set correctly?" she groaned and decided she would go get her laundry and put it away. She pulled everything out of the dryer, took it back to her room and hung it up in the closet, leaving out some things to wear after a shower. "I really lucked out with Sousa coming in last night," she thought to herself. "He's been above and beyond cool to me."

The bathroom was incredibly clean. "Not usual band practice space level dirt at all," she muttered to herself while she showered. "Seriously impressed."

After she got dressed, there was still no sign of Sousa. She called out, "Souz? You around? I was gonna make some breakfast, you want in?" Nothing. She decided after nosing around that there was everything available for pancakes and bacon, so she would make a lot – Sousa could reheat it later if he wanted, or she'd eat the rest later.

She ate, then she roamed around the room looking at things because there wasn't a lot else to do. That's when she found the note addressed to her with the key stuck to it.

It said, "Vali, I might be gone for a bit, here's a key so you're not trapped

– come and go all you want, just don't bring other people here, k?" It was signed with a scrawl that she could barely make out to be his name.

"Well, all right then," she said out loud. "Guess I'll see what it's like outside."

It was still snowing. She had stuck her head out the door, saw the piles of snow everywhere, and got the radical idea that she'd never done a piece during a snowstorm. It felt dark enough if she stuck to the alleys, and she could always claim it was a piece of performance art if she got caught. Though it was rare that anyone spotted her at work – she seemed to have an almost magical ability to graffiti and never be seen doing it, even the few times she had felt extremely reckless and done pieces that were highly visible.

She knew just the place, really close to The Maithe. It was a big wall that got hit up so often that there were tags and big pieces overlaid, paint so thick that you couldn't even see the brick texture of the wall anymore. It was a little exposed, but no one would bat an eye at her working there. She wanted to do a throw-up that wouldn't take too long but still give her the satisfaction of the accomplishment. If, of course, her cans would even work in the cold.

She took the note that Sousa had left, turned it over, and wrote on it, "Souz – stepped out around the corner to do some crimes and get some air. Be back soon, or come find me if you want. – Vali"

The trek to the big wall was actually tougher than she expected. "Good thing I wore double socks," she thought, as she stomped through the snow. No one at all was out, it was like the city was deserted. "Ah, I love it when the city is mine!" she said to herself, happily.

The wall had recently been buffed – either the city or the building owner covered over the pieces that were already there – but a few people had hit up the wall since then, so she wasn't the first. But there was an open, coveted spot she always looked for – close enough to the street that her tag would be seen, but far enough away from traffic that she probably wouldn't be noticed as she worked, especially with her usual luck. She started out with a color outline of the letters of her tag – EARF – in a sky blue. She had to rattle the cans a lot to get them going, which was annoying, but in this weather, she had to suck it up and deal with it.

She was really into what she was doing, when something set off her instincts, a "ping" that made her stop, freeze in place. She heard a noise, muffled in the snow, and quick as she could, she grabbed her bag and ducked down the alley and behind a dumpster. She couldn't see well past it, so she crouched there as quietly as possible, imagining that she was invisible. The noise became louder, and she realized it was footsteps crunching lightly in the snow, and two low voices.

"That's the one, right there – Earf. That's the one to look for," a growly, deep voice said.

At first Vali was elated – someone was paying attention to her work! Maybe she was getting a good rep, finally. But then the second voice, which sounded like nothing she'd ever heard before, said, "The Camlin wants it alive. Bring it to the Grimshaw. That is The Camlin orders. I obey."

The voice reminded Vali of the sound of branches creaking in the wind. It was terrifying. She tried to calm her breathing because it felt like she was gasping for air, and her heart was pounding.

She heard sniffling, then the first voice said, "I can't smell anything in this snow but wet paint. Earf was here recently, we should keep looking, or Camlin will have my hide."

The noise in response must have been laughter for the one making it, but to Vali it sounded like a tree scraping against a window, shrill and dissonant. The noises moved away and finally she heard nothing but the wind and the snow falling.

When she finally came out from hiding, the snow was really blowing and she could feel it getting colder. She knew she should get back to Sousa's, but there was a stubborn streak in her that hated leaving her work unfinished, and it wouldn't take her long to finish up – just the black needed to be added, really. She decided that she was going to do it then beat feet back to The Maithe, pulled out her black can of paint, and got to work.

While she was spraying, she chanted to herself, "You can't see me, I'm not here, you can't find me," until she'd slipped back into that zone and found herself adding tiny white stars across the letters, making the tag into a sky that went from light blue through darker blues, then purples to black – maybe it was stars, maybe snowflakes. Didn't matter. It was perfect.

She added a date because why not, and "snow cru" because it made it sound like there were more people than just her out here freezing her ass off.

And then she heard another sound, and that sound was her name.

"Vali? Are you still around?"

She stood stock still, then realized it was Sousa calling her name – but he didn't seem to see her? She was right here!

He walked up to the fresh tag she was standing right next to and said, "Damn, that's really nice! And fresh – I wonder if that's her work?"

She blinked in confusion, and said, "Souz? Hey?"

He almost jumped out of his skin at the sound of her voice. "Oh shit! How did you sneak up on me like that? You're quieter than a cat!"

Obviously, her face was betraying a lot, because his next words were, "Are you okay? You look even more freaked out than I am – did something happen?"

She bit her lip, then said, "Yes. No. I don't know. Can we get back to your place, and I'll tell you? You won't believe me, but I've gotta tell someone."

Sousa shook his head and said, "You'll be surprised at just how much I will believe. Let's get back and I'll make you some cheap hot chocolate and get you warmed up first, then you can tell me everything."

"Hold on one sec, let me take a pic of this piece first," she said, pulled out her phone, and grabbed a shot. "I feel like I need to commemorate the first piece I ever did in the snow."

He grinned and said, "It is really fucking good, Vali! You have a distinctive style."

As they started walking back to The Maithe, she explained, "My style is definitely more unique, I guess because I don't roll with a crew. I started doing street art on my own and never had anyone to show me the ropes, and I had to build my rep without knowing anyone."

She jumped over a snow-covered bike that was lying in the middle of the sidewalk, and all her paint cans clanged, which amused Sousa. "It's fun to go to places like Graffiti Alley and hear people talk about my work like I'm some wild mystery. I'm like an urban cryptid or something."

At the door to The Maithe, Sousa said, "You checked your key to make sure it worked, right? Good. Let's get you warmed up!"

They took their boots off at the door, and he got to work making some hot chocolate for them both. He made sure to put a ridiculous amount of whipped cream on them. He sat across from her on the couch and said, "Okay, hit me up with what happened."

"Oh jeez, this is going to sound so weird and/or dumb," she started, and Sousa gently interrupted her, "Let me be the judge of that, okay?"

She nodded and continued on with what happened, and as she went, Sousa's face got more serious, then actively worried. "You don't know anything about what they're talking about, do you," he asked, but it was less of a question than a confirmation.

"I have no earthly clue. And the one guy talked so odd. And had the weirdest voice. Like... well, like trees, if evil trees could talk. I know that sounds stupid."

"ArDonnath. You totally described ArDonnath. Which is nuts, because people almost never hear them speak."

She looked lost, and really upset.

"I'm sorry, Vali. I don't mean to make this worse, I know you have no idea what I'm talking about."

Her voice rose in pitch a bit as she agreed, "No, I absolutely do not. Who or what is Aredonneth? Why would it be interested in me? Did I tag the wrong building or something? Did I step into a turf war?"

Sousa reached over and put his hand on her knee. "Hey. Don't panic. Of all the places you could be, this is the safest. And I will explain everything I know, and it'll be your turn to think I'm the weirdo. Okay?"

Music: Cranes
Lilies

Sousa knew that he was taking a risk to tell her about him and what he knew – but it was obvious that somehow, the Grimshaw had an interest in her. He didn't think it had anything to do with being with him; the timing was too soon, and they were tracking her through her graffiti, which meant they had to have seen her art prior to her coming to The Maithe. And anyway, if they had known that Vali was linked to him, they probably would have just come to The Maithe.

He took a deep breath and started to explain. "Okay. So... you didn't see anything, you just heard voices. At least one of those voices belonged to an ArDonnath. That's – ugh, here's where I steal your line, because you aren't going to believe me."

She said, quietly, "I will suspend disbelief and let you talk before I interrupt to challenge anything you say. I promise. I am too freaked out to do anything else."

Relieved, he said, "Cool. Because this is going to sound super bizarro, and if I weren't me, I wouldn't believe me either."

He went on, "So, the ArDonnath. If you'd seen them, you would have seriously freaked out, because they look extremely spooky, like they're made of, well, sticks." He stopped to gauge her reaction, but she waved him on, her face expressionless.

He tilted his head and made an impressed face, then continued, "It is very rare to hear one speak, especially a... well, a mortal. Like you."

Vali blinked, but said nothing. Sousa added, "The Grimshaw are a bit of recent information for me. They are something new to this area, at least that we are aware of – and they are causing a lot of trouble."

He sighed, and said, "I know you're thinking 'who is we?' and that's what's got me hesitating so much, because it's what is most likely to have you turn around and march out of here, which would be a horrific idea, knowing what we know. But – let me ask you something?"

She nodded, and he queried, "So how is it that I was standing right next to you and I didn't see you? Is this a thing that happens to you often?"

She sighed, "Not like that. Though I have this thing that I've noticed – I thought it was just incredible luck or something. It's really hard for me to get caught when I throw pieces. For a while, when I was feeling really fatalistic, I would try to take the craziest risks, tag right out in the open, maybe right by a cop car or on a main street just to see if I would get caught. If I'm in the right frame of mind, I seem to just disappear. It's like no one sees me, even as I'm making art right under their noses. I tried to tap into that hard today, so that those whatever-they-are wouldn't see or hear me. And then when you showed up, I was really in the zone, trying to finish up quickly. I know, that was stupid. I just get so hard-headed about leaving my work unfinished."

Sousa said, "Hmm. So, it's something you think you can control. Can you show me now? Do you mind?"

She said, "I usually am making art when it happens, though I guess I did it when I was hiding. Though there's no way to know if they just didn't know I was there, or I was functionally not visible to them. I can try, though." She took a few deep breaths, becoming very still. He could see her lips moving, like she was talking to herself, and her eyes looked like they were focused on a point in front of her that Sousa couldn't see.

And then he was sitting there looking at nothing at all, and he blinked a bunch of times, trying to see what his eyes told him wasn't there anymore. "Wow, Vali!" He stuck his hand out to see if she had actually disappeared and jabbed her in the shoulder.

"Ow!" she said and reappeared in front of him. "Did it work? What did you see?"

He answered her with awe in his voice. "You were gone! Invisible! Really impressive, lady. That, I did not expect. Have you ever shown this to anyone else?"

She said, looking a little dazed, "No, never. Who would believe me? And honestly, I never actually tested it in this way until today. It was always just something I thought of as luck. Not a thing I could control!"

"All right, then. Please allow me to either blow your mind or piss you off so much that you get up and leave, though I really hope you don't do that." He got up, stood in front of her with a bit of a nervousness about him, and she had no idea why.

He said, "I've got some tricks, too. Here, rub this on your eyelids." He handed her a small tub that he'd picked up out of a bowl on one of the tables. She looked at him curiously but did what he said. As she did, he explained, "Look, I don't look like it right now, but I'm something more than just a dirty punk. If you ever loved old faery tales, you might recognize me from those pages, I guess."

She looked up, blinked a couple of times as she tried to refocus, and said, "Your ears."

He laughed, self-consciously, and said, "Yeah, not as pointy as some. I'm not nearly as showy as some of the Eleriannan." She looked confused, and before she could ask, he added, "Good Neighbors. The Fae. Fair Folk. Faery, I guess, though we don't really like that term much. Seelie is okay, I guess – reactions are mixed. And there are others, the Gwyliannan, who have a bit of a different philosophy. You could also call them the Unseelie, but they're more complex than that, so it's not really fair." He shrugged. "And then the Grimshaw, that's new. And really bad. They are enemies to all, and for some reason they seem to want you."

He stopped rambling and looked at her now very pale face. She was sitting there with her mouth open a little, very still, just looking at him. "Oh no, I broke her," he thought.

She finally said something, very quietly, "So. You are really handsome. I mean, I thought you were cute, but why do you make yourself look less handsome?"

Sousa made a funny face, like he wasn't sure how to react. "I... I have never had anyone ask me that before. I guess... wow, this is awkward. I try to blend? I don't want to get a second look. I hide in plain sight. A different way than you do, I suppose. It's called glamour, a way to make things seem more, or less attractive to mortals."

She was incredulous. "Mortals? So – so you are not mortal, you're saying?"

He shrugged again. "Mortal is a kinda weak way to differentiate but calling you human is even more problematic. But yeah. I can be killed, though it takes an awful lot to do that. But I won't die outright from old age or the like. I can will myself to die." He seemed like he wanted to reassure her. "Take all the time you need with this. Ask me anything you want."

She jumped up off the couch, flailing her arms around in front of her to blow off all the nervousness she was feeling. Sousa watched, wondering what she was thinking.

Finally, she calmed down a bit, turned to him, and asked, "So I can do a glamour or something like that. What does that make me? Is that normal behavior for a mortal? Wow, I hate being called that in ways that must be programmed in somehow. Damn."

He tried to stifle a laugh but failed. "I am not thrilled with calling you that, either. But yeah, glamour isn't something that mortals come equipped with standard – though you can have an aptitude for it and pick it up or be taught it. Mortals usually need extra help with these sorts of workings, like using a talisman or having a power kickstarted by someone like me.

"The fact that you are able to do this all on your own, that you figured it out on your own time, tells me that either you are exceptionally talented for a mortal, or you're what we call a half-blood. Either option is pretty rare and exciting."

Vali looked frustrated. "There's no way to know? I can't exactly ask my parents. Dad's dead and my mother threw me at some relatives and disappeared."

Sousa said, reassuringly, "There's other ways we can find out. Don't stress. I know some people. They'll figure it out." He smiled, then. "So, you are taking this amazingly well. How do you feel about all of this?"

She shrugged. "Honestly? If anyone else in the world told me all of this, I would be calling bullshit. But even if you hadn't shown me the real you – the ridiculously good-looking version of already attractive you, I might add – I think I would have believed it from you. My disappearing thing, I can't ignore that."

Sousa grinned at her aside about him, and said, "If you keep that up, it will go to my head. And we don't need that. But I'm glad you believe me. And soon enough, you'll meet some of my friends who will really blow your mind, if you need more visual proof."

She raised an eyebrow. "You have friends coming in this snow?"

"Well, some are coming… and some I'll need to go get. They're not big on driving. Or technology, in general. Luckily for them, I have no problem with it; in fact, I have developed a bit of skill in that area." She shot him a skeptical look. "I don't have to get them until tomorrow, thankfully, so the snow might be less plentiful by then."

"So do your people not have any weather control powers, then?" she asked, playfully.

"What? No! We're not witches, just your general Fair Folk. Weather powers, jeez," he grumbled, but with a look that said he might – might! – be joking. She absolutely couldn't tell for sure.

He nudged her with his elbow and said, "Hey, wanna see the rest of the place? I think as a new member of the family, even maybe once removed, you get a free pass to check it out. Keep in mind, no one's seen it in a very long time, so it's still a bit messy…"

She grabbed his arm and squealed, "Really? I have always been so curious about what it looks like inside here!"

She then realized what he'd said, and her eyes grew wide. "What are you thinking?" he asked her, and she replied in a quiet voice, "Two things. One: so, you really think I'm a half-blood? Related to you, in a way?"

He ran a hand through his hair thoughtfully and said, "Yes. I do. Like I said, you could be a mortal who is exceptionally talented, but I don't think that's the case here. But what's the second thing?"

She shifted nervously, obviously unsure she should ask. "You said it's been a very long time since someone had been in the main part of the house. What's a very long time? Is it rude to ask how old you are? Do I want to know?"

He winced. "Well, I hate those questions, but no, you have every right to ask them. This house was built in 1879. I had the house built. I was not young then. Unlike a lot of the others I know, I was born here – there are not many like me that I'm aware of, most of my kind were born in the Old World.

"So… I have a connection with this area that is different from most of them. And it sets me apart from them in other ways, too." He watched her nervously, waiting for the reaction that would send her running away – but to her credit, she was made of stronger stuff than that.

"I guess I should be freaking out. Maybe I'm in shock? All I know is right now, everything you add to this crazy story just hits me like, 'Well, why would that be surprising?' And I'm just like… okay. What's next? So, keep going, I seem to be drinking this in."

He took a deep breath, exhaled slowly. "O-oh kay. Please let me know if you suddenly reach the saturation point and are ready to snap, would you?"

She gave him a thumbs up and a weak smile, and he decided that maybe a distraction was in order. "Follow me and I'll show you around. That's your reward for all of my nonsense."

He led her back toward the bedrooms, then to a door she hadn't really noticed, over by the laundry. He smiled at her and said, "You didn't really see this before, did you? That's because I didn't want you to. Hidden in plain sight."

He took out a ring of the most beautiful keys she'd ever seen – they were all old, ornately scrolled metal – unlocked the door, and swung it open to reveal darkness. He stuck his hand in, something clicked, and the lights turned on to reveal a huge basement, as long as the building, though not as wide. She could see various large things covered by dusty white tarps.

"So… what's under those?" she asked as they walked past them.

"Old things. Furniture, carriages, things that I probably could get a pretty penny for if I ever wanted to sell them. I keep hoping I'll find a reason to use them again, which is probably ridiculous." Sadness tinged his voice, surprising Vali with his sentimentality.

"I'd love to see everything someday. They sound like treasures," she said, comfortingly.

They came to a door at the other end of the basement, and again, Sousa opened it with one of the keys. There was another click, and this time Vali saw that it was a push button switch, something she'd only seen once in her life, at a historic mansion. She must have made a noise of recognition, because he turned to her and said, "I had everything rewired to modern standards a while back, I've got no desire to burn down the whole palace."

Then she turned and gasped. "Wow, this is beautiful!" she intoned, touching the curved banister of the stairs that curved up and away from her.

The staircase was a spiral of dark, shining wood that curved up one of the turrets on the ends of the building, from the basement to the fifth floor. "That's a lot of stairs!" she added, as she looked up, catching a glimpse of the sky through the windows at the top of the turret.

"This is one of my favorite parts of this building. There's one in the other turret, as well. You'll see this wood all throughout The Maithe."

They came into the first floor and Vali's mouth dropped. There was an entryway to their left, then beyond that was a huge ballroom area, complete with tables and chairs, a stage along the inside wall, and giant crystal chandeliers hanging above.

"Sousa! How have you been keeping this to yourself?" she exclaimed. She wandered into the room, and admired her reflection in the impeccable, shining hardwood of the ballroom floor. "This is astonishing!"

Sousa just grinned, enjoying watching her reactions. She twirled around on the floor, laughing, and then said, "Those windows!" They ran from almost floor to ceiling, and she ducked over to look out one.

"This faces the front, okay. I've got my bearings now. Wow, this must have been amazing to walk by when it was in use, filled with beautiful people dancing."

Sousa smiled, wistfully. "It was a sight to see. There were balls, salons, revels galore. But things changed, and people stopped coming. Eventually, I closed everything up and became the caretaker only. There's so much more here you haven't seen."

The building was triangle shaped, and you could walk around the building via the corridors that ran around it. They went through the other end of the ballroom and past the second staircase. As they continued down the hall, they traveled by a smaller dining area, and some sitting rooms and salons, all with the huge windows around. Each one was beautifully decorated, with gorgeous furniture upholstered in velvets and brocade styles, bookshelves filled with all sorts of books, and stone fireplaces.

As they continued, Vali got the sense that she was missing something extremely important, something right under her nose that should be so obvious... what could it be? As they approached what would be the apex of the triangle, it hit her. "What's behind these walls, Sousa? There's a huge amount of unused space here!" He looked at her with an intrigued expression. "You noticed that? Hmm, interesting. Tell me, what are you feeling right now?"

She stopped right at the turn of the corridor and faced the flat wall on the inside part of the bend. She cocked her head, like she was listening for something. Then she walked up to the wall and put her hands on it, and her eyes slowly closed. She could hear Sousa's breathing, as if he was excited or scared, then she felt a sensation rush over her like the greatest need she'd ever felt, a loud calling for her to get on the other side of the wall. She wasn't even thinking now, she just started pounding on the wall like someone who was trapped and wanted to escape, and then her fist punched through the wall -

No. Not through the plaster, but through the wall itself, like it wasn't even there. She stumbled and lurched forward, and then the rest of her was through, and the wall wasn't even there anymore. She was standing in an alcove, against a door, and Sousa was looking at her, shocked.

"How – how did you do that?" he breathed. "You shouldn't have been able to break through that illusion, Vali."

She looked at him, wild-eyed, and said, "Do you have the key for this door? Don't make me break it."

Sousa pulled out the keyring, hands shaking, and it took him a moment to be able to fit the key in the lock and turn it. The door opened, and she stepped through, blown away at what she'd found.

The door opened into a three-sided brick chamber, two sides with windows. To her left was an arched opening, and when she stepped out through that, she was standing on a landing that led down into a green space. Well, it wasn't a green space like a courtyard, not exactly... Because it was a forest.

Walls rose up on either side of what she now saw was a tower, like the ones that had staircases in them, on the outer part of the building. The walls had balconies that looked out over the wooded area. As they spread away into their triangle lines, they seemed to vanish – in fact, she could not see the other side of the space at all from where she was. It looked endless.

She turned to Sousa and said, "How?"

He looked like he didn't even know how to answer her. "You shouldn't have been able to find this. You shouldn't even be able to see it! It should look like a simple courtyard to you, with some trees and benches."

She looked away from him for a moment, then looked back, and there were tears rolling down her face. "I can't believe this. This is the most amazing thing I've ever seen. And I'm supposed to be here."

Sousa, taken aback, said, "What?"

But she was already stepping onto the grass, moving along the path there under the trees, drawn like she was being called. "Well, maybe she is," he thought, and followed her. She was laughing, delighted by everything surrounding her – the trees and underbrush, the unexpected flowers, the lack of snow – and Sousa picked up that contagious energy.

She suddenly stopped, and he saw why. There was an open space, and in the middle of that space was a huge oak tree. Its canopy hung over the open space like the sky above, and it commanded attention just by being there. Vali's hands flew to her mouth, and she said, "ohhhh," and ran up to it.

Sousa muttered to himself, "This was never here before, not that I've seen."

Vali turned back to the great tree, and her arms opened wide. The next thing Sousa saw was a bright flash, and there was darkness as he blacked out.

As he slowly came back to awareness, he heard voices, and he had to strain to understand what they were saying.

"I chose you because I see how you care for this city, and for those in it. For me."

The voice sounded so familiar to Sousa, yet he couldn't place it at all. It was feminine, but with some gravel to it, the depth that only comes from someone who has seen things. The next voice he heard he recognized as Vali's.

"Chose me for what? I don't understand, ma'am. I'm just some homeless punk, this is all too much." She sounded both confused and extremely emotional.

The deeper voice answered with a chuckle. "I chose you for all this, Vali! That one, lying there? He has been my steward. And you? You will be my voice, my representative."

Suddenly, Sousa knew who – what – the voice belonged to. Mustering as much strength as he could, he sat up and forced his eyes open.

The first thing he saw was Vali, on her knees, a perplexed look on her face. And standing in front of her, barely taller than the kneeling woman before her, was a grandmotherly figure – if your grandmother was made of bark, and stone, and mud, and asphalt.

She was stout, with a wrinkled, round face. Her hair was the color of concrete and steel and cobblestones, and it flowed down and around her to brush the ground. Where it touched the earth, it was the green-blue of algae and mosses. Her skin was a rich, dark color, but her eyes were the same green-blue as the ends of her hair, and gleamed between the wrinkles of her face.

She turned to gesture to Sousa, and as she did, the colors and textures that made her up shifted and moved, so asphalt and earth and brick and steel all slid and spun together. It made Sousa's head almost hurt to watch; she was like a landslide in motion to his eyes. He took a deep breath to stabilize himself and heard her cackle like a witch.

"All these years he's served, yet the first true sight of his mistress and he's green at the gills! Joseph Sousa, you know full well who I am."

"Y-you are the City. The Genius Loci. The protective spirit."

She made a dismissive noise. "You have it jumbled up, child. You are the protector, and now this one here is to join you. I am the one you must protect. Darkness has tried to infiltrate this place – me – and I need those who are both strong and sensitive, to stand for me and by me." She gestured around her grandly. "Here you have endeavored to protect the heart of your city, enclosing it within these walls for safekeeping. But while my heart was safe, sickness took hold outside, and now threatens to engulf all. If that happens, none are safe."

He sat there, blinking, while all of this sank in. "I guess this isn't really news to me," he said, finally. "We have planned a meeting with others like me. Upon reflection, it all feels related – we have darkness pursuing us, as well."

She nodded sagely. "They are a threat to all, far beyond the petty squabbles of Seelie and Unseelie, as you call them. It is up to you," and she pointed at Sousa, "To bring your peoples together and defend me." She turned to Vali. "You will be my voice and presence. In return, you will be able to tap into my strength and wisdom, and what is mine will be as yours.

"I have spoken."

She looked as if she would leave, and Vali cried out, "Wait! I don't know what to call you, how to address you. And how will I know what your voice is, or your will?" All good questions, Sousa thought.

The wizened woman cackled again. "You shall know. If you wish to grow closer to me, to know my will and my mind, sleep on my grounds. Bathe in my waters and be restored. Those are my gifts to you. And you may address me as Grandmother, or The Lady of the City. Never call me by the name the mortals gave me, that is not my true name."

With that, she vanished in a slow fade that left a lingering odor of ozone, brackish water, and salt.

Sousa's attention turned to Vali, who was still on her knees but curled up on herself, shaking. He struggled to get up and ended up crawling over on his hands and knees to her. When he reached her, he realized she was laughing, tears streaming down her face at the same time.

"Are you all right?" She collapsed into his arms, still full of emotion. "I don't think those words are ever going to apply to me again," she gasped, her laughs edging closer to hysteria at this point. He sat there, his arms around her, while she exhausted herself of her feelings.

"Sousa, I still don't understand why she chose me. I guess I could spend more time here and it would become clear?"

He thought about it a moment, then tentatively posed an idea. "I think I have a hunch or two about why she wants you. But I also suspect that resting here, as she suggested, might give us both more clarity. Nothing will hurt us here; we could lie down and see if dreams give us any more direction than the Lady's words did. What d'you say?"

Vali looked at him and tilted her head, considering. "It's true that I am exhausted. And I've slept in worse places, and with people I've trusted less." She winked, keeping her face utterly emotionless, and he made a raspberry noise at her.

"As far as recommendations go, it's not the crappiest one I've gotten," he joked, and stretched out on his back, folded his arms under his head, and closed his eyes. Vali looked at him for a moment, considering, then did the same. Sleep overtook her in no time at all.

Music: Virgin Prunes
Don't Look Back

Merrick and Lucee were both nervous. Cullen watched them from his seat in one of the big couches, as they paced back and forth like caged tigers, and he felt exhausted just watching them.

"Hey mortals!" he yelled across the room at them. "Why don't you try to come sit with me and relax a little. Sousa will be here in plenty of time. All will go well tonight. Working yourselves up into a froth of anxiety won't help a thing."

Merrick gave him a weak smile and went back to pacing. Aisling went over to talk some sense into him, and Lucee came over and sat next to Cullen. She perched on the very edge of the cushion, ready to pop back up at any given moment if invited to do so.

Cullen reached over and took her hand, and said, "Seriously, Lucee, you are too wound up. This will be fine. Or at least it will be what it will be, and you will do fine in handling whatever it is."

She turned to him, brow furrowed. "It isn't me that I'm worried about. Really, I'll be following Fallon's lead in things unless my big mouth gets in the way, but Merrick is what's got me anxious. There's a lot on his shoulders, and he knows it."

"True but keeping calm while he carries that burden is a fine gift that we can give him. Let him know you believe in him by standing steadfast and without trace of internal doubt, and he will fly true. I believe in him. Don't you?"

She huffed, "Of course I do! But this is big, and uncharted territory -"

He cut her off, gently. "Don't you think all of this has been uncharted territory? And look how well he has handled himself. Your friend learned how to shapeshift this week! That right there is amazing, especially for a mortal. And he has proven himself wise and clever. He will be fine."

Cullen kissed the hand he was holding, gently, and said, "If you can't help but doubt, then hide it well. Confide in me and I will buoy your spirits and bolster your belief." She nodded and leaned her head on his shoulder. He managed not to look entirely too pleased about that while he comforted her.

Across the room, Aisling was trying to do the same thing for Merrick, with about as much success. "I don't know what I'm doing, Aisling. I am terrified I am going to screw this up and drive the Eleriannan and Gwyliannan further apart. And right now, that would be the worst thing that could happen."

Aisling tsked at him and said, "Merrick, you are creating problems that are not even in existence yet. And you have handled yourself extremely well, especially in situations where you knew nothing about what was really going on. You trust your instincts; you know to lean on your friends. You will be fine, stop borrowing trouble." She slipped her arms around him and gave him a hug, and he took that opportunity to pull her closer.

"I couldn't do this without you," he whispered into her hair, and he felt her hands deliver a gentle acknowledgement of his words with a squeeze.

Finally, Sousa arrived. Both Merrick and Lucee could tell immediately that he had things on his mind.

"Hey, did something happen while you were gone?" Merrick asked, and Sousa replied, "I'll tell you all when we're on the way back. It's gonna blow your minds."

"Never a dull moment, is it."

"Not in the least! Fortunately, this is a good – though weird – story."

They loaded Sousa's van with people – mortal and Eleriannan – and he started back toward the city. Tully was in the far back, along with Edana, who looked utterly out of place in Souz's shabby van. Merrick sat behind Sousa, with Aisling between him and Cullen, and Lucee took the front seat.

Sousa said, "I trust everyone else found their own ways to The Maithe?"

Lucee's eyes shone with the memory as she replied, "It was the most magnificent thing I've ever seen. A regular menagerie took off from House Mirabilis! Birds, deer, animals I didn't recognize... mist... I don't know. I've never seen anything like it, Sousa."

He couldn't hide his amusement at that, and Lucee frowned. "Aw, don't laugh at me, Souz. It was the stuff of dreams."

He protested, "I would never laugh at that! I actually love your sense of wonder, and how your time with the Eleriannan has inspired it. You make me see things in a whole new light that I had learned to take for granted." That made her beam at him.

"But hey, you were going to tell us something that happened," Merrick reminded Sousa, who took a deep breath, then began to spin the story about what had happened with him and Vali.

They listened raptly, loath to interrupt. He finally was silent, and Aisling asked, gently, "Where is Vali now?"

"I left her to sleep in the woods, under the tree, as directed by the Lady of the City. She is trying to understand her role more fully, and why she was chosen. She is, as you might expect, a bit freaked out. Up until now, she had not really understood that she might have something different about her."

Lucee said, "Honestly, the thing about Vali isn't even fazing me. What I can't get over is that you have a forest inside The Maithe? How is that even possible? Or is that a stupid question? It's a dumb question, isn't it?"

She elbowed Cullen, who was silently shaking with laughter until she nudged him, then his laughs burst free and he covered his mouth with his hands. Lucee shook her head in mock exasperation.

"Hey, it's old news to you, but not to me, okay? And for some ridiculous reason my boyfriend being able to turn into a fox doesn't seem to ping me as much as a forest inside a city building, but what can you do?"

Merrick rolled his eyes at both of them and said to Sousa, "So she can basically disappear? That is wild! And she's a street artist, too – I wonder if she can work magic with her tags. That might be really useful."

Sousa's eyebrow shot up in surprise, and Aisling turned in her seat to stare at Merrick at the same time.

"Sousa, do you think Vali could do that?" Aisling asked.

"I do. Her work buzzes with energy. For all I know, she's doing it already and just doesn't realize it. Hey, Merrick," he added, with the sort of offhand air that said he was downplaying the importance of his question, "What kind of magic were you thinking about when you asked that? What would you do with that ability?"

"Protection of vulnerable or important areas? That was my first thought." A memory was tugging at the corner of Merrick's mind, a familiarity about all of this – something like deja vu. He continued on, figuring it would become clear to him soon enough. "They might be good for leaving messages for our people, too – warnings, for example, about areas that give us trouble?"

Aisling caught Cullen's smug smile at that response and said, "What?"

Cullen looked like a proud dad. "I knew our boy was going to blow us all away, but he impresses even beyond what I thought I saw on that first day."

Aisling giggled at that. "I didn't know you looked so deep, but alright. I thought you were along for the amusement when all this began."

He made a shocked face, and said, "Are you saying I was shallow? Self-centered? A wastrel?"

"I said not a one of those things! However..." And she squinted at him in a way that made everyone laugh, including Cullen.

"You would have been correct, anyway," he conceded. "Not worthy of any of our current adventures." He squeezed Lucee's hand, and she smiled and blushed a little.

From the back of the van, Edana's voice cut through their laughter. "So how does this Vali fit into our plans?"

Sousa sighed and said, "I honestly do not know. All I know for sure is that she is now more than my guest, and in some ways has more rights to The Maithe than I do."

That drew gasps from the Eleriannan in the van, and Sousa replied, "I know, I know. It is a really shocking situation we find ourselves in. And the fact that The Grimshaw want her means that we are lucky indeed to have her on our side. And... the Lady of The City wants her and me to work together. So, she hasn't rejected me.

"Which is good, because who wants to be rejected by a spirit of place that you never for sure knew existed until they showed up in your secret Heart of the City forest, right?"

Tully's quiet voice cut through the silence that followed Sousa's statement. "I would like to meet her. I feel like I've been on the wrong side of everything."

Merrick turned around and said, "You haven't been on the wrong side, Tully. That would be like The Grimshaw. There have been some wrong turns, maybe, but the path is still there for you, for us."

Tully made a sad noise. "I've spent so much time trying to bring more people into House Mirabilis, away from the city. I never thought about what that was doing to the balance of power, or even if that was the best choice for those I tried to recruit."

Cullen turned and told her, "My friend, we didn't know that was what we were doing. We were ignorant of the far-reaching effects of what we did, which isn't an excuse, but it is the reality. Now we know better, so we must do better. We can't change what we have or have not done, but we can make more informed choices going forward. That's what I intend to do, at least."

Tully smiled gratefully at Cullen. "You are wise. I will take your words to heart."

Edana added, "I said previously that you've changed, Cullen. When first I said it, it was with disdain. I see now that I was wrong. You have changed, but I should laud you for that, not disparage you. You have grown, when we have not." She took a deep breath, and said, "I have much to think on."

Cullen touched his forehead and bowed his head to her. "I respect that," he said. This time, Lucee squeezed his hand, and Cullen smiled to himself at that.

The snow was still piled up around The Maithe, but the streets and sidewalks were all clear; as predicted by Vali, everything had started to melt away. Sousa parked in the usual spot, but when Merrick and Lucee started to head towards the practice space, he corrected them.

"Let's use the front door. I want you to get the full experience of what The Maithe is really like, and anyway, we need to have the door open for the others."

He pulled out his ring of keys, and Merrick whistled when he saw them. "Dang! Those are proper keys! Souz, how is it we've never seen those before? Also, how the heck do they not jingle constantly?"

Sousa rolled his eyes. "Fae, remember? You think I don't have a fix for jingling keys? I've also got one for keeping people restricted to only the parts of the house I want 'em in. More properly, I guess, the House does."

He opened the door and gestured them in with a flourish, then grinned ear to ear at the awed reactions when they entered.

They oohed and aahed over the great spiral staircase, then when they saw the great sprawl of the ballroom. Lucee, in particular, was awestruck by the chandeliers, and spun around in the middle of the floor with her arms wide open, laughter bubbling out of her.

"This is so grand!" she gasped between laughs. "I never in my life expected this!" Sousa watched her and remembered how Vali had reacted, how she had been charmed by the shiny wood floors.

"You'll have to excuse me for a moment," he said to the group, "I need to collect our newest member."

When he came back with Vali, he found that the group had discovered a great spread of food and drink set out on banquet tables and had poured some drinks while they waited. Vali looked like she had just woken up and was still getting her bearings, but her face changed to one of excitement as she approached the Eleriannan. She spoke to Sousa, and whatever she said made him laugh heartily.

"Friends, this is Vali, who I told you about on the trip here. Vali, this is some of the folks from House Mirabilis. There will be many more of our kind here soon, so this is your chance to get all the gawking you need before you get thrown into the deep of things." Sousa stepped back a little, letting her take center stage. He wasn't surprised to find Merrick introduce himself first.

"Hey, I'm Merrick Moore. I'm in the band with Sousa, I think I remember you from around? You look so familiar to me! I'm also an adopted Eleriannan, I guess you could say. They call me the Blackbird." He gave her an awkward grin.

Sousa added, "He's one of two mortals here. The other's my guitar player."

"I'm Lucee Fearney, hi. I'm Merrick's sidekick, also freshly adopted to the Eleriannan – Merrick, I like how you put that! Still getting used to everything but I'd never want to go back."

Sousa mentioned to Vali, "She's also the newly minted heir to House Mirabilis. So, she's a good one to talk to about sudden rises to power."

Vali asked, confused, "But you are mortal? How did you become heir?"

Lucee answered, "Ask me later and I'll tell you the whole tale. There's a whole story, right there."

Each of the others introduced themselves and explained who they were. Vali was deeply interested in Aisling. "I think you might be of help later, at the Great Oak? The tree speaks through dreams."

Aisling, with a knowing look on her face, nodded. "I think I can assist you there."

The other Eleriannan sparked wonder in Vali, with their more obviously fey features, and Sousa said, "You haven't seen anything yet, Vali – the guests are arriving. I should greet them."

Sousa walked over to the entrance and began ushering in folks. First to arrive was the Eleriannan contingent, and they swept in like a cloud of silks, velvets, sparkles, and enchantment.

Fallon led the procession, and when Vali saw her, she breathed in sharply enough that Lucee turned to her and asked, "Are you okay? I know it can be very overwhelming the first time you see everyone."

Vali nodded, mutely, watching first as Ffyn waltzed by with their swaying, gliding gait, then The Ladies followed, in a haze of green and black. Vali turned to Lucee and said, "They are surely not children? And those – what were those being made of branches?"

"The small ones are known as The Ladies, and do not confuse their small size for immaturity or lack of power, they are intense as hell and extremely powerful. And old!" Vali looked at her in shock. Lucee went on, "The twig people are very lovely. They are properly called Ffyn, but they don't mind being referred to as twig people. Oh, did Sousa explain the rules to you?"

Vali, desperately trying to keep her mouth from gaping as she watched the assembly of Eleriannan, said, "Rules? No, he didn't mention rules?"

Lucee sighed deeply and said, "I swear, he's such a lunk sometimes. Look, you need to know these things." She stepped directly in front of Vali so that she would pay attention, because Lucee knew how distracted she was.

"Maybe it won't matter if you're some sort of emissary for the city, but best not to piss anyone off or mortally insult them. Number one: don't thank anyone, ever. They love attention, but thanking them is insulting, and some of them will totally cut you off if you do it. You can express gratitude, just be clever."

She waited for Vali's nod, and continued. "Two: our group is trustworthy, but in general, don't tell anyone more info than you need to. Don't make bargains if you can help it. Don't say anything like 'I owe you.' Basically, anything that traditional faery tales or ballads warn you against, don't do it. Three: manners are everything with these folks. Usually, being deferential will get you through a lot. Oh, and they hate hate hate being called fairies. Don't do it."

Vali snorted, "Oh, that's all? Suuuure, I am sure I'll remember all that."

Lucee said brightly, "Oh I am positive we will be here to help you. I know it's a lot, but I promise, these folks are so worth it. My life has become so much more interesting, even if I can't tell many people about how it has changed!" She touched Vali's arm and pointed toward the door, "Oh look, the Gwyliannan have arrived! Oh, they are all so different, and so beautiful."

Vali and Lucee both tried hard not to stare. Whereas the Eleriannan had some in their cohort who were not, as Aisling had explained to Merrick, "Gentry" – in other words, what a mortal might classify as "elven-appearing" – the Gwyliannan were wildly varying.

First to enter were the Court, the ones that Merrick, Cullen, and Sousa had met with. Leading the group were Daro and Genaine; Daro was dressed in robes of gold and black that trailed behind him, and on his arms were golden bracers that glinted and gleamed in the light from the chandeliers.

Genaine wore all black silk; her dress had a labradorite beaded bodice that matched the goat-horned headdress she was wearing. Her arms were bare, decorated only in the tattoos of vines – thin lines that swirled up her arms from the back of her hands to disappear into the armscye of her dress. She had a look on her face like she wanted to be anywhere but where she was.

Karstyn walked behind them, clothed in what could only be described as leather armor – a full outfit of leather pants, an actual metal breastplate, and a leather biker's jacket. Their combat boots had spikes on them, and they had pushed back their sinuous hair with a pair of bronze goggles that any Steampunk would have killed to get their hands on.

Behind them, Brenna followed nervously, her head swiveling back and forth, her wide eyes unblinking as she took in everything. She had completed the owl-like persona with a full cape of brown and white feathers, and they fluttered lightly as she walked through the ballroom.

Dermot was the last of the Court, though his was the least remarkable entrance. He was dressed in very plain brown, and if it was not for his talons, Lucee and Vali might have thought him a shy mortal. He tried to stay near Brenna, who did not give him even a glance as they walked.

They were followed by a small group of Gwyliannan, including a few ArDonnath, which drew a few gasps from the Eleriannan. Lucee felt her heart speed up at the sight of them, and Vali asked, "What on earth are they? They don't look like the Ffyn. They scare me."

Lucee agreed, "They are scary! They are ArDonnath, though I call them Stickmen. Cullen told me that some of them were with the Gwyliannan and would do me no harm, but I can't help but be afraid. My last meeting with Stickmen almost killed me."

Vali turned to Lucee with wide eyes. "Killed? There was one who wanted to capture or kill me, too. But I never saw it, I only heard it."

"Souz told us about that. I wonder how these Stickmen are different?"

Sousa's voice boomed through the ballroom, interrupting them. "Are all here, now? I wish to close the doors if we are all in attendance."

Fallon called out, "The Eleriannan are here."

Daro responded, "As are the Gwyliannan."

Sousa said, "Then let us begin this meeting. Welcome to The Maithe, or as some of you call it, Maithe House. I have not had another being inside the main part of this house in years and years; I can't think of a better place to have this gathering, in this uncertain time. Please feel free to avail yourselves of all that the first floor has to offer. I don't know who wants to go first, discuss amongst yourselves."

He waved everyone over to the tables, arranged cleverly so that each group could sit or stand together, with space in front for people to speak, and the banquet table between and behind the whole setup.

Daro spoke first. "As you came to us at the outset, we shall initiate this evening. A New Moon is a time for new beginnings, let that inform our actions and discussions tonight." He gave that a moment to sink in, then continued.

"I am Daro of the Gwyliannan. When your emissaries came to Tiennan House, we were in turn amused and affronted by your reasons for parley, then shocked and dismayed to learn what was happening right under our noses. It seems that what once drove our houses apart, needs must bring them together again. We talked long after The Blackbird and Sousa left, and then sent out scouts beyond our own lands to see what we could learn beyond what was discussed." He paused, and looked around his audience, daring them to guess what happened next.

Merrick raised a hand and asked, "Did you find anything new? Because we have things to tell on that front."

Daro's eyes widened in surprise. "Something happened? We found no evidence of new activity, no. Please tell us what you have seen?"

So first, Merrick told the story of the attack by ArDonnath on their walk around the property of House Mirabilis, and when they described the fight, some hisses and unsettled noise rose from the Stickmen in the Gwyliannan's ranks. Merrick assured them, "I promise, we mean you no disrespect! We understand that they are under the control of this Camlin person, and you are much different."

Brenna cocked her head and then said, "They think that if it had been them, there would have been a different victor. Perhaps I am not being charitable to interpret that."

Privately, Merrick felt his skin crawl, but he replied evenly, "Perhaps they are correct. I would prefer that we never come to that, though." He turned to the ArDonnath. "I don't expect that you'll ever like us, but I hope that we may be allies. I feel that you've been done a disservice by the Grimshaw, one I'd be honored to help rectify."

There was a general rumbling from the ArDonnath, and Brenna said, "Unexpectedly, you have pleased them. They are disposed to dislike mortals, so I would count that as a success."

Merrick tried to keep the surprise off his face, and merely bowed to them. That seemed to score points with the rest of the Gwyliannan.

He finished telling the tale, and there was much consternation when he finished. Daro asked, "It was just ArDonnath? How many attacked?"

Merrick said, "I was running around a lot, so my accounting might not be reliable – ten, maybe?" He looked to Fallon, who nodded agreement.

She added, "They very nearly killed one of the mortals under our care, we were quite overwhelmed. Our tale might have been different if the Blackbird had not drawn them off."

Genaine, whose face had grown tight when Fallon started to speak, burst in then. "You have taken in more than one mortal now? Ah, you Eleriannan never learn!"

Lucee piped up then. "Hey, I'm that mortal, and I don't appreciate that! I am certain it wasn't in the plan to take me in, as you say – I'm the Blackbird's sidekick, where he goes, I'm going."

Genaine gave her a haughty once over, and Lucee got the distinct feeling that she came out of it lacking, but she wasn't going to let that bother her. But Fallon spoke up next, to confirm what Lucee said.

"I understand that you do not approve of our ways, and your words to us, through your chastisement of Cullen, did take roost in our hearts. But Lucee is correct – we could no more abandon her than we could Merrick, as she is the most loyal companion to him. And when the battle ensued and she was injured, she became even more so to us."

Genaine made a dismissive face, and Sousa spoke up. "Fallon doesn't need to get your approval, but you might want to know that she was hurt defending me and Sheridan. She put her life on the line to save two Eleriannan. As terrifying as that scene was, she never hesitated. And Fallon rewarded her for that bravery in kind."

The entire delegation of Gwyliannan stood still at that, and Genaine said, "Excuse me, what?" Fallon said, "She is of our clan now. And my heir. So adjust your reactions appropriately."

At first, Genaine blinked, genuinely surprised. But then her anger came back in a flash, and she spit out, "Who are you to school me in appropriate reactions? You, who let your whole House ignore the distress of Tiennan House, and left me there to die?"

The tension in the room was so thick you could have sliced it with a knife. And at first, Fallon hung her head, and let Genaine's anger wash over her. After a moment, while all looked on in silence, she raised her head and looked Genaine in the eyes. She could feel Genaine's anger like a wall of heat, burning into her. She sighed, softly, and then spoke.

"I cannot undo the choices I made then. I told Lucee when I made her my heir that being a ruler is about making the best choices for those who look to you for leadership, making good decisions. And sometimes the criteria used for making good decisions is flawed. I made a flawed decision, based on beliefs that have been long held, but incorrect. My lack of action cost you everything, and it is imperative that I take responsibility for that, as the one who leads this group."

Suddenly, she dropped to her knees before Genaine, and bent her head to the floor, sweeping her long hair away to expose her neck. She called out, "Quillan!" and he rushed over and seemingly out of thin air pulled forth a gleaming sword of gold and silver.

Cullen and Aisling gasped at the same time, and Tully cried, "No!" as Quillan offered the sword, blade laid across his hand, to Genaine.

"My life is forfeit to you, Genaine, as only blood can assuage blood," Fallon said. Her voice raised so that all could hear. "None shall fault you for taking what is yours."

Music: Siouxsie and the Banshees
Take Me Back

Genaine's face went pale, and she almost stepped back from Quillan, but then reached out and took the sword. She turned it in her hand, feeling the heft of it, looking at the blade, while Fallon knelt below her. It felt like everyone in the room was holding their breath as Genaine debated what she would do.

Lucee was clutching Cullen's arm so hard he knew there would proba- bly be bruises, but he didn't stop her. She whispered to him, "Why is no one objecting to this? It's grotesque!"

"It is one of the oldest rules. Blood for blood. A life to atone for loss of life. She is looking to absolve all of us for our inaction, by taking the blame and the punishment." His gaze never left Genaine's grip on the sword.

Lucee growled, "It is stupid."

Genaine's gaze snapped up to meet Lucee's and she said, "What did you say, mortal?" Cullen tensed up, but Lucee wasn't so easily cowed.

"I said: this is stupid! What will this solve? Not only will killing Fallon not bring your people back, it will take from us another powerful per- son, someone we will need in this fight! How will that resolve anything? Reparations are one thing but taking a life for the loss of others will never bring peace between us. It's just another step to helping the Grimshaw to tear us apart." She stood there, defiant, with her arms crossed, daring any- one to deny her logic.

Genaine stood stock still while Lucee ranted at her, then gave her a long look, sizing her up. She pointed at Lucee with the sword. "YOU."

Again, there were gasps from the Eleriannan, and Cullen inhaled sharply. Lucee, to her credit, did not budge.

Genaine repeated, "You." She threw back her head and laughed, then continued, "I have changed my mind about you. Fallon chose well."

Lucee's eyebrow shot up, but her face otherwise stayed unreadable. Genaine walked over to her, the sword still pointed at Lucee, but Lucee refused to flinch. Merrick watched with his fists balled up, afraid to say anything lest he change the mood and send Genaine into doing something rash.

Genaine stopped right in front of Lucee, with the point of the sword right at her heart. She inspected Lucee's face, looking for any weakness. Lucee could sense Cullen's distress but she couldn't let it sway her. She was not going to give in on this, not going to let Genaine's anger best them all.

Genaine sniffed, then, and in one swift motion, she flipped the sword so that the pommel was pointing upward, and she was holding it by the bottom of the grip and the cross-guard. She presented it to Lucee, who reached out in one smooth gesture and took it from Genaine.

Lucee gestured briefly at Quillan, who ran over and took the sword from her with a grateful smile. She patted his shoulder as he ran back to Fallon and helped her up.

Lucee looked at Genaine with pity in her eyes. "You've been through so much," she said. "Having to handle the things you went through, with no one you thought would save you showing up – that is a lot to ask of anyone. You deserve recompense. But this? This is not the way. Let us create different solutions, ones that build bridges, rather than continue the trauma that happened. I promise to do everything I can to help mend those rifts."

There was a shimmer in the air, and Merrick whispered, "Oh, Lucee. You made a promise."

A flurry of surprised noises and chatter from the crowd punctuated Merrick's reaction, and Lucee snapped, "I know what I did! I meant it. This obviously is part of the work I've got in front of me and I'm not going to abandon it. The promise is important. It's the least I can give to Genaine for what she went through."

Genaine blinked, a flush coloring her face and the points of her ears. "You know what you are saying. And yet you are making the pledge anyway."

She took a sudden breath, like a gasp, and said, "I am Genaine, of the Gwyliannan, formerly the Eleriannan. And I think that Fallon was right to choose you as her successor. You've got more guts than the lot of them, other than the other mortal, the Blackbird. Though I suppose we can't call either of you mortals anymore, can we?"

Lucee turned her head to look at Merrick, and he said, "No, I suppose you can't, at that. Things that have happened weren't exactly planned, but neither of us would have it differently. That doesn't change what I said to you at Tiennan House. I respect you. My goal is to reunite us in purpose, to truly do good, not just good that benefits the members of one house." Genaine inclined her head, the closest he'd seen her come to a bow.

Lucee turned back to Genaine, and said, "I'm Lucee Fearney, somehow heir to Fallon of House Mirabilis, and guitarist for The Drawback." That drew a guffaw from Sousa, and Lucee grinned in his general direction. She turned back to Genaine and said, "How about we do some amazing things together?"

A palpable sense of relief washed through the room, and Merrick came over to the two women and said, "There's so much we still need to talk about. Why don't we take a few minutes to regroup and then sit with some food and drink and talk more?"

Daro nodded and said, "I am ready for a drink at this point." He leaned in towards Lucee and said, "I would take some moments to see to your Lady, first." He touched her arm gently, then escorted Genaine away.

When she went to Fallon, she was surprised to find Vali by her side, along with Aisling and Tully. "Lady, that was brave, but foolhardy," Lucee said to Fallon, who closed her eyes and sighed at Lucee's admonishment.

"I took a risk. Someone needed to address her pain, and our failure to her and her people, and as the leader, that falls to me. But you! You were dazzling in that moment," Fallon praised Lucee. "If nothing else came from that, you showed them all why you are the correct choice to follow me."

Lucee screwed up her face in frustration. "That is not the way I want to prove that! Genaine was seriously contemplating killing you. What would I have done to salvage the situation then? And how would that have served anyone, especially when we need to face the Grimshaw, too?" She threw her hands in the air and walked away, exasperated.

She saw Merrick and Cullen sitting at a table, waving her over. She sat down and said, "Tell me there's a beer here with my name on it. We've just started and I'm already exhausted." The guys started talking at the same time, and she put a hand up and shushed them. "Don't. Do. That. I know what you're going to say. That was stupid, Lucee what do you think you're doing, you could have been killed, blah blah. I know. I couldn't just stand there and let that happen, though."

Merrick held up a finger, then said, "Would you give me a second to not put words in my mouth? I was worried as hell, yes! But Lucee, you managed that like a badass. I hate seeing you in danger, but you aren't some weakling who needs rescuing or lecturing."

She closed her eyes and sighed deeply. "I appreciate you saying that."

He added, "I don't really have room to throw stones, anyway. We really are a lot alike in that ability to jump into the middle of madness."

She snorted and rolled her eyes at that. "Master of understatements, you are." She turned to Cullen and said, "Go ahead. Tell me what you were going to say."

He bit his lip, then said, "I am not known as a fighter. But if she had killed you, none of us would be left standing by the time I was finished." He looked away, and Lucee couldn't tell if he was angry, embarrassed, or sad. Merrick, on the other hand, looked properly shocked at what Cullen had said.

They sat there a moment like that, and then Cullen added, "You need to do what you are meant to do. I may not like it, but it is not my place to keep you from it. I can't even properly keep you safe – I guess if you needed that, you might get it from Merrick or Sousa. But you've taught me the value of loyalty, and that I can give to you."

Lucee said, softly, "Loyalty and love are more than enough, Cullen. And you respect me, which is something I don't think you give enough credit." He turned to her then, and she took his hands. "I'm sorry that I scared you. I was scared, too. It's funny – I don't get scared for me, really. I get scared that if something happens to me, it will hurt you, and Merrick, and Sousa. That's my guiding light."

Merrick said, "That's pretty much how I feel all the time, too. That, and the fear if something happens to me, I'll have let everyone down."

Cullen laughed, a small, sharp sound. "You two are the bravest of the Eleriannan, and you aren't even born of us. And you worry about letting us down? What fools these mortals be. Brave, but dumb." Lucee had to hold back a laugh at that.

"Merrick, I think we found our next slogan. 'Brave, but dumb.' Maybe Tully will make us a banner with that, so we can carry it into battle."

Aisling, Sousa, Vali, and Tully, who were escorting Fallon, joined them at the table. Tully pulled out a chair for her and sat her so that she was near Merrick and Lucee.

Fallon said, stiffly, "I will not ask for forgiveness. You must understand that. A leader does what is best for her people, even if she risks her own destruction."

Lucee broke in, "Jeez, for people who are supposed to live for wordplay and getting the best out of a bargain, you don't seem to be good at strategy. Surely you know that you aren't supposed to lay all the cards on the table right away! You leapfrogged right over talking or bargaining to offering your life – that is not my idea of *détente*!"

Everyone at the table shifted uncomfortably, and Fallon stared off into the distance. Something sparked in Lucee's eyes then, and she asked, pointedly, "You've been planning this for a while. This is why you chose me, isn't it?"

Fallon looked incredibly tired. "I could not see another way out that would not destroy us."

Aisling spoke up then, her voice thick with emotion. "You would rather sacrifice yourself than force these changes on the Eleriannan. You would rather choose oblivion than do the work."

Merrick's face drained of color. "Is that true, Fallon? Because when we went to parley, we all knew it would be difficult work to bring the Eleriannan back into the modern world. But I never thought you would be one of the ones who would resist change."

People had begun to listen to the conversation, especially as voices had become raised through emotion and frustration. Fallon looked around the circle of Eleriannan and Gwyliannan that had gathered, and she began to look ill.

"I did not see it as such," she said, a catch in her voice. "But you are holding a mirror to me, and I do not like what I am seeing."

There was an audible reaction from the Fae as they realized what she was saying.

"You would have abdicated to the mortal heir rather than face change!" a voice rang out.

The crowd became noisy, arguing and yelling, the din growing in volume until finally a loud voice broke through.

"ENOUGH!" yelled an exasperated Vali, who climbed up on a chair so all could see her.

Someone in the crowd said, audibly, "Who does that mortal think she is?"

In that moment, Vali seemed to expand, and a crackling aura of purple and green surrounded her. She transformed from a homeless punk girl to something much older and wilder while the entire crowd of Eleriannan and Gwyliannan gasped as one.

She addressed the crowd then, and her voice was thunderous and commanding, not Vali's voice at all.

"I have stood here and watched your petty arguments, your disregard for each other, when you could have stood together and been true stewards to this land and the people on it, and I have had enough.

"I am speaking through this one called Vali, the emissary for the Lady of the City, the Grandmother of these lands – now called Baltimore but with names so much older and more meaningful – older than any of you!

"I have waited for you until I could not anymore, so now I speak to you directly, and I call you to take action. I see the movement of those upon my lands who would not only destroy both of your houses, they would usher the destruction of those who live here as part of my ecosystem, who try to grow and do better but are too easily swayed by the powers of these creatures.

"They are of your people, and they are your responsibility to divert away from these lands that you call yours so cavalierly. How can you claim home when you do nothing to ensure the safety and growth of it?" She glared at Fallon with eyes that flashed in anger.

Then she turned to Genaine and Daro. "And you, so ready to save your surrounds but not to cast your protection wider, or to let your anger sit to the side in order to fight a bigger evil. You will destroy yourselves with the poison of anger and squander the powers that could sway the balance toward the light."

Genaine clenched her fists at that, and shot back at the Lady, occupying Vali's body, "And who are you to condemn us? You say you are the embodiment of the city, but how do we know that to be true?"

Vali seemed to grow more intense, the colors around her pulsating in ever deeper shades. "Follow me, then, and I will show you."

She jumped from the chair and began walking through the crowd, which parted ways for her as if they were afraid to touch any part of her. They fell behind her as she led them to the hidden door, and threw it open to gasps and sighs from the crowd. She gestured them to enter, then walked through, down the steps, and stopped to turn in the grass and address them.

"I am not just the City. I am the Land. The Spirit. The People who live on this Land. I am all, and more beyond that. Before the buildings were built, before the people came in boats, and earlier still when they hunted here and slept under my trees – I was here. I grow and change as time and the people do, but when you are all gone, I will remain."

She looked around at each of those standing before her. "I am changing for the worse these days. I am troubled by the struggles of the people, the divisions over things that should not matter. Pollution ruins the wildlife, makes my streams and my harbor dangerous. All of these things change me in ways that make me a stranger to myself. You, immortal ones – you are not native to these lands, but still you were designed to caretake. Some of you have forgotten your original charge. Others follow your calling but have divided yourselves off from the rest of those who need you and your strengths.

"I need you, children."

Vali's body slumped at the last words, and she stumbled around for a moment, before sitting down hard, with an "oof!"

Sousa ran over to her, and she looked up at him, dazed, and said, "That was really difficult, I'm not gonna lie." Everyone else was deadly quiet, and she cocked her head and asked Souz, "So I'm guessing no one was expecting that? Let me tell you, neither was I."

Sousa gingerly helped her up, and asked, "Are you okay? Did she just – take you over? That was something else."

She nodded, holding her head. "Left me with a bit of a headache, too." She addressed the others, "Is that enough to get you to stop arguing? Getting yelled at by a primordial being via some dirtbag mortal who got left with a headache? I sure hope it was."

Lucee couldn't help herself; she busted out laughing at that, putting both hands over her mouth to try and contain it. She managed to choke out, "I thought I was the badass here today, but nope!" She buried her face against Cullen's shoulder, laughing uncontrollably.

The Eleriannan and Gwyliannan, on the other hand, looked totally nonplussed for the most part. Finally, it was Tully, of all people, who spoke up.

"So... fighting the Grimshaw, together, will help The Lady?"

Vali replied, "And coming back to the city regularly, ceasing the urge to withdraw and lock up your resources just for your benefit. Basically, do what the Gwyliannan are doing, but even more so. That goes for both Houses."

Sousa added, "It helps everyone, not just the City. The benefits are widespread. You can't just dam up your magic forever, it needs outlets or you truly will fade away. What the Eleriannan have been doing by dazzling the occasional mortal is nothing more than putting a bandage on things, limping along when you could be and do so much more. Come back into the world, share your light. That's what she's asking."

The Gwyliannan had been quietly looking around them while Vali and Sousa were talking, dazzled by the woodsy heart of the City. "Who knew that such a thing existed?" Genaine asked of no one in particular.

Brenna, though, had an answer. "I had heard the tales of hidden ancient lands, still here somewhere, like a memory forgotten amongst the streets of the city. But I had thought it a tale, or something we had lost long ago. Never did I dream that it lived within the walls of Maithe House!"

Sousa gestured around them and said, "This was here in plain sight, and slowly getting choked out as the city built up around it, so I bought the plot and the ones around it, and had The Maithe built up around it, to my specifications and with some magical help."

He got a bemused look and added, "You know, I've never been able to find the end of the woods. I know it's there, but I don't have the right sort of connection to find all the things this place hides. It's been waiting for Vali, I think. I'm just the caretaker. She's the conduit."

Brenna's big eyes blinked slowly, and she asked, "Might I take a flight around here? I could see more from the sky in my owl form..."

Sousa looked at Vali, who nodded and said, "That is a smart plan. Shall we await your report on what you see?"

"I will tell you all I find, but I can seek you out in the ballroom if you wish to continue the council while I fly." She paused, then touched her chest and said, "My name is Brenna, of the Gwyliannan. If you are so kind to trust me in your secret forest, I can entrust you with my name."

That made Vali smile in a way she hadn't all night so far. "I am Vali. Vali Dawe, but the last name doesn't matter. I can't wait to hear about what you find."

Brenna took two steps and with a jump and a wave of her arms, she shifted to a full owl form and flew off with almost no sound at all. Vali stood there, dumbstruck. "That was the coolest!"

Lucee said to Vali, "So far, seeing stuff like that has not gotten old, let me tell you." They grinned at each other with the shared joy of two mortals caught up in something enchanting.

Sousa said, "There's so much here to see, you could spend years combing through it all. But we have important things to discuss, in the here and now."

Karstyn – who until that moment had not spoken much – said in their soft, clear voice, "I am unsure what our plans for the future will be. But I know that this is not the right place to speak of battles."

Their hair curled and uncurled as they spoke, and they pushed a few of the moving tendrils back. "Let us go to the ballroom and eat and drink and decide how we want to partner. Then if Sousa and Vali allow, perhaps we could come back here to this garden of delights?"

Vali nodded, and Sousa agreed, "The forest should be something we can all access, if we are going to do The Lady and this land any good at all. And now we will have a goal to work towards."

They trooped back to the ballroom and gathered themselves around the tables. The discussions seemed to go on all night – what were their goals, how could they fight the Grimshaw, were they to wait for an attack or go forth and attempt to challenge them? And how could they bring the Eleriannan and Gwyliannan together in purpose, so that they could become truly united?

At one point, Lucee looked over and saw that Aisling had fallen asleep, her head in Merrick's lap. She sighed, desperate to do the same on Cullen. "I might not be bright, so I'd better be awake," she thought, trying to keep her face from showing her exhaustion.

Sousa shook himself awake with a groan, and said, "What have we decided? I might have lost a moment there."

Dermot piped up, his soft voice able to cut through the group thanks to their exhaustion. "We were discussing that we are spread out, and that makes us vulnerable. We need a way to easily stay in contact."

Brenna, returned from her survey of the forest, piped up from the doorway, "I think I may have an answer to that, in part." She held her hands up to quiet the rising commotion. "I found a gate."

Sousa perked up at that. "A gate? Where was that – is it easily accessible, or do I need to attempt growing wings to reach it? I had no idea, there truly is an untapped wilderness within these walls."

Brenna shrugged, "It is no great feat to get there, if you follow the wall to the left. What I found is that if you travel along the walls, the trip is as long as it would be outside the building. But if you cut across the 'spanse, the lands roll on before you. I feared becoming lost, so I turned back to the boundaries."

Merrick raised a hand. "Can I butt in here and just ask what's going on? A gate? Like a garden gate, or a trans-dimensional gate, or..." Aisling stifled a sleepy laugh.

Fallon, who had been quiet for some time, answered in a wary voice, "You are not so off with that question, Blackbird. One of our gates can take you to many places, depending on how it was created to operate. Some only connect between one place and another. Others are more valuable – and dangerous – because they are what we call 'open gates' – they can convey you to many places, including the Misty Realms.

"Those gates are usually highly guarded, because anyone with the power and wherewithal can use them to travel unfettered from one gated location to another. It makes sense that one would be here, and that it would be relatively hidden to any but those who hold the house."

Merrick raised an eyebrow. "That sounds like a really helpful thing to have in your possession! But where else are there gates? Can you only travel between gates, or can you emerge anywhere you want?"

Fallon looked pleased. "Good questions. Second question first: one may only emerge where there is a gate. They all connect to a shared, liminal space. As for the first question: only a few gates are known to me. It is generally considered foolish to travel indiscriminately to any open gate without knowing where it opens, as one has no idea what will be waiting for them upon passage. Once, all the great Houses had one. But the only one I know of that is still open is Gentry House, though it is well-guarded."

Merrick paused a beat, then asked when the answer wasn't forthcoming, "And House Mirabilis?"

Fallon lifted her chin a little. "We closed it. When I say we withdrew, I meant it. We closed ourselves off from the mortal world and also all the Houses. I have been," and she stopped for a moment to look around the room, "I have been made aware of my folly."

Merrick could feel his heart beating a little faster as he asked the next question. "And could that gate – could it be reopened?"

There was a little explosion of noise at that, many voices talking at once. Fallon held up a hand and the room fell silent.

"Aye, that it could. But who will take the charge of guarding it? That is a full-time occupation. And Blackbird, say you not that you would, for you have your own responsibilities to attend."

Merrick thought about it for a moment, then answered, "Surely there must be some sort of magic we could call upon to only let the right people through? And can you explain how no one has come through the one here at The Maithe, if it is not guarded?"

At this, Morgance spoke up. "No one has come through this portal because no one has been close enough to it on this end to know it. One must truly know the portal in order to come through it without risking ruin. It is not like walking through a door one finds randomly. The key is one's understanding of the door."

Merrick furrowed his brow. "So… to use it, I would have to communicate with it, in a way?"

"Think on it, Blackbird. It is not dissimilar to you taking the Raven's shape."

She tapped one finger on her other hand and looked thoughtful for a moment. "Your first question has me intrigued. I see a puzzle here that I and my sisters might be able to solve. Let us think on this. But I do believe that reopening the portal at House Mirabilis should be a priority."

Fallon raised an eyebrow. "Will you be taking watch to guard it then, Ladies?"

Morgance grinned at her, all pointy teeth. "Mayhap we will, my Lady. If that is where our path lies, of course."

Merrick blinked, shocked – The Ladies were so full of surprises lately! – and then turned to the Gwyliannan contingent. "And what of Tiennan House? If all great houses had gates, it should follow -"

Genaine cut him off. "I have no knowledge of this." Daro, beside her, squinted almost imperceptibly. Dermot, on the other hand, had a tortured look. He was tucked away towards the back of the crowd, but somehow Merrick saw his grimace and took note.

"Perhaps you don't, but Dermot seems to know of something. Dermot?" Merrick called out, drawing attention to the reclusive Fae.

"I... I am not sure. There is something in the lot at the bottom of the hill," he stammered. "By the cold Gwynns Falls, where they call it a city park, but it still is ruled by us. I do not know if it is working. But the rudiments are there." He ducked his head, shy or afraid – Merrick couldn't tell.

He looked back to Genaine and noted that her hands were in fists in her lap. Daro had also noticed and leaned over to whisper something in Genaine's ear. It did not improve her reaction.

Merrick asked, "Are there any at Tiennan House who know how to use these gates?"

Karstyn raised their hand. "I have a bit of experience. Not much. But I can learn. And if there are any who might give me any tips, I will graciously accept." Merrick gave them a thumbs-up, and unexpectedly, they smiled at him. He couldn't help it, he smiled back.

"So, I guess we're not trying the gate any time soon then," he said, only a little dejected about it.

Fallon said, "The only other open gate that I know is Gentry House, and they will not like anyone just dropping in unexpectedly. But we have another task to add to our list, and that is a good goal to have. And then we will have a much easier way to respond in times of need, or travel to all the Houses."

Tully added, softly, "As it was before." The Eleriannan nodded along, a mixture of sadness and regret on their faces.

Lucee looked around the room with bleary eyes. "I am utterly exhausted. What else do we have to discuss? I am enjoying being with you all, but with all respect, I would enjoy sleeping even more."

Music: Japan
Ghosts

They decided that they should adjourn for the next few days, to work on the gate situation. Merrick turned to Aisling and murmured, "Is there a way I can get both sides to pledge a bond to help each other? To be allies? Is that too forward?"

Aisling squeezed his hand and said, "You can be the link between them. You are the link, actually."

Merrick thought on it a moment, then rose from his chair. "Before we part ways, I ask only one thing from you all." Everyone in the room grew quiet and turned to Merrick, expectantly.

"I am the champion of House Mirabilis, and that makes me friends with all in that House, as it should be." He bowed to the Eleriannan contingent, and they clapped politely and made approving noises.

He turned to the Gwyliannan then and addressed them. "I have no such formal bond with you, but I would be pleased to call you friends. May we cast a bond of friendship between you and I?" He extended a hand to them, and he was pleased to see Daro move forward first.

"I will gladly take your hand in friendship. You have been fair and advocated for us when you had no benefit to do so." He put his large hand over Merrick's.

Karstyn came next, then Brenna, and Dermot. Genaine stood alone, with a wary look on her face.

Merrick said, "I will call you friend, Genaine, even if you do not believe me." She closed her eyes and exhaled hard, then walked over and put her hand on the others' hands.

"I will take your hand in friendship," she said, sounding defeated.

The others in the Gwyliannan contingent cheered, and rushed up to touch Merrick, to get in on the moment. There was a palpable ball of energy around them, the physical manifestation of the bond they were creating together.

The Eleriannan looked uncomfortable. Aisling sighed, stood up, and went over to grab Lucee, and Sousa. "You need to bond with them before they leave. Get over there and make an impression. This is important."

Lucee looked from her to the group around Merrick. "I get it." She took Cullen's hand and pulled him over to Merrick, who saw them and grinned.

"I hope you will accept my friends as readily as you have me," Merrick said to the crowd, and pulled Lucee in next to him.

"I would be honored to call you friends. Together, we can do so much good," Lucee declared.

The Gwyliannan seemed pleased to have her in their circle, and again, cheered. Genaine even kept her silence about her dislike for Cullen.

Sousa also joined in and said, "You are friends of The Maithe and welcome here." That was also well received. Slowly, the Eleriannan drifted over and were drawn in.

Aisling, chatting with a few of the Gwyliannan who were very interested in her uniqueness, noticed Fallon at the edge of the group – a part of it, but barely. "Your actions will be noticed," she thought to herself, but decided for now, there was nothing she could do, and let it go.

Sousa addressed everyone, "Let us get to work on our tasks, so that we can reconvene and test everything. I think if our plans work, something more along the lines of a party will be in order, what do you say?" Cheering from the people answered his question, and he grinned. "Bring things to make music, be ready to dance. I have a good feeling about all of this!"

The Gwyliannan left slowly, hesitant to call the evening done after that rousing end to the council. Aisling pulled aside Merrick to whisper in his ear, "Well done! You allowed them to leave on a positive note, which will do much to foster good feelings about this alliance."

He turned and gave her a quick kiss. "All credit goes to where it is due – to my clever girlfriend."

She blushed a little and squeezed his arm. "I just didn't want them to leave feeling like they wasted their time, you know?"

He agreed. "Something needed to re-energize us."

Sousa had extended an invitation to whomever wanted to stay the night at The Maithe and looked excited for people to take him up on it. Fallon and The Ladies excused themselves, saying that they wanted to work on the gate in the morning.

Edana, looking less sure of herself than usual, said, "If you will convey me home tomorrow?" Tully, perpetually where the action was happening, stayed also. And, of course, Merrick and Aisling, and Lucee and Cullen.

Sousa directed them upstairs and indicated that Vali should go first. They heard her pleased gasps as she came out of the stairwell and into the hall, and soon after they could see what got that response.

To the left, corresponding to where the ballroom was below, was a long open gallery, all dark woods and rich brocaded wallpapers. There were bookcases along the short wall that bracketed a fireplace, and tables and chairs scattered through the room in comfortable configurations. The windows along the outside were framed by burgundy velvet curtains, and the inside was all glass French doors. It felt like an airy cross between a private library and an atrium.

Turning to the right, there were windows that faced the street along the corridor, each framed with the same burgundy curtains. On the opposite side, doors to rooms lined the wall. The doors were open, and they could see that each room was set up as a private room. The rooms were large, with fireplaces and plenty of furniture for lounging around. And these rooms also had French doors; Vali opened one to reveal a balcony that looked over the forest contained in the center of The Maithe.

"Oh!" she exclaimed. "I should have guessed, but this is so unexpected!"

Sousa couldn't contain his pleasure. "These have just been waiting for someone to come enjoy them again! There are also two bathrooms in each section, because I know how we all love a bath." Cullen raised a hand at that, which made his friends laugh.

Sousa indicated that they should choose whatever room appealed to them, and anything they needed would be there. So, they broke off to sleep, leaving Sousa and Vali standing in the hallway.

He turned to her and said, "Any of these can be yours forever. You don't have to stay in the crappy little practice space rooms. I would have offered them before, but as you can see... things have changed." He gave her a sheepish look, and she chuckled.

"Huge changes! I am still processing all of this, honestly. I – I don't know if you'll go for it, but if I could convince you to stay in the same room with me –"

He cut her off, "Yes. I can do that."

It was her turn to look sheepish. "Normally I'm fine on my own, but I just feel so off kilter right now. Can I tell you something?" He indicated that she should go on. "I haven't slept in a bed in so long, I'm not sure I'd even be able to handle that level of normalcy. I'd be happy just sleeping on the couch or even on the floor in front of the fireplace."

"Like a dog? No, no, no. You can sleep on the couch and I'll drag it in front of the fireplace, how's that? We'll make this work for you. I get it."

She looked relieved and said, "Honestly, Sousa, you are the best. Luck was on my side when you came into the coffee shop."

They had taken the room next to the other staircase, and Sousa went about moving the furniture around while they were talking. He plopped down on the newly repositioned couch and said, "I hope you remember that the next time the Grimshaw come at us. Meeting me put you in danger. I regret that. Though I fear they would have figured out who you were soon enough."

She raised an eyebrow and sat next to him. "Do you think so? I guess replaying the scene in my head, they must have known who I was before you came into the Bean – so... meeting you didn't put me in danger, it keeps me safe because I'm in here with you, where all the magic is. I know I'm not supposed to thank you, so..." She leaned over and kissed his cheek, then noted with quiet satisfaction that he was blushing. She decided to give him an out. "I should clean up before sleep, right? I'll be right back."

She moved to get up, but he put his hand over hers before she could rise. "Hold on." She turned towards him, expectantly. His face was unreadable to her.

"Vali, I wanna be honest. I wasn't planning on meeting someone I liked as much as I like you, especially not now, with everything that's happening. I mean, bad enough that I'm this immortal Fae thing in a punk shell, who owns a giant house with a magical forest in the middle of it – that just happens to be the heart of the city. But then there's maybe a war beginning, between factions that are full of dangerous powers, and with our side comprised of allies who are barely allied."

He made a face, because he knew how ludicrous it all sounded when laid out like that. "And here you are, already dealing with so much, including a whole new facet of yourself being revealed to you in a pretty dramatic fashion. That seems like a lot to handle already, without putting a potential attraction on top of it all."

She snorted. "Seriously, listen to you. You go through in great detail about all the weird ass stuff that's happening, but when you get to what you and I are feeling, you gloss over it. Are you afraid of admitting your emotions, Souz? Because I really like you. I'm attracted to you; I think I made that clear. And I really want your friendship. All of those things. I don't think any of this is incompatible."

She sighed, and stood up, pulling her hand out from under his. "I am going to go wash up, and when I get back, I'm going to operate under the things I just said to you, just like I have been. You do what seems right to you. It's cool." Her smile was colored by resignation.

Sousa watched her leave and said to the empty room, "Well, that didn't go as planned. I am such a dumbass."

When she returned, she saw that Sousa had started a fire in the fireplace and made approving noises as she sat back down on the couch. He sat there for a second, thinking, then reached over and took her hand. She smiled, squeezed his hand, then slid over and leaned her head on his shoulder.

In the early morning, with the sun just starting to peek through the windows, Merrick woke up with a start. After trying to convince himself that he should fall back asleep to no avail, he carefully unwound himself from Aisling's embrace. He dressed and decided to walk down to what he was calling the study.

"I won't wake Aisling up this way," he thought. Most of the doors to the various rooms were closed, but one was standing open and Merrick couldn't help himself, he peeked in as he passed.

He caught a glimpse of Sousa, on the couch with his head resting on the arm, his legs up on an ottoman. Stretched out along the length of the couch with her head in his lap was a sleeping Vali. They looked so incongruous in that well-appointed room that Merrick almost laughed out loud but caught himself in time.

He decided he'd better move along, and he passed the staircase and moved into the study space, to find that he wasn't the only one awake.

"What ho, Merrick?" called Cullen, from an overstuffed armchair situated by the fireplace. Merrick shook his head in disbelief.

"I see you've discovered this ungodly hour as well," he answered, then he caught the smell of coffee and added, "And you made coffee, too? Amazing."

"No, no, that was no work of mine. It was ready and waiting for me when I arose. There is breakfast, as well," and he pointed to a long table filled with baskets of muffins and biscuits, an urn of coffee and all the fixings for it, and several silver domes. When Merrick lifted one, he discovered French toast.

Cullen advised, "There are eggs and bacon and sausage too. But no waffles, Lucee will have to do without." He took a swig from his mug and added, "The coffee is very good."

Merrick fixed coffee and took a biscuit and some bacon, then sat by

Cullen, in another of the fabulous armchairs, with a happy sigh. "At least when you get recruited by the Fae, you eat well," he said around bites of bacon.

"We do enjoy some food and drink," Cullen agreed. He sipped from his coffee for a moment, then asked Merrick, "So... could you not sleep anymore either? I was awakened from a deep sleep as if pulled from the depths."

Merrick nodded, his mouth full of biscuit – they really were good! – then answered, "Awoke with a jolt. I wonder if it's because I really want these gates to work, and to do that, I need to go there."

Cullen made a face. "What do you think you can add to that effort? Fallon and The Ladies know more about those sorts of endeavors than probably all of the other occupants of House Mirabilis combined."

One side of Merrick's mouth twisted downward for a moment, and he looked askance. Cullen asked, "What? Do you not trust them all of a sudden?"

Merrick deflated a little as he admitted, "Not them. Fallon. She is... something is wrong with her, Cullen. Something is off, and I don't understand what exactly. I don't think she'd actively sabotage anything, but she seems to be – well, just off."

Cullen pondered what Merrick had said for a moment, then said in a soft voice, "I do believe that she is in the end stages of her life amongst us, Merrick."

Merrick grew very still, and he felt his heart start pounding. He managed to spit out, "I don't believe that."

"I wouldn't pose the possibility if I did not think it true, because it is a terrible thing to suspect. But Lucee and I were just talking about this before sleep last night, and we both see what you are seeing, and my supposition is the only answer that fits. I am just not certain if it is because she is disenchanted with life, or if she feels that she cannot move forward with us. Or perhaps some other reason I have no way to guess." He sighed deeply. "I do not know what is in her mind. But it is obvious that she is moving away from our path forward."

Merrick drained the cup of coffee, then stared into the cup like it might somehow refill itself. "So, I shouldn't be worried about her work on the gate, then?"

Cullen waved that thought away with one hand. "Oak and Ash, not in the least. You see, if she's thinking of leaving, that's her easiest way out."

"I'm afraid I'm not following."

Cullen clenched his jaw, then his face took on an incredible sadness. "The gates don't just connect to each other. If you keep walking, without a destination in mind, eventually you will travel to the Misty Lands. And if you do that... Well, there is no returning. It is a one-way trip."

Merrick didn't know what to make of this.

"Does that mean that she dies? Or is there something beyond? I vaguely remember you mentioning something about the Misty Lands once."

"There's no way to know, I'm afraid," Cullen confessed. "It is as much the subject of great spiritual debate as Heaven is to mortals. Do we reach some great land on another plane of existence, where our ancestors that have gone before still reside? Or do we just walk into oblivion?

"We were once known to have the skill to walk between worlds, but none of us that I know has done that in ages. It is all but the stuff of legends now. You saw how many of the younger ones last night were surprised by the idea of gates! All of these skills risk being lost because of our choices." He looked disgusted and slammed back the last of his coffee to hide his emotions.

Merrick asked, in a subdued voice, "What do we do, then? Far be it from me to step between a supernatural being and her ideas of destiny, but it would be a loss in so many ways, an incredible loss. But this is why she picked Lucee, then?"

"I suspect that she'd been playing with the idea since she first met Lucee and gave her the Book. But the attack and Lucee's injuries forced her hand much sooner than she expected, and now she's feeling a sense of the light at the end of the tunnel. She hadn't planned on being a leader, you know. It came to her as unexpectedly as it has come to Lucee."

Cullen stood, started fixing more coffee and offered to do the same for Merrick. Merrick handed him the mug and queried, "Should I even ask what happened?"

Cullen's grip tightened on the spoon as he stirred his coffee. "They left us. All the oldest ones, all at once. Fallon's parents, the leaders of Gentry House, and Tiennan House too."

"They all left? That is horrible! And that's something that would be really difficult to recover from – no wonder all the Houses split like they did. I guess no one knew what to do, left with that sort of trauma."

"And you have seen that we are not the best at addressing hurts. We get angry, we hold grudges, we use ceremony to carry us through. Again, I think this is why Fallon has invested so heavily in you and Lucee. You are visionary, where we are staid and narrow-minded. You speak honestly, forthrightly – and we are used to dancing circles around the truth, leaning on tradition to keep us from diving deeply."

He paused, then leaned forward in emphasis. "We may have the magic, but you? You are the magic. We use it, but you embody it. And now you know why your tales are filled with faerie courts taking on mortals; you are the only ones able to give us inspiration, to change us. We seem to be incapable of doing that on our own." He turned away, disgusted with himself and his kind, and Merrick looked around, uncomfortably.

Finally, Merrick said, "I think you're unnecessarily harsh on yourself and your people. From what I've seen, you've just needed a small push, a glimpse of possibilities. But after that, you have all taken on the challenges offered with a full head of steam. Cullen, look how much you yourself have changed! And look at the progress made in healing the rift between the Eleriannan and Gwyliannan here."

Sousa, standing in the doorway, interrupted him. "I would say that, in an historical sense, these changes are happening at an astronomical rate. Cullen, you and I know how long it usually takes our kind to shift in any way."

Cullen snorted, and said, "True enough. How long have you been standing there, anyway?"

Sousa grinned widely and answered, "Just long enough to hear almost all of that conversation. I didn't say anything because I wanted to hear how Merrick would answer. And dude," he addressed this to Merrick, "When did you get so wise? I've gotta admit, I've felt much the same as Cullen. You answered that well, with a good but gentle kick to the ass."

Merrick chuckled at that. "That's what I'm here for, compassionate ass-kicking."

The rest of the Eleriannan who had stayed over wandered in, and then Vali, who made appreciative noises about bacon and eggs and drank three mugs of coffee before she spoke to anyone.

Lucee poked Sousa and muttered, "You'd better take note of that for the future, me bucko." She burst into laughter when Sousa blushed, then stammered, "I, um, sure!"

Vali seemed oblivious, concentrating instead on eating, then finally looking up with an apology. "Poor habits, my bad. When you live like me, and get offered really good food, you make sure you get enough before the offer runs out."

There was a flash of sadness on Sousa's face that no one but Lucee caught before he reassured Vali, "You will never have to worry about that as long as you live here. And you'll find that your favorite things will start to show up as you express a liking for them. Just never say thank you. You know, the usual."

Vali asked, "Is saying 'Compliments to the Chef' too much? Because this was delicious. And the coffee? Amazing! Better than what I make, and I take pride in my joe."

"No, I think that's just the right thing to say. Genuine compliments are always a boon, in my experience." Sousa grabbed her mug and refilled it, then commented, "Now I know how you work those late night hours."

She stuck her tongue out and blew carefully on her coffee. "Mmm, still piping hot, too. What a treat."

Merrick said, "So if I'm not going to House Mirabilis today, and we need to wait for Tiennan to get their gate working – what should we do? I have two ideas, and I personally think both are awesome, but I should let you be the judge."

He looked pleased with himself, and Sousa answered, "Okay, I'll bite. What are your awesome ideas?"

"First, I wanted to work with Vali and see if my idea about working magic with her tags is a solid one. If you're up for it, of course," he directed this at Vali, who gave him a thumbs up. She was sitting on the floor, leaned back against the front of the chair and Sousa's knees, with his feet on either side. She had balanced a plate with biscuits on it precariously on one of his feet.

"When I'm done eating all this food, I'll go get my sketchbook. It helps to have things mapped out on paper first before I pull out the cans. This should be fun," she said, brightly.

Edana, who had been quietly eating until that point, leaned forward and offered, "I might enjoy being included in that task, if you would have me."

Merrick was surprised, but kept it off his face as he replied, "Certainly! I am sure you will have many insights." She looked pleased as she went back to picking delicately at a muffin.

Merrick then pointed at Lucee and Sousa. "And after that? Us. Downstairs. Band practice. Or I guess we could haul everything up and do it in the ballroom? That doesn't sound fun, but it needs to be done. Playing sounds way more fun."

Lucee grinned and cheered, "Yes! I have been missing my guitar something fierce! And we'd better be sharp if we're playing for the whole host of Faerie." Cullen made a face at that, and Lucee said, "Look, it gets tiring to refer to everyone by their dang factions, okay? Y'all could have picked something shorter to call yourselves. Both sides!"

Tully snickered and said, "The more syllables, the longer our names are on your tongue. That is just the thing that appeals to our egos."

Lucee responded, "Oh daaaaaaang!" and that set them all to laughing.

Music: New Model Army
##

S ousa decided that while Merrick, Vali, and Edana were puzzling out the idea of graffiti magic, he would bring up the equipment to the ballroom. Lucee and Cullen jumped up to help. Aisling and Tully decided to hang around and watch Vali at work.

Aisling pointed out, "You might need test subjects, right?" Edana got a slightly wicked look at that suggestion.

Vali followed along to the practice space, noting that Sousa walked them around the outside of the building, rather than through the secret cellar. She went ahead while she was there and grabbed her entire backpack, which she had repacked after washing everything the other night, out of habit. She looked over at the equipment stacked up to go, grabbed an amp on rollers, and started rolling it out the door of the practice space.

Sousa raised an eyebrow, and Lucee said, "You're damn well keeping her around." Vali grinned and kept dragging the amp.

The ballroom had a small stage set-up ready for the equipment – just a platform, really, but enough that a decent number of people could get up on it at once. "When did Souz have time to put that up?" she thought, then shrugged to herself and went to find Merrick.

She found everyone in the study, sitting at the type of table you'd find in any library, and at first, she thought they were playing with a toy on the table. But it turned out that they had their hands open in front of them on the table, and they were taking turns pushing a leaf back and forth between the four of them, without touching or blowing on it – at least as far as Vali could see.

"What are you doing?" she asked, puzzled.

"This is a game we play as children," Tully explained, "One that helps us learn to hone our powers and build control. Merrick is still learning, so we thought it would be a fun way to help him and to pass the time. You can try to move it toward another player, or make it dance in patterns and keep others from taking it over. Want to try?"

Vali studied the game for a moment, watching as Merrick fought to keep possession of the leaf from Edana. Both of them were furrowing their brows in concentration, until with a laugh, Aisling caught the leaf from them and made it do a series of loops in the air.

Merrick chuckled, "Aw man," and Edana made a "pfft" sound.

Vali cracked up and said, "So how do I do it?"

Edana gestured for her to sit down. "Put your hands like mine. That helps you concentrate where you want your attention to go, but it also keeps you from cheating." She winked at Vali, who caught, out of the corner of her eye, Merrick's wide eyes at Edana's wink.

Edana continued, "Now just imagine the leaf moving. Everyone has their own way to visualize it – a wind, your hand, your breath, a string – none are wrong, just find the one that works for you. Once you can move it, then you'll start to get the feel for doing tricks with it."

Vali put her hands out as instructed and thought about the leaf moving. She imagined that she was controlling a breeze that moved it, sliding it across the table... did it move right then? Aisling made an approving noise, and Vali continued to imagine the leaf moving across the table. Suddenly, the leaf did just that, flying right into Aisling's lap! Vali squeaked with surprise and slammed her hands down on the table, and Aisling cheered.

"You did well!" Edana said! "The Blackbird took longer to get the leaf to move than you just did."

Vali looked around the table, her eyes big with amazement. "I – I have never done anything like that before." She swallowed hard, then said, "I wanna do it again."

They let her try a few more times, until she got the leaf moving fairly reliably, and was even able to keep Edana from stealing it from her once. She finally decided to step away, saying, "I'll never stop if you let me keep playing, this is fun! But Merrick, you and I have a challenge in front of us to tackle."

She pulled out a hardback sketchbook from her backpack and tossed it onto the table.

"This is my black book; I keep all my sketches and ideas for pieces in here. See anything that strikes you?" She grabbed a pencil bag filled with markers and colored pencils and spilled them out on the table and said, "Let's see what we can come up with."

When Sousa, Lucee, and Cullen rejoined everyone in the study, they found everyone standing around Vali as she was finishing a drawing, humming energy billowing around her like sparkling clouds of steam and glitter as she drew with sweeping gestures.

Edana exclaimed, "That might work!" and Tully clapped her hands.

Vali flopped down in a chair with an audible "oof" and said, "That might be the most satisfying piece I've ever done!"

Merrick noticed his friends and waved them over. "Look at this!" He picked up the sketchbook and waved it, and the tag on it – all yellow and pink and blues and greens, done in some incomprehensible style – seemed to waver in the air, above the page.

"Oak and Ash," Cullen murmured. "That's some powerful stuff. What's the intention, Vali?"

"Go out of the room."

He shrugged and walked over to the staircase, outside of the study room. She took the open book and sat it next to the wall by the entry and touched it briefly.

"Come back in now," she directed, and he raised his eyebrows, but obeyed – until he was repelled back at the entry with a hard bounce, as if someone had erected a barrier of clear plastic over the doorway and he'd run directly into it.

"Yikes!"

Vali laughed and ruefully said, "I should have warned you, but I wanted to see how it would work if you didn't know. I'm sorry."

Sousa said, "Hot DAMN!"

She turned to him and said, "Now you walk to Cullen."

He warily walked to the threshold, with his hands stretched out in front of him, and his face changed to delight as he walked through the door untouched.

"It's one way?" he asked.

She grinned at him and said, "Try walking back!"

He did so, without impediment. He looked at her with amazement. "This is like nothing I've ever seen, Vali."

She looked pleased. "Okay, now walk back, and bring Cullen through with you. You need to touch him, skin to skin like hands – you can grab his wrist even."

Sousa walked through, held his hand out, and Cullen sighed and took it. "I had better not get beat up by invisible walls again." To his bafflement, they both walked through without issue.

"Now, Cullen, you try to walk through without Sousa." Cullen found that now he was unimpeded.

"Well, Wind and Water, I did not expect that! So, because someone on the inside brought me in, I'm now free to move back and forth?"

Vali nodded. "I wasn't sure I got all the details right, but it seems that I did! This can go on our gates, and more importantly, on our Houses. It doesn't need to be a large piece to work – obviously, that's just a sketchbook sized tag and it was fine. You put it on the side you want protected for the gates.

"I can do one for the outside of properties, too, and that will guard them. And clothing, for people. I see how to do it, now, so the possibilities are endless."

Merrick added, "It's like working with sigils, from what I can see. Not that I'm an expert, I read a book once from the occult bookshop and thought it was a really neat idea. When I explained it to Vali, she got it right away and just went to town, making these pieces."

Sousa turned to Vali and asked, "Can you put this up inside the entrances to The Maithe? And on our gate?" He could tell by her face that she thought that was a dumb question.

"That's the plan, Stan," she chirped at him, and added, "I'm starving. AGAIN. When are y'all going to do your band practice?"

Sousa made a face. "Magic expends serious energy. Ask Merrick there, he's constantly hungry or sleepy. Me, I run on beer and drums. Which I'm going to get revved up on as soon as these fools in my band get it together and come down to practice."

Lucee sighed. "I hope there are sandwiches down there or something. Music revs me up, too, but I know I'm gonna be hungry soon. And a beer might be nice, yeah."

Sousa confided, "I am pretty sure if you want sandwiches, they will be there. Vali, you might find something good to fill you up, too."

So, they all trooped downstairs, where there were indeed sandwiches, and Vali sat at a table and devoured one, then drank a beer while the band got set up and started warming up. They sounded really good, she decided, even just jamming out in a practice. They managed to get a really full sound from just the three of them and some electronic loops. She thought it would be fun to hear what the Fae would add to the mix later.

She decided that paint pens were the way to handle putting the piece on the doorways, so she grabbed her bag full of pens, the original work-up of the sigil, and headed to the front door.

The Drawback were winding into a blistering cover of "First And Last And Always" by the Sisters of Mercy, Lucee pacing around the stage in a circle while her fingers flew over her fretboard. Vali bounced out of the ballroom in time to Sousa's sped-up beat.

She managed to get the front door and the door to the practice space finished faster than she expected. She had to laugh when she walked into the practice space and saw the giant mess that was left behind from moving all the equipment so quickly.

"Typical musicians," she laughed to herself.

As she was coming back up the stairs, she thought she heard something, like a noise at the edge of her hearing that sent her senses on alert. She tilted her head, trying to suss out where the sound was coming from, and finally realized that it was someone at the front door.

"We're gonna need a bell," she muttered to herself, as she walked up to look out the door's glass. She was pleased to find Karstyn, Dermot, and Genaine standing there.

She swung open the thick door and greeted the Gwyliannan. "Hey friends, come in," and she gestured to them to enter with a grand sweep of her arm.

Karstyn smiled and said, "We bring you news of success – at least we think it is success, we just need to try out the repaired gate."

Vali led them to the ballroom, her bouncing steps giving away her pleasure at this development. "I have something to show you all, too – a way to keep the gate a little safer. at least. And your House, as well!"

As they came into the Ballroom, The Drawback was crashing through a version of a Siouxsie and the Banshees song, Lucee at the mic yelping and playing guitar at the same time, Merrick standing with one foot on a monitor, his bass pointed out to an imaginary audience. Sousa was standing up at his drum kit, jumping up and down while hitting the snare and a cymbal. The song crashed to a halt as they saw the Gwyliannan enter, with Lucee yelping a few extra times into the sudden silence, then laughing hysterically.

"WHY IS THAT SO FUN," she yelled into the mic, which made Sousa answer with a drum roll and a bass drum thump.

Vali applauded, joined by Karstyn and only a little grudgingly, Genaine. Dermot looked confused, and said, "I don't understand this music."

Cullen, over at a table to the side, chuckled at that. "I didn't either, for a long time. It grows on you, though."

Dermot nodded thoughtfully and walked over to Cullen. "Maybe you can explain it to me at some point? I want to understand, it seems important to keep connected to this time and place."

Merrick came bounding over, gesturing for the rest of them to come to the table.

"We're going to play some at the next meeting, if you wanna try to get what rocking out is all about," Merrick told Dermot, with a friendly thump to the shoulder. Surprisingly, the usually nervous looking Dermot responded with a tentative smile.

Genaine asked Vali, "What is it that you wanted to show us?"

Vali winked at her and said, "Right, right, let's get to business." She slapped the page with her art on it down on the table and said, "This."

Genaine made an unimpressed face, Dermot looked confused, but Karstyn – after a moment of studying it – breathed out an, "Ohhhhh."

Genaine whipped around to look at Karstyn. "You understand this?"

Karstyn looked at her, then said, "Maybe if you touch it. I'm surprised you don't feel it, though."

Genaine looked irritated at that but extended a finger and touched the center of the drawing. "Ugh!" she exclaimed. "That is so peculiar!"

She turned to Vali. "What is this, exactly? I can feel how it is charged with energy, but not how one would use it."

Vali gave them the same demonstration that she'd done with Cullen, who watched the whole thing, amused.

Genaine asked, "What if we want to withdraw someone's permission after the fact? Is the sigil that sophisticated?"

Vali's face scrunched up as she thought. "I think you'd have to keep them out by other means. I am just learning how to create these, but they are only limited by my ability. I could create a new one if situations change. For your House, I can make one just like this, on paper or a board, that you can take down or put up as needed. But for your gate, I will have to paint it on."

Genaine nodded. "I can see that your next ones will be even better, you are learning even now. My kind is very good at looking for and exploiting loopholes, so it is in my nature to question. But this is well done, Vali!"

Behind Genaine, Cullen looked impressed that she had awarded Vali a compliment. Vali was glowing from the praise.

Sousa leaned over and gave her a side hug. "You are amazing. We are so lucky to have found you."

Obviously pleased, she waved a hand, warding off the compliments. "But we are supposed to be seeing this new gate!" she said, in an attempt to change the subject and get the focus off of her.

They trooped down to the secret forest inside the courtyard, and Sousa pointed to the left.

"Brenna said that it was along the wall on this side, so we just need to follow it."

A short walk later, they came upon was obviously was the gate, a great upright circle made of the same sort of stone that could be found as some old curbstones and building foundations in the city, a bluestone that was cut into irregular, thick slabs and stacked up and mortared to form the shape of the gate. It had three small steps that led up to the inside of the circle on the side away from the wall; the side facing the wall had no steps.

Sousa said, bemused, "What's amazing is that I didn't put this here."

Everyone in the group turned to look at Sousa, shock or confusion on their faces.

"Um – Sousa, if you didn't, then who possibly could have?" Aisling asked.

Sousa shrugged. "I have to tell you, this house has a mind of its own," he confessed. "I don't know if it's the influence of The Lady, or there's something or someone else's work at play, but as much as I built this house and live here, this place is in no way under my control."

He looked around for a moment, then added, "And I am glad of that. This house has never been about me."

Merrick was nodding, and Lucee made an approving noise. The Gwyliannan appreciated his words as well, Genaine in particular.

She asserted, "Any would be proud to call Maithe House their home."

Sousa gave her a half-smile, one that acknowledged her compliment, but didn't take any of the acclaim for himself. He turned back to the gate and asked, "What do we need to do to familiarize ourselves with this gate, so we can get back here?"

Dermot spoke up, "My understanding is that you don't need much. Touch the gate, lock the feel of it in your mind, where it is located. As this gate is inside your own domicile, you should already have a deep connection with it."

He looked over at the gate and saw that Vali was deep at work, using paint pens to add the sigil tag to one of the stones that made up the gate. The surface was flat but not the smoothest, so she was working carefully. Dermot walked over to her and said, "Will this last on the rock?"

She shook her head. "Not forever, no. I will have to either touch these up eventually, or redo them with better paint at some point. But for these times, it will do." She grinned at Dermot, and added, "Gives me more practice at this!" Dermot seemed to be loosening up a little, as he managed an actual smile for Vali.

"All done!" she declared and turned to the group. "Are we all going? I know I need to, who else is coming? I personally think it should be all of us."

Merrick spoke up and said, "No. We need to do this in teams."

Sousa was nodding. "He's right. We need to make sure that someone is here. Vali, you should go first, with Merrick and…" He looked around, then decided, "Lucee and Tully. Dermot, will you accompany them? Genaine can take the second round."

Tully said, "I have used a gate before, long ago. I can get us there and back." Sousa gave her a thumbs up.

"This had better go well," he thought to himself.

Vali said, "Don't panic if we don't return immediately, I need to add the tag to their gate before we return, okay?" She caught Sousa's eye and said in a low voice meant just for him, "I won't be long. I promise."

He smiled bravely. "Tough girl," he replied, but she could tell he was putting on a show for her.

She squashed the sudden urge to hug him and instead winked and said, "You know it," and turned to walk with Dermot, Merrick, Lucee, and Tully through the gate.

As they walked through, Tully was explaining, "This gate has what we call an open connection – that is, you can get from here to any other open gate."

Her lesson was cut short by gasps from the others as they felt an odd wrenching feeling, and what felt like vertigo for just a moment – and they found themselves in a different sort of woods from what they'd left a moment before.

The atmosphere was greyed and heavy, with the sort of fog that curled around the trees and oozed through the undergrowth. There was a path that spread out before them, and they could see further along that there were many other pathways that branched off.

"Ohhh," breathed Merrick, in awe. "How do we know which one we want?"

Dermot stood with his eyes closed for a moment, then opened them and said, "This is the way we want." He pointed to a path that peeled off to the left, just up ahead.

Merrick looked impressed. "How do you know that, Dermot?"

Dermot shrugged, but it was obvious he was pleased. "I can feel my home. It has its own special energy. You paid attention to the gate you just walked through, yes?" Merrick nodded, and Dermot continued, "'S the same thing. You get to recognize the energy signatures of places, especially ones full of our kind. They're each unique. That's how you move between these."

Lucee asked, "What if you didn't know anywhere else when you came through one of these? Can you just jump out anywhere?"

Tully answered, "Yes, but that's a terrible idea, if you ask me. You could find yourself anywhere in this world, including possibly under the ocean. I know there were gates that were lost, long ago, and there's no reason to expect them to be closed just because they are now inaccessible." Lucee looked horrified, and Tully nodded wisely.

"Look, there's the gate we want!" Dermot cried, and to Lucee's surprise, grabbed her arm in delight.

She grinned and said, "Lead on, friend!"

They emerged from the gate and found themselves coming through what looked to be the remnants of an old arched stone doorway. It had obviously once been the front wall and entry of a stone building, but all that remained now was the doorway, which leaned slightly askew from age and settling in the soft earth. They were flanked on their right by the gentle curve of swift moving water.

"That's what they call the Gwynns Falls," Dermot told them. "It marks one of our boundaries, I think we used to have more buildings here, long ago. But now all that is left is this gate."

Vali plopped down next to the stone arch with a loud sigh of resignation.

"Why is it that I've been possessed by the personified spirit of the city, and I've learned how to keep people out of rooms with my graffiti, but this is what breaks my brain? It beggars belief," she grumbled.

Her face was much paler than usual, and Merrick leaned over and asked, "You feeling okay?"

"I feel weird as hell, but I guess that's to be expected! I guess this is our life now, eh?"

Merrick had to laugh at that. "I say that to myself at least half a dozen times on any given day."

She decided to work down low, so she stayed seated and got to drawing, carefully moving her paint pens over the stone surface.

While she worked, Merrick asked, "Where is Tiennan House in relation to here?"

Dermot showed him by walking up the hill a bit and pointing to where Merrick could see the shadow of Tiennan's form looming in the distance.

"Not too far, this is at the edge of what I'd call our territory. But not many come down this way, it's too soft for bicyclists or hikers, and too unreliably wet for homeless folk or anyone looking to do anything clandestine. It's a bit uncomfortable, I guess like we are." Dermot snorted at that, like it was wildly funny.

Tully tilted her head and said, "I don't find you or yours uncomfortable. I thought I might, as I've been long under the misunderstanding that the Gwyliannan were enemies, opposites to us. But no – you are different in a way that complements us. Or we complement you. All I know is that it seems to me that together, we are better."

She smiled brilliantly, and it seemed to Merrick that Dermot glowed in response, and it changed everything about him. Where he usually looked worried or sullen, he was now handsome and at ease. Merrick was struck by the change, and how easily Tully had brought it about.

Vali said, "Okay, that's done! Dermot, you understand how this works, right? You will have to manually bring anyone through who has not passed from this side of the gate first. But once they've been through, the sigil will know them, and they will be able to pass in either direction unhindered."

"Got it. That seems simple enough, yet effective to keep traffic from the other side lessened, at least."

She bobbed her head once, then said, "I know I won't forget the feel of this gate. Is everyone ready to go back?"

They bade Dermot farewell and came back through, this time feeling more sure about the process. Lucee said, "I get what he was saying now, I think. There was a sort of pull this direction when I thought about where I wanted to go. Neat!"

Sousa looked wildly nervous as they came into view through the portal.

"What happened? Did it work? Is everyone okay?"

"Dust and ashes, Sousa, you need to calm yourself!" The usually placid Tully looked exasperated. "I know that I am useless decoration next to most of you, but I can take our friends through a gate and back!"

Sousa had the grace to look embarrassed. "I didn't mean to imply that, Tully, I am truly sorry. I just…" He trailed off as she waved a hand of dismissal at him.

"Go see for yourself, it is fine. The Gwyliannan did a marvelous job with the gate."

Suddenly, Vali's hand popped up to cover her mouth, and she said, "Oops. I need to go this time, too." The group turned to look at her, and she explained, "I went in the first round and placed the sigil. Someone that's been through the gate since I threw the tag needs to take the second group through, or they won't be able to pass."

Sousa smacked his head with his palm. "Of course! I'm glad you thought of that now, rather than after we'd left!"

Genaine escorted all who were left through the gate next, asking Vali endless questions about the sigils and how they worked.

"I cannot seem to get my mind around the technique, I am sorry," Genaine apologized, which Vali waved off with a grin.

"I don't get it either, and I'm the one doing it! But Merrick was the one who thought of the idea; he's brilliant at this stuff. I knew what he meant as soon as he began to explain."

Vali made a "mind blowing" gesture, and Cullen snorted. Edana looked at Cullen in confusion, and he leaned over and whispered, "She means astonishing, eye-opening."

Edana rolled her eyes and said, "Mortal idioms, fah."

They found the gate, and Genaine started to walk through first, but experienced first hand the repellent power of the sigil, and Vali said, "Whoops! But at least we know it is working properly!"

She stepped up and held a hand out to Genaine. "You'll need to be touching me to get through, as I'm the only one who has been here since I tagged up your gate. We need to hold each other's hands with me in the front." Genaine hesitated, and Vali laughed and said, "I promise my hands are only covered with paint. Otherwise, I'm pretty clean."

Karstyn sighed and walked up to take Vali's hand instead. "Foolish. I am glad to take your hand." Karstyn turned to take a hand and exchange a scathing look with Genaine, who exhaled hard and turned to take Aisling's hand. They made a chain with Sousa at the far end, and Vali walked through the gate leading them all.

Karstyn took the time to point out for their group where Tiennan House was, while Genaine stood a bit away, wearing a rueful look. They confirmed the upcoming party plans, with a reminder to bring musical instruments if they had them, and parted ways.

Vali went out of her way to smile at Genaine and wave goodbye as they stepped back through, and Sousa caught a glimpse of Karstyn yelling at Genaine before he finished stepping through.

The walk back to the gate for The Maithe was a lot quieter, with only Cullen commenting.

"That felt odd, right? I know she hates me, but I thought she liked you, Vali."

Vali just shrugged. "People sometimes get weird around me. She looked like she didn't want to touch me, I'm used to that. I'm covered in paint and have mud on my ass, I'm not the most discerning."

Sousa broke the tension, replying, "And that's why I like you!"

They all laughed, and Vali said, "You would, you dirty punk."

They were still laughing when they popped out of the gate back into the Forest, and were met with cheers from those waiting for them.

Merrick said, "Now we just need House Mirabilis' gate online, and we will be set!"

Sousa relied, "Guess we'd better get out there and see where they're at with this, eh?"

Music: Love Is Colder Than Death

Wild World

T he drive to House Mirabilis was just Sousa and Vali, and instead of talking, they put old punk albums on the crappy CD player in Sousa's van, turned them up loud, and yelled along.

When they got to House Mirabilis and Sousa turned off the van, Vali turned to him and said, "That was seriously just what I needed. I know, I'm not supposed to thank you... but man. You totally nailed that."

Sousa shrugged comically. "Like I need an excuse to rock out? But nah, I get it. There's been a lot of weird happening, you needed something to ground you, something just fun. And for that, oddly enough, I'm your guy." He reached over, awkwardly, took her hand, and squeezed it for a moment. That got a smile out of her, which pleased him to no end.

Fallon met them at the door. "We have success! And how did you know to come now?"

Sousa replied, "We just got finished with Tiennan House, so I figured you must be at about the same point. I'm glad I was right!"

The sun was getting low in the sky by this point, so they hustled down to the gate so that Vali could get her art on it before she lost all light.

"I'm good, but not drawing a complex tag in a pitch-black night in the country good," she said.

Fallon waved her hand, and a sphere of light appeared in her palm. "We would not leave you in darkness, child."

Vali shook her head in amazement. "There's always something new with you all, and I love it!"

Fallon beckoned with her other hand, and Quillan, always near her side, ran up and took the sphere. He walked next to Vali with it, to light her way when she would need it.

The gate was near the water, very close to where the battle with the ArDonnath had taken place. It made Sousa a little nervous, and it must have been obvious to Fallon, because she reassured him, "We have been doing regular sweeps of the property, and no sign of the ArDonnath remains. No fear."

Vali had a harder time working with the material of this gate, as it was formed from a tree trunk that grew up from the ground, made a natural arc, then returned to the ground.

She made a funny face as she worked on the sigil, and asked, "Is this tree still living?"

Fallon walked over and touched it, reverently. "It does live still. It was asked before it was shaped into its current form, many years ago. In the Spring, it will even bring forth leaves." She paused a moment, and added, "It does not mind your new addition to its bark, either. It feels... fancy." She was amused, like someone had whispered a private joke into her ear.

Vali patted the tree's trunk and said, "I'm glad you like it, friend." She turned to Fallon and said, "Let us do this, then?"

The trip through, to The Maithe, was uneventful, and Fallon smiled when they arrived.

"Ah, I had forgotten what this mode of travel is like! So much more efficient."

They spent the next stretch of time getting those through the Gate and back again who needed it, while Sousa had to go back so that he could drive the van to The Maithe again. Merrick volunteered to ride back with him, and the ride home was a bit less loud than the ride there, with Vali, had been.

Riding back through the curving, dark roads that led back to the city, Merrick glanced at Sousa's profile, illuminated in an eerie green from the dashboard lights. In this moment, Merrick thought, even someone who wasn't in the know might feel the magic around them.

Sousa must have sensed Merrick's stare, because he asked, "What's on your mind, man?"

Merrick felt at a loss for words. "I'm not sure I can explain it. I guess – well, I've been in the thick of this for a couple of months now, and I'm beginning to feel like... how did I not see all this before? Was I really that unaware? I mean, I know I was, but it just seems like..."

He stopped for a second, to gather his thoughts, and Sousa stayed quiet, giving him room to think.

"It must be like only being able to see in black and white, all your life, and then suddenly not only being given the gift of full color vision, but then finding out that there are others who have always been able to see all of the spectrum. And to realize that all those colors were always there, you were just not equipped to see them... and now I wonder what else I've been missing, my entire life."

Sousa was nodding along with Merrick's words, and once he was sure Merrick was finished, he said, "You know there's tons out there that we don't know about, either. It's levels and levels of knowing. I think it's a natural response for someone as thoughtful as you, for you to feel this way. Honestly, if you weren't feeling like this, I might wonder what had happened to my friend."

He glanced over at Merrick for a moment, then focused back on the road, curvy enough to warrant his full attention. "You used to like to play it small, and you know what? I take it back, what I said about wishing that you'd ended up living a normal life. I do think that the Eleriannan have been terrible at using mortals for their own ends, but damn if you and Lucee haven't started to turn that around. And you? You are more alive than I've ever seen you. So, something good has come out of your adventure, which is something I'd never expected to say about dealings between the Eleriannan and mortals before now."

Merrick took a deep breath, let it out slowly. "Weirdly, you saying that feels like a weight lifted off of me. Your opinion matters, for some dumb reason."

Sousa chuckled at that. "I'm sure it is a very dumb reason."

The day of the party was filled with tension – despite the original plan to have a celebration, free from all of the pressures the Fae and mortals had been facing recently.

Sousa had offered regular rooms to any of the Fae who wanted to use The Maithe as a regular meeting place, saying, "Think of The Maithe as a halfway house or an inn, but with a room that's functionally yours. The Maithe doesn't really have members, so think of it as a neutral space for all."

In theory, that news had been met with enthusiasm, but the fallout from it left things a bit chilly between Cullen and Lucee when he discovered that she had moved all of her possessions out of her rented room, and into the room they had shared at The Maithe. He tried to play off the hurt he was feeling, telling her that he understood that she needed a space of her own.

"But we can provide that at House Mirabilis, Lucee! You would live away from your people?"

Cullen tried to keep his face neutral, but that had never been his strong point, and he was afraid he was going to end up pushing her farther away. Lucee, to her credit, was doing her best to be calm and logical about the whole thing.

"Cullen, it's just a place to keep my things for now, and where I can hide sometimes when I need to reset, you know? I promise that it doesn't mean I'm less available. This is all nothing. You have nothing to worry about." She tried to take his hand, and he let her do it for a moment, but then pulled away as gently as he could manage.

"I think I just need to take a walk and bring my head and heart to an agreement. Please forgive me."

He walked off, head hanging low, and Lucee stood there and watched him go with her mouth open. Aisling, who had caught the tail end of the argument as she'd walked into the room, tried to comfort Lucee.

"He'll get over this. He knows that you are an independent woman, one who is trying to be careful to take care of her needs. Unfortunately, that's not the sort of woman he's used to dealing with, so his ego needs to readjust when you don't behave the way he's expecting. It's not about you, really. It's about him learning how to be vulnerable."

"Yeah. I get it. And I do appreciate that he walked away to think, rather than continuing to push me. That's a pretty smart way to handle me, honestly. But... gah!" She threw her hands up, letting her exasperation out.

"Oh, I guarantee you are not the only woman that has had that reaction to our Cullen! Though unlike those ladies, he actually cares about what you think." She winked at Lucee, who tried to grin, but managed only a lopsided smirk.

"Wanna help me pick out an outfit for tonight?" she asked Aisling, who clapped her hands in excitement.

"Oh yes! Let's make you sparkle!"

It turned out that Fallon wasn't particularly happy about Merrick moving everything from his apartment into a room at The Maithe, either. His explanation went over with her about as well as Lucee's did with Cullen. He pacified her by promising that after the party, he'd look into claiming a room at House Mirabilis, with the intention that it would be his main roost, as she called it.

Merrick muttered to himself after Fallon walked away, "My girlfriend was fine with it, but I guess no one cares about that?"

Sousa, in earshot of the whole thing as he tinkered with the stage setup for later that night, just shook his head. "Just like Eleriannan," he thought. "I swear they never learn."

Vali seemed to be the only one in a good mood. She had walked down to the Frisky Bean to quit her job, and came back with a huge, fancy latte for Sousa, one for herself, and a chocolate chip cookie that she shared with him.

"You are a goddess," he declared, then shoved half the cookie in his mouth like it might disappear.

"And you have chocolate on your nose!" she laughed.

He wiped the chocolate off and wiped his hand on his pants. "Yes, I will be changing, before you say anything." Vali made a "who me?" gesture, and Sousa continued, "So how did it go?"

"They don't want me to outright quit. Pleaded me to keep my options open with them, so I did, because I'm a sucker like that, and I kinda miss the late-night shifts. Maybe I'll actually be able to do that again someday, when the fairy army isn't after my ass."

Sousa's head whipped up from the snare he'd been tightening.

"Hey. Just a warning – don't use that word, okay? It is the height of insults to our people. Seriously, pretend like you've never heard it before."

Vali's brow furrowed. "Oh! Oh no, I didn't mean to, I am so so sorry -"

He cut her off, telling her in a gentle voice, "Hey, it's okay. You didn't hurt my feelings. But there are others who will never rally with us, and will curse your family line backwards and forwards, if they hear that word come from your mouth. Fae is fine. Faery is less acceptable coming from mortals, even a half-blood like yourself. Fairy can start wars and end friendships."

Vali looked anxious. "I am sure I will screw that up at some point, Souz. There's so much stress on etiquette and unspoken rules with you all. Except you, of course. You mostly don't seem to care. I'm glad for that."

"Well, once a black sheep, always the black sheep. It's why, after the horrible event at Tiennan House, I distanced myself from the Eleriannan. All those protocols and rules, yet no one could be bothered to help each other when the time came. So now, with everything happening, I'm sitting here hopeful – but cautious. Maybe having The Lady show up like she did will be the catalyst that actually creates meaningful change."

Vali had sat down on the drum throne and was spinning back and forth while he talked, but as he finished, she used her boots to come to a hard stop, facing him.

"Sousa, I believe they can do better. If you can't, it's okay. I'll believe for you. I've seen a lot of awful things in my time on this planet, but I have never, not once, thought that anyone was beyond saving."

She thumped the bass drum to emphasize her next words. "I'm not going to start now."

She looked over to Sousa, who was looking away, and she realized he had tears in his eyes.

He finally said, "Look, don't you ever change, okay? Especially not because of my jaded ass. You are a breath of fresh air that this world desperately needs."

She decided the room was feeling a bit too serious for right before a party, and the best way to fix that was humor.

"Dammit, don't make me get all sappy, we will both end up a wet mess. How about you train me to be your back up drummer?" She picked up the sticks and attempted a drum roll.

He yelled, "Nooooo that's terrible," so she jumped off and ran away from him, brandishing the sticks in her hand like a trophy while laughing maniacally.

It was finally time for everyone to start gathering for the party, and somehow the ballroom was transformed from an already elegant space into something truly fantastical. The tables had been spread out more, with the buffet tables – laden with the most scrumptious array of food and drink ever – at each end of the ballroom space. Each table had a glittering centerpiece piled with candles and flowers and mosses and crystals, and ivy that flowed out and trailed off the table edges.

Besides the gorgeous chandeliers that hung from the ceiling, a huge mirror ball turned slowly, reflecting light both from spotlights and the candles everywhere. Lucee was the first to walk in, and she gasped with delight and spun around, the tulle of her skirt bouncing with her twirl.

"Look at this place, it's even grander than before! Where's Sousa, that man deserves a hug for this!"

Sousa was busy bringing in a wooden wagon filled with several kegs. Merrick was on the other side of the wagon, trying to keep the kegs balanced as they rolled up to the buffet tables. Lucee wolf whistled at them and yelled, "Looking good, guys!"

Merrick, dressed in all black, with his high leather boots laced up to his knees, strutted around like a peacock for Lucee. Sousa, who had put his mohawk up for the night, flexed for her, laughing. He had taken a black dress jacket and cut the sleeves off, then studded the edges and around the lapels. Paired with the fanciest pants he owned – red plaid trousers with random zippers – he looked about as spiffy as Lucee had ever seen him.

People were starting to show up, and the party began in earnest when Sheridan walked in with a complement of Eleriannan, yelled, "Where's the beer!" Karstyn met him with a giant tankard.

Daro and Genaine were holding camp at a table with Tully and Vali, while The Ladies chatted with Brenna. Merrick looked around the room with pride as he watched Eleriannan and Gwyliannan mixing together as they ate and drank and talked.

He leaned over to Aisling and said, "I'm not asleep, am I? Because so far, this seems to be going swimmingly, and that makes me think it's too easy, too much like a dream to be real."

She kissed his cheek and said, "I think I'd know if this was a dream! Just wait until you start the music, you will have the happiest room in the city!"

She was right. When The Drawback went up to play a set, the room cheered. Lucee ripped into the opening chords of the Dead Boys' "Sonic Reducer," and grinned when Vali whooped with joy. Merrick paced back and forth when he wasn't singing, or would join Lucee on her mic for the chorus. The audience was eating it up, singing along.

They plowed through their set like they were on fire, and the only way to put it out was to keep playing. Lucee even took the vocals for a blazing cover of Siouxsie and the Banshees' *Love In A Void*, bouncing up and down with the beat as she sang, strutting and dancing around during her guitar parts. Sousa pounded on the drums like he was trying to wake the dead.

Their last song, and Merrick stepped up and said, "This one's for all of you. For us." It was the same song they had ended with at Club Marcada, at the show that felt like it had happened so long ago – and now, with all that had happened since then, the song meant even more. It felt like Merrick had written it just for this moment.

The whole room sang out the chorus in unison at the end, repeating as Sousa led them on with just the drums to guide them.

"Our shared bond is our strength
Together we are stronger than one
And when we face adversity
Nothing will make us undone
Stand with me, I will fight for you
As I know you fight for me
And know that our bond conquers all –
Friends for eternity."

The chorus trailed off into a cacophony of applause, whistles, and stamping feet, until Merrick yelled out, "Who is playing next? I want to see dancing!"

Musicians took over the stage and pulled out guitars, hand drums, a fiddle, and even a set of uilleann pipes. They struck up the notes of a reel and the room broke into movement. Some folks danced in pairs or groups, while others danced alone, with wildly joyous movements.

At one point he saw Vali doing some sort of square dance with Lucee and some of the Ffyn, and it was so uninhibited and energetic that he had to throw back his head and laugh, overjoyed by the sight.

They danced and partied long into the night, and as the sky was just beginning to turn from deep purple-black to the deep blue that heralded the eventual dawn, the last few stragglers had left. Sousa and Lucee looked over the beautiful mess that was the aftermath of a perfect party.

Lucee sighed, "Nothing's going to beat this night, Souz." He grinned and pointed over to where Merrick and Aisling were slow dancing together, to no music – none that anyone else could hear, at least.

Sousa sniffed and said, "They're using up all the romance in the room. They should consider leaving some for the rest of us."

Lucee raised an eyebrow and teased, "Got someone in mind, Mr. Mohawk?"

Sousa looked around and frowned a little. "It's hard to make your move when she's nowhere to be seen. I wonder if she went to bed?"

Lucee snorted and said, "I knew it, and you two seem perfect for each other!" She punched Sousa lightly on the arm. "I saw her a while back, walking the Ffyn out. She seems to like 'em as much as I do. I'll ask Cullen, if he's talking to me now."

Sousa grimaced. "I didn't mean to make things awkward between you two. It just seemed like a smart solution -"

"You did nothing wrong; in fact, it was a generous offer and makes a lot of sense. He's just... he's got to learn how to be in love, I guess. He wants, without understanding what those wants really entail. And that's okay, we'll get through it, as long as we can talk about it eventually."

She shrugged, and added, "Figures that I finally date someone substantially older than me, and I'm still the emotionally mature one."

Sousa tried to keep his face blank as he replied, "Your mistake is that you date guys, Lucee. We're all a mess."

She peered at him with pursed lips and said, "Bah, this would happen no matter who or what I dated. Maybe I should hook up with the Ffyn. No gender, and they just like to dance. I can get with that."

There was a soft sound, like a throat clearing, that made everyone's heads turn to the entrance to the ballroom, then a tentative "Hello?"

Lucee smiled as she saw Genaine standing there, and indicated that she should come in. "Hell-ooo! What brings you back here so soon? Did you forget something? Want some coffee?"

Genaine looked uncharacteristically nervous, and like she had been crying. She said, "No. I came back because there is someone who wants to meet you."

Then, so soft they could hardly hear her, "I am so sorry."

Something about her tone set the room on edge; Sousa immediately stepped smoothly in front of Lucee and spoke out, "Who is there? Show yourself!"

A tall figure in dark clothes stepped into the room, a hooded sweatshirt pulled up to hide their face. There was something about the figure's energy, a palpable wrongness, that put them all into defense mode.

Merrick and Aisling were the closest and stepped back quickly to put some space between themselves and the shadowy figure. Cullen, who had been sullenly staring out a window until now, and hence was farthest away, tried to calculate how fast he would need to move in order to reach Sousa and Lucee.

A soft, male voice spoke up, "Greetings, strangers."

Pale hands pushed back the hood and revealed short, pure white hair and a clear, youthful face with a strong jaw and very fine features. His eyes were a clear blue, like arctic ice; when he smiled disarmingly at them, the smile didn't reach his eyes.

He held his arms open, a gesture that said "I come in peace" though he spoke nothing that supported that impression. Instead, he said, "I come to bring you a message from The Grimshaw. No one loves the messenger who brings bad news, but surely I can expect safe passage as the envoy?"

Merrick started to answer, but Sousa held up a finger as he spoke over him.

"None shall harm you here while you deliver your message. As soon as you are finished, you will leave, and no more will we be bound to give you safety."

The man nodded once, and said, "Very well. Here is the message I bring to you."

He drew himself up tall, and Merrick thought to himself, "He's not as confident as he wants us to think." The man began to speak, first turning to Merrick and Aisling.

"The Grimshaw know of you, Blackbird, with your Dreamlands lover.

You have done much to bring Eleriannan and Gwyliannan together, which we find ironic from a mortal such as you be." For a moment, the mask seemed to slip, and Merrick could see the contempt in this man's eyes when he spoke of mortals.

"There is no love for your kind, I admit. But you – you are different. You intrigue us. We see potential in you that is wasted on these dreamers, these relics that refuse to move away from glory days of past honor and awe, who refuse to see that the mortal world and our place in it have changed greatly."

He turned to Sousa, then. "Not you, of course. You were sensible to withdraw from all of their nonsense. And look at you now! Pulled back in, when you have the greatest treasure of all, one they cannot fully fathom and hardly respect."

Sousa's eyes narrowed, but he said nothing to address what the man from The Grimshaw had addressed, but merely asked, "What is the message you bring us?"

The man's face tightened, a small furrow forming between his brows.

"I have come to extend a hand to you. Join us, forge a new power here in the midst of these mortals. We do not need them, despite what the Eleriannan have told you. We could have this city for our own. We could push away the mortals who poison the land and fight amongst each other, who are cruel and destructive and focused only on money and getting ahead. Let us craft something loftier by causing them to leave and letting She Who Is The City return to her untarnished and poison-free state."

Sousa's eyes were wide, and Merrick could see his chest rising and falling as he breathed hard, in fear or anxiousness. Was this common knowledge in the world of the Fae? Everyone had seemed surprised to see The Lady of the City appear. Merrick had to believe that this was a surprise to Sousa.

"What would we gain from that? What can you offer that we do not already have?" Sousa's voice was deeper than usual, and Merrick could tell that he was doing his best to control his emotions.

The man raised his chin, looked at Sousa haughtily. "I can offer you supremacy over these mortals. No offense, Blackbird, we all know you are no typical mortal," he said in Merrick's direction. "I can offer you power beyond what we wield in this world right now, and a cohesive vision that the Eleriannan could never create."

He stood there, looking between Sousa and Merrick for a moment, then said, with a trace of humor in his voice, "No? Then perhaps telling you that your precious half-blood is in our hands might sway you. I am sure I can sway her to my purposes. Or of course you could just yield this place to me, and do what the Eleriannan do best – retreat further away and leave us to do the difficult work here of making a land that is truly ours."

Lucee, still shielded behind Sousa, had to put a hand on him to keep him from reacting out of anger. He spat out, "We are not surrendering The Maithe to you. This is my charge to keep, a task I took on when none other would. What makes you think I would give it up to you, even if you have the half-blood?"

Merrick nervously bit the inside of his cheek, afraid that Sousa would push this agent of The Grimshaw too far. Suddenly, he remembered something he had heard at the first meeting with the Gwyliannan. "I know who you are, now. You are Camlin, the leader of The Grimshaw! We have heard about what you did, and how you treated those under you."

Camlin laughed, a bitter sound. "You are indeed the clever Raven, as I have heard. If you know that, you know that I can just as easily turn the half-blood to my side as I can destroy her. And I know that she is of value to you. My little spy has told me all."

He snapped his fingers, then, and Genaine slunk in, head hanging low. "What a pretty little traitor she is, too. Perhaps you should explain to them how this will go if they fail to bend to my will?"

Music: Shriekback
Faded Flowers

Genaine shook her head, eyes averted. "Please don't make me," she whispered. Camlin laughed again, this time mockingly, as he grabbed her chin and forced her head up. "You will tell them what to expect, clearly and in detail. Now."

Genaine took a deep breath, and slowly turned to face the others. "The Grimshaw will only extend their generous offer to join them once. If you refuse, they will bring a war to your doorstep and fight you without rest or peace until you are destroyed. The half-blood will remain in their possession, and when you know defeat, the last thing you will see is Camlin's blade slitting her neck." She paused, a look of disgust at the words she was speaking on her face.

"So have The Grimshaw spoken."

Camlin spoke in a silken voice. "Well done, my broken poppet. And so, you may see my mercy," he addressed the room, "I am giving you some time to prepare yourself to give me an answer. Tonight, at the first moment of twilight, we will assemble here and you may come to stand with us, or we will slay you. Your half mortal child will be returned to you if you bend your knee. Otherwise, you have heard your fate."

He turned on his heel to leave, then turned back for a moment. His face was a perfect, handsome mask that sat ill with his words.

"Oh. You may keep this ruined piece of garbage; she will prove to be rather useless, I fear, but consider it a gift of goodwill."

He pushed Genaine towards them and was out the front door in the blink of an eye.

Genaine, sobbing uncontrollably, stumbled and fell in front of Sousa. Merrick ran to the front door to make sure that Camlin was truly gone, turned the lock and pushed on the door just to be certain, before he came back.

"How did the sigil not work?" he asked the room, visibly upset. Aisling pointed at Genaine, who was in a pile at Sousa's booted feet.

"That one. She let him in. That's the only way."

Sousa sank down on his heels to eye level with Genaine, and said to her in a voice that was soft, but full of steel, "How could you? You have destroyed everything in a moment's work, and for what?"

Genaine sobbed, "I had no control. He found me and it was like I never escaped; he somehow still rules my mind. All that I have been through, and I still bend to his will like a reed in the wind, and I can never escape the betrayal I brought to everyone!"

Lucee sank down to sit next to her on the floor, releasing a great, stuttering breath as she did. "Oh Genaine. I promised that I would help you, and now I don't know if I can. So now you are a traitor, and I am forsworn, and Vali is in the hands of that monster."

Genaine buried her face in her hands, sobbing.

Lucee looked up at the faces of her friends and asked, "What do we do with her? What can we do now?"

Cullen, who had been silent through everything, spoke up then. "Aisling. You can hold her."

Aisling looked distraught. "You know that goes against everything I believe in, Cullen."

He inclined his head, and answered, "Do you think I would bring it up if I didn't think it was the only way? At least until we can bring The Ladies here. Then they can keep her."

Merrick shook his head. "I have an idea. My bead charm – could it not hold someone in as well as it holds others out? Could we keep her in that, until we have a better plan? I hate the idea of imprisoning anyone, but if we can keep her out of play until we find a way to free her mind from Camlin's influence, that might be a kindness as well as one less thing for us to worry about."

He looked at Genaine, who was nodding. "I would want you to lock me up, honestly. I can't trust myself. I wish none ill but I seem to have no control over acting in accordance with my wishes."

Aisling said, "Let me work from your premise, Merrick. You will have enough on your plate without having to maintain a charm like that, as well."

Merrick looked to Sousa. "Souz? What do you say?"

Sousa looked at Genaine for a moment, and all could read the anger and disgust in his eyes. He then locked eyes with Merrick and said, "I don't care. Just get her away from me. Maybe later I will feel more compassion, but right now? That's low on my list."

Cullen spoke into the silence that followed, "I can round up the Houses. We need to bring everyone here. If The Maithe falls into the hands of The Grimshaw, none will be safe."

Genaine agreed, her voice raspy and soft. "Camlin hates you all. He would do his best to twist Merrick to his will, believing that as a mortal, he would be easy to warp. He thought the same of Vali, but she has proven unbreakable so far, and he cannot do much with her for fear she will break loose with the power of the Lady of the City."

She paused, then added, "I might have given him the impression that she is much more in control of that connection than she truly is. Any fighting chance I could give her to stay alive – to escape this mess I helped make..."

Lucee frowned. "You could have helped her get away. Or loosed her so she could call on The Lady. Something."

Genaine gestured, uselessly. "I could not. When he is near, I can no more fight against his control than you can fight gravity. His powers are considerable, though he must be careful not to stretch them too thin. He works to build slavish loyalty with his followers, most of whom are Fae like us. Fae who were already filled with hatred for mortals, and possibly the Gentry as well. It was easy enough to turn them into his army, fill their ears with what they wanted to hear."

Aisling asked, "Genaine, will you tell us all you know? You cannot change what has happened, but perhaps there is information you possess that could help turn things to our favor."

Genaine nodded, eyes cast downwards. "Anything I know, I will share."

Cullen broke away to find coffee at the buffet table. As he was filling his mug, he was interrupted by a soft tug at his sleeve and turned to find Lucee standing by his side. He gave her a rueful, sad look.

"You are a spot of beauty on this dark day, Lucee Fearney. Too bad this fool doesn't know how to properly appreciate that until it is too late."

She reached over, and gently took the mug from his hand and sat it on the table, then pulled him in for the tightest hug she could muster, arms wrapped around him, her head against his chest. He gasped a little, emotions flaring perilously close to the surface, as he pulled her more tightly against him. He knew he couldn't afford to lose it now, not when there was so much to do before the battle. But at this moment, repairing things with Lucee was the most important thing he could think to do.

"I cry you mercy, my lady. I am, as ever and always, a fool – but I am your fool, as much as anyone can be another's. And I would not run off on this errand without mending this rift between us."

He ran his hand over her hair, lingering on the texture of her braids, as if he was committing that feeling to memory. He then stepped back just enough so that she would look up at him, and he told her, his voice quavering just a little, "You have my heart. I beseech you, keep it safe for me."

Tears welled up in her eyes. "Oh Foxy... I love you and every bit of your stubbornness, your charm, and your willingness to be better – even when change is so hard for you. We will get through this. And then we can get back to fussing about all the unimportant details again."

She kissed him, tilting her head up with an almost blissful look on her face that somehow managed to calm him for the time being.

"I don't want to leave you, but I should get this news to the Houses, so we can prepare." At that moment, he looked so tired, bone weary.

Lucee frowned. "You need to eat, at least. And drink the coffee you poured. You need something."

She made him have a small breakfast, then walked down with him to the Gate. He said, "I will be back as soon as I possibly can. I am first going to Tiennan House, and yes, I will be as careful as I can."

He kissed her again, then stepped through the Gate, while she watched him leave, her jaw set with worry. As she came back to the stairs that led out of the forest courtyard, she found Merrick waiting for her.

"We have some information from Genaine, and the beginnings of a plan. But I need your input – and you need to eat and rest at least a little, okay?"

She waved her hand impatiently and retorted, "It's not the first all-nighter I've pulled, I'm sure it won't be the last. Though I guess this is my first inter-species war."

He snorted and quipped, "Is that any way to refer to your relationship?" She rolled her eyes, and he continued, "Sousa is waiting for us. And I know for a fact that you have got to be starving. Can't plan for war on an empty stomach, now, can we?"

The five left at The Maithe – Merrick, Aisling, Lucee, Sousa, and the disgraced Genaine – gathered at a table in the ballroom, laying out their plans. At first, Sousa and Lucee had argued over including Genaine.

"She can't know what we plan, we can't trust her to not run to Camlin somehow!" Sousa yelled, slamming a fist down on the table.

Merrick sat there with his mouth open; he had never seen his friend angry like this. But Lucee wasn't afraid to push back, and she did so earnestly.

"Souz – Aisling will have her confined, for her own good as well as ours." She looked at Aisling and Genaine, sitting together, and they both nodded in agreement. "Genaine knows how he thinks. I believe her when she says she is not currently under his control. Let it be on me if I am wrong, but I think we'd be fools not to use her knowledge to help us."

Merrick spoke up then. "I agree with Lucee. Sousa, one of our biggest strengths is that we see the best in people. Genaine has been through so much. Let's give her a chance to help us."

Sousa glared at both of them, then sighed, his face softening as he considered what they were saying. "If it was anyone else but you two, I would argue this until I died." He turned to Aisling. "You can hold her if he finds a way to get to her, or compels her to come to him?"

"If things look bad, I can put her to sleep. If I send her to dreams, even Camlin won't be able to force her to wake up."

She looked to Genaine, who said in a small voice, "You are too kind. My gratitude knows no depths."

The plan began to shape itself as they discussed everything they knew. Genaine admitted that she did not know the strength of The Grimshaw, but estimated there were probably thirty or forty, including the ArDonnath and the ex-Gwyliannan whom she knew.

"For someone who detests Gentry, he does have a few of us in his inner circle, as I was," Genaine explained. "He prizes us because we Gentry are difficult to rule over and subvert." The unasked question hung there, none willing to ask it: why had she been dominated so thoroughly, then?

She looked at each of them and said, "I hear the unspoken query, and here is the answer: Anger. He was able to tap into my anger at the Eleriannan, at the Gentry for how they have acted and treated so many they felt under them. That's how he ruled me so completely – he told me what I wanted, what I needed to hear, and I ate it up. But I never thought it would come to anything. Then when he attacked Tiennan House, and my friends – I was angry again, because I knew I had been used. He left me there to die, after he took advantage of me to get everything he needed to know."

Sousa commented, in a tight voice, "Yet you went after Cullen and his lack of action. For a tragedy you precipitated. Fallon offered her life to you for the slights you leveled at her – for a tragedy that was your responsibility!"

Genaine spread her hands in front of her, palms open. "I own my part in all of this. I have been paying for it, and I will pay a steeper fee now that the truth is revealed. I accept that. But it is also true that House Mirabilis did not come. They did not save my people, even as I was the one at fault for their peril. Now, they understand what part they played in this, too. And now you know how we have all been changed, and ruined, by Camlin and The Grimshaw." She slumped a little after that, and Merrick could see the tears in her eyes that Sousa could not.

It was difficult to plan, with so many unknowns that they had no way to calculate, but they did their best. They knew Aisling would hold Genaine, and Merrick and Sousa would be leading the charge.

Sousa gave Lucee one of the mic stands, which had a heavy round base, and he took the mic clip off.

"Practice swinging that around. Since it telescopes, you can find the length that feels most natural for hefting about."

She picked it up and did as she was told, a truly fierce look on her face only marred by her tongue sticking out of her mouth as she concentrated.

"You're gonna bite that off if you do that in a fight!" Merrick told her.

Sousa disappeared for a bit, and when he returned, he smelled like campfires. Lucee gave him a questioning look, and he said, "Fire barrels. I set some up outside. It's cold as hell, no one will even notice – and with the wood I left nearby, we can light torches against the ArDonnath and whatever else doesn't like fire." Lucee made an appropriately impressed and slightly apprehensive face.

Finally, Cullen returned, with a number of angry, armed Eleriannan in tow. Fallon was at the forefront, wearing the sort of clothing one might expect a warrior in a fantasy film to don for battle – shining, beautiful, but not obviously useful. She had her sword of silver and gold hanging at her side; the rubies in the pommel were gleaming softly in the light.

The Ladies were mounted on ponies, shining black with long, streaming manes. Sheridan was wearing only a kilt and the sort of grin that bode his enemies no good at all. Even the sweet, gentle Ffyn were there, which made Lucee both glad and sad in equal measure.

Quillan ran up to Lucee and hugged her, which surprised and pleased her. He then reached into a bag he had slung across his back, and pulled out a piece of armor, a chest plate in shining silver tones, covered in etching of knotworks. Set at the neck were three peridots, which were almost as green as her hair.

"This is for you. It will help to protect you in this battle," he told her.

He then brought out vambraces to match, and she made pleased sounds while he showed her how to put them on. She had changed into black BDU pants and a black thermal shirt earlier, so everything together made her look quite ready for anything that might come her way.

Fallon had a shirt of chainmail for Merrick, light and supple.

"This should not weigh you down, especially if you need to change shape," she explained. He had dressed much like Lucee, so he slipped the tunic over his clothes and tested moving around a bit.

"Magnificently light!" he told her.

Lucee winked at Cullen, who wore leather – a dark brown padded vest that buckled up the front, and leather bracers laced up over billowing black sleeves. His pants tucked into tall leather boots that matched the set. All of it looked old and authentic enough that Lucee wondered if it had seen battle before now. He had pulled his hair back into a loose braid.

"Looking intimidatingly handsome, Foxy," she called to him. He gave her a sweeping bow, but she could tell he was trying to cover his anxiety about what was to come.

Sousa looked them all over, then asked Cullen, "Did the Gwyliannan not come?"

"They are not here? They were in quite a state when I left." His volume fell a little. "Especially when they learned about Genaine's part in all of this."

Sousa shook his head. "We haven't heard or seen them at all yet. They had better hurry up, it's beginning to get darker out there. Not too much longer."

No one liked this; until this point, Merrick had just been moving forward with the plans in order to keep himself from thinking about possibilities, but now everything was becoming too real. What if it was just the people in the room when everything went down?

He said quietly to Sousa, "We are going to be outnumbered by quite a bit, Souz."

Sousa grimaced. "Yes. We are going to have to be smart about this."

Fallon broke into the conversation, her voice strained, "The light grows dim. We should take to the street."

Sousa nodded curtly, and pulled on a thick black leather biker jacket, covered in metal spikes and some chains. It matched the leather pants he was wearing, tucked into his usual combat boots.

He had a baseball bat, and Merrick asked, "Is that all you're bringing?"

Sousa winked at him and said, "Made of ash wood. Trust me, that makes it better than swords to me."

Merrick had nothing in his hands. He couldn't imagine what he could carry as a weapon, nothing seemed adequate.

The Ladies trotted up next to him as they slowly filed out to the battle-field, the street that ran before The Maithe. He greeted them as courteously as his shaking voice could manage.

"Well met, Ladies – if we must fight, I'm glad we are on the same side."

Morgance held a hand up in greeting, the welcome of equals – though Merrick was unaware of that detail.

"Hail, Blackbird! Off we go to battle, and we are here to defend your back and help you as we may. Be afraid, but know you are not alone."

He sighed, "That's only so comforting, Morgance."

To his surprise, she threw her head back and laughed, the most genuine laugh he had ever heard from one of the Sisters.

"Ah, Merrick, you know better than to look to us for comfort! But your fear can be your aide, if you let it. Know that it will make you sharp, if you do not let it rule you. And we will watch over you as best we can, as well."

Morgandy leaned over and told Merrick in a bell-like voice, "He is the thorn in your side. Be you his on this day."

Merrick blinked, not knowing what to make of that. "I'll keep that in mind, Morgandy."

Ula said, "You had best. When my sister speaks, all bend to heed her words."

Morgance yelled, "To the forefront, Sisters!"

Her tiny heels nudged her pony, and they pulled away, stopping next to Sousa, who was standing on the double yellow line in the middle of Park Street, the road in front of The Maithe. The street was eerily deserted, despite it only being late afternoon.

The buildings across from The Maithe were grey hulks, a warehouse and offices, lifeless and dark. Even the streetlights, which had begun to flicker on as the sun sank low, didn't seem to provide much illumination. Only the fire barrels, set at each end point and in the middle of the stretch of sidewalk that ran in front of The Maithe, seemed to brighten things.

The Eleriannan spread out, The Maithe behind them, Sousa and their Champion before them. Lucee stood with Fallon, who was a proud, regal figure beside her. And watching from the ballroom windows in The Maithe, Aisling and Genaine stood inside a protection spell.

Merrick muttered to himself, "We're just standing here out in the open, The Grimshaw could just pick us off. What are we doing?"

Sousa heard him and answered, "That won't happen. There are, weirdly enough, rules for these things. And if there's one thing we're sticklers about, it's rules – even ones we impose on ourselves. They won't fight until we officially turn down the request to forfeit The Maithe."

Merrick said, "I don't know how to react to that. Yay?"

He didn't get to hear Sousa's response, because a terrifyingly loud sound like a pack of wolves howling echoed through the street, bouncing off the buildings until it finally faded out. And from the alley between the grey buildings across the street emerged The Grimshaw.

Camlin led them, dressed head to toe in shining silver mail, and what looked like silver leather armor as well. With his shining white hair and pale skin, he looked like what any movie elf desperately wanted to be, and Merrick thought to himself, "This is why the Gwyliannan believed him. Surely no one this beautiful could be that evil."

But flanking him were some of the ArDonnath, and nothing could hide their vileness, their absolute wrongness. Some of the Ffyn recoiled, and it dawned on Merrick, "They look like an awful parody of the Ffyn!"

Behind them was a mixed host of ArDonnath and Fae, and Merrick realized that these were the Eleriannan and Gwyliannan that Camlin had somehow swayed to his cause. These were going to be the real problem, because there was no way to know what they could do in battle.

ArDonnath, he understood. But these Fae were unknowable, unpredictable, and extremely focused. "Or are they?" Merrick thought. "Maybe they actually aren't all here. They look a little vacant."

Camlin had reached Sousa and Merrick, and he looked them both up and down and made an unimpressed noise before addressing Sousa.

"So, I doubt by the reception we have received that your answer will be the wise one, but I am duty bound to ask: have you considered the offer I have made you?"

Sousa rolled his eyes, but answered in an even, booming voice, "Before I answer anything, show me the half-blood."

Camlin raised his right hand, and from the alley where the horde had emerged, two ArDonnath brought forth Vali, bound and gagged. She looked furious, and Merrick wondered how hard they'd had to work to keep her under control.

"There she is, hale and unharmed. Now do you have an answer for me?" Camlin had a bored look on his face, but Merrick could see a gleam in his eyes that told him that the leader of The Grimshaw was hoping for a fight.

Sousa nudged Merrick. "D'you believe this guy? Like I'd ever give over The Maithe to him."

He addressed Camlin then, and his voice was steely and sharp, a tone Merrick had never heard from Sousa. "You pledged to keep her alive until you defeated me. No matter how this battle goes, you will live to regret those words."

Camlin glared at Sousa through narrowed eyes. "You choose war?"

Sousa laughed bitterly, "Man, you're the one who wants war, I never asked for any of this. But if you want it, you got it." He raised his baseball bat into a defensive stance, and glared at Camlin defiantly. Camlin looked almost astonished at this turn of events, but not for long.

"It is War!" Camlin cried, and jumped back far enough to make some space between himself and Sousa. The Grimshaw horde behind him shouted and began to surge forward.

Sousa yelled to the Eleriannan, "They come! Prepare to fight!"

Two ArDonnath rushed at him and slashed at him with their sharp sticks and branches, as he struck at them with the bat. A branch flew off of one, and there was an unearthly shriek of pain. Sousa shouted and began to batter at them while yelling at the top of his lungs.

Merrick gasped, and dropped into a defensive stance, the first thing his instincts told him to do. He realized Camlin was standing there, laughing at him, and for just a moment, he felt extremely foolish, like maybe this had all been a misunderstanding.

"Oh, the Blackbird has been tasked with taking me on, has he? Have they explained to you that you are severely outclassed? No mortal can match the powers that I wield, Raven. What a waste it would be for me to have to destroy you, and so needless."

Camlin sounded reasonable, his face a mask of pleasantness and regret that things had come to this.

No. It was a mask. That was the magic, of course – a glamour that he was trying to spin around Merrick with his words, his influence. Merrick shook his head, both as a denial of what Camlin was saying and as a way to clear his own mind.

"I'm only tasked with championing my friends, and that is hardly a burden. Perhaps I'm outclassed. But I will use all that I have, even as a mere mortal, to keep them safe."

Merrick took a moment, gathered himself, concentrating his energy. "And if there's one thing I know for sure, it's that when people tell me that I'm not good enough, it's because they're not sure if they are."

He made a quick feint to his right, and Camlin shot a beam of energy at him, missing him by inches. As Merrick dodged, he released the energy he'd been building, and had the satisfaction of seeing Camlin get thrown back, hard.

"Is that all, Mortal?" Camlin drew himself up, his face looking angrier than his words belied.

Merrick took a breath, his heart pounding, then answered, "I guess you'll have to find out!"

Music: Modern English
Someone's Calling

The street was alive with magic and the sounds of weapons clashing. When the ArDonnath came at Sousa, it felt like everyone had been standing there like patrons at a bar, watching a fight to see how far it would go before they needed to step in. It took Camlin's first strike at Merrick to really set everyone in motion and fighting seemed to spread out from them in waves.

As Merrick struck back at Camlin, Fallon stood tall and yelled, "Eleriannan, to battle!"

The host surged forward, charging into the fray with swords and clubs raised, hands alight with blasts, or in the case of the Ffyn, branches waving. Lucee watched the Ffyn go and her heart ached, knowing that her gentle friends should never have had to be in a fight like this. Then she gasped as she saw one pick up and rip apart an ArDonnath that threatened the small, squat Eleriannan that reminded Lucee of a hedgehog.

Fallon looked down at her heir and said, "We do what we must, today." She blasted away at some magic-wielding Grimshaw, who had turned in the direction of Fallon and Lucee.

Lucee swung her mic stand for all it was worth, smashing a path forward through clawed branches and a group of imp-like creatures who had laughed at her until her weapon struck them; then they ran off yelping like hit dogs.

Quillan, on the other side of Fallon, shifted between boy and flock of birds as needed, using the flock form to sow confusion amongst the enemy ranks as they flew through in dizzying configurations. Lucee thought that it would have been an amazing spectacle to watch in a movie, but as a participant, she was just grateful that it scattered their opponents.

She glanced around for Cullen but couldn't see him anywhere in the mass confusion. "Let him be safe," she sent out like a prayer, before turning to swing her mic stand at a couple of ArDonnath who lunged at her.

One was thrown to the side by the power of her swing, but the second managed to grab the pole and base and yanked it out of her hands. She yelled in frustration and prepared to take it on with her hands if she had to – even though she knew she was outmatched without a weapon. Before the ArDonnath could reach her, Fallon had turned and blasted it away. It flew backwards into the fray and disappeared.

Fallon turned to Lucee and said, "Here, take this. You need it more," and pulled her sword out of the scabbard and handed it to her. Lucee took it gingerly, surprised again by how light it actually was.

"I don't know how to use this!" she exclaimed.

"You will learn now!" She pointed at the ArDonnath, rushing back towards them at full steam.

Lucee swallowed hard and took a defensive stance, the sword in both of her sweaty hands. She could feel her heart pounding as the creature moved to attack, and she swung the sword desperately.

One part of her mind was thrilled and relieved to see it slice effortlessly through the ArDonnath, as the creature's face changed from malice to shock as she cut it down. The other part of her mind was horrified; she had never killed anything before, and despite her target being an otherworldly stickman who wanted to harm her, she didn't want to kill it.

It fell into a pile of branches and mud at her feet, and she had to fight back being sick, right there on the battlefield.

She could hear Fallon's shout of approval, and Quillan touched her arm for a moment and whispered, "It will pass."

Then she had no more time to consider what she had done, because there was more fighting to do.

Elsewhere on the field of battle, Merrick and Sousa were having their own trials. Sousa was desperate to get to where Vali was held, but the alley was well-guarded by ArDonnath and they just kept coming, even as he beat them down. He could feel himself starting to tire as yet another group of stickmen came at him and wondered if this was where he would go down.

He swung his bat at one stickman just as another jumped on his back and tried to get at his eyes with one bristly arm. He thought he was a goner, but suddenly the ArDonnath on his back was gone. As he lunged forward to smash the other one, he found his blows matched by the great tattooed fists of Sheridan, who laughed like a madman as he pummeled the foe.

"Ah, y'should see the look on yer face, friend!" Sheridan shouted glee-fully. "C'mon, this is best done in pairs!" Sousa grinned and side by side, they met the next wave of assailants.

Aisling and Genaine watched from the window, while Genaine twisted her hands into tight knots, and Aisling paced back and forth, looking for Merrick.

"Do you see him anywhere, Genaine?"

Genaine shook her head at first, and then said, "Oh no. I see him. He is not where you want him to be, I fear."

She pointed, and Aisling spotted him toward the center of the battle. She could see that he was facing off against Camlin, and she bit her lip in fear.

"You can do this, my Raven," she murmured, and Genaine touched her arm reassuringly.

"I know my words mean less than nothing, but I am a big believer in your Blackbird. He just must be very careful. Camlin is treacherous."

"Does he know about who Merrick is? Did you tell him anything?"

Genaine grimaced and said, "I told him all I knew, because he com-pelled me. But he did not seem to put much stock in it, and that may be a point in the Blackbird's favor. He discounts the idea that a mortal could be any sort of challenge to his superiority."

She made a surprised noise then, and pointed across the battle, to the grey building that hemmed them in to the East. "Look, Sousa is fighting his way to Vali. But there are two of the Grimshaw-converted Gwyliannan there, guarding her. They are going to be difficult for him to overcome."

She turned to Aisling, a desperate look in her eyes. "Aisling. You have no reason to trust me. I know that. But I can help."

Aisling looked skeptical, and Genaine went on, emphatically. "They know me, I could distract them then help Sousa. You could release Vali while we did that. We could make a difference!"

Aisling knew that Sousa was going to need more help than just Sheridan – mere brawn wasn't going to beat those Fae holding Vali. And Aisling was no fighter, but she could make herself almost unseen when needed, which gave her a shot at getting close enough to release Vali. But the plan hinged on trusting Genaine.

Aisling didn't know if she could do that.

"Genaine, if you betrayed me, we would be undone. Even if you are earnest, what would keep Camlin from controlling you if he spots you?"

Genaine looked askance, then met Aisling's gaze, her eyes begging her to believe. "If he takes me over, you will need to kill me. I would want you to. I cannot betray you again and live with myself." A tear slipped down her face. "As for trusting me, pull me into the Dreamtime and ask me. I want you to. I know that I can't lie to you there; you can ask me anything."

Aisling scowled. "I hate this. I hate every bit of this." She reached out and grabbed Genaine's wrist, and the perspective shifted as they connected in the Dreamtime.

Merrick, in the meantime, had been running a fast-paced game of cat and mouse with Camlin. Trading energy blasts, they moved through the battle dodging and feinting, neither gaining an upper hand.

Camlin was looking as if his patience was starting to wear thin. He unexpectedly lunged at Merrick and in the attempt to get away from him, Merrick felt his feet go out from him as tripped over a body sprawled out in the street.

Merrick felt a moment of clarity sweep over him as he was in the air – he had only one choice. He closed his eyes for a moment, and felt himself shoot up, wings beating strongly as he flew straight up and away. He cawed loudly, a cheer at his success, as Camlin went from a cackle of glee to a gasp.

He recovered his composure quickly enough, yelling at Merrick, "Two may play this game, Blackbird!"

Then he shifted into a peregrine falcon.

He let out a shrill call, and the chase was on, weaving and dive bombing through the melee. Merrick was moving at top speed, using every trick he could think of to elude his pursuer, but he realized that Camlin chose a form that could easily outpace him. And unfortunately, Merrick was running out of ideas.

He did a twisting roll through the air, narrowly missing someone's head as he darted between two of the Eleriannan as they fought some ArDonnath. They yelled and swatted at him as he zipped by.

"I need to change form into something that gives me a fighting chance," he thought, wildly flipping through possibilities as Camlin got closer and closer.

Merrick decided that he had to try, he had run out of time. He barreled toward the ground, held the feeling of running in his mind, a compact feline body, and prompted the shift...

He tumbled to the ground, recovering quickly as he got his legs back under him, his paws scrambling for purchase then finding it on the asphalt.

He zoomed through the crowd, now in bobcat form, to circle back and find Camlin.

He crouched in a stalking posture behind a body strewn across the road and caught sight of the falcon, who was swooping over the field of battle, scanning for any sign of Merrick. Could he jump up and catch Camlin unaware?

He managed to do just that, as the falcon swept by much too low to evade the sudden leap that came its way from the bobcat that was Merrick. There was a flash of feathers, a loud screech, and a quick sear of pain before Merrick tumbled back to the ground with a mouthful of feathers and blood. He quickly changed back into his human shape, appalled by what had happened.

He realized that not all the blood was from Camlin, that he had a cut down his cheek – not enough to be concerned, but it hurt. He spit out feathers and looked for his foe, who had made a less graceful landing than Merrick had, and looked a bit worse for the wear, too. Camlin's right arm was wounded, bloody and at an odd angle.

Merrick took a deep breath and stood up. "This can't end soon enough," he thought.

Camlin was struggling to stand but seemed to shake it off. He snarled at Merrick, "Don't get too cocky, mortal. Look around you and see how outclassed you are."

It was true. The Eleriannan weren't necessarily outclassed, but they were outnumbered, and that was wearing them down. Despite the bodies of ArDonnath he saw lying here and there on the street, there were also some casualties to the Eleriannan, a high price to pay.

The noises of the battle rang out and bounced between the buildings, echoing with clangs and clatters and shouts.

Camlin shouted over the din, "You are going to lose, and badly! Surrender now and you might still find your way with us. Continue to fight and I guarantee that none will live through today!"

Merrick felt an anger like he'd never experienced wash over him in a flash. It wasn't a hot passion that made him want to charge at his enemy. No, it was a calm anger, what he supposed that people would refer to as a righteous indignation. It was disgust at what the Grimshaw were and what they represented, and the knowledge that fighting them was the most important task he was ever going to have in his life.

Nothing would be the same after today, but at least he was on the right side of the battle.

That sense of purpose filled him with an energy that flowed freely through him and pushed all the aches and pains he was feeling from his fight into the back of his mind. He lifted his chin in defiance.

"Don't be so sure, Camlin. This mortal's still got some tricks." He grinned, because he heard something that Camlin had not. "Tell me that noise comes from your troops, Grimshaw."

The noise in question was the roar of motorcycles, near at hand and getting closer every moment – when there had been no city sounds during the entire fight until that point. Merrick hoped beyond hope he was right, and Camlin's confusion confirmed his guess – the riders were none else but the Gwyliannan.

They drove headfirst into the battle, swinging swords and pikes – Dermot even had a bow, aiming shots as he rode behind another Gwyliannan.

Brenna rode behind Daro, swinging a weapon that looked like a pole with three sharp, clawed talons that spun around at the end of a chain.

And behind Karstyn rode Cullen, brandishing a polearm and yelling at the top of his lungs. The rest of the Gwyliannan, even some that were unfamiliar to Merrick, followed behind.

Camlin cursed loudly. "You will not win this fight, I swear it!" He raised his left arm up, then brought it down in a swift motion, and a blast of red, crackling energy boomed out in a circle away from him. Everyone standing nearby was knocked down, including Merrick, and when he looked back up, Camlin was not there.

"Shit! Where did he go!" Merrick yelled, trying to see around the crowd of fighters in his way. He couldn't decide – would he head toward Fallon and try to take her out, as the ruler of the Eleriannan? Or would he go after Sousa, the one who could cede The Maithe to him?

He cast his eye toward the direction of the alley, and it became crystal clear when he saw Genaine, inexplicably standing there talking to one of the Fae guards.

He was going to go after Vali.

He wouldn't go against what he had promised them, that he would give Vali back if they surrendered. But if he could make Genaine do it, it would not have happened by the hands of The Grimshaw. And of course, Aisling had told him: the Fae might not lie outright, but they will bend their words to suit as needed.

He made a quick calculation in his head and decided switching back to the raven form would get him there fastest. He saw Genaine, all smiles and simpering, as Camlin approached, and knew he had little time. How had she escaped Aisling? He pushed his worry for the Dreamling out of his mind for the moment, because he needed to focus completely on the task at hand.

He yelled out to whoever might be nearby to hear, "He's going for Vali!" and took off, beating his wings as hard as he could. Taking a huge risk, he flew in front of Camlin's face, his feathers actually brushing the man's face as he zoomed between Camlin and Genaine.

Camlin yelled out, and made a too-slow grab for Merrick, throwing himself off-balance and making him stumble. Merrick could feel just how angry Camlin was becoming, which Merrick welcomed.

"That's right, direct it at me, maybe you'll make a mistake," he thought. He landed far enough away that Camlin would have to come to him and away from Vali if he took the bait.

Camlin shouted something at Genaine, who looked like he'd slapped her, then ran toward Merrick. The last thing Merrick caught before Camlin struck at him and they engaged again, was a glimpse of Aisling, barely visible in the shadows behind Vali.

Camlin steamrolled into him full-force, leaving weapons by the wayside in order to grapple hand-to-hand in a punishing fight. Merrick wasn't proficient by any means at this sort of fighting and found himself hanging on through sheer will and using the energy at his call to reinforce his blows.

They parted for a moment, both breathing heavily, and he slowly became aware that fighters from both sides surrounded them. They were more interested in watching the outcome of this battle than their own part in it.

Merrick sighed, feeling every place he'd been hit, then raised his hands back into a fighting stance. Camlin laughed bitterly and spit at him, "You thought it would be easier than this, eh Blackbird? Spending time with all your soft Eleriannan."

Merrick shrugged a shoulder dismissively. "You thought the same, though. How embarrassing that a mere mortal is giving you such a terrible time."

Hissing and laughter spread through the crowd. Merrick spied both Fallon and Genaine off to the side of Camlin – Fallon to his left, Genaine to his right. He saw no sign of Vali, for better or ill.

Lucee was near Fallon, and he caught her eye for a moment, and winked at her. It wasn't very mirthful, but hopefully she would know that he was okay so far. She had a look of someone who had seen terrible things, and maybe had done them too. In that moment, he hated the man in front of him more than anything, because he was the cause of that pain on his friend's face.

Camlin turned toward Genaine and said, "Have you chosen your side, finally?"

She looked to Merrick for a moment, and he couldn't read what was in her eyes. She then turned back to Camlin and replied in an emotionless voice, "I choose you."

Merrick's fists tightened at Camlin's look of smug satisfaction. "Once mine, always mine, Blackbird. You see? And all this will be mine once I kill you."

He raised his left hand, and his right one weakly followed. Merrick noted that Camlin was still sorely hurt there but kept his face unreadable.

He cocked his head and said, "You keep threatening me, but I'm still standing."

Camlin screamed in rage and shot a beam of crackling energy at Merrick, who rolled to his left and did the same to Camlin, aimed directly at the damaged arm. Camlin howled in pain and fell back, then charged at Merrick like a bull at a toreador.

They came together hard, and Merrick felt himself falling backward. "No no no," he thought desperately as he hit the ground, Camlin on top of him. Camlin's fist connected with his head, and Merrick groaned with the pain, then instinct kicked in and he was trying everything possible to get away. No longer brave, his only drive was to get out of this compromising position, and he managed to flip over somehow and scrabble on the asphalt on his stomach.

Camlin wrapped his strong left arm around Merrick's neck and started choking him, and nothing that Merrick did seemed to move him. He could hear a buzzing in his ears, and the sounds of the fighters around him began to fade away.

"Think, man, think!" he told himself in desperation, and tried to fight off the darkness beginning to encroach his vision. His arms flailed helplessly, striking Camlin ineffectively when he could actually reach him.

His mind began to drift, and he thought about flying, and how much it thrilled him... he wished he could summon the raven now, but that form seemed as far away as hope in that moment. He flashed back to the ceremony when he had become pledged to the Eleriannan, each gift falling onto his chest as he laid there, his mind in as much disarray then as it was now. A flower, a berry, a glass bead, a tiny key... a thorn.

Suddenly, he had never wanted more to move his arms. He flopped around for a moment, trying to move his hand up to his charm bag around his neck. Camlin must have thought he was planning to try and pry his arm away, because he started laughing, a chilling sound. Merrick ignored him and worked his fingers into the bag carefully, urgently trying to get the thorn out before he passed out and all was lost.

There was a sudden flash, a crackling and burning like being hit by electricity, and then he could breathe again. Camlin's arm loosened in the aftermath of the blast he'd taken from... Genaine? Merrick saw her standing there, arms extended in the position of attack, a defiant look on her face.

"I never said what I choose you FOR, you pestilent creep," she shouted.

Her voice took on an unearthly tone. "Hear me now! You shall have no rest, no growth, no success, no home. Watch it all rot away!" A ripple of energy moved over them, then the crowd, and then faded away.

Camlin howled in anger and dropped Merrick in order to blast Genaine full on with his still-strong left hand. Merrick looked up and saw his opportunity.

"Be the thorn in his side," Morgandy has said, and he took her at his word as he swung his hand with the thorn in it upward and into Camlin's exposed side. The thorn hit and expanded into the size of a dagger, cutting up and through the other side of him. When the thorn erupted through, it burst into white flowers.

Merrick gasped and tried his best to back away, and Camlin screamed and fell to the ground, where he writhed in pain. Merrick felt arms around him and tried to fight them off with wild blows, until he heard Lucee's "Ow! Merrick, it's us!" and realized that she and Fallon were pulling him away.

Across the battlefield, there was a loud scream and a flash of light, then a wave of energy that blasted them all back. Lucee helped Merrick up in time for him to see Vali finally burst free from her bonds. She looked crazed, and energy was flaring all around her as she turned to blast the ArDonnath nearest to her.

Merrick cried out, "Aisling!" as the buildings around Vali began to fall down, and the asphalt surged and rolled under their feet.

Steam tunnels that ran under the city streets burst, and hot steam and manhole covers shot to the sky. Fallon ran to Genaine's body, lying on the street unprotected.

Merrick turned to Lucee and said, "We need to get out of here! She's going to bring it all down!"

Lucee pointed toward Vali and said, "Look!"

Walls were collapsing over on Grimshaw, Eleriannan, and Gwyliannan alike, and steam and fire was shooting out of any vent in the pavement, but somehow Sousa had made it over to Vali. As Merrick and Lucee watched in horror, he fought his way to her, yelling her name, and grabbed her by the shoulders.

"Vali! Vali, stop! You will kill us all!"

She turned to him, a goddess in rage, not the clever punk he knew at all. But he wasn't going to let that stop him. "Vali! Come back to us!"

Energy crackled, and Sousa knew he was the next target. He did the only thing he knew to do. He pulled her into him, wrapped his arms around her.

"If you hurt me, you hurt yourself. And you don't want that. Vali, you don't want to hurt me. It's Sousa. It's me. C'mon, punk girl, you know me."

For a moment it was silent, like the entire city had gone to sleep, and into that silence, Vali spoke.

"Sousa? Why is everything on fire?"

MUSIC: KILLING JOKE

Requiem

The sound of sirens in the distance told them that the battle was truly over and the Mortal world was once again imposing itself over whatever liminal space they'd been fighting inside. Merrick knew he had to get up, get everyone inside – but where was Aisling?

"Have you seen Aisling? She was in the alley, trying to release Vali before everything went wild," Merrick cried out, trying to get anyone's attention.

Lucee tried to get him to calm down. "We'll look for her, Merrick. You need to get into The Maithe and get looked at by someone. You almost died, dumbass!" She looked like she was going to cry.

Cullen, who looked like he'd been through some hell himself, came running up to them. His face lit up with relief to see Lucee unharmed, but it darkened again when Lucee turned to him and begged him, "Help me find Aisling? She was in the alley before everything went sideways!"

Cullen recruited Quillan and Karstyn to the search. Merrick saw Quillan take off and split into his small flock of birds, flying over the burning wreck.

Lucee said to Merrick, "They'll find her. You know you can trust them to find her." She put an arm around his back. "C'mon. Let's find someone to make sure you're not seriously hurt."

Once inside, they found triage spread out across the ballroom – a huge change from the party that had happened so recently. Merrick looked around, trying to spot his friends. Someone brought him a glass – water, he didn't remember any of the Fae ever handing him water before today – and he drank it in one gulp.

He saw some of the Ffyn gathered around one of their friends, obviously hurt, though Merrick couldn't tell how. He spied Tully running around, giving aid where needed. Sheridan was there as well, which surprised Merrick until he thought about it a moment – of course, the man who was most comfortable in the woods would know how to give first aid.

There was a commotion at the door, and Quillan came, followed by Cullen carrying Aisling in his arms. "Is she hurt?" Merrick yelled as he ran over.

Quillan grabbed his arm and patted it. "She will be fine," he reassured in his soft voice. Cullen eased her to her feet gently, and she collapsed into Merrick's arms with a sob.

"Found her trapped between rubble and a dumpster," Cullen explained, "We had to dig her out, but she's mostly just scraped and bruised."

Merrick held her tightly, and mouthed to Cullen, "I owe you."

"You do not. You are my friends, my family. We all save each other. That is how this works."

Merrick smoothed Aisling's hair back. "Do you need Tully to look at you, love? What can I do?" She leaned against him, her arms tight around him.

"Just stay close. Just hold me," she whispered. He smiled and kissed the top of her head.

"That's the easiest thing anyone's asked of me today."

Cullen muttered, "Oak and Ash, what goes on there?" Merrick turned to look.

Quillan said, in solemn tones, "The Queen mourns."

They slowly limped over to the group gathered around Fallon. She knelt in the middle of the circle, cradling Genaine in her lap. Merrick and Aisling both gasped as one, and Cullen put a hand to his heart and whispered, "She is dead?"

Fallon looked up to see them standing there and gestured them close.

"Pray tell, where is Lucee? Bring her hence," she spoke, and though it was an order, there was no power in her voice, only sorrow. Quillan ran off – "Of course he did," thought Merrick – and fetched Lucee, who walked slowly to them in a way that said she was feeling every moment of the night's battle.

She sank to her knees in front of Fallon. "What can I do? Whatever you need-"

"I need you to lead now, more than ever," Fallon told her. "You must be the one to heal the Eleriannan, Lucee. It is time for me to leave this place and travel onwards to the Misty Lands. No, don't cry, little one. You have everything you need, and the people love you. Cullen will guide you. The Blackbird will champion you. And perhaps now the true healing between Eleriannan and Gwyliannan will begin."

Cullen made a terrible noise, one of sadness and horror both. "You can't do this. You know what it means. You know!"

She shook her head, a slow denial. "I know nothing, and neither do you. It is the Great Mystery now, Cullen, and I am going to go out and find the meaning of it. I believe that I will join those who went before and will see with my own eyes how it was before we let the mortal world change us. I will take Genaine with me, and she may rest there, or perhaps they will find a way to bring her back again. I do not know."

She looked down at Genaine's face, peaceful in death. "*Nom sum qualis eram*," she whispered.

Cullen turned away, his face buried in his hands as he sobbed. Lucee's face was as emotionless as stone as she asked, "What do I need to do, then?"

Fallon gestured her close and laid her right hand on Lucee's chest. "Do you love these people as your own, Lucee Fearney?"

"I do. I love them with all my heart," she answered, her voice shaking.

"Then you now have all that I have carried with me. You speak for the Eleriannan, and they will follow you. If you are scared, or unsure, ask the Book, and it will advise you more wisely than I might have. You are now the queen here, Lucee."

There was a sparkle, a golden light that danced from Fallon's fingertips and swirled up and around Lucee, and just as quickly was gone. As Fallon took her hand away, Lucee covered the place where it had laid over her heart with her own hand, and a tear ran down her cheek.

Fallon then addressed Merrick.

"Blackbird, come to me." He did, dropping to one knee before her, tears in his eyes. She reached over and wiped them away gently.

"No tears, my Raven, you are far too brave for that. I need you to continue the work you have started, Merrick Moore. You are the glue that keeps us together, and the balm that soothes all the hurts we have foolishly inflicted on each other. Always keep that wonder about you," and she touched Lucee's arm, "Both of you. Together, you will lead our people into the change we need. I know I am leaving here with everything in strong, capable hands."

Merrick saw that tears sparkled in her eyes, as well.

"Now. I will take this brave child, and we will leave. No, none shall escort me. This is my journey, to undertake on my own."

Fallon stood and took Genaine's body in her arms. "Farewell, my beautiful children. We shall meet again, in the Misty Lands."

And with those words, she turned – still and always a regal figure – and walked across the ballroom and out the door.

Epilogue:
Einstürzende Neubauten
Grundstück

The healing of the Eleriannan and the Gwyliannan took some time. Sousa, who had combed the wreckage of the street with Vali at his side, never found Camlin's body. He had been the one to field questions from the first responders, telling them that he lived at The Maithe and had come to help when he heard the explosions.

Reports claimed that no one could explain the preponderance of charred and broken branches everywhere. They found a few bodies, but they were all destroyed beyond recognition. Sousa commented to the mortals in the Fae council, as they were calling themselves for now, "We are good at taking care of that sort of evidence." Lucee looked a little ill at that thought.

Daro argued, with a tinge of anger in his voice, "I don't believe that Camlin is dead. They will be back. We should have made sure to take the body ourselves."

Merrick made a face and said, "Next time I stab my enemy with an expanding thorn that turns into a blossoming tree inside his chest, I'll try to remember to recover the body before I'm squashed by a half-blood channeling the spirit of the city. Ok?"

There were several folks who snickered at that, both Fae and mortal alike, though Daro's glare cut that off quickly.

Sousa said, "I believe that The Grimshaw have gone back underground for now, down to the steam tunnels and hidden spaces under the cityscape. They know that we know what to expect from them now – they will be back, but they will be more cautious. And we are united, which makes us more dangerous to fight."

They laid out plans to meet each month at The Maithe, during the full moon – an easy schedule to keep.

Lucee declared that she despised using the names of their old factions, and instead of being Eleriannan or Gwyliannan, she was just going to refer to them by their names or House names or just the Fae, and she was in charge, the end. Sousa stood up on one of the tables and applauded. Edana made faces about it but confided in Cullen later on that she had more hope than she had held in ages.

Lucee and Merrick both kept rooms at The Maithe, but mostly stayed at House Mirabilis. Lucee moved most of her things into Cullen's room, which pleased him to no end. They made it through the winter and well into spring without a sign from The Grimshaw, and finally everyone started to breathe easier.

And one very wet April afternoon, The Drawback got together for one of their regular band practices, which they were holding in the ballroom these days. Often one or several of the Fae would sit in or hang out and listen to them practice, but this day it was just Sousa banging away on the drums, and Merrick doing some vocal warm-ups, as they waited for Lucee to show up.

"She's never late, I wonder what's going on," Sousa yelled over some loud thumps from his bass drum.

Merrick laughed, "You know you could stop hitting that thing while you spoke, right?"

Sousa answered by thumping it louder and flashing Merrick a cheesy grin.

There was a bang as the front door flew open, and both Sousa and Merrick pivoted together to look at the entry to the ballroom with not a small amount of trepidation. They were relieved when it was only Lucee who burst in, wearing a grin from ear to ear.

"Good news, guys! Guess who got us a GIG!"

CPSIA information can be obtained
at www.ICGtesting.com
Printed in the USA
LVHW050715271021
701668LV00010B/615